LOVE & THEFT: A Story of White Collar Thieves, Government Agents, and Marriage

Published by 718 Stories

Cumming, Georgia

ISBN: 979-8-9884627-0-5

FICTION / Romance / Police & Law Enforcement

FICTION / Romance / Romantic Comedy

Cover and design by 100 Covers, copyright owned by 718 Stories

Printed in the United States of America.

718 STORIES

Contents

Song of Songs 7:6-10 V

1. In Which My Contentedly Waddling Life Exploded 1

2. In Which a Thoroughly Interesting Proposition Presented Itself 11

3. In Which I Rediscovered the Simple Pleasures of Returning Home 23

4. In Which a Thief Became a Cop 37

5. In Which I Discovered the Joys and Excitement of Office Work 51

6. In Which We Enjoyed the Aphrodisiacal Qualities of Playing Hard to Get 63

7. In Which I Received Some Answers and Much Delayed Gratification 75

8. In Which We Reunited New Friends and an Old Associate 85

9. In Which I Engaged in Golf and Other Physical Pursuits 97

10. In Which I Issued Invitations and Received a Delivery 111

11. In Which No Good Deed Goes Unpunished 125

12. In Which Plans Began to Take Shape 135

13. In Which Costumes Removed Our Masks 145

14. In Which Devised Plans Became Complicated 161

15. In Which I Took a Boy Home for the First Time 175

16. In Which We Explored the Various Incarnations of Chess 189

17. In Which Trees Revealed Their Magic 201

18. In Which Set Plans Utterly Imploded 213

19. In Which New Plans Began to Take Shape 227

20. In Which Remembering was the Final Stage of the Pleasure 235

21. In Which I Implored for a Terrible Sacrifice 253

22. In Which an Ending Loomed Heavily 267

23. In Which My Heart Learned to Beat Again 279

Acknowledgments 289

About the Author 291

Song of Songs 7:6–10

How beautiful you are and how pleasant, my love, with such delights!

Your stature is like a palm tree; your breasts are clusters of fruit.

I said, "I will climb the palm tree and take hold of its fruit."

May your breasts be like clusters of grapes, and the fragrance of your breath like apricots.

Your mouth is like fine wine —

flowing smoothly for my love, gliding past my lips and teeth!

I am my love's, and his desire is for me.

From the Christian Standard Bible (CSB)

Chapter One

In Which My Contentedly Waddling Life Exploded

I always loved how champagne and diamonds sparkle. Poor lighting doesn't even matter. Not that the Morgensterns had a poorly lit home. Quite the contrary. The interior lighting melded with the Manhattan skyline, begging an art studio to pop up in their triplex penthouse.

Mrs. Morgenstern convinced her husband to purchase the top-level duplex and the condo below some six months ago. She wanted a humble abode for their golden years. So began the arduous process of joining two independent units and renovating the whole thing to Mrs. Morgenstern's specifications.

That night's party celebrated the unveiling of her passion project and refined tastes. And what a *refined* palate she had. A shallow chandelier of multi-colored glass crawled along the ceiling above the twelve-person dining room table, projecting a glare onto the mismatched China place settings. The whole room looked rather like a rainbow on a bad acid trip.

Honestly, if you're gonna be ostentatiously gaudy, at least go all out and have a crystal chandelier. And where on earth did she find those atrocious place settings? Can we make a law banning hideous China? It's just too much effort to produce something so astoundingly ugly. Although, anything of true beauty would look entirely out of place in this gallery of poor taste.

Hardly any empty space existed in their house. Paintings and photographs pretending to be art contaminated the walls. Sculptures of modern shrapnel polluted poorly designed rooms full of uncomfortable furniture. At least the view from the upper-level terrace overlooking Central Park remained enchanting.

Even if she had tried to taint it with an amateur metal sculpture of...whatever the crap she thought that monstrosity in the corner was.

Fortunately, my interest in the Morgenstern's party had nothing to do with her definition of art and everything to do with his. But I had to wait for the opportune moment before admiring and acquiring my reason for crashing this party.

In the meantime, I contented myself with mingling and making new friends. Having dressed for the occasion, making those new friends was not difficult. I came clothed in my Audrey Hepburn-approved little black dress and stilettos, with my hair dyed a striking blonde and curled to perfection.

I looked like I'd stepped from the pages of a glamor magazine. A set of pearl earrings and a matching bracelet were added for good measure. A single, commanding diamond accented my right hand. Even the wedding band and engagement ring on my left hand—humble as they may have been—never deterred wealthy old geezers from flirting with me.

But hey! Makes my job easier. The more men flirt, the more they brag.

Floating between conversations with real estate moguls, investment bankers, international businessmen and women, and people who had money, though no one quite seemed to know how—the category under which Mr. Morgenstern fell—one learned an awful lot about the world and developed numerous conversation topics:

"Now is the time to buy stock in my new company. We go public next week, and demand will skyrocket."

"You are so right, *madame*. After eating Argentinian steak, one can never again have anything less."

"Isn't Croatia just beautiful? You must take a private yacht along the Dalmatian Coast. It's the most amazing vacation my husband and I have ever done."

"Have you seen the Met's new exhibit? The Renaissance Masters are unparalleled. Who's your favorite?"

"Wasn't ABT's production of *Swan Lake* magnificent? Their new *prima ballerina* is nothing short of divine."

"You own a unit in the Waldorf? We're neighbors! We must meet for a salad one afternoon."

I nodded periodically and made alternatingly agreeable or disappointed noises through a monologue concerning the impact of tariffs and third-world emigration on the global economy, only further muddled the aftermath of Brexit. Then, a passing comment from a neighboring conversation caught my ear.

"Did you hear about what happened in Atlanta?"

"You mean the bombing? A partner told me the FBI's already launched an investigation. Apparently, one of their agents was caught in the blast."

My heart stopped. Fortunately, my conversation partner remained too consumed by his passionate diatribe to notice that I neither paid him any mind nor continued to breathe.

Atlanta housed hundreds of FBI agents. That didn't matter. My emotional, terrified heart overpowered my rational brain to not merely assume but unequivocally know that the worst had occurred.

I needed to casually insert my curiosities into discovering more about what happened in Atlanta. My mind raced as I pieced together a cover story about having friends in the Candler family to allow me a passing interest in the goings-on of the South's empire city.

The trouble would come in feigning only a passing concern in the matter. In truth, I had to still my wildly terrified heart to avoid betraying the reality that my entire life hung in the balance of their answer.

I attempted to graciously exit the trade conversation. With each of my companion's rambling sentences, I tried extricating myself by taking gentle steps away from the enthusiastic gentleman.

But he merely stepped with me. He did not want me to miss a moment of his exhilarating, detailed analysis.

To make matters worse, the conversation that had captured my mind and soul also took to traveling.

“Of course, there are both sides to every situation,” I answered without having the faintest idea of the position posed.

The two unknown gentlemen wandered about the main room, examining the artwork and periodically setting aside the bombing to converse with assorted guests. As they ventured to the bar for a top-off, I knew I had to quickly follow.

“Yes, indeed,” my merchant companion agreed, “but what do you think?”

When they finally disappeared, I abandoned all sense of decorum, leaving the poor fellow with a most unhelpful answer.

“I find I am inclined to agree with them. Excuse me.”

Before the bewildered man could scratch his head, I took off at a most unceremonious trot across the condo. Sixty seconds passed like sixty years before I found them. Marching directly to the isolated duo, I inserted myself into their conversation in a horridly unladylike fashion.

“Excuse me, but I happened to overhear you make a comment about a bombing in Atlanta?”

“Yes! A most terrible thing.”

Thanks to my attire, neither gentleman hesitated to welcome me into their circle. My entirely forgotten aloofness provided an emotional dishevelment that helped my cause. Not my intention, but men can’t resist a damsel in distress.

“It seems some lunatic blew up a section of the interstate.”

“Which, uh, do, do you happen to know which interstate? And, uh, which section?” The emotion clogging my throat stole all suavity from my speech.

“I-85. Somewhere between the Perimeter and Midtown, I think.”

The second man nodded in agreement as he took a swig of gin. I made no effort to hide my sigh of partial relief. The offices sat nowhere near that location. He had no reason to drive through that area of town. Still, his sporadic unpredictability had drawn me to him.

“You said something of an FBI agent caught in the blast?” I prompted. “Has the name been released?”

“No, but I did hear it was someone in the white-collar division.”

All hope crumbled as my throat constricted. My heart dissolved, leaking into a puddle at my feet.

Without a word or the merest suggestion of decorum, I ripped my phone from the noir clutch I carried and abandoned the two men. Using the phone call as cover to innocently withdraw from the party, I quickly checked that neither Morgenstern could see. Clear, I slipped into the private area of the condo.

The phone rang.

And rang.

"Come on, pick up," I pleaded.

And rang.

"Please. Please answer your phone."

And rang.

When the voicemail *beep* shrilled in my ear, my unabashed concern had ignited into fear-fueled indignation.

"Answer your phone, you bastard!" I screamed into the receiver.

How dare he ignore my call!

All logic drowned in fervid distress. My heart wouldn't allow my mind the simple interjection that the eastern seaboard had already passed well into the night, and he went to bed early without me home to keep him awake. I dropped my mobile, letting it plunk down the carpeted stairs. My knees gave out.

Not three hours ago, I selected my attire for maximum effect during reconnaissance flirtation and slipping away unnoticed. My dress pressed to perfection, I dared not sit. The subtlest of wrinkles might have marred my meticulously curated appearance.

I even walked instead of taking a cab. On said walk, I wore a driving scarf wrapped loosely around my stylized hairdo, lest a stray gust flew through the city, leaving me disheveled.

But sitting on those stairs, the terror that my world and heart had exploded loomed about me. I wanted nothing other than to cast off my posh, tailored image and cuddle under a woolen blanket with him. I wanted wrinkles and disheveled hair.

I wanted neither glittering jewels, shining crystal ware, nor sparkling champagne. Only fleece pajamas, cheap mugs, and steaming tea. My fingers caressed the simple diamond and unadorned gold band on my left hand.

No less emotional but slightly less hysterical, I scooted my butt down the few stairs to reach my abused mobile. I redialed the number, convinced he would answer now. Again, the phone rang uninterrupted. A generic voicemail greeting clicked on. Taking a deep, steadying breath, I calmly left my recording.

"Call me back as soon as you get this. I need to talk to you."

My breath caught in my throat. Gasping to swallow that suffocating clump of emotion, I finished.

"Until we meet again."

And prayed I had not just lied.

Taking controlled, steadying breaths, I reminded myself I had a job to do. Focusing on that would help distract me until the return call came. I put away my phone and stood slowly. The shifting of every muscle came punctuated with another determined breath.

I will not fall into a helpless, emotional mess. I infiltrated this party for a reason, and I will not fail my client, by goodness.

Taking one more calming breath, I put everything but the thrill of the task at hand from my thoughts. Just as I took my first step, I saw what I hoped was a grandchild's finger painting displayed in a multi-hundred-dollar frame on prime wall placement. It hung directly at eye-level on an outcropping as you turned the corner at the bottom of the stairs.

The evident pride the Morgensterns felt about this particular piece of... *art*... caused a disgusted shiver to creep along my spine. It banished thoughts of all other horrors from my mind. I quickly continued down the hallway into the master bedroom.

When studying the condo's floor plan, I wondered why they had sequestered the master to what essentially acted as their basement. Why wasn't it left on the terrace level like in the original blueprints? Apparently, Mr. Morgenstern had rather a terrible time sleeping. The faintest light kept him awake.

Wonder if 'light's out' in prison engrained that?

As members of the Baby Boomer generation, they had no particular fondness for people trapesing through their private rooms. However, they wouldn't dare hinder guests' use of the upper floor. Thus, we found ourselves with a basement master bedroom.

Winding around the bed, I stopped in front of the larger, sturdier end table and squatted. I grabbed two felt gloves from my clutch and slipped off my rings. A quick popping open of the cabinet door revealed the safe tucked inside.

I fiddled with the single-dial combination lock to feel how the tumblers and bolts interacted in this design. Satisfied with my own knowledge of how this kind of safe behaves and the just-acquired intimate understanding of these particular tumblers, I set about feeling out the combination.

Each wrong tumbler made the faintest clicking sound as the lock spun around. A *thunk* barely louder than the clicking signified success upon reaching the correct numbers. To the trained ear, it sounded like a song. The final bolt released.

Aw. It's their anniversary.

The safe's door swung open, and my eyes landed on why I'd come to New York. I withdrew a cleaning wipe of my own design—a combination of bleach and 180-proof moonshine left to soak and mingle for 48 hours—and my calling card.

A smile of giddiness and pride stretched across my face as I stared at the beauty glistening in the lamplight. No matter the piece's final destination, I always adored the sensation of thieving.

Cradled on a silk pillow rested the only thing in Mr. Morgenstern's safe: a twenty-carat princess-cut white gold diamond necklace.

A contented sigh slid from my soul as I gazed upon that evening's prize. I knew I mustn't waste too much time in admiration, but she was just so pretty. Both hands still gloved, I removed the necklace from its hiding place and hung it around my neck.

Well, I tried to.

No matter how often I don jewelry, I can never work these stupid clasps.

Biting the tip of my glove, I ripped my hand free and used my naked fingers to latch the necklace. I used my gloved hand to place a tented piece of cardstock where the necklace once rested. The printed words read:

"Taken from you, courtesy of the Parisian Sapphire."

I locked the door before cleaning the safe with my wipe and closing the cabinet. Returning all my tools to my clutch, I turned off the lamp and went back upstairs. No one saw me emerge from the basement or slip out the door.

With neither need nor desire to linger in this abysmal excuse for a personal art gallery, I bade goodnight to the doorman and disappeared into the New York City night in search of pancakes.

The following day, I sat on the edge of Central Park's iconic Bethesda fountain. A depleted cuppa tea barely warmed my hand. I bemoaned my dislike of coffee on mornings such as this. The little sleep I managed to steal last night came in sporadic, restless fits plagued by cruel dreams and a racing mind.

My phone sat uncomfortably dormant through the long darkness of the night, and I had yet to receive any messages. I had the ringer firmly flipped to 'on,' and the ringtone volume raised to the max. Still, I spent most of last night compulsively checking for calls or texts. My heart sank a little further with each blank screen.

Fortunately, I had prearranged this morning's meeting to occur early—early for me, anyway—and had to stop by the bank first. That left only a short time to kill before something else distracted me. If only for a moment.

I waited for my client in sneakers, jeans, a hoodie from *The Phantom of the Opera,* purchased one size up, and an 'I heart NYC' baseball cap. Holding a brochure about the Statue of Liberty, I looked just like every other unmemorable tourist.

With timing not even I could have planned, my contact appeared just as I swallowed my last sip of tea. I tucked the brochure into my 'pickpocket-safe' travel bag and wandered to the trash can.

"Walk with me," I told the client without slowing my stride.

The scraggly young man fidgeted for a moment before dutifully falling into place. He came on behalf of his grandmother, as she could no longer amble around the park and might catch a cold in the chill of an autumn morning. Having learned of me through her extended 'family' connections, I never did get to meet the old woman. She seemed a colorful character.

Beginning our promenade down the Mall, I withdrew an envelope from my hoodie.

"This is the key to a safety deposit box at Goldman Sachs. The index card has the details and address. In the box, you'll find letters of authenticity and ownership. If anyone like Mr. Morgenstern ever tries to come after you again, you'll have the documentation to retrieve what's yours. And send him to jail.

"Natalie Blackwood is the manager. Refuse to conduct business with anyone besides her."

I took a dramatic pause. Though he had not said a word, the poor boy needed to breathe. Looking at him for the first time, I broke my frown with a smile.

"That's all there is to it. The heirloom will be back in your family's possession as soon as you pick it up."

"Thank you," the young man exhaled.

He tried to stop, to look me in the eye as we spoke, but I would not allow him. He tripped over his shoes, and his hands trembled as he took the envelope.

"You don't know what that necklace means to my family."

I smiled but said nothing. My mind was too distracted by my fiddling with the rings tucked in my hoodie pocket. The motion typically granted me a particular type of security and comfort. Nothing doing with the autumnal air, the metal felt cold this morning.

"Anything else?" he asked after realizing I would say nothing.

Brought back to the task at hand, I smiled again and told him, "Cross this street and wait until you are outside the zoo to open the envelope. Ignore the urge to look back."

Unable to forego a Shakespeare quote—we stood in the shadow of his Central Park statue, after all—I added:

" 'He no more shall see my face.' "

With a final 'thank you,' the young man grasped the envelope tightly and jogged between cars, crossing into the park's southern section. When he reached the far sidewalk, I turned and disappeared into the interior.

Before taking five steps, the dulcet tones of Josh Turner's baritone voice floated from my back pocket. Having spent the last twelve hours waiting for that sound, I nearly flipped my phone into the street as I yanked it free from the hug of my jeans.

"Well, it bloody well took you long enough to call me back, you bastard! What have you been doing for the last twelve hours!"

The voice on the other end came through calmly and clearly. Frankly, the fact my outburst had remained so condensed probably surprised him.

"Yes, I heard about the explosion. Why else do you think I was so desperate to talk to you? I heard an agent died! No? Of course, that's a good thing, but it does make me wonder why you couldn't call me sooner! Do you have any idea how dithery I was all last night?

"Yes, the party was fine," I answered his blatant attempt to change the subject and set my mind at ease. "That woman's sense of taste is atrocious," I lamented, "but no matter."

Going off on a new tangent, I remarked, "I think myself well suited to life in Victorian England. Dinner at 8. Parties begin 10 or later, and no one goes home until sunrise."

He had, once again, succeeded in subtly, or not so subtly, bending me to his will.

"Obviously, I'd be a member of the aristocracy!" I protested. "Who do you think I am? Why can't you just ask me on the phone?" I inquired about his final topical shift. "Fine, I can swing by the club. All told, it should take me about four hours. I'll find you."

Forgetting all jokes and pretenses, I smiled at the man over 800 miles away from me and promised:

"Until we meet again."

Chapter Two

In Which a Thoroughly Interesting Proposition Presented Itself

I spent the rest of my morning in a luxurious private plane, sipping mimosas and chatting with an old friend. I really must advocate for the befriending of the fabulously wealthy.

Needing to dress for the occasion, I changed clothes upon boarding. I sported a sky-blue sundress, wicker-style wedges, and a fashionably floppy beach hat. No one could be blamed for thinking I was flying to Martha's Vineyard, not Atlanta. Especially with my adornments of fine diamond and sapphire jewelry.

Much as I admired my new diamond and sapphire tennis bracelet, the rings on my left hand were the ones continuously catching my eye. The single stone—barely substantial enough to be called a diamond—on a simple gold band made me smile more than all the world's crown jewels.

"Another mimosa?" a man's voice asked in French.

"Hmm?" Once again, the rings tempted me into remembrance and delicious anticipation, so I had to be brought back to the present moment.

"Would you care for another mimosa before disembarking?" Gustave asked again in his native French.

Though wearing a custom-made velvet, three-piece, royal purple Yves Saint Laurent suit that only a black man can properly wear, diamond-studded cufflinks, and shoes more expensive than my entire outfit, Gustave Dubois' greatest accessories remained his smile and sultry French accent.

I have always felt something immensely sexy about a black man speaking French, particularly a well-dressed one, but perhaps that's just me. I looked over the cut crystal champagne flute in my hand and noted that only a few sips remained. But we would shortly finish taxiing to the hangar, and I had to drive to my meeting and then home.

"No, thank you." I took one of my final sips. I continued the conversation in his French. One must always do their utmost to accommodate their host when cashing in favors. "Thank you again for the lift, Gustave. It is so much more convenient than having to fly commercial."

"But, of course, *Madame* Kati!" He assured most emphatically, holding his arms out for a hug. "I am forever in your debt due to your tireless efforts to acquire all the pieces for my personal Degas collection."

"Forever in my debt?" I mused. "That's a dangerous claim to make."

"And yet, I still freely make it for as long as I live."

I raised my glass to the pristinely groomed and immaculately dressed Frenchman. He gladly reciprocated my toast. By that time, I'd known *Monsieur* Dubois for about five years. Only last year did I finally complete acquisitions for his prized Degas gallery.

He never had lacked for visitors. Now, his chateau in Saint-Tropez had become a mecca for the elite art lovers who marveled over his fantastic collection of sculpted and painted dancers. Gustave extended a standing invitation to me to visit the estate as another expression of his endless gratitude. I'd have to take him up on that offer sometime.

One of Gustave's stewardesses informed me the valet had brought my car around. I thanked her and finished my mimosa. Gustave set down his glass and stood with me. He buttoned his suit jacket as he did.

I switched to English to tell him, "I best not tarry."

Some things simply don't translate properly.

"I've a meeting I must get to. As always, Gustave, it has been a pleasure."

I gingerly held out my hand, which Gustave took in his to lightly kiss.

"I assure you, *Madame* Kati, the pleasure has been mine. Give my best to your husband."

"I shall. Thank you again."

"Au revoir!"

Thwack. Pfft. Thwack. Pfft. Thwack.

The cadence of a friendly round of tennis bounced off the ivy-draped walls of Fox Glen Country Club. Nestled in the heart of the luxurious Buckhead community, Fox Glen emerged in a refurbished antebellum estate some decades after Sherman burnt the city. It spent many years as an at-hand retreat until Atlanta grew to envelop it. Now, the club served as an oasis for members without even having to leave their zip code.

The crown jewel of Atlanta's elite social scene, Fox Glen boasted an exclusive member's list to rival any. Most white-collar folks spent years—if not their whole lives—clawing for the opportunity to join.

Me? I took the easy route. I stole my way in.

The CliffNotes version involves several mysteriously vanished masterpieces, exploitation of multiple staff members' desires, and the knowledge that denial or revocation of my membership would promptly result in numerous arrests, none of which would be my own. But those details are a story for another time.

With my hands resting on the railing, I stood on the terrace overlooking the tennis courts. Beneath me, Special Agent Garth Harmon of the FBI's White-Collar division played a friendly match. The presence of a government agent devoted to hunting and arresting people like me would, understandably, deter me from becoming a member here.

However, he was only here because of me. And I immensely enjoyed watching him sweat beneath me. I tell you, forbidden desire constitutes at least half the fun of foreplay.

Unfortunately, those gym shorts do nothing to show off his immaculately sculpted posterior.

Agent Harmon's lean build was one of subtle muscles. It all lent itself perfectly to his chipper but professional demeanor. He bounced the ball off his racquet in preparation for his next serve. Feeling my presence, Garth suddenly looked up as though a sound only he heard caught his ear.

Our eyes locked.

I meant to hold a dominating stance and unfeeling expression of examination over this infiltrated kingdom. But seeing his cinnamon-colored eyes latch onto mine for the first time in over a week broke me. My smile was entirely different from the one I had during the theft.

That had radiated from a place of subterfuge, power, and the adrenaline rush that only comes from getting away with something. This smile held nothing but pure unbridled joy and devotion. It was evoked by only one person in all the world.

And he was safe.

Agent Harmon made his apologies to his playing partner before trotting toward the locker rooms. Garth glanced up at me with a perfectly timed wink and smile before disappearing beneath the veranda.

My, am I glad to be home!

Allowing my fingertips to linger as I pulled away from the banister, I left my post, strolling towards our secluded meeting locale. Fox Glen had a patch of land on the far side of a two-acre pond that no one else ever bothered to visit. And on this half-acre of seclusion stood a gazebo.

In a most striking moment of design inspiration, the artist constructed this gazebo from dark mahogany wood and sculpted wrought iron. The sculptor used wrought iron to craft the main structure, while the wood created the gazebo's floor, bench, and roofing tiles.

Carved in the guise of petrified trees, the six support beams wrapped around themselves with knots and bark lines to solidify the illusion of the artistry. Beautiful as the beams looked, the bottom half proved the crowning jewel.

Perfect ebony rose bushes were forever frozen in various stages of bloom, twisted and intertwined around themselves. As my fingertip glided across the glossed, thorn-less blooms, I heard Agent Harmon's voice behind me quote from *Le Petit Prince.*

" 'The stars are beautiful because of a flower that cannot be seen.' "

I smiled and let my eyes close as I fell into the comfortable intimacy of his recitation and the feeling of his heat near me.

I sighed and replied, " 'That which is essential is invisible to the eye.' "

"Strange sentiment for a thief."

"Who's to say I keep all the things I steal?"

Though he still stood behind me, I could tell by Garth's pause he acknowledged this point.

"Was your trip productive?" he finally asked.

"Indeed, all pieces have returned to their proper place. Though I'll never understand why the family doesn't sell that necklace. You have any idea how much money that thing's worth?"

"Some people value sentiment over money," he explained.

"Some people are idiots."

Relaying the partial tease in my retort, I sent Agent Harmon a sidelong glance and the subtlest of half-smiles. I admired one of the sculpted roses for a moment, unsuccessfully attempting to hide my giddiness. Clearing my throat, I stepped around to the other side of the gazebo as Agent Harmon sat on the bench opposite me.

To distract myself, I got down to business. "You said you needed something of me?"

"I need your expertise."

"I help you with cases all the time. Why treat this one so formally?"

"We require your services in a slightly different capacity."

I perked and looked over my shoulder to meet Garth's eyes. With a toothy smile and wide eyes burning with anticipation, I guessed:

"The FBI wants me to steal something?"

"No," he answered blankly, shattering the prospect of my joy.

All excitement drained from my face, leaving a thin-lipped, unamused expression.

"You'd act as an official consultant," he answered the unspoken question behind my scowl.

"And allow the FBI to know about me?" I gasped, turning back outward.

"The FBI already knows about you."

"The only things the FBI know about me are that they have no idea who I am and have no hope of catching me," I reminded with a dismissive twirl of my wrist.

I heard Garth chuckle behind me as he made his pitch. "The night we met, you wore a twelve-karat diamond and sapphire ring to dinner that you had stolen from Cartier earlier that same day."

He sauntered over behind me to whisper in my ear, "You can't expect me to believe you wouldn't relish the chance to be invited in, knowing that not one of those agents could touch you or even know your real identity."

"I do hope one of them will touch me," I sighed.

Spinning within the frame of his arms, the teasing smile I meant to display melted. Seeing him healthy and whole stole all coy elusiveness from my mind. Our faces hovered hardly a breath apart. With their flecks of gold, his cinnamon eyes shone in the sun.

I could no longer keep the charade. I sighed again but without the tease of desire. Only now as an outpouring of relief and contentment. Without a word passing between us—the welling of alleviation in my eyes told him more than words would have explained—I threw my arms around Garth.

I clutched him against my chest until I felt his heart beating in time with mine. Finally confident in his safety, I released my hold and relaxed against the gazebo's railing.

Returning to business, I admitted, "You make an enticing offer. But is the thrill ultimately worth the risk of giving away my anonymity? More to the point..."

I looked up to meet his eyes anew, my lips curling upward in a desirous half-smile. With the matter of devout sentiment settled, I could now return to our game and resume my sexily aloof facade. I bit my lower lip.

"Why are you suddenly so desperate for me?"

"Is it sudden?" he teased, shifting his weight to close the gap.

I acted to meet him but rolled backward just before he could reach me.

"But what makes the FBI desperate?"

Garth laughed in resignation. He knew I would only keep extending my teasing foreplay. He pushed himself off the railing and padded across the gazebo.

"We have evidence to believe Mancini was behind the explosion."

"Mancini's a thief," I reminded. "Why would he commit what you seem to think is a terrorist act?"

"CSI collected fragments which match a bomb he's suspected of having used seven years ago as a diversion while he robbed the Uffizi."

"But as you said, that explosion, which may or may not have had anything to do with Mancini," —I pointed out with the raised single finger of a school teacher— "was used as a distraction for a theft. Was anything stolen around the time of the 85 explosion?"

"Not that we know of," he admitted.

"Oh, you'd know. That's a heck of a distraction; he would have stolen something incredible."

"You don't think it's Mancini?"

"I'm curious why the FBI is so convinced," I corrected. "To such a degree they'd hire the likes of me."

I turned around to stare contemplatively across the lake. I kept spinning as I realized something Agent Harmon had yet to explain.

"How *did* the prospect of my cooperation come about?"

"Well..."

He told how one of his coworkers jokingly suggested hiring someone who thinks like Mancini to get in his head and anticipate his next actions. The outlandish suggestion made Agent Harmon consider me and how I helped him catch a rival thief when we first met. He told the pertinent details of our professional camaraderie and suggested he contact me about consulting.

He paused before adding, "We're prepared to meet your demands."

"Any demand?" I asked with a cocked eyebrow.

"Possibly."

Turning back outward, I mused over all my options. "I want..."

I tapped a finger on my lips, pondering, "Immunity for all former crimes."

"Former crimes?" I could hear Agent Harmon's rise in pitch. "Nothing about future crimes?"

Once more spinning to him, I protested, "What's the fun in immunity for future crimes? That's totally cheating and robs at least half the excitement out of it."

Garth crinkled his eyes and looked sideways at me. "There is something wrong with you. Are you aware of that?"

"Acutely," I whispered with a wink.

Garth's eyes shone with such a hunger that I thought he might fly across the gazebo and force himself on me right then and there. Not that I would protest. With every heave of his chest, every labored and stunted breath as he fought to temporarily squelch that burning desire, my own built.

My smile creased deeper into my cheeks. My own hunger shone in my eyes as heat billowed throughout my body. My heart raced. It pounded within my chest to such an extent that I feared my breast might burst.

But then was not the time. Terms needed setting. Serious matters required discussion. And we both knew it.

"So," Agent Harmon asked after we finally managed to calm ourselves, "will you help us?"

"What happens to my immunity if it's nothing to do with Mancini?"

"The terms aren't contingent," he assured me. "If you help us find who's behind this, or who isn't, as the case may be, you'll get your immunity."

I considered for a moment. "And you believe your boss will actually grant my immunity?"

"I do. Mainly because he's desperate and doesn't have a choice." He shrugged. "The attack wasn't exactly subtle. There's a lot of pressure around this one."

"Alright." I held up my hand to still his excitement. His mouth hung open mid-breath. "I will consider your proposal. I make no promise other than that I will genuinely think about it."

Agent Harmon nodded diplomatically. "That'll do."

Knowing the conversation had ended, but neither wishing to leave, a bored, waiting silence settled over the gazebo. Garth fell into a habit retained from childhood. When caught in a situation more boring than uncomfortable, he tapped his finger and stared off into space while blowing air bubbles out of the corner of his mouth. I took the far more dignified pastime of an in-depth examination of my cuticles and conducting Rorschach tests of the clouds.

With an exasperated sigh incorporating a slight raspberry, I announced, "I'm hungry. You want some lunch? Perhaps a pint at Clover and Crown?"

"I shouldn't," he sighed. "I oughta get back to work."

"Spoilsport. But just as well. I should probably actually start preparing for the party."

Agent Harmon stood and buttoned his suit jacket. Though tailored to perfection, it still came off a Dillard's clearance rack. It gave me the slight urge to vomit whenever I saw him wear one of those work suits.

Honestly! The man owns custom-made suits from Brooks Brothers yet voluntarily wears those hobo suits! I digress.

"Think about the offer," he said. "We could really use your help."

"I told you I would, and I will. But not on an empty stomach."

Agent Harmon paused in the entryway of the gazebo. Looking over his shoulder to meet my eyes, he added:

"Try not to steal anything *too* valuable while you make up your mind."

"What else would I steal?" I teased with a shrug and head tilt more seductive than inquisitive.

Garth only smiled contentedly and promised, "Until we meet again."

Watching him go, I couldn't help but think back to the first time we met. I had traveled to Paris for work, spending much of my time visiting the Louvre and Cartier. Agent Harmon had taken it upon himself to use vacation days to track a hunch about Mancini.

I still wonder, can a woman find anything sexier than a man impassioned?

Five Years Earlier...

I sat enjoying my morning chai at a café in the *Jardín des Tuileries* and watching the most intriguing man sitting alone across the patio. He was generally attractive. The kind of man who caused your gaze to linger as you passed but weren't likely to fantasize about.

But his physical appearance did not draw me to him. His hair didn't hold the milk chocolate shine I would come to love; it just looked brown. The glimpses I caught of his eyes looked sandier than like cinnamon. His ill-fitting, off-the-rack suit did nothing to impress my eye.

Even still, something I couldn't—nor wanted to—resist compelled my gaze.

He had a folder and several papers sprawled across his table, all held down by a cup of coffee on a saucer. He studied each document with lightning speed and sporadic scrambling. It reminded me of a squirrel.

A rogue gust of wind blew through the café on this otherwise still day. One of the papers sat beyond the saucer's reach and blew off the table. Without looking away from the paper he studied, Agent Harmon extended his arm and snatched the fleeing paper mid-flight.

The speed of his nonchalant reflexes elicited a justly amazed, though silent, reaction from me. I had to know who this man was. I casually stood from my seat and made a sweep around the café. My route just *happened* to take me by Agent Harmon's table, and I caught a glimpse of a surveillance photo he held.

I instantly recognized the bald, olive-skinned man as Arsenio Mancini. This revelation only piqued my interest in the ill-dressed suit. I continued my sweep under the guise of going to the toilet and left him be.

For about 60 seconds.

"You'll never catch him here," I said, standing behind the agent.

"Excuse me?" He turned to see who had interrupted him.

I moved in the opposite direction around the table so his eyes couldn't catch me.

"You'll never catch him here," I repeated, knowing he heard me the first time. "In Paris, I mean."

I sat in the chair across from him without waiting for an invitation. I always have valued forgiveness over permission, though rarely seeking either.

"Not even in France, really. He doesn't much like France," I explained to the man's dumbfounded expression. "He's essentially the antithesis of a Francophile. He greatly prefers Tuscany."

"One might describe that as a Francophobe," he quipped, finding his bearings. A half-smile stretched up one cheek.

My heart jumped a beat in response.

Agent Harmon used the lingering silence to evaluate his new tablemate. If the camisole plastered against my bra beneath the open button-down shirt did anything for him, his eyes didn't betray it.

Instead, he seemed most interested in the magnificent diamond-encircled sapphire ring I wore. He stared at it, trying to recall where he'd seen it before. He may have seen it had he wandered through the Cartier store recently. Somehow, he didn't strike me as the kind to frequent high-end jewelry houses.

"That is quite the ring," he finally said, nodding to my right hand.

"Oh, why, thank you." I raised my hand to rest my chin on the back of my fingers and display the ring more prominently. "It has become one of my favorites."

He continued staring at the ring. I could see the gears in his mind grinding together as he struggled to pin its familiarity. Finally giving up—I assumed only temporarily—he returned to the question of Mancini.

"You claim I won't find this man in France," he leaned forward as he spoke. I realized, then, the relaxed composure he'd maintained throughout our conversation. Even now, he looked more interested than concerned. "Are you familiar with him?"

"Relatively," I shrugged in a decidedly noncommittal manner.

"And how do you know him? Relatively speaking," he added with a playful glint in his eyes.

This man understood the game and took to it with remarkable ease. Though unquestionably a man, his face retained a boy's delicate features and wide-eyed innocence. But innocence alone did not shine in his eyes.

A mischievous twinkle flashed behind that disarming smile in a way that sent flares of desire coursing through my body. My body's reaction to those twinkles would only become more poignant as anticipation joined desire.

I leaned forward to meet Agent Harmon's gaze.

"We've worked together."

For the first time in our encounter, Agent Harmon's composure broke. His mouth fell open as his eyes matched the saucer holding his coffee. He shifted with the very first stages of beginning to move towards me. The waitress, appearing with his pastry, blocked him.

Capitalizing on his trapped position, I bade the enchantingly mysterious man enjoy his breakfast and disappeared into the throngs of tourists. I imagined him attempting to follow me but wouldn't allow myself to look back and see. I only smiled and kept moving further away.

As I soon learned, some distances can always be breached no matter their length.

Chapter Three

In Which I Rediscovered the Simple Pleasures of Returning Home

Is there anything more pleasurable in all the world than driving down a country backroad on a crisp fall day in a pristinely tuned convertible? Well, maybe not nothing, *but nothing that one can do by oneself.*

The deep, sultry red of my Shelby Cobra melded perfectly with the changing colors of the leaves that decorated both the branches and the road. The gray racing stripe bisecting the custom paint job and the wood interior only heightened my belief that Hermie and I belonged on this road.

Always needing proper color coordination, I'd slipped on my red driving gloves. My *Breakfast at Tiffany's* sunglasses completed the ensemble for driving from Fox Glen to the manor, which stood about half an hour south of the city.

To keep my hair from flying and tangling every which way, I wrapped it up and contained every strand in an orange and blue driving scarf. Unfortunately, the color coordination simply went all to splinters with this inclusion. But I'd adopted that combination from my husband's alma mater and favored football team.

The only games I grew up on used neurolinguistic programming and weren't something one could discuss in polite society. As such, I brought no rivalries to the romance. I acquiesced soon enough to my husband's devotion to something other than me.

Coming out of a dipping curve in the road, I downshifted and floored the gas. Off Hermie and I went. The name of my favored car came from a diminutive of Hermes, the Master Thief of Olympus. My smile grew into pure elation as I hugged every curve, flew between them on the straightaways, and generally enjoyed myself on this gorgeous autumnal day.

I never much understood the concept of a casual Sunday afternoon drive. One could deduce such from the '10-80' vanity plate adorning Hermie. Also known as the police code for a high-speed chase. Drives like this, however, forever remained a pastime that never failed to thrill me.

Upon reaching the driveway, I slowed from speeding and turned between two ivy-draped stone walls. An entrance better suited to a European country estate was rather the idea when designing and building my home. A simple, wrought-iron gate stood perpetually open, hanging off both sides of the walls flanking the dirt driveway.

My back tires spun ever so slightly as they momentarily struggled to grip the new loose road. I soon disappeared beyond the curve in the forest, which blocked all but the first dozen feet of the driveway from the view of prying eyes. After two full minutes of wending my way through the trail we called a driveway, the trees suddenly fell away.

The driveway split from a single-lane dirt track to a full circle of finely manicured pea gravel perfectly contained and separated from the mown grass. Looming above the perfection of my tailor-made entryway stood a three-story Edwardian-style country home to do Downton Abbey justice.

Growing up mainly on a ranching estate in Argentina, I never felt truly at home unless my abode covered at least 10,000 square feet. After spending no insignificant amount of time traveling throughout Europe and visiting various estates, villas, and chalets, the simple ostentatiousness of the Jacobethan block homes drew me more than anything else.

I never intended to share this home with anyone other than my husband, so I didn't need anything exceedingly gorgeous to show off. I built the manor home for me and my pleasure alone. The addition of a husband merely added to that pleasure.

Knowing I'd soon leave to formally accept my offer in the FBI offices, I parked Hermie in front of the main door. I put my scarf and gloves back in the glove box and retrieved my overnight bag from the trunk before heading inside.

My desire for a muted opulence on the house's exterior did not extend inside the walls. A polished marble foyer magnified the light from the Waterford crystal chandelier hanging overhead. It all expertly illuminated various tapestries and paintings I'd collected throughout my years.

The uneducated eye would see my private gallery as pretty and impressive. Any curator or scholar worth their salt would murder for the chance to examine the works I had mounted. With the ivy-draped walls, manicured yard, and polished entryway, one would be forgiven for believing that this house did contain a small museum.

But step beyond the foyer to discover just how intimate a home it was. I wandered to a swirling pink and black marble dresser to drop my keys in their bowl. Beside the bowl stood a picture of my husband and me, taken while on vacation at some nondescript tourist beach along the eastern seaboard for our first anniversary.

I had intended to pose smiling for the picture, but he blindsided me with a kiss. Our Good Samaritan photographer managed to perfectly capture the moment. We knew no other photo could occupy this place of honor. Further down the dresser spun a statuette of one of Degas' dancers, forever suspended in mid-pirouette. I winked at her before heading up the floating marble staircase.

Hardly an inch of space remained on the hallway leading to the master bedroom. Photographs of me and my husband or posters from various movies, operas, ballets, plays, and musicals we'd attended covered the paint. Many would fetch a pretty penny for any serious collector with several of the posters signed.

For my part, I wouldn't dare allow a single one of them out of my possession for all the crown jewels in the world. Each poster elicited a priceless memory shared between my husband and me. That simplicity overpowered any material thing I could ever covet.

I flung my suitcase onto the king-sized, mahogany sleigh bed dominating the master suite, kicked my heels off, and sank into the plush leather armchair with a sigh. I considered everything Garth had told me about the attack and weighed it against everything I personally knew about Mancini.

None of it made sense. But perhaps I didn't know Mancini as well as I thought.

Pushing myself up from the chair, I crossed around the foot of the bed. Our TV hung mounted on the wall as an expansive cabinet with glass doors housed the extensive collection of movies ranging from Blu-rays to VHS tapes. All of these came courtesy of my husband.

Though I enjoy an evening at the cinema, I never cared for watching any movie repeatedly and certainly had no interest in owning my own copy. My husband, however, adored films and made a habit of collecting them. I never complained. Some of our best nights at home began as movie nights.

I fished my phone out of my bag in an act that took me several seconds longer than it should have. After boarding Gustave's plane, I had haphazardly tossed it into my luggage and didn't think anything more of it. The blasted thing sank to the bottom of my bag, and found it amusing to run about and hide under clothes as I searched for it.

Finally locating and trapping the bastard, I yanked my phone from the bag in a moment of triumph. Only to lose my grip and send it flying across the room. Fortunately, it landed harmlessly on the carpeted floor, faceplanting with a dull *thud.* I spit a raspberry at the pesky piece of technology before circling the bed to retrieve my phone.

I finally set about making my phone call. I dialed the number of an Argentine-based cell phone from memory, put the call on speaker, and stuffed the phone in my bra strap as I set about unpacking from my trip.

As the phone rang, I remembered the last time I went home to visit Uncle César. Though we talked on the phone regularly, nearly five years had passed since I last saw him. I had returned to Argentina after a job in Paris, but the memory of an unexpected meeting at a park café and subsequent dinner distracted me.

Five Years Earlier...

The day glowed with gorgeous autumnal beauty as the cab drove me across the rolling hills of Uncle César's estate. Of course, we barely traversed a tenth of the massive ranch he'd acquired in retirement as we drove up the endless approach road from the main gate. I told the driver to drop me off at the villa's second gate. I'd walk from there.

I did not explain to the driver that dropping me just outside the gate substantially decreased the likelihood of him being shot. Javier had not won the position of Uncle César's head of security due to his leniency. I intended my return trip to surprise Uncle César. Else he certainly would have sent his helicopter to fetch me from the airport and deposit me right at the front steps.

A sprawling mansion to dwarf my country manor towered above me. The Mediterranean-style Spanish revival home boasted a smooth adobe façade with sweeping archways and wrought iron decorations complementing the soft tonal colors of the exterior.

While gorgeous in its custom design, the physical appearance of Uncle César's villa didn't captivate me near as much as the emotional resonance of returning to my first home.

I still have no idea how I found myself in Argentina as an approximate twelve-year-old. I only remember wandering aimlessly through the picturesque countryside and avoiding the *gauchos* when I stumbled upon the grandest house I'd ever seen.

They had just completed construction on the house. Many furnishings were still arriving at their new home. As such, the doors stood open for easy passage. Through careful observations and silent movements, I slipped inside after watching the last group of workmen leave for the evening.

Inside, I discovered a wonderland of priceless art and artifacts. Approaching footsteps kept me from reveling in the beauty. I searched for an escape and tore up the staircase at the end of the room. I wandered dumbfounded through breathtaking frescos, gracefully shifting to new scenes with each turn.

Eventually, I found myself in the master bedroom. A single room more massive than some houses I'd lived in. But what truly caught my eye rested on a nightstand beside the poster bed. An open ring box captured the setting sun's light streaming through the window and sent refractions dancing all along the walls and ceiling.

Someone less captivated by the light source might have noticed the magical way the jeweled beams perfectly highlighted the frescos painted within the room. Once close enough to realize what reflected the light, I discovered a ring with the most massive blue stone I'd ever seen.

My mouth hung open as I marveled at its beauty and no longer had to wonder how it caught the sun's full power with such ease. The approaching footsteps came for me again. I grabbed the box and ducked into the bathroom.

Two men's voices talking in Spanish came near before one suddenly stopped midsentence. I was sure I'd been caught. The voices remained quiet for an eternity before I finally heard another sound. The sound of a gun cocking. I sucked in my breath. The bathroom door ripped open to my scream and hiding place.

To my surprise, the man who opened the door didn't immediately shoot me. He didn't even hold the gun. The tanned skin I'd seen on the *gauchos* also appeared on this man. He, however, wore a three-piece suit and no hat. He stared at me for a long moment as his face shifted from rage to confusion. He couldn't quite seem to figure out what had happened.

How had I found my way into his house? And why did I hold his ring?

I believe he recognized the fear on my face because he raised two fingers. The man behind him put away the gun. The man said something that sounded like a question, but I had no idea what it meant. I clutched the ring box tighter.

Though I had no idea what would happen, I knew it best to have something with which to barter. The man knelt before me to move from looking down on me to looking me in the eye.

"Do you speak English?" he asked with a heavily accented voice.

I opened my mouth to speak but found I could only silently nod.

"Who are you? How did you get here?"

This time I didn't bother trying to move my lips. I only shrugged and shook my head. I didn't know the answer to either of his questions.

His eyes dropped to the ring box I clutched against my training bra. He slowly lifted one finger and gently tapped it against the box. He was careful to avoid touching me.

"Do you know what this is?"

"A sapphire ring," I answered.

His eyes shot up to meet mine again. They'd grown in shock as though the mute had just learned to speak. For all he knew, that was precisely what had happened.

"Why do you want to take it from me?" His voice held little accusation or annoyance. Confused curiosity overshadowed every other emotion.

I hesitated before responding, "It's expensive and will buy me things."

"What sorts of things?" With each question, any angry, accusatory sound in voice further dissipated, lightening into gentle, curious prodding.

I hesitated again before answering. Not because I searched for an answer, but because the answer seemed completely obvious.

"Whatever I want."

My response drew an unfiltered laugh from the man kneeling before me. He twisted to look at the man behind him and said something in Spanish. It must have been a joke. The other man smiled and gave a stifled laugh.

"Do you have anywhere to go?" the man asked after turning back to me.

I shook my head.

"Would you like to spend the night here? I have a spare bed and plenty of food." His eyes dropped to the ring box again. "But, if you want to stay, I need two things from you. I will need that ring back and the promise that you will never try to steal it again. *¿Claro?*"

I watched the man's eyes for several seconds as I wondered what to do. The idea of a real bed and hot food enticed me to accept his offer for the night. Something about his eyes made me want to stay longer. I relinquished my hold of the ring box and placed it in his waiting hand.

He smiled and said something else. The box that had required both of my hands to securely hold rested easily in one of his. He clutched it so tight that I thought he might need it to live. Like that sapphire ring acted as his version of Iron Man's arc reactor.

"My name is César. What is yours?"

I stared at him in silence again for a far longer moment than I should have needed to answer a simple question. For me, however, the question wasn't simple. My eyes slipped from focus as I looked inward and frantically searched for the answer to his question. Finally, I steadied my gaze on his.

"You can call me Kati."

Returning as a 25ish-year-old, I marched past the armed security and waltzed inside undisturbed. I paused a moment in the stone foyer to listen. It took less than a full second for me to hear Uncle César's billowing laugh rolling through the open doors leading onto the grand terrace.

No surprise there. The balcony overlooked 100 acres of pastureland and had always been Uncle César's favorite part of the house. I handed my bags to the butler coming to greet me, then wandered through to the back of the house.

"By the time *la policía* knew anything, I was already lounging in my pool with my brand-new bottle of Chardonnay," Uncle César told his guest. He laughed hysterically at his own story. His guest laughed obligingly.

Though I did not join in the laughter, a joyously contented smile crossed my face. Instead of saying hello and announcing myself like any sane person, I decided to surprise everyone by diving headlong into the conversation.

"I have missed your stories, Uncle César."

A man in his early 60s whose face aged far more gracefully than his joints, Uncle César leapt to greet me with a speed and dexterity I'd never seen. Though I'd known the man for over a decade at that point, I still saw his beaming smile and somewhat rotund build the same way I did in that first moment when I knew he'd shield me and keep me safe.

He lumbered towards me with arms outstretched and unbridled giddiness on his face. Wrapping his arms around me in a hug I could never escape, he lifted me into the air as though still a child. At that moment, I felt like one again. I stood in the lavish security of the first place I'd ever called home and settled into the cradling—or squishing—of the only man who had yet loved and cared for me.

The feeling of Uncle César's casual linen suit and his perpetual smell of Cuban cigars washed over me. I was transported to the comfort of a beautiful childhood. Even if it had a delayed start.

"¡Mi pequeña ladróna!" He all but screamed in my ear while he still held my arms pinned against me. *"¿Cómo estás?* I'm so glad to see you!"

He squeezed me tighter before returning me to my feet. "Why did you not tell me you're coming home?" Having grown up in Argentina, Uncle César spoke with the sultry melody of the Rioplatense Spanish accent.

"I wanted it to be a surprise," I told him. Throwing my arms out wide, I yelled back at him, *"¡Sorpresa!"*

Greeting my outstretched arms, we hugged again.

"How are you?" he inquired.

"I'm doing well. Great, actually."

"I can tell. You smile."

"Do I not usually?"

"Yes, but you smile different than I know. Something happened on your trip."

I responded with a giggle, which I attempted to suppress by exhaling and pretending to clear my throat. The whole endeavor failed miserably. I coughed long enough to hack up a lung. Uncle César offered me a glass of water with paternal concern over whether or not I'd survive the ordeal.

I eventually did. A gulp of water washed down my embarrassment in front of Uncle César's unknown guest. I thanked Uncle César as I returned the emptied glass to him.

Before I could say anything more or make excuses why I couldn't divulge this information in front of the stranger, Uncle César told the man to leave. Without delay or protest, the man stood, shook Uncle César's hand, made a slight nod of recognition to me, and departed without a word.

Though retired from our line of work, Uncle César still demanded the respect of those who came searching for him.

"Come here." He crossed the porch to the table and pulled out the chair for me. "Sit. Sit."

Once I settled, Uncle César moved around to where the other man had sat. "Tell me all about your travels. Where were you last?"

"Paris," I told him.

"¡Dios mío!" He threw condescending arms in the air. "No wonder you look so hungry. The Parisians and their over-praised food."

His hands dropped to the table as he slammed a pointed finger repeatedly onto the glass tabletop. I feared he might shatter the glass and send his finger slicing right through the table.

"Tonight, you dine on real Argentinian steak!"

I couldn't contain my smile and chortle. "If you insist."

"Now, about this smile." He leaned forward, studying my face. His eyes watched me like the answer to my giddiness lay written just beneath the crinkle of my eyes. "Who brought this about? What is his name?"

"Who's to say it was a man?" I attempted to remain as coy as possible, but we both knew Uncle César was spot-on. I continued with my charade. "Perhaps I did extremely well for myself in Paris." I sat back triumphantly in my chair with my fingers laced authoritatively.

"No. I know the smug, devious smile of a job well done. This is not it. This is a smile of pure, untainted joy. This is a smile of love."

"Infatuation, perhaps. Love is far too strong a word." I waved my hand dismissively as though I could shoo the word away.

Uncle César watched me with his emblematic, versatile stare. He never scowled, sneered, raised eyebrows, or looked down at you. His eyes narrowed slightly to form a straight line that matched his mouth. The expression itself conveyed no meaning and would seem disinterested to an outsider.

The recipient, however, knew precisely what Uncle César desired to gain through that gaze. Whether waiting for my 13-year-old-self to confess about borrowing one of his cars for a joyride or convincing bounty hunters to leave him alone, Uncle César's ability to make anyone crack under that stare became the bane of many people's secrets.

I leaned forward in a futile attempt to meet his stare and beat him at his own game. After several seconds of returned focus—a feat I'm still quite proud of—I finally broke.

"Fine." I slumped back into my chair in abject failure.

Overselling my indignation, I slammed harder into the wrought iron chair than I'd intended. A throbbing pain shot through my shoulder. Sitting forward again, I rotated and stretched the bruised muscle as I acquiesced to Uncle César's questions.

"Did you meet him while in Paris?"

I nodded.

"Who is this master thief?"

Another chuckle escaped me as I thought of my man as a master thief.

"He is no thief," I corrected.

"But a thief he must be, for he has stolen your gaze. What a thief a man must be to steal the heart of one such as you. So, what does this master thief do? Is he honest?"

I sighed with a nostalgic comfort that surprised me as I thought of the enchanting man I'd only met a few days before. I released my hold on my shoulder and leaned back—gently—into the chair.

"Honest as they come," I finally said with a contentedly enraptured smile I knew I couldn't hide.

"I see, and does he know you?"

I nodded again.

"And he let you go?" The surprise of Uncle César's voice couldn't be missed.

"As if he could catch me," I teased.

"I hate to break it to you, *mi pequeña ladróna*, but it seems he already has."

I smiled once more and didn't try to deny it. I wouldn't dare lie to Uncle César.

The click of an answered phone drew me back to the present moment.

"*¿Hola?* Who is it?"

"Uncle César, you know who it is," I scoffed as I pulled my black dress out of the bag and examined the wrinkles. It hadn't crinkled enough to need extra attention. I passed through the bathroom into the closet and returned it to its hanger.

"And you know that I always verify before I start talking," he reminded me. "One can never be too careful in our line of business. A great many people don't like us, you know."

"A great many people *love* me," I retorted, tossing my reading glasses and current book onto the matching mahogany nightstand. "Clearly, you're doing something wrong."

I withdrew a silk bag tucked into my suitcase pocket and carried it back into the bathroom.

"Yes, I've heard about your..." he paused, trying to settle on the right word, "philanthropic pursuits."

I froze in mid-squat, hesitating at eye-level with the copper sink. My hand rested on the cabinet handle. "You aren't disappointed, are you?"

"Disappointed! *¿Eres loco?*"

A relieved smile slid across my face. I proceeded with my unpacking. Opening the unassuming cabinet door, I moved a piece of cardboard aside to reveal a stainless-steel safe between the Q-tips and hair ties.

"You've found a way to thieve with almost no risk of getting caught. You have all the thrill with none of the risks."

I input the combination, then scanned my thumbprint and retina before the safe clicked open.

"I'm jealous I never thought of it myself! Besides, it's not like you need the income to support yourself."

In perfectly timed agreement, the door to the safe popped open. It housed millions of dollars' worth of rings, necklaces, earrings, and bracelets. Diamonds, sapphires, emeralds, rubies, onyx, gold, silver, and countless combinations collected over the years from various sources. I withdrew my necklace of Tahitian pearls from the silk bag to return to their resting place.

"How have you been, *mi pequeña ladróna*?"

"I'm great, but I called because I need to ask you a question. I need information."

"About what?"

Returning all the jewelry that had traveled with me to New York, I closed the safe. I wandered back into the bedroom to finish the rest of my unpacking.

"Have you heard about what's happened in Atlanta?"

"*Sí,* of course. You live there. I always monitor the news of every city you're living in. Every city that you tell me you're living in, anyway."

Though he couldn't see it, I'm sure Uncle César knew I smiled at his additional comment.

"You aren't in danger from it, are you?"

"No, no. I'm fine. I'm safe. I need to know if Mancini could have been behind it."

"Mancini? Why Mancini?" He stuttered before adding, "Why do you need to know?"

I hesitated for a moment before deciding to tell him the truth. "I'm helping the FBI with the case."

Silence.

"I take it you're working with the honest thief?" he finally asked.

"I am."

"And the FBI? What do they know of you?"

"Not a damn thing," I reported with proud confidence.

"No blackmail?"

I sneered at the phone on behalf of both our points of pride. "You taught me better than that."

"Then why work with them?"

I paused again as I wondered about my answer. Honestly, I hadn't given any consideration to why. I certainly hadn't thought about it well enough to explain or justify my decision to someone else.

Of course, I played coy when presented with the opportunity. I would continue to do so until officially accepting, but that was all part of the game.

The truth of the matter simply remained that Garth had asked. That settled it. Finally, I gave Uncle César the only answer he'd accept and believe.

"Because I'm in love with him."

"Then, that's all there is to it," he replied with an audible smile. "What do you need to know?"

Chapter Four

In Which a Thief Became a Cop

After a lovely conversation with the sweetest lady at the security desk—an adorably sassy mother of four with a husband who cries at Nicholas Sparks movies—she told me I'd find Special Agent Harmon on the fifth floor.

Pathetic. This abysmally bland government building stood only eight stories tall, and he couldn't even manage a penthouse office? What a slacker I'd hitched myself to.

Never one to deny myself the pleasure of a jaunt through private and restricted locations, I went promptly to the elevators and pressed the button labeled '2'. I knew the first level only housed the lobby and cafeteria. I had no qualms bypassing it. The dull pencil-pushing jobs constituted the whole of the second floor.

Surprisingly, I did meet an amusing young man in Accounts Receivable named Allan. We spent several minutes discussing our love of E. M. Forster's *A Room with a View* and our staunch conviction that Alexis Bledel is a clone of Helena Bonham Carter from her early twenties.

I bypassed the fourth floor. Human resources and building security. If my hunch that I'd soon move in and out of this building came to fruition, I thought it best to meet building security as the protected guest of an active special agent. The GBI contaminated the third floor. Their jurisdiction and authority sat well below my level of interest.

A lovely southern gentleman asked where I was headed upon returning to the elevator. I wanted to sojourn the building but couldn't readily give him a false reply. I acquiesced and told him 'white-collar division.' He dutifully tapped the button for the fifth floor before hitting the button labeled '7' for himself.

Seventh floor? I'll have to acquaint myself with this man.

"Excuse me," I called to a woman passing with a stack of folders. "Do you know where I might find Special Agent Garth Harmon?"

"Oh, yes," she cheerily replied. "He's just gone to Moller's office. I can show you."

"Lovely!"

I held my hand out for her to proceed down the hall and through a maze of cubicles. As she pointed me down the final hallway, I heard Garth's and another man's—whom I assumed to be this Moller person—voices coming through the open door.

"What's their demand?" Moller asked.

"Immunity for all former crimes," Garth reported.

"How many crimes is that?"

"I honestly don't know, but it isn't a small number."

A self-satisfied smile crossed my face as I stood beyond their door and listened for a proper entrance.

"What kind of crimes?"

"All white-collar in nature. Nothing terribly severe."

Though I understood his meaning, I silently scoffed at the idea that he considered none of my thefts 'terribly severe'. I assure you, they stung as 'terribly severe' to the people on the receiving end.

As I considered ways to later reprimand Agent Harmon for his casual disregard of my skills and prowess, a phone call interrupted their conversation. The voice I took as Moller's answered it.

"Yes, ma'am. Of course. We'll take every available resource to handle this situation. Understood." He hung up. "Top Brass wants Mancini stopped before anything else can happen. They've just offered permission for whatever we need. Bring your thief in. Full immunity for former crimes. We don't have another option."

And there's my cue.

I stepped inside the door and began talking before any of the men had time to notice my presence. "I am so glad you agree. Otherwise, this meeting could be quite the awkward introduction."

As well they should with my flawlessly invasive entrance and immaculate attire, Agent Harmon and the two other men stared dumbfounded. My form-fitting red dress, heels to match, re-curled and still-blonde hair, and fine diamond and ruby jewelry caused jaws to sag and eyes to travel.

Only Agent Harmon's eyes gave any mind to the simple silver chain that disappeared into my cleavage. I cocked my eyebrows at Agent Harmon. Whether intended as a flirtation tactic or a subtle gesture for him to make the proper introductions, suffice it to say that I have always had a talent for multi-tasking.

Quickly collecting himself, Agent Harmon walked over to join me in the doorway. He made an impressively platonic introduction.

"Agent Moller, this is my thief consultant."

"You may call me Bonnie," I told Moller as I extended my hand.

I purposely stopped short, so he would have to move to greet me properly. He dutifully did so but looked at my hand, confused. He seemed unsure whether I intended for him to shake my hand or kiss it. Either would have proved acceptable options. He eventually settled on a suspicious shake.

Hoping for a better response from the third man, I turned to the silent stranger in the room. "And who might you be?"

"Thaddeus James Wilmington IV," he proudly answered without delay and firmly took my hand in his and kissed it. I saw Garth barely shifting out of the corner of my eye.

Oh, I will have great fun working with this man.

"Now, that is a name. Might I call you Thad?"

"One of my many nicknames," he informed me with a flirty smile.

"Good."

"How did you get up here?" Moller demanded, apparently significantly less amused with this game than I was.

"Don't you recall, Special Agent Moller?" I asked the sardonically rhetorical question in a tone I'd spent years perfecting.

The bristling of his arm hair and grinding teeth immediately betrayed how easily I would get under this man's skin.

Oh yes, this will be great fun.

"I'm a thief."

Ever the gallant knight, Agent Harmon jumped into the conversation before Moller could respond.

"Miss Ka— Bonnie," Garth quickly recovered from having almost instinctively used my real-ish—it was still adopted—name. After all, he hadn't much practice with my various pseudonyms. "Why don't we go to my desk, and we can discuss what you'll be doing."

"Of course," I agreed, still holding Moller's eye contact. I turned to Agent Harmon with a delightfully wicked smile and reminded him, "I am here to serve at your pleasure."

"No," Moller interrupted. He pointed a meaty finger at me. His massive hands appeared better built for constricting throats than typing reports. "You and I will go to interrogation."

I calmly nodded both my acknowledgment and permission.

"Follow me." His tone brokered neither argument nor delay.

I nonchalantly followed the storming hulk known as Special Agent Moller. Though I would later learn he was already in his early fifties, the man looked nothing of the sort. The towering black man was built far more like a sturdy bouncer than a wimpy paper pusher.

I wondered if I could lug him around as my personal security. He'd never have to do anything, of course. I'm no wilting flower. However, some events do require the added clout of private security.

As we walked out, I could still hear the commentary of Agent Thad goading Agent Harmon.

"How did you meet her, again?"

"She gave me a lucky tip that led to my assisting INTERPOL in apprehending Tobias Jorgensen," Agent Harmon responded with admirable disinterest.

"A *very* lucky tip, I'd say,"

I imagined the eyeroll accompanying Agent Harmon's sigh as he refused to play Thad's game.

"I have to go make sure Miss" —an almost imperceptible hesitation— "Bonnie doesn't wander somewhere she's not supposed to go."

"I've a feeling that's about the only place she does go."

Though I desperately wanted to turn and see, I wouldn't dare debase myself by giving away my eavesdropping. But I didn't need to see to know Garth shared my smile at the acuteness of Thad's observation.

If those boys only knew.

As I sat alone in the interrogation room waiting for Agent Moller to return, I knew Agent Harmon stood on the opposite side of the two-way mirror. He had been left to guard me and ensure I didn't go anywhere until Agent Moller returned. Just like having an addict keep an eye on their dealer.

I'd no idea if Agent Thad stayed in the observation room with him. I secretly hoped he had. I could've only enjoyed the whole ordeal more had I the ability to go back in time and watch their reactions from beyond the mirror. Alas, my imagination and intimate knowledge of Agent Harmon served as entertainment enough while I waited.

It began innocently, of course. I gently brushed some debris from the fabric that covered my breasts and adjusted the shoulder strap of my bra. I realized my dress had ridden up and needed to pull it back down. Most unfortunately, I accidentally pulled it too far down and showed off just a bit more cleavage than I'd intended.

Naturally, I needed to briefly fondle myself to sort the whole mess. I discovered a particularly tenacious crumb still clinging to my finger upon my fondling. A proper cleansing required that I stick well beyond my fingertip in my mouth to suck on for the removal of the pesky particulate.

Freed from clothing discomforts and comestible interlopers, I began a practiced nonchalant examination of the silver chain disappearing between my bosoms. Sliding my finger along the smooth surface of the precious metal, I drew my audience's eyes to and fro between my clavicle and the first signs of the line between my breasts.

Agent Moller reentered the interrogation room with a manila folder in hand. I raised my head at an amused, cocked angle to meet his glare.

"Are you done?" he asked. He was once again far less amused with the situation.

I wholly ignored Agent Moller as I looked back through the two-way mirror and allowed a devilish half-smile to curl up my cheek. My voice little more than a breathy whisper, I informed them all:

"Oh, I am just getting started."

Agent Moller huffed as he closed the door. He stomped to the table bolted to the ground and perfectly centered in the small room.

For the first time since entering the room, I took the time to look around. With a contentedly nostalgic sigh, I made an observation.

"You know, there's something oddly comforting that all interrogation rooms look and feel basically the same. Of course, you'll find they're made of different materials: brick, cinder block, concrete, carved out of a mountain, hole in the ground. And some are more..." I paused, searching for the best word, "colorfully decorated than others. Still, you always know it's an interrogation room. Even if they drag you there blindfolded."

Ignoring my observation, Moller told me to state my name for the record.

With the smile of a troll, I told him, "Bonnie Anne Clyde."

The glare Moller sent boring through me suggested he did not share the amusement in my overt trollery.

"What?" I asked, playing innocent. "You asked for my name, and that is one I use."

"State your birth name," he grumbled.

"Ah. Well," I hesitated, "that, you see, is a far more complicated matter."

Wanting to hurry off the topic, I hastily laid out my hand. I leaned forward, my arms resting on the table. "Listen, let's just skip this nonsense and have you go ahead and agree to call me Miss Bonnie."

Sliding back into my nonchalant posture, I taunted him further. "Why do you need my name, anyway? Agent Harmon promised me immunity.

According to him, you folks desperately need my help. It's either Miss Bonnie Anne Clyde, or you never see my face again, on any terms."

Agent Moller smacked his hand on the metal table with impressive force as he demanded, "Why are you here?"

How his hand isn't throbbing is beyond me.

Feigning shock by the accusatory nature of the question, I put a hand to my chest to still my insulted heart. Answering his question with all the arrogance of one who saw the answer hovering plain as day before them, I said:

"I was invited. And I was always taught it's rude to dismiss an invitation without proper reasoning."

Apparently, Agent Moller didn't take kindly to my tone of this seeming the simplest and most obvious explanation in all the world. I let him seethe a moment before continuing with my fun.

"An impressive power play using a bomb, even for Mancini. Quite the master of subtly, if you ask me."

"I don't recall asking you."

"I'm here for some reason."

Flustered and in no mood for my games, Agent Moller tilted the manila folder towards him and opened it. He started looking over whatever useless pages he held inside.

Before he flipped to the second page, I said, "Oh, let's cut the charade, shall we? We both know there's nothing of consequence in that folder. There's not even anything about me."

His indignation grew at every sound uttered from my pretty little mouth. The defiant smile shining in my eyes didn't help. Struggling to maintain composure, Moller angrily flipped the folder closed and threw it back on the table. The paper slid across the smooth surface to almost fall in my lap from the force he put behind it.

My curiosity burned as I wondered what he'd come in here with as my pretend rap sheet. But, to retain the upper hand, I knew I had to remain more amused than intrigued by this game. Fortunately, Agent Moller began his questioning and drew my attention from the beckoning folder.

"What do you want?"

"Immunity for all former crimes was the agreed-upon price by Agent Harmon and myself."

"What are your former crimes?" he pressed.

"Inconsequential now that I've been granted immunity from them."

"You've been granted nothing."

I intentionally let Moller feel the lingering silence as I waited to respond. I abandoned my relaxed pose to lean forward without breaking my hold on his gaze. My forearms rested on the table. I called Agent Moller's bluff with my most patronizing smile.

"Then I wish you the best of luck in finding Mancini."

The metal chair screamed as it scraped across the floor. I stood and casually sauntered towards the door. To Agent Moller's credit, he allowed me to grasp the handle before he caved.

"Wait. Immunity for all former crimes, granted." His own chair ground across the floor. Agent Moller turned and pointed at me with another stern warning finger.

"But if you are manipulating us in any way or still stealing while working for us, I'll arrest you for every possible crime I can. Are we agreed?"

His question sounded far more like a statement than a question. Either way, I considered for a moment before replying, "I do love a challenge. Agreed. And what of my name?"

Moller glared at me again. "Do not overexert your advantage."

"You have to call me something," I pointed out.

"Take your seat..." he gritted his teeth and hissed the pseudonym, "Miss Clyde."

I released my hold of the door handle and retook my seat across from him. Having waited for me to resettle, Moller steadied himself and continued the interrogation.

"How's it that you're familiar with Mancini?"

"Relatively."

"Pardon?"

"I am only relatively familiar with Mancini."

I mightily struggled to contain my genuine smile as I recalled a nearly identical conversation I had five years earlier.

"Fine," Moller sighed. "How is it that you are *relatively* familiar with Mancini?"

"We worked together."

Agent Moller grabbed the manila folder and clicked open his pen. "What was the job?"

I clicked my tongue at him. "I can't tell you that. You could start building a file on me. I'm right proud of my spotless reputation."

That proved the final straw for Agent Moller. He stood so quickly that his chair skipped the scrapping process and immediately fell backward, clattering to the floor. He almost made me jump.

"Spotless reputation! You're a thief! And, by your own confession, an accessory to a terrorist! Your reputation is anything but spotless! You're just a—"

"Moller!" Agent Harmon cut off his boss as he threw open the door and rushed into the interrogation room. Having calmed the immediate tension in the room, he asked, "Can I have a word with you? Privately."

I wiggled my fingers in a wave goodbye as the two men departed to the hallway, leaving me alone again. Muffled one-sided yelling seeped through the closed door as Agent Harmon tried—and evidently failed—to calm Agent Moller.

Though I couldn't hear the specific words of the conversation, it sounded like I'd made quite the impression on the unflappable special agent. I smiled, imagining the lexical web Agent Harmon spun to keep Agent Moller from arresting me for obstruction of justice, disorderly conduct, or some other nonsensical charge.

I thoroughly examined my cuticles and the fresh coat of red paint while waiting for the maelstrom to subside. Finally, after a solid minute of heated deliberation, I heard Agent Moller's heavy steps pounding down the hallway.

Another minute passed as I heard calmer conversations on which I couldn't drop any eaves. One of the voices sounded dainty. A woman had replaced Agent Moller. The voices stopped, and the door slowly opened. Agent Harmon stepped inside.

The smile I'd sported for Agent Moller lost its smugness. I struggled not to appear giddy. Clearing my throat, I reset myself and returned to my teasingly uninterested facade, complete with head tilt and eyebrows raised and slightly creased.

"Agent Harmon," I observed in the voice to match my countenance. "Alone at last."

He took the seat across from me and adjusted his tie.

"Don't get too excited. Agents Wilmington and Jolene are still watching you from the observation room."

"But you're here, and you just make me all sorts of excited." I slipped into my old, deep south, southern belle accent. The kind of timbre that sounds like the speaker is just makin' love to every syllable that comes out their mouth.

Would that we were makin' love. Where were we? Right! The interrogation room.

"You are here on official business, Miss Bonnie."

Curse that man for so calmly shooting me down.

He did have an impressive dedication to his work. Fortunately, he had just as equal a dedication to other interests. While terribly fun, that day did turn out to become painstakingly long. With an indignant sigh, I collapsed back into my chair.

"Is it ever anything but with you? One of these days, Agent Harmon, I will break you."

"I'm not sure my wife would appreciate that."

"No?" I sat forward in my chair. He'd piqued my interest again. Not that he didn't do that regularly. "I should think her rather flattered. Knowing my husband so desirable to have other women wanting him would be quite the turn-on for me."

"You have a husband?"

"You know there's no other man for me than you."

He admirably ignored the wink accompanying my compliment. But I knew one thing that would force a reaction. I slid my foot from a red heel and slowly slipped it into his lap. I wiggled my toes and stretched as far as possible without becoming conspicuous to our audience.

And a *reaction* I received. Although, I realized that most of that hardening had already occurred throughout our conversation. Words always did provide some of the best foreplay.

After allowing me to taunt him for a few seconds, Agent Harmon calmly slid his chair back just enough so I could no longer reach him. He casually dropped a hand as though adjusting his position on the chair. His hand subtly but forcefully pushed my foot out of his lap. His face never broke from its professionally stoic expression.

My! he is good. That's alright. All these pent-up reactions to my teasing only mean for a more fantastic release at the appropriate time.

"How do we catch Mancini?" he platonically asked.

"But first," I said, leaning forward in my seat, "you mentioned an Agent Jolene. I'm not familiar with that one. Have you been keeping secrets, Agent Harmon?"

"You'll meet her soon enough."

"Her? Does your wife know about this mystery woman?"

"Miss Bonnie." He said the name like a trainer trying desperately to educate a particularly troublesome puppy with a knack for exploring places it ought not go. His voice rang long and sonorous. It sent a shiver across my body in the best possible way.

Retaining that gently corrective tone, he asked again, "How do we catch Mancini?"

I sighed and acquiesced to the knowledge that I wouldn't get any more fun out of Agent Harmon here.

"We don't," I told him.

"What do you mean, 'we don't'? If we can't catch him, why are you here?"

"Because I have contacts who can tell us what *actually* happened."

"What does that mean?"

"It means Mancini is not behind this, you adorable dunce."

Agent Harmon looked at me with the tired, mildly-annoyed-but-uninjured glare that only two people in a long, affable relationship can adequately convey to each other. I stared back with a cocked head and raised eyebrows, which related a sardonic 'you asked' defense. His eyes narrowed as he fought to keep himself from breaking.

I've yet to figure it out, but my innocent spunkiness in such entanglements often prompted physical entanglements. Being a smartass can prove just as sexy as having a good ass. To further taunt the poor boy—

Because, really, what other such pure joys are there in life?

—I curled the edges of my mouth upward in a devilish smile and sent him a wink. Agent Harmon released a long, controlled exhale before continuing.

"If Mancini is innocent, why not go to him directly? Find out if he knows anyone looking to settle a score? You are friendly with him, yes?"

His unamused expression returned when I replied with the sound of what a wince looks like.

"About that. When last I saw Mancini, we did not part on the friendliest of terms. I fear direct contact would prove rather counterproductive to your investigation."

"You?" His voice rose with exaggerated sarcasm. "Exacerbating people and making situations more complicated than they should be? No. I don't believe it."

It then became my turn to produce that particular glare. Though not nearly so charming as mine, Agent Harmon retorted with his own smirk.

Before any more silent exchanges could occur, Agent Harmon wondered, "In light of your," he paused, "complicated relationship, how is your presence here helpful?"

I scoffed. "That was your job to figure out before you hired me." Leaning back against my chair, I reclaimed a diplomatic tone. "Look, whoever is behind your bombing clearly went through a heap of trouble to frame Mancini. Only I have the connections to help you hopelessly decent folk find out who and why."

"We do have ways of doing these things on our own," Agent Harmon informed me in a futile attempt at saving face for his agency.

"I'm sure you do," I cooed in the same voice that southern ladies don when blessing someone's heart. "But Mancini is a big fish who's not been regularly active for years. You need deep coffers to successfully go after him. Fortunately, I have friends and favors."

"Fine," he acquiesced. "What do we need to do?"

"Give me some time. I'll send out a message and let you know once I hear anything. In the meantime," I leaned forward again as though I planned to suggest some sordid secret meant only for Agent Harmon's ears.

Likewise, he leaned close, fully aware that my next comment may sound sordid in nature.

"Perhaps you could show me where the bathroom is?"

He breathed a half-exhale, half-laugh, and broke his professional demeanor again. We sat for a moment longer than we probably ought to, smiling in the silence.

Chapter Five

In Which I Discovered the Joys and Excitement of Office Work

Vacating the interrogation room, Agent Harmon provided me a brief tour of the building. He remained unaware that I'd already acquainted myself with most of the places we visited. Even a few we didn't. He instructed me where I had permission to go. And quite forcefully insisted where I was *not* allowed.

As expected, part of my initiation involved meeting building security to receive clearance for entering at any time without an escort. Much to my pleasure, the gentleman entering me into the security system made several comments about my beauty. Were I his guest, he insisted I'd never go anywhere without him.

Naturally, I returned the flirtation and egged him on in the most suggestively nuanced of ways. Agent Harmon had no choice but to stoically look on. He tried convincing us that the conversation did not fall under the 'appropriate office intercourse' umbrella.

Blast that man for his word choice!

That singular remark almost caused me to lose my composure and nearly crumbled my entire vixen persona. And that bastard knew it, too. Unfortunately, our elevator ride back to the fifth floor carried several others. Our tour of the accessible parts of the building complete, Agent Harmon took me to his desk space.

Near a small collection of prison windows sat four desks arranged in a square facing each other. Three desks were scattered or organized, revealing their regular use suiting their occupant. The fourth desk stood abandoned in the corner. It only had a purpose when an outsider temporarily joined the group or another department had overflow agents. This became my desk despite having no use for one.

Evaluating the desk where Agent Harmon took a seat, I marveled at how organized the whole thing appeared. He had folders tucked away in various filing systems. He readily jumped between the different drawers and stacks to fetch precisely what he needed at any one thought. He never searched frantically for what he wanted. Instead, he immediately located the file he desired and the particular page within the file.

I watched, amazed that this man could readily remember all this interchangeable information with the slightest of ease yet regularly failed to recall his own phone number. Neither other desk was currently occupied. They were presumably out and about performing various government agent responsibilities. I capitalized on their absence to examine their working spaces and profile them based on such.

The desk across from me looked like a second explosion had occurred. A sweating fast-food cup stood proudly beside the keyboard without any coaster or napkin to catch the slipping water. A crumpled to-go bag poked out of the trashcan positioned between the desk and the industrial shredder.

The precariously piled legal folders made me question if anyone ever knew when the desk's occupant sat at his—so I assumed—post or not. I thought to ask Agent Harmon on that matter before noticing how engrossed he had become on a particular document. I waved away the question.

Turning my attention to the desk diagonal from me, I did a double take at the dichotomy between the two workspaces. The final desk had such organization to put Agent Harmon's to shame. The tabletop sat so seemingly untouched and empty that I almost wondered if anyone presently used it.

I saw nothing more than the computer monitor, essential accessories, and a bottle of hand sanitizer resting atop it. I assumed everything must live inside the drawers and be withdrawn only when required. Receiving so few clues, I couldn't decide if another man or a lone woman used that desk.

I knew Agent Harmon would strongly frown upon my actively going through the drawers of each desk to examine their contents. So, I sank back into my chair and briefly explored the empty drawers of my new desk. That 30-second task complete, I blew an exaggerated raspberry and spun in my chair.

Having still not captured Agent Harmon's attention through my subtle antics, I decided to take a more direct approach.

"What am I supposed to be doing?" I inquired with no lack of disdainful annoyance at my forced presence.

"I don't know," he answered without breaking concentration from the document left on his desk while questioning me. "Twiddle your thumbs and whistle Dixie until we find something useful, I guess."

Knowing my response would possess no level of kindness, Agent Harmon purposefully didn't look at me. Even still, I saw the slightest smile creep across his lips at the thought of keeping me detained in this way. I stuck my tongue out at him in protest. Fortunately, I found something far more entertaining with which to occupy my time.

The crash site directly across from me belonged to Agent Thad. I gasped in delight. The most generous smile I could muster consumed my face as he returned to his desk.

"Special Agent Thaddeus James Wilmington IV." I stood from my chair to perch on the corner of my new desk. I positioned my legs just so for the men to have a proper view. "Do we really get to work together?"

"It certainly appears that way, Madam Bonnie." Thad echoed my hyperbolic excitement with a slight bow reminiscent of antebellum gentlemen.

I slipped into my *Gone with the Wind* voice to maintain the quixotic nature of our exchange.

"Well, I do declare. Just color me a beautiful magnolia pink, for I do believe I'm blushin'."

"Think nothin' of it, my dear," Thad continued, matching me step for step, "The nat'ral rouge only serves to beautify your already lovely face."

"Oh, you tease me, young man—"

"Enough!" Agent Harmon demanded, finally breaking his concentration. "I can't take listening to you two minstrels anymore. Will, you have work to do.

"Miss Bonnie," he hesitated, trying to determine an appropriate order for me. I looked at him with a playful yet challenging smile as I, too, waited for what he wanted me to do for him. I saw his resolve begin to crack with the shape of my leg and the glint in my eye.

"Stop distracting my team," he finally blurted out before promptly returning to his work.

I retorted with an unkind Spanish insult whispered only slightly under my breath.

"¿Hablas español?" Thad inquired of my comment.

"Por supuesto." I proceeded to tell him that all good thieves are multilingual. Continuing in Spanish, we discussed becoming fluent. I learned that Thad had a Mexican mother and grew up speaking Spanish.

Not surprising. His coffee-color skin and jet-black hair gave him the stereotypical Mexican appearance. He must've taken after his mother's physicality. A man of short, stocky build—only slightly taller than me when not wearing heels—I wondered if he took after his mother or father in that respect.

"I told you to quit distracting my team," Agent Harmon finally butted in.

I added, still speaking Spanish, "He's just jealous he doesn't speak anything else."

"Gringo," Thad lamented.

I shook my head in agreement.

"You guys suck."

"Come now, Agent Harmon. You don't really mean that." I attempted to persuade him. Leaving my perch, I sashayed across the open floor to his desk. He fought to keep his focus on the computer screen and ignore my approach. Still, I saw Agent Harmon's eyes darting a peek at me as he hurriedly examined the sway of my hips and the curve of my breasts with each step closer.

Upon reaching his desk, I placed both hands on the corner and leaned over beside the monitor. Poor lad, his eyes had nowhere to go. I opened my mouth to tease him further, but another woman's voice cut in.

"Garth, did you see that file I left on you—"

A plain, but not unattractive, woman dressed in an abysmally boring and poorly cut grey pants suit cantered into the desk area with an open folder in her hand. She examined the pages within as she approached. She froze stone cold when she saw me.

I stood slowly and thoroughly examined her from the old lady pumps to her frizzy brown hair pulled back in much too tight of a bun that tugged at the skin on her face,

"Ah. Desk number three."

The poor girl visibly shrunk at my evaluation. Possibly at my mere presence. She looked hopelessly at Agent Harmon for help. Ever the gallant knight and proper gentleman, he promptly made the introductions.

"Miss Bonnie, this is Special Agent Jolene. Brynn, Miss Bonnie Anne Clyde. She's the consultant I mentioned in the meeting yesterday."

"Hi!" I greeted with an enthusiasm I think only frightened the girl further.

"Hello," she mumbled back. I imagine she would've wrung her hands had she not held the folder.

"You were saying something as you came up?" Agent Harmon dove in once more to the rescue.

"Uh— um— yes. The— the— uh— the report I left on your desk. Did you get it?"

"Yes, the ballistic findings of the bomb?"

She nodded.

"Right here," he said, holding up the document he'd been examining.

"Oh! I'll take that." I snatched the paper out of Agent Harmon's hand. He promptly snatched it back and informed me I could look at it only after he finished.

"Go sit at your desk and wait until I have something for you to do," he told me.

I stuck my nose up at him but returned to my sequestered confinement all the same. I could feel his eyes watching me go and the smile accompanying his gaze.

As the workday hours drudged on, Agent Harmon's desk space became quite the hotbed of activity. Apparently, word of my arrival had spread surprisingly quickly through the masses. They all came under the pretense of consulting with Garth's team.

Garth later revealed that he only knew two of the dozen people who came to see the legend-in-flesh. He recognized most of them from office Christmas parties and such, but he did admit that he had never seen one or two of them.

"They could've been random strangers off the street, for all I know!" he exclaimed.

Only one lady who came to investigate had any actual business to conduct with my new handlers. In fact, aside from when our eyes briefly met upon her arrival, she entirely ignored me. The obvious deliberateness of it sat ill within my stomach.

Eventually, the stream of tourists visiting the newest exhibit ceased. Boredom quickly descended upon the land.

I propped my legs on the desk and shot rubber bands at the ceiling.

"I want to see the crime scene," I blurted without changing my posture.

"What?" Agent Harmon inquired. His neck craned toward me, but his eyes and fingers stayed focused on whatever he typed. Finishing his thought, Agent Harmon turned his attention to me. "What'd you say?"

"I said that I want to see the crime scene."

"You mean the explosion site?" Brynn inquired.

"No, I mean the other case I'm working with you people."

"Miss Bonnie," Agent Harmon gently chastised again, sultrily drawing out the final sound of each word. I had to sigh in mock contrition and shoot my last rubber band at him to keep my distance. Removing my legs from their propped position, I turned back to Brynn and made my apology.

"Yes, I mean the explosion site."

"Why do you need to go there?" Agent Harmon pestered me further.

"You hired me to consult. Let me consult. This is part of my process for working with the feds."

"You have a process for working with the feds?" Thad jumped in.

With a shrug, I explained, "Figure now's as good a time as any to develop one."

Finding no fault in my logic, Thad nodded and returned to his work.

"So?" I asked, twisting my chair to face Agent Harmon's desk. "Take me out?"

"Sure." Agent Harmon did an admirable job keeping his composure and making his acquiescence sound like my request burdened him. I bit back a smile, knowing the truth of what lay behind that groan. He saved his work, grabbed his suit jacket, and led me to the underground parking garage.

Unsure of the areas covered by cameras or the diligence of those who monitored the feeds, I maintained my distance and platonic interest as I slipped through the car door he held open for me. We rode silently for several minutes as the car crawled through chaotic Atlanta traffic.

Nothing works faster as an anti-aphrodisiac than rush hour traffic.

I smiled despite the hundreds of cars creeping along while attempting to occupy the same place in space and time. My smile grew as I reflected on the day and the prospect of entertainment to come.

"I didn't expect to actually enjoy this," I finally commented.

"What? Atlanta traffic?" he joked.

"Gracious, no," I scoffed. "Working with you. I love being able to do this. To see this forbidden side of you. You're different at work."

"How so?"

"I don't know, exactly. You're more in your element. You thrive and take command, but not authoritatively like Moller."

"I don't thrive or take command at home?" he teased.

"Only when I let you," I replied with a matching devilish smile.

He turned to me with a lingering look suggesting, in no uncertain terms, that he didn't believe me. My smile lost a touch of its devil at his gaze.

"In all seriousness," I continued after all sets of eyes had returned to the road, "your authority in the office is different. I don't know how to describe it. Yet. But I will watch you until I figure it out," I threatened with a smile.

"Just don't watch me too closely," he cautioned. "It might draw suspicion. And you are already under scrutinous eyeballs."

"And a great number of them." I thought back to the parade of suits.

Though I smiled at the joking advisory, Garth recognized the mirthless appearance of my grin. "What's the matter?"

I sighed and shook my head. "I put on a show at the office, but in all sincerity, I don't think Mancini's behind this. I talked to Uncle César and—"

"How is he?" Garth interrupted.

"He's good. He asked about you. But he agrees. This does not look like Mancini."

"Why not?"

"Mancini's like me. Get in, do the job, get out. No muss. No fuss. But this," I waved my arm at the still-standing interstate, "this is *all* muss and *all* fuss. It just doesn't fit."

"People change," he offered.

A disparaging snort served as my thoughts on the matter. "People change clothes; that's about it."

"You've changed," he countered.

"I've redirected my end goal, but I haven't changed," I corrected.

Garth placed his hand over mine. "And I'd never want you to."

I smiled again, a different smile than any so far in that car ride.

"Mancini's really being framed, then?"

"But I've no idea how. Or why, for that matter. None of it makes sense."

"Well, that's why you're here. To recognize something we don't."

We arrived at the explosion site with the impeccable timing of Garth's finishing. I waited for him to open my door before getting out. Agent Harmon offered me his hand so I might disembark with the grace I always demanded, whether in a dress or jeans. He gripped my hand tighter and longer than required. I didn't protest.

Garth finally relinquished his hold to allow me to explore the sight as I saw fit. I'd seen my fair share of damage throughout my travels and never once acquired the adjective of squeamish. But something about this sight struck me.

The crumbled concrete, exposed rebar, and mangled metal of cars not yet recovered from the wreckage twisted a knot in my stomach that human tragedies rarely touched. Perhaps because that catastrophe had touched closer to home than any had previously.

Literally. This site lay destroyed less than ten miles from my city condo and less than an hour from the impenetrable protection of the manor. Any other attacks occurred in cities I'd visited and possibly temporarily lived in. But I always retreated from those cities back to home. The location of this onslaught offered me no retreat.

"What did you hope to find out here, anyway?" Garth's voice brought me from my retrospection back to our shared reality.

Turning away from the edge of the remaining bridge to face him, I shrugged. "Beats me. I just couldn't stand to be in that office anymore."

Garth dropped his head and laughed at my response, not questioning the truth of it for a second.

"Besides," I continued as he still laughed at me, "there's something I've desperately wanted to do that I wasn't allowed to in that stuffy government building."

"Since when has that ever stopped you?"

Taking a pause, Agent Harmon opened his mouth as though to guess what that forbidden action might be. Realizing that countless acts fell into that category and he could eliminate very few with me as the perpetrator, he curiously studied me.

"And what might it be?"

Leaving the wreckage behind me, I crossed with a purpose to the parked car. Had I not worn heels, I would've sprinted. Alas, I had to content myself to move quickly as I could in the stilettos completing my ensemble.

Gracious, how I wish I could run.

Garth remained propped up against his government-issue black sedan and had his arms crossed lazily over his chest. Poised just so, he reminded me of a James Dean-type fella. He knew exactly who he was, what he was about, and didn't have to show off to anybody.

That nonchalant confidence and lackadaisical fortitude combined with the look in his eyes as he watched my body sauntering towards him sent the most pleasurable shivers down my spine and a delectable burning in other areas.

Recognizing a similar look in my eyes, Agent Harmon dropped his crossed arms, opening himself up for a full-frontal attack. I grasped his face between my hands and promptly buried my lips against his. He enclosed my hips in his arms and pulled me in tight. He was just as desperate for the taste of me.

One hand traveled further south to grip me, but I had already pressed all my bodyweight against him, pinning us to his car. As the kissing continued, I had to fight the urge to remove his suit jacket.

"I still don't understand how we ever manage to spend a single night apart," I finally admitted after regaining enough breath from our kiss.

"Because temporary abnegation makes for wonderful reunions," he explained before pulling my mouth back over his.

After acceptable, but not nearly enough, kissing, I wondered, "I don't suppose you could just skip out on the rest of today?"

"Don't tempt me," Garth countered with an anticipating smile.

"Oh, but that is my favorite pastime," I reminded him in a breathy whisper. "But, if you're to maintain your moniker as an honest thief, I suppose the honesty part means you need to go back to work."

Garth gave a slight hum of response. I couldn't tell whether he agreed with me, meant to seduce me, or was resigning himself to his fate. Likely a combination thereof. As he moved to kiss my neck and make up for lost time, I definitively labeled it as a combined response.

"However, if you're set on returning to the office, I recommend dinner beforehand."

"Why? Are you hungry?" He did not pause from exploring the sensitive skin connecting my neck and lower jaw.

"Not so much, but I am terribly thirsty." I felt his lips curl in a smile against me. "And it would seem, my dear, that you are as well."

I reached down to the seam of his pants to illustrate my observation. His breath hitched as the kisses momentarily paused.

"Unless you want a heap of questions upon our return, I'd recommend a cool-down period." We both looked down before I added, "Or perhaps an ice bath."

Chapter Six

In Which We Enjoyed the Aphrodisiacal Qualities of Playing Hard to Get

Clover and Crown became one of my favorite Atlanta restaurants when I first stepped inside. The owners emigrated from Ireland and England and erected a proper pub on American soil. Something about an authentic pub always comforted me with its cozy, homely glow to warm the cockles of my soul.

The dark wood interiors that created an intimate space and the hearty food and abundant alcohol made for a serenity where I preferred to take my meals. Though he lived in Atlanta for several years before me, my husband knew nothing of this hidden gem. Introducing him to the Clover and Crown only heightened my love of the appropriately rustic-looking pub.

"So, I realize we might should've addressed this before you signed on, but what exactly is your tangible plan for helping us investigate?" Garth inquired before taking another bite of his shepherd's pie.

"I told you at the office: talk to friends," I replied.

"And that's really all you've got?"

"For now." My pitch rose in defense.

My phone violently shook in my purse. Looking to see who dared interrupt this time with a text, I didn't recognize the number. But that proved no great cause for concern. Most of the people with whom I communicated regularly changed cell phones and numbers and frequently incorporated the use of burner phones in their lives.

Though I couldn't place the number, the message revealed all I needed to know about the mysterious sender. '*Piedmont Park. Half an hour. Consider it payment for Budapest.*'

"Anything of interest?" Garth wondered.

"Not particularly," I lied and slipped it back into my purse. "Where were we?"

"I don't know about you, but I couldn't help wondering where I'll sleep tonight."

I raised an anticipating eyebrow at him and smiled at his future plans. "Do you honestly think I'd be willing to wait for you to drive to the manor after you finally leave work?" I teased.

"To be perfectly honest, I'm surprised you've lasted this long." His eyes shone as he spoke of our future entanglements.

"Well, as you pointed out earlier, delayed gratification can prove glorious."

We silently watched each other over our Guinness and entrees for several seconds. Though we'd finished most of the meal already, our hunger did nothing but grow with each passing moment.

Knowing my half-hour deadline approached, and I'd still have to locate him within the park, I forcibly—and dearly distraught doing so—removed myself from the boiling, silent foreplay.

"If you'll excuse me, I must run to the loo," I said as I grabbed my purse and slid out of the booth.

"Shall I join you?" The desirous twinkle in his eye forced me to grab hold of the table's edge to keep from crumpling.

Releasing a deep sigh and fighting to keep myself from improper public action, I leaned to whisper in his ear, "Save all that for tonight." I left a lingering kiss on his cheek and wandered to the back.

As I passed the bar, I asked our waitress to deliver a note the next time she checked on our table. She agreed, and I left the napkin before disappearing out a back door and hailing a taxi. Written in a familiar calligraphic script, my note simply read:

'*Until we meet again.*'

The use of such a specific calling card and the anticipatory nature of its promise set my heart to fluttering as I recalled its first use.

Five Years Earlier...

"Housekeeping!" I called out in my adopted Argentinian accent.

I could hear my target finishing a phone conversation as he came to answer the door but couldn't make out what he said. The drawl of his southern accent made all the words run together in a delicious but undecipherable way.

The utter confusion and recognition on his face gave me the highest satisfaction of accurately anticipating his reaction to seeing me standing in his doorway. I had not anticipated catching him in the mid-stages of undress, and my response elicited therein.

My body committed a not-uncomfortable betrayal in my heart skipping a beat. The man from the café stood before me in a white undershirt plastered against his torso and unbuttoned suit pants revealing part of his boxer briefs. I should have taken insult to not garnering a more significant reaction on his part.

Then again, I understood he must have felt far too confused to become aroused. Besides, the appropriate outfit for that would come later. I quickly collected myself.

"Oh, good! You're already beginning to change."

Without waiting for a response, I brushed by him and rolled my cleaning cart into the room.

"Can I help you?" he inquired as I abandoned my cart for his closet.

"As a matter of fact, you can."

I began sorting through his clothes, trying desperately to find something suitable. He was apparently not terribly disturbed by my intrusion. He continued the conversation with great confusion but no discernable discomfort as I rummaged through his clothing.

"How did you find me?"

"Oh, let's not get into that right now. We must leave something to discuss over dinner," I explained with my head still buried in his closet.

"Over dinner?" His voice hitched slightly enough to make him sound like a nervous young man attempting to flirt with his first crush and, remarkably, succeeding.

I pulled my head back from his abysmal collection of suits, khakis, and polos to give him a cheeky smile.

"Over dinner." Returning to my search, I added, "At the hotel's restaurant."

Regaining his footing, Agent Harmon made his logical protest. "Unless I'm mistaken, the hotel's restaurant requires reservations." Despite this potential difficulty, Agent Harmon never attempted to stop my search.

"Well then," I removed my head from the closet to look at him.

Our eyes locked and held each other with a deliberate intimacy not yet experienced. Our mouths curled slightly upward in shy, unguarded smiles.

"It's a good thing we have reservations." I broke my gaze to check my watch and informed him, "They'll seat us in twenty minutes."

I once more buried my head in his closet as he pointed out a flaw in my plan. "The restaurant also enforces a stringent dress code."

"Perfect!" I withdrew the best black suit with matching dress shirt and tie I could find from his stash and tossed them at him in response. "Put those on."

I crossed back to my acquired maid's cart and withdrew a small duffle bag from the covered bottom level.

"Are you hoping they let their staff dine with their patrons?"

"Of course not," I retorted with a smile, recognizing the playful taunt in his voice. "Hurry up, now, and change. We haven't much time."

Again, not allowing him time to respond, I closed the door to the bathroom behind me. I turned on the fan so he wouldn't succumb to trying to talk through the door. I could only imagine his intrigued confusion at my whirlwind appearance and hoped the intrigue would outweigh the uncertainty and prompt him to change for dinner.

Several minutes later, I emerged from the bathroom, fully transformed. I wore the same red dress I would don for my grand entrance at the FBI but changed the jewelry accompaniment. I still wore the sapphire ring I'd worn that morning when we met. Now, I also had earrings, a bracelet, and a necklace to match.

The most significant omission of that first evening was the silver chain that would hide its contents beneath my dress.

I'd let my hair—colored a velvety black at that time—down from its bun to hang silky and smooth just past my shoulder blades. Agent Harmon stared at me with no level of feigned interest in my emergence.

"Think they'll let me in the restaurant, now?" I inquired to his wandering eye.

He began trying to respond but only managed to repeatedly trip over his tongue as he struggled and failed to keep his eyes above my neckline. Finally, he conceded to simply nodding his head.

"Excellent," I replied with an unflappable, sexy aloofness to my tone.

Fortunately for me, my reaction to seeing Agent Harmon in his finery was far subtler and more internal than his for me. Then again, women have always had the upper hand in the appealing clothing department. Not that the setback ever stopped Agent Harmon from discovering his own strengths in that regard.

"Put on your jacket," I told him. "Our reservation waits for no man."

Agent Harmon did as instructed. He rushed ahead to open the door as I pushed my maid's cart back into the hallway. Abandoning the cart, I looped my arm through Agent Harmon's. We proceeded downstairs to dinner.

The hotel's dining facilities sat in a sequestered section of the spacious lobby opposite the check-in desk. Though not the fanciest restaurant I'd ever dined in, the hotel's restaurant assuredly did not lack for class. Not for the first time, I found myself wondering how a commoner found himself staying at such a luxurious establishment.

With my arm draped across Agent Harmon's, I marched us directly to the tuxedo-clad host at the restaurant's marble entryway.

"*Bonjour, monsieur et madame.* Do you have a reservation?"

"*Oui*," I affirmed.

"May I have your name?"

"Harmon," I answered without delay.

Little did I know that not two years would pass before that became true.

I could see Agent Harmon look at me with an intrigued surprise at my knowledge of his name out the corner of my eye. His gaze on me and the amazement behind his expression forced an involuntary smile. Impressively, I retained the ability to refrain from looking back at him.

"If you please follow me, I will show you to your table," our host said, finding the not-yet-shared-name on his list.

"*Merci*."

Our host led us to a corner isolated from the other tables as per my instruction. Candles burned in the center of each table. A piano played softly somewhere on the other side of the restaurant. Of course, the candles served purely as atmospheric aesthetics. Several chandeliers scattered across the ceiling provided practical lighting.

Beginning early to play the gallant gentleman, Agent Harmon helped me with my chair before our host had the opportunity. Providing us our menus and a quick rundown of that evening's specials, our host bid us a good night and floated back to his stand.

Agent Harmon opened his mouth to ask the obvious question, but our sommelier interrupted us. After I ordered a bottle of *Chianti Classico*, Agent Harmon watched her go and waited a moment longer. He scanned the restaurant, ensuring no one else would interrupt us.

"Well," he began once confident we had found ourselves alone, "you apparently know my name. How do you know my name?"

"I did my homework."

"Did you?" Though he tried sounding less than pleased at yet another cryptic answer, I already detected the tease lacing his tone.

He asked the only logical next question. "Can I know your name?"

Though I knew the question had to arise during the meal and suspected it would appear early, I still found myself unprepared to answer. Though I possessed an arsenal of readily available aliases, something about this man gave me pause.

I suspected it was the same thing that captured my attention at the café. The thing which caused me to track him down and spring dinner on him without knowing the slightest bit about him. I still had no idea what that was.

To this day, I still question that initial, instantaneous possession. And I intend to spend every day left us investigating and studying that mystery.

Displaying a smile laced with nothing and brimming with undeserved contentment, I told him, "Kati."

"Just Kati?"

"For now," I promised him.

Even I didn't understand the significance of that promise at the time.

The sommelier returned with our wine. I inspected its bouquet and taste before granting my approval. When our sommelier looked to Agent Harmon for his confirmation, he merely smiled and said whatever I approved of sounded good enough for him.

"So, Mr. Garth Harmon, Special Agent for the FBI, how did you come to find yourself in Paris?"

"Wow," he commented with stunned amazement as he took another drink. "You really do your homework."

"I'm not always in the habit of lying. So, Paris?"

He hid his hesitation by taking another long sup of his wine. Placing his glass gently back on the table, Agent Harmon looked at me with inquiring eyes. He hoped to deduce information about me. Probably wondering if I met him to act as someone's spy. As I continued sipping my wine, I unflinchingly held his gaze with my own noncommittal intrigue.

Finally, he answered, "I'm investigating."

"Seems a bit outside your jurisdiction," I commented, relaxing back into my chair.

"Are you an expert on FBI procedures?"

"More of a novice," I retorted with a smirk over my glass. "So? How did the FBI manage to obtain jurisdiction in France?"

"We didn't."

"Oh?" I leaned forward again. "Are you a rogue investigator, then?"

"Of a sort. I still don't have the power to make any arrests, and everything I do must be cleared by the local police, but I felt it was something I needed to do. From a personal sense of duty."

I set aside my glass of wine. His conviction struck me in a way that required me to no longer retain hold of my prop but to direct all my attention at him. He felt strongly about whatever had happened.

That personal sense of duty of which he spoke called to something within me. Something I would begin cultivating within the following weeks but would not wholly realize I possessed until much later.

Recognizing my change in earnestness, Agent Harmon continued unprompted.

"Mancini slipped through our—" he caught himself and paused as though the memory pained him, "my fingers not long ago. It was the closest we've ever come to catching him. We had enough to put him away. I ran point for the sting, and it was my fault it fell apart. We lost an agent because of it."

"That doesn't seem right," I commented, not as a critique of his story but as commentary concerning his target.

Agent Harmon crinkled his brow at me in a look of both indignation and confusion.

"I just mean Mancini isn't violent. Whoever took your agent, it wasn't Mancini."

His investigative nature taking over his emotional lapse, Agent Harmon returned to a mild interrogation. "How exactly would you know that?"

"I told you at the café," I reminded him as I took hold of my wine glass. "We've worked together."

"You're a thief." I saw the emotion of revelation and subsequent confusion consume his face.

"In the flesh," I raised a glass to his investigative prowess.

Sinking back in his seat, Agent Harmon couldn't help but ask, "Why is a self-proclaimed thief eating dinner with a known FBI white-collar agent?"

"Don't worry," I assured him as I returned to my relaxed posture, "you're not allowed to arrest me. Even if you were, you couldn't. No one's ever been able to before."

"You seem awfully confident in yourself."

"I have reason to be." I ran a finger across my diamond necklace. He diligently watched my finger and studied the neckline of my dress.

"How many things have you stolen?"

Waving off his question, I assured him, "I don't keep count."

The face he made clearly suggested he didn't believe my answer. However, it convinced me I'd like to see this man out of his suit. Ignoring the flushing of my body and praising the ethnically androgynous tannish, olive color of my cheeks that kept me from blushing, I rebutted his disbelief.

"What? I'm not that conceited." I took another sip of wine before leaning forward again. "Where are you from? Specifically."

"Alabama."

"Ah. Your cadence suggests such. I don't hear much of that country boy twang, though," I teased.

"I've worked long and hard to tame it for my work," he insisted. "How about you?"

"Did I have to work hard to calm my country boy twang?"

"No." His smile made me glad I was already seated. "Where are you from?"

I teetered my head from side to side and shrugged my shoulders. "A little bit of everywhere."

We sat in silence for a moment, watching our tablemate. His eyes had softened throughout our conversation and now studied me, not as an investigator would study a suspect, but as a man would study a woman.

His eyes began to seem less brown and more like gold-flaked cinnamon. At one point, the corner of his mouth twitched upward in a reflexive smile, and I felt my heart silently giggling.

"How did you find me?" He finally asked. No interrogation laced his tone, merely pure curiosity, and a hint of gratitude. "And find out about me?"

"I'm a resourceful sort of girl," I told him with another shrug.

"And an enigma of one."

"Am I?"

"Seem to be. You openly admit to an FBI agent that you are a thief; apparently, a jewel thief who is partial to sapphires. Yet you play coy with everything else."

He paused for a moment as he realized why I seemed familiar with this attire. "It was you, wasn't it? The shipment of sapphires in Switzerland in route to LA three years ago. That's where your earrings came from."

"Not my ring? You seemed more intrigued by it this morning."

"Oh, I am. But no, not your ring. It came from somewhere else. I'm not sure where, but I intend to find out."

"Color me impressed, Special Agent Harmon," I sighed as I sat back in my chair. "My interest in you may be justified after all."

Our freshly born mutual respect resulted in a shared smile. The remainder of our meal passed in sporadic small talk as we were too hungry to devote much time to conversation.

Completing our meal, we strolled back out to the lobby. This time I did not slip my arm through Agent Harmon's. The fun of the facade had dissipated. We had not yet reached a point of comfortable touch.

"It was a pleasure to meet you, Garth Harmon."

"The pleasure was mine, Miss Kati."

His smile caused my legs to wobble as my name passed his lips. When he cleared his throat and could no longer hold my gaze, I knew precisely what he would say. Fortunately, I had already devised an escape route before ever going upstairs.

Taking the unobserved opportunity, I motioned to the desk attendant upon whom I'd hinged my escape. Agent Harmon began speaking before he could meet my eye.

"Knowing what I know about you, I can't, in good conscience, let you go."

When he finally lifted his head to meet my gaze, I saw him nervously biting his lower lip. With a flush I knew I couldn't tamp down, I imagined how those lips would taste.

Seeing the receptionist walk out from behind the desk with a folded sheet of paper in his hand, I forced myself to recover before I missed my opportunity.

"Don't worry, Agent Harmon, you won't be *letting* me go anywhere."

Perfectly cued, the receptionist called out for the recipient of my note. "Mr. Harmon! Mr. Garth Harmon!"

Agent Harmon turned to face whoever called to him, releasing me from his attention. As he turned away to receive the note from the receptionist, I promptly slipped out the doors, disappearing into the Parisian night.

I imagined Garth looking around the lobby for me before giving up and opening my note. I had left him a simple promise in calligraphic hand:

'*Until we meet again.*'

Chapter Seven

In Which I Received Some Answers and Much Delayed Gratification

I found C4 waiting for me on one of the isolated docks surrounding the park's pond. He stood alone, looking out over the water with a military stance and an aura that did not invite conversation. Not that most people would randomly wander up to talk to him anyway. Nothing about him made people feel comfortable.

Once an attractive man with the dark and delicate features typical of the Chinese, all that changed many years ago during a botched explosion. No one knew the story of what happened—just like virtually nobody knew his actual name—and C4 never discussed his life. But his appearance fast became legend within the underground networks of the world.

The entire left side of his body now looked mangled, pockmarked, and melted from the burn and shrapnel scars from where it took the brunt of the explosion. He wore an eye patch over that same eye and never donned attire that did not cover his arm. Sometimes he wore a glove on his left hand. This evening, he did not.

I crossed from the boathouse around the lake to join him on his dock. "Fancy running into you here."

Without directing his attention away from the gently rippling water, he observed, "I don't believe you've ever 'run into' anyone in your life."

I shrugged in silent agreement and stepped to the edge of the dock to stand beside him. "What brings you to Atlanta?"

"I go where the job is," he stated in the most impassive matter-of-fact tone.

"I was afraid of that." My voice dropped with concern. I turned to look at him, but still, he stared across the water. "Why?"

"You know I never ask questions. All I need to know is when and where." His disinterested tone never wavered.

"Then why'd you contact me?"

"Because I still owe you for Budapest." His voice showed the first signs of softening, but he recovered quickly.

"You already paid me." I turned my gaze across the water, mimicking his cold composure.

C4 turned to look at me for the first time. His dark eyes softened, and he watched me with a grateful longing.

"I can never fully repay you for that."

I met his gaze and made a slight nod of understanding. "And what is your payment?" I asked, turning my eyes to the reflection of the twilight city in the pond.

He hesitated as a family wandered down the dirt path behind us. He inhaled to speak but stifled it as a pair of runners came jogging by in the opposite direction.

"There are more isolated sections of the park, if you prefer," I informed him as the family stopped a few feet down the path to watch the turtles swimming along the surface.

He nodded, and I led us on a tour to the less populated back areas.

No matter where I've lived—from the isolation of Uncle César's ranch to the nonstop bustle of the world's major metropolises—I've found few sights more enjoyable than strolling through a city park at twilight. The sun painted the world in a gentle glow accentuated by the lights from the city skyscrapers. It always felt reminiscent of year-round Christmas lights.

The cooling air of a fall evening created the perfect time for families and couples to explore this urban Eden. It seemed all of them had taken advantage of the opportunity. I shivered slightly as a lazy breeze jostled the fallen leaves.

C4 silently removed his suit jacket for me. I gladly draped it across my shoulders as we moved further away from the gathered body heat of the city's inhabitants. We passed the play fountain on the opposite side of the park from the pond—already turned off for the season—and descended the stairs leading to the woodland section.

"There shouldn't be anybody in this section at this hour," I informed C4 once we reached a safe place to talk.

We continued wandering the path through the lowlands as our conversation resumed.

"Word is the feds believe Mancini's connected to the bombing," C4 reported. "Which is good; it means I did my job well. But he has nothing to do with it."

"You framed him?" I knew my tone sounded like I felt: torn between self-satisfaction and increasing concern for what the frame job meant.

"Not me," C4 said, sounding almost defensive as he did. "I'm only the hired gun."

"Whose gun?"

"I don't know. All exchanges were done through a third party." He took a long pause and a deep breath before continuing. Whatever he had to say, he didn't seem happy about it.

"Kati," he paused again, and I realized I had never heard him say my name before. Not even after Budapest.

"I don't think the location of this bombing was a coincidence."

"What do you mean?"

"There was no crime associated with the blast, and nothing points to its intention as a straight terrorist attack. I believe this bombing was meant to scare you."

I scoffed at his warning. "Scare me? From what? Mancini?"

"Rumor is you two had quite the falling out. Maybe he seemed like a logical perpetrator against you. I can only say that I recommend you drop it and get out while you still can. You're not a cop, an investigator, or a vigilante, and justice isn't your thing—"

"You don't know me anymore," I interrupted.

With a sigh of resignation, he recognized I would never take his advice. Still, he persisted, "Just leave it. It won't be pretty by the time this whole thing's over. I don't want to see you caught in the crosshairs."

I stopped short as we arrived at the sidewalk on the park's edge. C4 did likewise and turned his whole body to face me.

I sighed, thinking how much I'd changed since Budapest and who I'd become. I considered his words and knew his advice would keep me safest. I could flee to Uncle César's or go anywhere in the vast, wide world to disappear, entirely vanishing from this unknown threat.

But I couldn't. I thought of the single reason that spurned all that change, which now acted as my anchor.

Turning to meet C4 head-on, I told him plainly, "I can't go anywhere."

He slowly nodded. No one knew why I'd left the game and began working the way I had nearly four years ago or adopted Atlanta as my home base. Still, everyone understood it had to have been something significant enough to make me upend my life and something I wasn't likely to abandon. C4, more than anyone, had reason to suspect the truth and respect me for it.

"Then I've given you all the help I can," he said.

Reaching out with his non-mangled hand, he lightly gripped mine. Where I couldn't recall if he'd ever said my name, I knew for sure he'd never touched me.

"I wish you the best of luck."

I returned C4's jacket and watched him disappear in the bend of the path leading back the way we'd come. Once he vanished beyond my view, I turned to walk up to the main street and find a cab home.

The shot of noise from the condo's front door unlocking echoed through the penthouse just as the cherrywood granddaughter clock hanging in the entryway struck nine o'clock.

Stepping away from my perch that overlooked the city standing tall just beyond the forest, I took another sip from my nearly empty glass of wine. I had not gone out onto the porch that night due to the coolness of a fall night and the constant breeze blowing atop Vinings Mountain. I would have needed to change from my red dress to stay comfortable beyond the glass wall.

But I knew he'd never forgive me for stealing his fun.

I walked through the main room back to the kitchen, passing by our mostly-decorative piano. Both of us had learned the basics of how to play while younger, but neither remembered into adulthood. That said, no posh home ever looked complete without a baby grand on display. Besides, enough people came to visit with our parties that we found our home filled with live music regularly enough.

As I pulled another wine glass down from its holder, I noticed that Garth hadn't bothered to turn on the light when he entered. I supposed muscle memory and the lights from the city gave him enough to see what he needed. I heard him drop his keys and briefcase on the recliner across the main room from the piano and sigh as his shoes clunked on the faux-marble floor.

That sigh better be relief at finally coming home and not exhaustion. I have no intention of allowing that man to sleep anytime soon.

Flipping on the light illuminating the bar separating the main room from the kitchen, I uncorked the bottle of wine.

"Quite the long night at the office. Your poor little wife might get worried."

Garth let his other shoe fall to the tile as he replied, "My wife understands that late nights are sometimes part of the job."

"And she doesn't have any concerns that work might not be the only thing keeping you out?" I inquired, refilling my glass.

"What else could keep me from the woman I love?"

I poured a second glass.

"Well, I don't know. It seems to have taken you quite long enough to make it home."

"I thought we established at the bridge that my honest moniker required me to complete my work."

He stepped forward into the open space of the main room to meet me as I brought over the wine.

"Unfortunately, a lot is going on at work."

"Oh? Anything exciting?"

"Maybe." He took a long, slow sip, intentionally teasing me with his delay. Releasing a self-satisfied exhale, he continued:

"See, we've got this new consultant who I think will be more trouble than she's worth."

"Then why bother with the trouble?"

Garth's fingers examined the cut of my dress.

"Because I've been taught how powerful of an aphrodisiac it can be. Speaking of," he pulled his hand away slowly, emphasizing his intentions for me to make amends for ghosting him at dinner. "What happened to you? I felt stood up."

I turned away from him with a dismissive wrist flip while taking another sip of my wine. Crossing towards the floor-to-ceiling windows that looked across the city, I addressed him in my best holier-than-thou tone, as though his mock chastisement did nothing for me.

"It just so happens that I also had to go to work." I spun back to face him and wasn't surprised to find he'd followed me. "Clearly, I'm more efficient at my job, as I finished hours ago."

I lifted my glass in a triumphant toast before drinking again. Garth pried the glass from my fingers. Leaning forward to set the drinks down on the end table behind me, I became intoxicated for the first time that evening.

Having nothing to do with the alcohol, my head swam as the smell of him combining with the scent of the fermented grapes consumed me. His body ever so lightly pressing into mine to reach the table did nothing to quell the heat rising in my cheeks.

Garth whispered, "And now that we're both done for the day?"

My eyelids fluttered at his breath on my neck before finally sinking closed. A long, slow exhale of an entirely different nature from the one he'd exhibited before seemed the only reply I could manage. His fingers moved to my back. They examined the cut of my dress and the exposed skin between my shoulders.

"How many nights were you away?"

"Too many," I breathed. "Always too many."

I felt his lips curve into a smile against the nape of my neck. He accompanied the smile with a pleased hum as his fingers tickled my spine. My breathing became more labored. Pausing with that approach, Garth leaned back to aright himself and take another full view of my attire.

His eyes moved slowly and deliberately from my head to my toes and back again, allowing themselves to linger in a couple choice areas on each pass. He brought his eyes back to meet mine with his own desirous sigh.

"You just had to wear this dress,"—his eyes gave me another once over—"didn't you?"

Having regained my sea legs, I stepped towards him—a shuffle, he hadn't left much room between us—and momentarily retook control.

"But of course." With a sly smile and a thirsty twinkle in my eye, I wondered, "Would you prefer I take it off?"

Responding with far more tenderness and control than I had anticipated, Garth did not reach his arms around me to unzip the dress. Instead, a single finger ran down the silver chain hanging from my neck. He followed it to the top of the gap between my breasts and let his finger linger there. Pinching the chain between his fingers, he began to pull it from underneath my dress.

Looped around the end of that chain hung my engagement ring and wedding band. He held them in his hand, letting them rest alongside his own golden wedding band.

Looking up to meet my gaze again, I recognized the same desire shining back at me. He closed his hand around the rings and used the chain to gently pull my lips close.

Then he moved his hands towards unzipping my dress.

Effortlessly shimmying out of the fabric, I stood fully shucked in the moonlight. Indeed, I had worn underthings during the day but promptly removed them upon arriving home. I had made an unspoken promise to Garth that he could remove my dress. Still, I dare not extend the denial of our pleasure by leaving those pesky unmentionables in the way.

The golden flecks in my husband's tawny eyes glowed as they roved over my naked form. My husband reminded me of a wolf each time that unmitigated thirst consumed his gaze. I never have met a wolf alone in the wild, but I imagine a certain kind of shudder would pass down my spine if I did.

Alone and not a wolf, the desire my husband beheld me with in those moments did enough to change my mood at the drop of a hat. Not that my moods typically required much help.

Which reminds me...

I shifted my lips from a kiss to bite into Garth's shoulder.

"Ow!"

I had not bit hard enough to hurt him, only enough so he understood I had a bone to pick with him.

"What was that for?"

"For not returning my call and making me fear the worst! Gracious, why must you have a job that puts you in the crosshairs of criminals and thugs?"

"Oh, I'm the one constantly endangered by criminals? I spend most of my time in an office. You're the one spending day-in and day-out with those thugs."

"But they all want my help," I said with a flick of my wrist. Granting him a condescending once-over, I added, "You're the one they dislike."

"Well, I am sorry that my ethics and morals have put me in danger from your friends."

My jaw worked as I tried continuing the motions of annoyance. The sentiment had dispelled with the bite. Both unable and unwilling to maintain my ire, I acquiesced to his contrite smile.

"Fine," I huffed. Of course, I forgave him the moment I learned of his safety, but he didn't need to know that. "I forgive your morals and ethics but refuse to forgive your belatedness. A simple text would've sufficed for me to get some sleep."

His smile shifted from contrition to cheeky pride.

"You didn't sleep from worrying about me?"

"Must you look so pleased with yourself?"

Garth's eyes fell downcast in the most lighthearted of ways. Raising them to look at me through his eyelashes nearly caused a puddle on the floor.

"I am sorry I caused you a lack of sleep last night."

"And tonight?"

His eyes took to shining again as he examined my moonlit skin.

"I make no apologies for tonight's lack of sleep."

"Good, because you have work to do if you wish to find yourself back in my good graces."

My husband's kiss assured me of the dedication of his repentance in a way words could never suffice.

As a top-tier detective, it is literally my husband's job to pay attention to how people respond to certain stimuli and press when they give a desirable response. As less a skill and more a natural state of mind, it always served for some excellent lovemaking.

Our loving that night carried a connotation, I am sorry to say, became an occurrence with more frequency than I ever thought my mortal heart could bear. That night—that day, really—had begun with a hot and heavy lasciviousness well-suited to extended foreplay and the passions of a night before a planned separation.

But as the hour of our communion finally arrived, that same crude, unbridled passion dissipated in deference towards a love defined by tender touches and extended moments of mutual hesitation fueled by contentedness. We could not ravish each other with a desperate passion nor engage in mutual taunting and the whispering of sweet nothings.

Many nights of sex throughout our marriage occurred because we simply couldn't bear withstanding. That night was not such a one. Instead, that night acted as a reunion of body and soul.

We made love long, slow, and sweet. Not because our carnality drove us to, but because our shared appreciative love dictated for no other outcome. His love and my relief welled to such an overflowing extent that there became only one possible course of action. I was home, and he was safe.

And for those blessed hours before sunrise, nothing in all the world mattered.

Chapter Eight

In Which We Reunited New Friends and an Old Associate

The rising sun peeked through the uncovered glass of the windows comprising the condo's walls. Something has always felt so freeing and less confining while indoors when surrounded by floor-to-ceiling windows.

Shortly after marrying, we did some house hunting for a condo near the city to entertain and provide Garth with a shorter commute. Stepping inside, I instantly fell in love with the view from Vinings Mountain.

This morning, however, the city view does not hold my interest.

Garth awoke before me. A phenomenon so common in our marriage that I often did not set an alarm, allowing my husband to wake me. After all, even the most pleasant sounds from an alarm clock could not wake me as pleasingly as my husband did.

Himself a side-sleeper, Garth rolled over to face me. I felt his body shifting the covers and distribution of the bed and smiled, knowing what was to come. As a floppy sleeper, the following events were dictated by my position.

This morning, I lay on my side, meaning Garth wrapped his arm around my waist and tucked me close to him. Our bodies were perfectly aligned and, curve for curve, snuggled tightly. His lips moved to explore my neck and ear. His teeth left the gentlest of love bites while the flicking of the tip of his tongue removed their sting.

My body tensed in anticipation as his hot breath billowed across my exposed skin. With this confirmation that I no longer slept, my husband whispered sweet everythings in my ear, beginning with:

"Good morning, wifey."

Lovely as these one-sided amorous actions may be, a girl can only last so long without engaging her husband when he talks like that.

Delightfully trapped in his embrace, I twisted my body and reached back to grasp a full fist of that luscious hair, pulling his lips firmly against mine. His tongue no longer needed as a balm against his love bites, it took to filling the empty space of my mouth.

With my hand now the one holding us together, the hand Garth still had wrapped around my waist became free to explore. He slid down my stomach. He stopped to check the sculpting of my posterior with a few squeezes before tickling designs on my thigh with his fingertips.

Those delightful fingers slid into the gap between my thighs. But my mouth was too full of his tongue for me to respond.

"I always love it when you come home from a heist," my husband informed me as his fingers slid deeper.

Even with my mouth finally free, it took me a few moments to respond.

"Why is that?" I moaned.

"Two reasons. One: it means you're not out committing another crime."

I squirmed away in silent protest that he disapproved of my methods. My body rolled over to lie on top of him. Garth allowed me to pin his arms on the pillow as I glared down at him. He only smiled.

Curse that smile.

"And two?" I asked.

He no longer allowed me to pin him. In an impressively fluid motion, my husband moved my hands behind my back, rolled us over, and used my own body weight against me to pin my arms between me and the bed.

His muscular frame pressed atop me kept me from freeing my arms. Trapped as I was, I became entirely at my husband's disposal.

And what a glorious place to be!

I had only to lie there and enjoy Garth's hardy longsword coaxing as he rocked delectably back and forth, in and out.

"I should think you appreciate my thievery precisely for my return." My voice tumbled drowsily like when answering my masseuse's questions about pressure.

"People with legal modes of income do also travel for work," he countered without slowing.

"But is that anywhere near as exciting?"

My husband exhaled a growl of annoyance at my objectionable indiscretion and pleasure at my undeniable observation. A growl my tongue cut short.

Just then, at the most inopportune of times, the alarm on Garth's cell phone began to play. The grating sound of a preprogrammed horn grew louder as it traveled up the stairs and made its way into the bedroom. We both looked towards the sound, then back to each other.

"Don't you dare," I told my husband.

"You know if I don't turn it off, it'll keep getting louder," he protested.

With a tantalizing smile, I reminded him, "So can we."

Recognizing the immense superiority of my plan to any other alternative, my husband happily ignored his phone. Instead, returning his attention to my body and the delicious way we fit together.

The sound changed from a horn to police sirens. The ringtone for his office. I, however, had no intention of allowing him to leave that bed.

"Let it go to voicemail," I told him, hoping that my tongue may serve to persuade him once more.

"I can't," he mourned but made no move to lift himself off me. Trying to convince himself, he added, "That's my ringtone for the office. I'm sorry, wifey. I have to answer it."

He pulled out.

"No, Garth. No. Don't you da—"

But he had already rushed out of the room.

I collapsed onto the pillow with an exasperated sigh that I hoped carried into the hallway and followed him. I determined to retain my indignation until Garth returned so that I could make him work to regain my favor. Setting my face in a stern pout, I awaited his return.

Unfortunately, yet another aspect in which Garth existed as a dichotomy was in his coordination. Put him on a dance floor or a bed—

For what is dancing if not making love on hardwood?

—and he exhibits a grace to invoke the envy of Baryshnikov. Set him at the top of a set of hardwood stairs, however...

My pout broke into a giggling smile as I heard the distinctive squeak and rapid thudding of someone slipping and sliding down the stairs. My husband was unintentionally wont to do things like this, and classic slapstick never failed to bring a smile to my face. I had come to dub any 'flirtation' falling into this category as a 'use of lack of coordination'.

I pushed myself onto my elbows as I heard Garth ending the call and returning to the bedroom.

"What?" I sneered at the sheepish look on his face.

"I've gotta go in."

"Now? It's barely light out!"

He cocked his head and looked at me, trying to make sense of what I had just said.

"You do know that the sun rises later as we approach winter, yes? And," he paused to check the wristwatch we'd laid on the bedside table last night, "I really should've left already."

"Why? It's only one case."

Returning to the bed, Garth leaned down his fists on the duvet.

"Unlike you, Mancini is not the only criminal I'm trying to catch."

"Oh, come now." I raised a hand to run through his hair. "I cleared my schedule so we could spend the day together."

"What were you planning on doing all day?" His voice lilted, reminding me of a cat purring as my fingers caressed his body.

Though Garth's eyes closed as I ran my fingers through his hair, I couldn't help smiling at him as I considered my answer.

"I was planning on doing you for most of it."

Moving my massaging hand to his shoulder, I threw all my strength into that arm and shoved my husband down onto the bed. My own body too easily followed atop him, once more pinning his body beneath me. We recommenced our kissing.

I felt his body submitting to mine. A sensation not at all unfamiliar in our marriage. With each kiss, rub, squeeze, embrace, and passing moment of all his tension collecting in a single location, I knew the fight raging between his body and mind.

He seriously considered not going to work, or at least going in late, and I intended to convince him to give into the temptation. Unfortunately, one thing I always adored and admired about my husband was his sense of honor and duty. To that end, he reluctantly pulled his lips away.

"I really do have to go."

With an acquiescent sigh, I decided, "Well, I'm sure I can find *something* to occupy my time while you're gone."

"Why do I feel that tomorrow I'll find a new case file on my desk?"

I smiled cheekily but assured him, "No need to worry. I have to prepare for tomorrow's party."

"Oh yeah."

Honestly, this man remembers every minuscule detail about every case he's ever worked on but can't recall his own birthday.

"Well, I've never known previous plans to have stopped you before."

With another smile and a slight hum of anticipation, I reminded him, "Depends an awful lot on the plans."

We kissed again, and I wondered if I hadn't convinced him to stay. Just as I became ready to proclaim myself victorious, Garth sat up. He effortlessly pushed my dainty frame aside.

"I'll see you tonight," he promised, gently rolling me onto the bed before he stood and wandered into the bathroom. He called across the echoing tile, "Maybe we can pick up on your previous plans for today?"

"You don't want me to come in with you?" I yelled back.

The toilet flushed, and the sink stopped after washing his hands. Garth wandered back to the bed and hovered his body over mine.

"I don't want you around me at the office any more than required."

He leaned down to grant me another desirous, sensual kiss and point out why we oughtn't be around each other. It had to linger on both our lips until nightfall.

"Go on and get," I finally told him, knowing that if he kept kissing me like that, I'd be the one giving into the temptation of becoming unproductive. "If you don't leave now, I might change my mind and never let you go back to work."

He smiled and planted another kiss.

"I'll see you back here tonight."

"Yes, you will." My voice sank low and sultry, my body still drunk from his taste.

"Love you," my husband promised.

I hummed my approval and reciprocation. He kissed me again before disappearing into the closet to dress for work.

Still lying on the bed, I needed something to keep me occupied and keep my mind off my naked husband mere feet away from me. Deciding to kill two birds with one stone, I grabbed my phone to scroll through the news reports I'd missed from the previous day and night.

Few things served to kill the mood quite so effectively as receiving a bombardment of updates about the world going to shambles and everybody complaining about and blaming each other for it.

I pulled my charcoal, fully loaded Porsche Cayenne Turbo under the valet awning of Fox Glen and handed my key fob to the young man who'd opened my door for me.

While I always preferred driving Hermie over any other car, I quickly realized that I couldn't bring myself to drive him in the rain. I wouldn't dare allow another human being to operate him, even if for only long enough to take him to and from the valet lot.

Such was the case that spurred me to purchase my everyday driver. Some might consider it ostentatious to consider a top-of-the-line German luxury SUV that I'd customized to a price tag exceeding $150,000 an 'everyday driver'. I say that the only problem with being better than everyone else is that people tend to think you're pretentious.

Besides, who was I to pull into the finest social establishment in Atlanta driving some beater car, like Garth's antique F-150? Standards must be maintained, and I, certainly, was not one to break the mold.

The entryway of Fox Glen always seemed quite reminiscent of the manor's foyer. So much so that Garth had accused me of stealing the design as I constructed our home. I quickly corrected him by explaining that I had never set foot inside Fox Glen before building the manor. I also pointed out that I had genuine marble and crystal. Fox Glen had merely utilized excellent substitutes.

Ms. Parvati currently ran the front desk and greeted me by name as I passed. She immediately informed me that the ladies had taken up residence in the dining room since the rain ran us off the terrace we typically used. I nodded my thanks, turned down a short hallway, and proceeded directly to the casual dining room.

McCormick's served as Fox Glen's resident restaurant. Always available to members of the club, nonmembers required reservations made at least one month in advance to dine there. An upstairs ballroom served as the formal dining room whenever Fox Glen hosted various events for holidays and whatnot or if someone wanted to rent out the club for a private party.

As renting Fox Glen for personal use required quite the pretty penny, few people I knew of had ever done such a thing. Then again, since most people who would be invited to such a shindig were already members, the option of a private rental always seemed somewhat redundant to me.

I stopped at the hostess stand where *señorita* Marína Alvarado, McCormick's *maître d'*, filled in for a sick employee. I asked her once more when she would find a man to marry.

'Twould be an utter waste for a woman with those Latin hips and that gorgeous skin to go unproperly appreciated.

To which she observed that she felt no man worthy of her. While I couldn't argue with her viewpoint, I still told her that I'd find one with which to set her up. The unspoken trouble was that I didn't know how she felt about most men flashing through my mind working in unsavory careers.

I made a mental note to build a profile on *señorita* Alvarado to determine her comfortability with legally questionable gentlemen.

The girls had left the far chair open for me at the corner table. Only one had any inkling why I always positioned myself with the best vantage point of the room around me and all entrances and exits.

Today, that, unfortunately, meant I had to forego a view of the city through the floor-to-ceiling windows that created the dining room walls. Alas, as the day had quickly become shrouded in a dull, soggy, grey blanket, I needed only the option of listening to the rain to enjoy the ambiance.

With their backs facing the open space of the dining room, the silence of my footsteps even while wearing heels, and the story with which Jaylyn regaled the girls, I walked up unnoticed.

Unnoticed by all but Darcy, of course.

Darcy Rigby, a short Caribbean-born islander with skin like a dark rum and massive dreads that had to weigh at least half her body weight, also insisted on placing herself wherever she could best see everything around her.

She spotted me immediately after entering the dining room. We locked eyes and acknowledged each other's existence before she returned to listening to the story. She and I shared a particular secret amongst the girls and would never dare to spoil a grand entrance for the other.

Truth be told, I had always proved the one more prone to such appearances.

"And that's when I turned the corner to see her having the poor boy pinned up against the wall, not knowing what to do with himself!"

The girls laughed hysterically at Jaylyn's tale, not one doubting its validity. A natural-born storyteller with chocolate skin and hair dyed bright red, Jaylyn never had any trouble keeping the rapt attention of any crowd. Couple that with the lilting melody of her South African accent, and most of the work required in allowing me to sneak up unnoticed had been done by her.

"Telling stories on me when you think I'm not here to defend myself, are you?" I jokingly accused.

"No one would believe a word you say to deny it," Jaylyn replied. With a firm gaze on my hair, which I'd decided to dye a shimmering auburn color in honor of the season, she added, "I see you've taken after my style."

"Well, you just pull it off so well, I thought I'd give it a try." I continued around the table, taking my seat beside Darcy.

" 'Ow was your trip to New York?" Madeline inquired.

Despite having technically grown up in Connecticut, Mrs. Theobald attended a boarding secondary school and university in France. She desperately clung to the accent she had acquired.

"Very productive," I answered, pouring myself a glass of water. "I easily acquired the piece my client sought."

"I don't suppose you'd reveal who this client is?" Alexandria Hollins-Patel asked.

A woman with silky black hair, Indian chocolate for skin, and a fortune that made her easily the richest among us—except perhaps Darcy, whose total wealth proved near impossible to determine—Alexandria never lacked for suitors. More than once, I had inadvertently provided the requisite skill set for her current beau to acquire some piece of art or some such.

Of course, they typically thought the same as the girls—excluding Darcy—that I merely worked as an art curator for private collectors without ever stopping to think from where the acquisitions came. Ever since, Alexandria always wanted to know with whom I worked most recently, curious if she might know them.

"You know she won't," Jaylyn answered for me. "All that professionalism she wants to maintain."

"It's true," I affirmed. "You should know I won't ever reveal any of my clients. Cheers."

I raised my water glass, and the girls reciprocated with their own varying drinks. Alexandria Hollins-Patel, Jaylyn Mercer, Darcy Rigby, and Madeline Theobald were all fellow members of Fox Glen. We ladies had developed our own club within the already exclusive confines.

We met weekly to enjoy each other's company and catch up on the latest gossip from our various circles worldwide. None of us lacking in money or acquaintances, the stories typically stretched across borders and included people that TMZ and CNN to the *Louvre* and *La Scala* to Forbes and ESPN would've killed to know intimate details about.

"I see everyone present and accounted for," I slipped into a slight lull in the conversation. "Clearly, you all made it through the 85 episode unscathed. All husbands, friends, and consorts safe and well?"

Solemn head nods and mumbled general acknowledgments greeted my inquiry. Alexandria reported that a few people from the office had connections that got caught in the mayhem. One died, and three sustained various levels of injury.

Darcy told us that a delivery her company was transporting to a distribution center got caught in the middle of the blast. The truck plummeted to the surface street below the overpass. Miraculously, the driver escaped with only minor injuries.

While the other ladies let out sighs of relief at this news, my worry hadn't diminished. I stared at her with a concerned look the others didn't share. Understanding the hidden truth behind my wide eyes and open mouth, Darcy gave me a subtle head shake. I relaxed then.

"Where will you be heading next?" Jaylyn asked me, ready to move the conversation along. I later learned that Janko, her husband, should have been caught in the blast. A flat tire shortly after leaving the house delayed his commute.

"I'm actually in Atlanta for the foreseeable future."

A chorus of pleased cooing greeted my announcement. As I did the most amount of traveling for my job, I often proved the only one absent from any of our meetings.

"Taking an 'oliday?" Madeline wondered.

"More a temporary change in occupation. I've joined Garth's team and am now a consultant for Uncle Sam."

Darcy spat the swallow of mimosa back into her glass at my elaboration. The subsequent coughing from her spit-take allowed Darcy to cover for her reaction by saying her drink had gone down the wrong tube. After the fit subsided, it became her turn to stare at me with a misunderstood expression of concern.

"So, what exactly are you doing?" Alexandria inquired.

"What all consultants do," I answered with purposeful coyness. "I provide the services of my expertise to assist them with their work. Garth needed help within the white-collar world, and that is where I live. We decided it was time for a team-up." I leaned nonchalantly back in my chair as I took a sip of mimosa.

"Why now?" Darcy asked, her voice holding a slight twinge of accusation.

I'm sure none of the girls noticed the undertones, but I knew to listen for them. I shrugged and shook my head as though I had nothing to report and our working together seemed the most natural of courses to take.

I knew I needed to say something to temporarily assuage Darcy and keep the others from asking more questions. I quickly landed on the most enjoyable thing about my newest philanthropic endeavor.

"We felt we needed to spice up our marriage a bit."

Everyone else had their own turn at a spit-take. However, this unanimous reaction arose from laughter instead of shock.

"For some reason," Jaylyn began as the spokesperson to echo everyone's sentiments, "I very much doubt that."

"Fair," I conceded with my hands raised in surrender. "But!" I cried over the peals of laughter that continued rumbling around the table, "I am having great fun."

"Now, that I believe," Jaylyn admitted.

"And I'm quite certain Garth's more than happy to reap the benefits of your fun," Alexandria added with a smirk to do me proud.

I reciprocated her grin and raised my glass in a silent toast. We spent the next hour chatting like a roost of hens about everything under the sun. Madeline told us about her recent trip to France and recommended an up-and-coming vineyard in the Loire Valley.

The prodigal son of an established vintner family had decided to strike out on his own and make quality wines accessible to the non-elites. A kindred spirit of breaking away from their parents and gambling to strike it rich on your own, Madeline always sought to promote those worthy of her patronage.

Jaylyn had little to say about her life, preferring merely to add commentary about everyone else's. She'd stopped telling stories about her patients at the Shepherd Center after one particularly gruesome injury sent Darcy fleeing to the bathroom.

For someone in an unforgivable line of work, the idiosyncrasies concerning Darcy's squeamishness always amused me.

Alexandria divulged every detail concerning the three new men she went out on dates within the past week. Next, Darcy bored everyone to tears by going on a tirade about the alteration of shipping lanes due to increased pirate activity off the coast of Somalia and a typhoon tearing through the South China Sea and how all this set back her delivery dates and cost her company both time and money.

Truthfully, I just about passed out face down on my plate from the tapering rain and Darcy's droning. Jaylyn, fortunately, intervened just before my mashed potatoes became my pillow.

"That party of yours still on?"

"What?" I asked, snapping my head back into place. "Party? Mine? Yes! Yes, the party's still on. You best all come."

"Of course, we will come!" Madeline assured. "You 'ave the best 'ouse of us all! We never miss a chance to enjoy your 'ospitality and view."

"That's what I bought it for," I said with a cheeky smile.

The conversation fizzled out quickly after that. People had prior appointments to which they needed to attend. As neither of us had waiting engagements, Darcy and I remained as the last of the others paid their tabs and left. We sat in silence for a moment. Darcy looked past me to gaze out of the massive windows upon a wet and humid city.

"The rain's stopped," she commented.

Another silence stretched between us as Darcy stared out the window, and I disinterestedly nursed my mimosa.

"Join me for a round of golf."

She hadn't moved to look at me as she spoke. Had I not been acquainted with Darcy's business style, I might have thought her forceful suggestion was intended for someone awaiting her on the terrace.

"I only play golf when working a mark," I remarked.

"I know." She turned to face me. Her eyes were hard and determined, and I was reminded of her true colors. "But golf courses make for excellent conversation locations. Wide open spaces, quiet neighbors, and people keeping their distance. No prying ears to catch a stray word."

I nodded once, slowly, understanding that Darcy wanted to talk business. The part of her business that intersected with mine.

Chapter Nine

In Which I Engaged in Golf and Other Physical Pursuits

I followed Darcy to the Pro Shop across the lobby, where she booked the next available tee time. Realizing that, unlike her, I didn't have a golfing wardrobe or set of clubs at Fox Glen, Darcy rented a set of clubs and purchased me an outfit and shoes to wear that day.

She told me I could keep my clothes here, take them home, or burn them after today. I admitted that the latter sounded the most fun.

Looking across the landscape of the first tee box as Darcy took her practice swings, I noticed just how little visibility of the surrounding world existed from the first tee box.

It sat somewhat in a valley, with most of the course rising slightly above it. More trees lined its fairway than any other hole on this course. In fact, the F and G, winding together into the Fox Glen insignia towering above like a wrought iron weathervane, proved just about the only things one could see.

Still without a word about what she wanted to discuss, Darcy teed off. I dutifully followed suit. Admittedly, Darcy's drive, though having less distance than mine, did fly extraordinarily straight and landed on the fairway instead of the rough my ball inhabited.

I made a fuss about not having a golf glove, causing my poor drive. Darcy pointed out that I hadn't asked for one during her spending spree. I finally lost my composure when we'd made it to the third hole, and Darcy still hadn't said anything.

If she won't start the conversation, I'll force her into one.

As I waited for her to tee off, I said, "I've always wondered, but thought it indelicate to ask, about that time you ran off when Jaylyn told us the story about that one patient's horrific spinal cord injury, and you went all green around the gills. Was that real or just for show?"

"W'a' da ya t'ink?" Darcy asked, bringing down her driver without the slightest hindrance to her swing. No longer in the presence of our honest friends, Darcy let her natural calypso accent out in full force.

After seeing where her drive landed—perfectly centered on the fairway—she turned to me with a smile. "Good show, wasn't it?"

I didn't have to ask if she referred to her drive or the feigning sickness.

When we'd driven the hundred yards to where my pathetic drive landed, and I stared at my bag trying to decide which club to use, I wondered:

"When was the last time you beat someone with a driver?"

"Oh, no. You never use a driver ta beat someone," Darcy quickly corrected me as she jumped out to help me choose my club. Withdrawing her driver, she used the visual aid to explain.

"The club be much too pliant. The larger surface area distributes da blow for less impact upon your target. No, no." She put the driver away and pulled out another club. "When beating someone, always go for t'e 9-iron."

She handed me my own club with a smile. I stood beside the cart, examining the club in my hand and marveling at Darcy's multitasking talent. Noticing that I made no effort to find my ball and continue with the round, Darcy accurately guessed that an all-consuming thought had invaded my mind.

Wise enough to deduce that the intruder belonged under the category of the 85 tragedy, Darcy granted me mercy by finally broaching the topic requiring isolated conversation.

"What be this announcement t'at you be working with the FBI?"

Temporarily ignoring her question, I went to my ball for my next stroke. Still staring at the invisible flight path of the ball—which had landed several seconds ago—I informed her:

"I met with C4 yesterday." I allowed my club to drop, accompanied by a heavy sigh. Turning back to Darcy but not yet returning to the cart, I continued, "He's the bomber."

"Can't be saying I'm surprised," Darcy answered with an inherent nonchalance that always put my practiced indifference to shame. "There not many folks with his talent. But I ain't never known C4 ta do something without a paycheck. Who was his benefactor?"

"Anonymous third party." I slid my club back into its place.

My eyes absently stared at my contained clubs for a long moment. Someone called "fore" on a distant fairway, and a string of obscenities promptly followed the loud *thunk* of a golf ball bouncing off the roof of a golf cart.

Through it all, Darcy calmly waited for me to finish my tale.

I don't think a coherent, recoverable thought crossed my mind during the entire hesitation. C4's warning continuously drifted through, but I couldn't discern his cryptic meaning.

"He thinks the bomb was meant as a warning against me," I finally told Darcy.

"A warning?" Darcy sat straighter, and her eyes hardened. Though not technically a member of her company, our aged friendship caused Darcy to treat me as such.

"Who be wantin' to warn ya in such a fashion? Anybody willing to hire C4 ta get at ya be better suited hiring a sniper." Never one to be denied what she wanted, Darcy looped the conversation back around to her original question.

"But what in the world this got anything ta be doing with the FBI?"

Sliding back into the cart, I explained the FBI's belief that Mancini caused the bombing. I told her of Garth's idea to hire me as a consultant to catch Mancini and the details of my recent conversation with C4 that ironed out some of the unknowns.

It took three holes for me to finish the entire account. After teeing off, Darcy hesitated in the box, leaning on her driver like a cane.

"But if ya be knowing it ain't Mancini, and moreover, ya do know that it was C4, why ya still be working wit' the FBI?"

"I think it'll be fun," I quickly replied with a sly smile and a mischievous glint in my eye.

Far less susceptible to such things than Garth, Darcy merely gave an unamused grimace as she returned to the cart. With a sigh and a dramatic eye roll, I confessed:

"Truth is, I wanna know what this is about. I want to know who's supposedly after me, what they want, and why they chose this method."

Always the infallible poker player, Darcy called my bluff. "And ya can't be discovering that with your own resources?"

"Alright, fine," I surrendered. "I started 'cause it sounded fun and thought it'd be like a big joke."

"And now?" she prompted at my renewed hesitation.

I voiced my deep-seated concerns with a steady sigh as though holding something heavy inside. I needed to prep myself before letting it out.

"C4 reaching out to me yesterday—I'd never admit it to anyone but you—but it scared me. You know nothing ever shakes C4. Not since we got his family out. The fact that he tried to convince me to run made me believe that whatever's going on is serious and not something I can flit my way out of."

"And ya had ta always be making sure that Garth be safe," Darcy added, putting into words what I found myself unwilling to say aloud.

"I wouldn't know what to do without him."

After pausing to concentrate on her putt, Darcy said, "César and I be about the only two people who truly be understanding the change he's made in ya. Can't be saying I entirely approve," she added with a smile.

"But I must be saying that I ain't never seen ya consistently happier than since ya took up with him."

Darcy caught my arm, forcing us to hold each other's gaze. In a rare moment of mutual sincerity and dire seriousness, I knew Darcy shared some inkling of C4's concern for me.

"Whatever come of this whole mess, I'll always be here for ya. And if you and t'e Suit ever be needing me, ya know how ta reach me."

I responded with a nod and a weak smile. I placed my hand over hers and gave it a quick, reassuring squeeze of thankfulness.

Somewhere in the back nine—

I lost count through the course of the conversation and the minor detail that I didn't care.

—the rain from that morning began again. My interest in the insisted-upon round of golf fell swiftly from 'not' to 'contemplating taking Darcy's advice on beating someone with a nine iron'.

Our conversation concluded near the turn of the tenth green. I remained on the course only because Darcy chose one cart with the forethought of keeping me trapped.

The sudden downpour and Darcy's insistence that she finish her game—she couldn't care less whether I continued playing—made me quite the unhappy camper when I managed to scurry back into the Cayenne and drive to the condo.

Soaked to the bone and shivering, I unlocked the penthouse and made a b-line to the bath and a dry change of clothes. Never one to deny myself the pleasures of a long, hot shower, the stillness of a nice soak in the bath allows for more free-flowing thoughts when contemplating the inner workings of the universe and the vastness of the human psyche.

Having filled the free-standing, claw-footed, copper tub with water of the perfect temperature, the thinnest wisps of steam rose. I removed my robe and slipped into the therapeutic water.

Initially, I allowed myself no thoughts. Content to stew in the sauna of my own making, I closed my eyes and sank neck deep. A bird twittered as it flew by the window beside me.

Garth had thought me rather odd and possibly a bit kinky—not wrong on either count—for choosing to expand the tiny skylight when we purchased the condo. I removed the built-in tub, expanded the pathetic square into a bay window, and installed a copper tub like one I discovered at an Irish spa.

When questioning my adamancy concerning such a demand before moving in, I told him that I preferred a well-lit bathroom.

"You could just turn on the lights," Garth replied with such a well-executed snark I nearly had him right there in front of the contractor.

But he knew the importance of my ability to customize my home and offered no protest. Especially not after we'd completed all our business and returned to the privacy of the manor.

The real reason I desired a sizeable window had little to do with lighting. True, I've always preferred natural light and readily chose it over its artificial counterpart. But I wanted the panoramic floor plan for this precise moment: the countless hours I knew I would spend thinking and relaxing in the steaming water.

The bird's song drew my attention to the window, but the view halfway between me and the horizon kept me enthralled. Though compact compared to those found worldwide, no one will ever convince me that Atlanta does not boast one of the most picturesque skylines.

Each raindrop clinging to the window captured its own lumen emanating from the city. They glittered my view with dozens of year-round Christmas lights created by the beautiful marriage of nature and industry. The persistent rainfall had annoyed our real estate agent the first time we toured the condo.

When I'd told her I wanted somewhere with a view and a balcony, she banked on those features for selling this place. Alas, the downpour kept us from stepping onto the balcony. The thick sheets of rain rendered the skyline temporarily out of sight. The agent never realized that the rain only heightened my love of the view.

As we prepared to leave, the storm slacked just enough. I caught a glimpse of what could be mine. Taking one last appraising look as the agent escorted us out, I saw the faintest hint of those twinkling lights through the wall of windows. That tease proved enough to firmly cement the condo in my mind.

I refused to tour any other properties until seeing it again on a sunny day. We scheduled a follow-up for the following week. Since then, I've only managed to fall further enamored with the vista with each passing glance.

The condo door opened and closed. I glanced at the clock on the wall. The time displayed allowed me to accept the probability that Garth had just arrived home from work and not that robbers had broken in.

My eyelids fell as I hoped that he had something specific to do and wouldn't come upstairs to bother me. Though I usually immensely enjoyed it when my husband bothered me while in the bath, I needed the isolation to think that day.

Finally, I marshaled my thoughts towards productive means. I considered all that had occurred and my various conversations over the past three days. In my admission of C4's adamancy scaring me, I failed to mention how his warning also irked me. Something about it never sat right in my mind. The more I ruminated—

and by ruminate, I mean pondering, not chewing cud

—the more it didn't make sense. It wasn't until Darcy voiced the oddity that I realized what confused me so. If someone wanted to get at me, why not just kill me?

C4's prices steadily increased with each job. By now, anyone desiring to employ his services would find themselves shoveling out a small fortune. A decent hitman would have proved far more accessible. And quieter, for that matter. Whoever wanted me didn't just want me dead; they wanted to play with my mind first.

I must admit respect for anyone who chose to implement psychological warfare over a straightforward headshot, but who had I crossed so profoundly? And who would think or care to blame Mancini for it? Drawing him in consequently involved Uncle César skulking around the periphery.

Fortunately, though C4 knew nothing about his benefactor, the mere fact of his hiring significantly narrowed down the list of suspects. Few people had the disposable funds to employ C4 for a personal vendetta, even in my world of glittering jewels. But still, I had no idea who could populate such a list, limited as it may be.

Perhaps I'll ask Garth for help. His training ought to have provided him with ways of discerning suspects. I'm pretty sure that's literally what he gets paid to do.

Thinking of Garth caused a subconscious lifting of my eyes to the clock on the wall. I realized that he'd arrived home well over thirty minutes ago and thought it odd that he hadn't come upstairs.

Once more grateful for copper's heat capacity, I took a deep breath and savored my final moments in the still-warm water. Braving myself to step out into the chill of the bathroom, I grabbed the towel from the rack and immediately cocooned myself after stepping out.

My thoughts consumed with who could possibly dislike me and the usefulness of Garth's professional proclivities. They left little room for particularly amorous predilections that evening. I didn't bother to dry my hair, only throwing it into a messy bun to keep it out of my way.

Nor did I change into anything a casual observer would consider overwhelmingly sexy in which to greet my husband. I say 'not overwhelmingly sexy' because anything remotely formfitting and comfortable automatically fell under the 'innocently erotic' category I had a fondness for.

The pajama booty shorts and one of my husband's old, worn t-shirts hanging off my shoulders qualified.

Any amative feelings which may have developed between dressing and making my way downstairs promptly subsided. Utter confusion at the clanking sounds and wafts of cooking coming from the kitchen thoroughly replaced them.

I sniffed at the air. The acrid scent of burning garlic bread immediately accosted my nostrils. Grimacing my way past that, I detected pasta and vodka sauce, which seemed more vodka than sauce. A clattering baking sheet and a string of mild expletives briefly interrupted Garth's whistling. He resumed his nondescript, improvised tune.

"What are you doing?" My curiosity boiled over into a tone hovering between condescension and abject confusion.

Engrossed in his failing attempt at cooking, Garth hadn't noticed my entrance. His face shot up at my question. He nearly knocked the saucepan off the stove. Recovering quickly, he stretched out his arms over the train-wreck of a home-cooked meal.

"What does it look like I'm doing?"

"I'm not rightly sure," I confessed after another examination of the disemboweled kitchen.

Why must houses come with a kitchen but never a cook?

But even I sympathized with the poor thing. I wondered what crime it had committed deserving such harsh and thorough punishment.

Pausing his torturing, my husband kissed me in a way that finally allowed suspicion to inch in beside my confusion. Still unaware of what was happening, my reciprocating kiss felt terribly weak against his determination.

Garth removed something he'd hidden under his clothes on the bar behind me. My husband spun like a drunk Fred Astaire, causing me to question if this production arose from a failing attempt to seduce me. He then produced a sculpted red rose figurine, which I instantly recognized as Swarovski crystal.

The boy most certainly wants something.

As I reached out to take the piece of art, Garth caught my hand in his. He gave it a silent kiss before returning to the stove, having left the immortal rose in my care.

With an air as though nothing remotely out of the ordinary was occurring, he inquired, "How was your day?"

"Good," I answered slowly. The word drew across my lips with a hesitation having nothing to do with its truthfulness. My utter confusion once more spilled over so that the inflection of my answer caused it to sound more like a question than a response.

My eyes flitted between examining the rose and my husband. Realizing I couldn't fully appreciate the craftsmanship of the rose at that moment, I gingerly set it aside. I returned my perplexed attention to my odd husband.

"But really, what *are* you doing? I'm not sure I've ever seen you cook anything other than breakfast. Are we supposed to be celebrating something?"

"If you want to be," he answered in a decidedly noncommittal and unhelpful answer as he stirred the sauce.

My shoulders slumped, and my eyelids sagged. I silently glared at him for a moment. With an onerously controlled deep breath, I decided to play along. From his aloofness thus far, I knew Garth wouldn't come flat out with his intentions at any point.

Clearly, I won't be inclined to accept whatever he wants.

"What are we potentially celebrating?" I inquired.

"Our third anniversary?" he offered.

"Not for another six months."

"Our two-and-a-half anniversary?" he rapidly countered.

Having grown tired of his evasiveness and becoming queasy from the smell of botched cooking, I decided to forget the game and get to the point.

"Just tell me what it is," I groaned. "I know you want something from me."

"I always want something from you."

My husband finally abandoned his abysmal attempt at culinary enticement. He turned off both stove burners and threw down the oven mitt he still wore from removing the burnt bread.

Deciding to fall back on one of his seduction fail-safes, Garth turned to me with a glint in his eye that I'm proud to say I taught him how to conjure at will. And if there's anything my husband knew to do to make me agreeable to whatever he may want, flattering my ego always proved a solid choice.

Combine that with a well-timed whispered sweet nothing and a proper kiss—or several—from his blessed velveteen lips. I wondered why he bothered with this cooking nonsense.

My confusion was wholly superseded by a brain-melting heat flooding my body. I showed far more desire in my reciprocation than when he'd first kissed me.

"What is it you want?" I asked, still clinging to the desperate hope of regaining some semblance of control of the situation.

"I should think that rather obvious," he toyed.

"Ah, but you don't need to attempt cooking me dinner for that."

My calling his bluff encouraged Garth to prove how genuinely he felt that desire. And as he pinned me between the door frame and himself, I noticed that his body indeed reflected that genuine desire.

Loathe though I was to push his lips away from where they had traveled down to pay attention to my neck, I knew my husband wanted something he had to ask for. I wouldn't let him have me until I received a satisfactory explanation.

I summoned all my physical and mental strength to hold Garth at arm's length. Then, I repeated my question in a tone that allowed no more worming his way out of a direct answer.

"What do you want?"

The seductive twinkle and desire instantly faded from my husband's eyes. The change occurred with such rapidity that it actually concerned me. He looked away and seemed unable to return my inquiring gaze.

Afraid I had accidentally upset him, my worries promptly dissipated when I realized he hadn't removed the pressure of his chest from my hand. His interest in physical touch had always proved a tell-tale sign of Garth's mood. Maybe a male attribute, but Garth never allowed anyone to touch him, myself included, whenever mad about something.

Finally, raising his eyes back to me, I almost forgot all demands I had of him. All but the one where we remove each other's clothes with consummate rapidity. He still hadn't regained the amorous look. Instead, he appeared as an adorable little boy trying to ask an embarrassing question.

He chewed at his bottom lip and couldn't hold my gaze but flashed his eyes between mine and the floor. I felt myself suddenly travel back in time, imagining that I stood in the shoes of a little girl with pigtails as Garth tried to figure out how to tell his first crush that he 'liked liked' her.

Fortunately, my husband found his voice before I lost all my resolve.

"It's not what I want, but what Moller has ordered."

I raised my eyebrows, silently instructing him to elaborate.

"You have to come into the office with me every day," he continued. "You are to be kept on a very short leash."

"A leash? We've not tried that before."

"Wifey."

He said my pet name in that long, slow southern drawl. It dripped from his tongue like honey. My husband knew exactly what that accent did to me. Though I still intended to withdraw all his information, we both knew I'd already given in to whatever he wanted.

"Focus." He explained, "Moller wants to always keep an eye on you."

Countless wonderful ways in which to spend the night occupied my mind. But my playful demeanor fell flat on its face when the realization struck me.

"You mean to tell me that I'm going to be stuck in an office surrounded by a bunch of suits all day?"

"That's about the size of things."

I groaned like a petulant teenager who'd just learned how they would spend their summer holidays doing absolutely nothing fun.

"You do realize I'm just going to go bored out of my mind and end up getting into trouble anyway?"

"It'll be a struggle," Garth agreed with an unenthused shrug. "But," his eyes lightened at the word and firmly held mine once more, "at least this way, you can't be off stealing things."

Another moment of realization dawned on me. I looked at my husband with an annoyed admiration towards his surreptitious conniving. It almost proved enough to make me forget my impending doom of relegation to an office.

Almost.

"Are you sure this wasn't *your* plan?"

My husband again attempted a nonchalant shrug. He could do nothing to hide the grin flashing across his face this time. He tried admirably to subdue it, but each attempt at straight-lipped composure only made the smile breakthrough, beaming twice as much.

His eyes again shone like a little boy's. Now, glittering with the innocent mischief of one who knew he'd gotten away with something. And the man behind it, who knew he was about to get away with even more.

With a sigh of submission to the spoken work request and the unspoken private desire, I wondered:

"Why'd you have to be so darn cute?" I released the tension in my arm, allowing Garth to bring his body back to mine. "I should have left you in that café and never helped you catch Jorgensen or gone to dinner with you."

"You realize you were the one that set up the dinner and drug me along?" Garth reminded me as his chest pressed against mine. His lips hovered beyond my reach for one tantalizing moment before continuing.

"Speaking of dinner—"

"Uh, no," I interrupted, pulling my body the few centimeters available between him and the kitchen door frame. "I am not attempting to eat whatever monstrosity it is you've butchered in this kitchen tonight."

Not losing his stride for a second with my sassy outburst, Garth closed the barely existing gap between us.

"Well, what would you like to do for dinner, then?"

Without awaiting the answer he already knew, my husband slid his hands under the hem of his tattered t-shirt and swiftly lifted it over my head. Tossing the shirt to fall limp across the bar with the first of his discarded clothes, his hands promptly found their way back to me and set to work on my bra clasp.

"Oh," I began, pretending to consider my answer.

My fingers had already unbuckled his belt and moved along to unzipping his pants. As his slacks fell to the floor, I told him:

"I'm sure we can find something to satisfy ourselves."

Chapter Ten

In Which I Issued Invitations and Received a Delivery

Having received neither permission nor—more importantly—access to park in the employee deck beneath the building, I found myself forced to park in the one across the street from the FBI offices.

And they made me pay for it, myself!

I later asked Agent Harmon if I could submit a compensation form for the personal money required for the deck in question. His response was less than promising. Except it had occurred while in bed, and I promptly forgot I had asked a question.

I stood waiting to cross the street and watched my husband pacing back and forth in front of the building's entrance. I was curious why he chose to wait for me when I already had clearance to enter independently.

I suspected it had something to do with the likely fact that he didn't trust me to go straight to my new desk without first wandering to make new friends.

Honestly, after all these years, he still doesn't trust me?

It almost proved enough to make me ignore all pretense and kiss him in front of the whole FBI.

The tails of his nondescript work suit fluttered in the breeze Garth made with each heel turn before passing back in front of the glass doors leading into the FBI lobby. He must have completed this circuit nearly a dozen times in the few minutes I spent watching him as I waited for the light to turn.

An aura of nervousness or annoyance hovered about him. Given the circumstances, either—or perhaps both—proved appropriate options.

Finally, the light changed, and I could safely cross.

Reaching the end of another cycle, Agent Harmon checked his watch for the twentieth time. Turning around again, he saw me stepping onto his sidewalk and promptly marched to meet me.

"You're late," he reprimanded me in no uncertain terms.

"Good morning to you too," I snipped back.

"Hardly. Most people start work by at least 9 a.m." He held out his arm to examine the time displayed on his watch for myself.

Ignoring the timepiece shoved at my face, I reminded him, "You should know that I greatly prefer being active at night."

Garth paused. He gritted his teeth and stared at me with a harshness that conveyed that this confrontation wasn't one of banter on his end. Releasing a strong, controlled exhale, my husband chose to bite his tongue and move on.

For the first time since he approached me, his eyes released mine and took in an appraisal of my wardrobe change. My significant tardiness partially arose from the need to dress appropriately. To that end, I wore a pencil skirt, a prudish blouse, and a black blazer.

I'd even scrounged up a pair of detested hosiery for the affair!

I capped my outfit with modest, close-toed heels. My auburn hair was pulled back into a tight bun I felt confident would give me a headache before the day had ended. And I wore a pair of reading glasses for purely aesthetic purposes. I also carried an appropriately boring briefcase, which held little more than my semi-permanent visitor badge and keys.

Still completing his scrutiny of my attire, Garth wondered, "This is why you had to go to the manor and got here so late?"

Giving myself my own once-over, I explained, "I thought it only appropriate I dress for the occasion."

Any slacking in his annoyance of me that may have occurred after him biting his tongue returned in full force at my last comment. Garth groaned something fierce while dropping his face into his hand. He grimaced and muttered something under his breath, which sounded most unfit for a lady's ear.

"Kati, we are under enough of a gun as is. You can't pull stuff like this, okay?" He finally looked at me, only long enough to gesture at my clothing.

Turning away from me—something I knew he only did to keep from lashing out further during an argument—he took a few gapping moments to calm himself. Each second was punctuated with another deep breath as my husband fought to contain his annoyance and composure against me.

Though I wanted to say something—even if not an apology—I had learned not to interrupt Garth during times like this. I had only to wait in the deafening silence until he had said his piece. He eventually continued, his voice steady but obviously measured.

"When I proposed you become a consultant, I never anticipated you actually coming into the office with regularity."

Though I had asked no question, I knew Garth felt the need to explain his outburst. He always behaved healthier in conflicts than me concerning things like that.

My entire life had consisted substantially of isolation and things unsaid. I typically found this an asset in cutting ties and moving on to whatever I wanted next. It took several years of living with Uncle César to wonder if it might become a detriment in particular relationships.

Not until beginning my courtship with Garth had the gravity of the reality set upon me. Only upon realizing that there existed nothing beyond him to which I wanted to move did I exert any effort into healthy conflict resolution. I was still a severe work in progress.

In line with hashing things out and not leaving any questions unasked, I wondered, "Then why'd you make me official? Why not just let me help you from the shadows like always?"

"Because this case is high profile, and I knew I couldn't get away with my usual midnight epiphanies," he answered with resolute calmness.

"It's not always midnight," I imprudently quipped. "They tend to occur at any point during the day."

"Kati, please!" Garth snapped, whipping around to face me.

"You're really shaken up about this." I felt the slight quiver in my voice. It didn't arise from any fear of my husband but, instead, fear over his genuine fear.

"We could both suffer serious consequences if the truth came out." All venom had fallen away from his voice. He spoke now with unabashed worry.

"You've never shown concern like this before."

"You were never in danger before."

He reached forward to take my hand in his but stopped himself. We could get away with any random passerby seeing us argue but explaining away holding hands to a fellow agent could prove exceedingly challenging.

"Come on," he finally said. He'd made an admirable attempt at forcing his voice to sound as detached and platonic as possible. I could still trace the lingering annoyance from the consuming concern lacing his words. "It's well past time we get inside."

Without waiting for a response, Agent Harmon held open the door and followed me inside. The interior of the building looked as dreary as ever. Still, I did feel delighted to see Gloria working the security desk again. We chatted briefly as Agent Harmon and I walked by. I dared not linger for fear of exacerbating my husband's concerns.

With another smile from fate, Allan from Accounts Receivable happened to join Garth and me in the elevator as we headed upstairs. He had just returned from an early lunch and was happy to tell me all about the delightful restaurant he frequented just down the block from the office.

The poor lad just beamed with excitement at revealing this treasure to a kindred spirit. I hadn't the heart to tell him that I never liked Indian food and found curry particularly distasteful. I heard Garth suppress a snorting laugh when I promised Allan I'd try the bodega soon and how much I looked forward to the exotic cuisine.

After Allan exited the elevator, Agent Harmon and I rode the remainder of the three-story ascent alone. While I would've enjoyed nothing more than capitalizing on the lack of security cameras in the elevators by sneaking around like a couple of teenagers out past curfew, I knew Garth wouldn't respond well.

I couldn't think of that last time I'd seen him so anxious and worked up about something. He stood stock-still, never spoke to or acknowledged Allan or Gloria, and refused to look anywhere but dead ahead. His stoic aloofness set me ill at ease for a man who typically had a bounce in his step, darting, observant eyes, and a kind greeting to total strangers.

"Good morning, Garth!" Brynn greeted with what I typically would've described as unbearable perkiness but found it ambrosial in light of Garth's sour mood.

"Why you so late?" Thad questioned, only barely glancing up. "You're never late."

Agent Harmon slid silently into his desk, but Brynn instantly jumped to his defense.

"I'm sure he has a good reason for what kept him this morning— oh!"

Having trailed several steps behind Garth, I only just appeared in Brynn's field of vision. Turning the corner into their cubicle area, the unchanged sights of Thad and Brynn's desks comforted and calmed me most unexpectedly.

"Miss Clyde."

Thad looked up at the sound of my name but did not interrupt.

"I didn't realize you were coming in with Garth."

Having regained my footing, I responded with my emblematic wit and flippancy.

"It seems I have been mandated to accompany Agent Harmon. Terribly unfair, if you ask me, but I suppose there are worse people to be shackled to."

I heard Brynn's dismayed 'oh' as I sauntered by to my new desk.

Much desiring to move the conversation away from me and settle into business, Agent Harmon demanded, "Anything new?"

Collecting one impressively thick folder and one flat folder from her desk, Brynn carried them over to Agent Harmon.

"It seems your Parisian Sapphire has been hard at work."

Unwilling to ignore any opportunity to poke fun at Agent Harmon and the FBI—even if it required self-deprecating humor—I quipped, "Parisian Sapphire? Are you tracking strippers now?"

"See!" Thad interjected. "I'm not the only one who thinks it sounds like a stripper."

Ignoring the coupled outbursts, Agent Harmon inquired, "What's missing from where now?"

"20-carat diamond necklace from a private collector in New York. Stolen four days ago," Brynn dutifully reported.

Fortunately, Brynn and Thad remained too engrossed in the photo of the missing piece to notice the look of confusion on my face. I found it remarkably odd that Mr. Morgenstern had reported the theft. And why had it taken him four days to do so? No matter. Nothing could tie to me, and the man had no chance of getting his hands back on that necklace.

A thought flashed across my mind with such speed that I couldn't catch it before it vanished. I'd had an epiphany of who hunted me but lost the thought before I could make good on it.

It certainly had nothing to do with Mr. Morgenstern, so why should his unexpected behavior trigger such an elusive memory? Someone else I had robbed?

Brynn withdrew another photo from the larger folder, she handed it to Garth, who held it for Thad to view.

I couldn't risk blowing my cover by appearing uninterested even though I knew precisely what the photo showed. I leaned over Thad's shoulder to have my own look. A tented piece of cardstock sat directly in the center of the safe with the words *'Taken from you, courtesy of the Parisian Sapphire'* printed on it.

"Interesting," I commented with unenthused curiosity. "It wouldn't be my personal choice, but I admire their forthrightness."

Thad tilted his head to look at me as I still draped across his back. My head hovered above his shoulder. Thad neither flinched nor pulled away at my encroachment on his personal space.

I felt passably confident that he was not a man unused to the advancements of women. He might have even found the flirtatious pastime just as entertaining as I.

"You know them?"

I played dumb. "Know who?"

"The Parisian Sapphire."

"No," I breathed my answer across Thad's neck. His expression never faltered, and I received my confirmation. "No, I can't say I know any strippers who answer by that name. Not that I know many strippers to begin with," I added as an afterthought to quell any follow-up questions Thad may ask concerning my connections.

"What about thieves?" Brynn pressed.

My head shot up off Thad's shoulder, affronted by the audacity and tactlessness of Brynn's question. I took a small step backward from the trio of suits as though the insinuation might taint me if I remained too near the hovering words.

With a hand to my aggrieved heart, I told her, "Terribly rude to call a stripper a thief. It is legal work, you know."

Finally fed up with my game and Brynn's unwitting contributions, Agent Harmon set his pen down on the desk with far more force than required and called me out.

"Miss Bonnie. If you're going to work with us, you'll need to cooperate."

"I'm working with you to catch Mancini, not whoever this is," I promptly pointed out with a wave towards the—my—massive, untitled file.

And to think, I only became the "Parisian Sapphire" four years ago.

"You don't know who this is, then?" Brynn asked again, still not realizing that every word out of her mouth only gave me more fodder.

Catching Garth's peeved sidelong glance held firmly on my face, I could hear his teeth grinding. Instead, I bit my tongue like a good stooge, opting for a less derogatory response. I stepped back to Agent Harmon's desk and took the photo of the note to examine for myself.

"This seems like a calling card between law enforcement and the thief," I finally answered, most diplomatically. "Besides, I don't know any thief who would voluntarily refer to themselves as the 'Parisian Sapphire'."

I leaned further across Agent Harmon's desk than necessary to hand the photo back. "It sounds like a name used to mock someone."

"Who is being mocked, I wonder?" Agent Harmon commented.

He took the photo, allowing his fingertips to graze my hand as he did. My knees rapidly losing their ability to support my body, I returned to my desk. Agent Harmon kept my file as Brynn and Thad dispersed to their desks.

Everyone diligently set about their work for the day. Because I had nothing else to do, I withdrew a notebook from my briefcase and began making my own case notes.

Thad taps his feet to a beat and bobs his head along in time. Likely not allowed to listen to music while at work, he keeps the tunes rocking in his mind to keep him occupied while he works. Probably thrives when given field assignments.

Brynn types like a mad woman. When was the last time she looked down at the keyboard? Her case notes probably keep this whole department running. Why does she keep glancing at Garth? Adoration or validation?

Agent Harmon, well, I already have plenty of notes about him.

"Why haven't we arrested you yet?" Thad's voice cut through the occupational silence.

"Huh?" I responded, most unladylike, my mind still distracted by thoughts of Agent Harmon.

"I mean, no offense, but why haven't we arrested you?" he repeated.

"I was granted immunity for all former crimes," I promptly and proudly informed him.

"I'm talking before you ever came to work with us. Garth's known you were a thief for a few years, yeah?" He turned his attention to Garth. "Why didn't you ever arrest her before?"

My maniacal chuckling seemed to set Brynn on edge. Thad merely appeared intrigued, though slightly nervous. Garth ignored me.

"Knowing she's a thief and proving she's a thief are two very different things," Agent Harmon conceded.

"It's true," I agreed after my laughter subsided. "You can't connect me to any crimes."

"Cocky, aren't we?" Thad retorted with equal parts admiration and annoyance.

I blew him a kiss.

Taking a moment to recover from grinding his jaw, Agent Harmon finally continued his admission. "Extremely."

Turning my attention from Thad to Agent Harmon, I awaited with bated breath and a knowingly thirsty smile for what he might say next. Garth held my longing for an extended moment I hoped would last until the end-shift whistle blew.

His face betrayed neither interest nor excitement. My face fell as I wondered if he was merely an excellent actor or still harbored feelings of annoyance at my delayed, nonchalant entrance. But I'd seen that man's attempts at role-playing and knew his acting skills left something to be desired.

Fortunately, the rest of him did not.

"But unfortunately, it's not unfounded," Agent Harmon admitted, still holding my gaze. Shifting his eyes to Thad, he added, "She's right in that we can't actually connect her to anything."

"Well, let's take her prints and run them now," Thad suggested. He seemed to think it the most obvious thing in the world.

"Why?" I wondered. "I have immunity. Do you really want to know what crimes I've committed when you can't punish me for them?"

As Thad and Brynn shared a dumbfounded expression, I seized the moment to send a wink Agent Harmon's way. I silently reminded him that he—and only he—could punish me for whatever he wanted.

Garth collected the photos Brynn had given him and donned his jacket with a sigh and eyeroll. I knew he utilized those as defenses against any genuine reactions. Addressing Thad and Brynn as though I were some mischievous puppy, he told them:

"Keep an eye on her. I'll be back in a minute." Turning to me, he added, "You, stay put, Miss Bonnie. Please don't get any of us in trouble."

I made my mock salute as Agent Harmon disappeared into another section of the office.

Leaning eagerly forward, I whispered across the room, "Now that he's gone, we can talk about him. What sort of gossip do you have for me?"

"You're crazy if you think we're going to talk about Garth behind his back," Brynn shot back in no uncertain terms. She still didn't look away from her computer screen.

I narrowed my eyes at her but didn't linger on the defeat. Deftly switching gears to what I expected as a readier wellspring of information, I singled out Thad.

"What about you, Thad? What've you got?"

Grinning at me like the Cheshire Cat, my mind tingled with the gossip Thad would surely unload. All excitement deflated when he responded:

"Loyalty, Miss Bonnie."

"Well," I bemoaned, falling back against my chair, "you two certainly are boring."

But I would not be deterred. An idea of convivial subterfuge stretched a conniving smile across my face.

"But I can see how this," I motioned to the whole office around us, "might not be the right environment. Perhaps we need something a bit more informal?" I offered. "Something more festive?"

Finally capturing Brynn's attention to draw her eyes away from her computer and pause her incessant typing, she looked at me with curiosity and concern. I felt she recognized an invitation when she heard one but was not accustomed to receiving it.

Speaking slowly as though the words might cause some terrible backlash, she asked, "Something like what?"

I'm reasonably positive the smile I gave her did little to put poor Brynn at ease.

Agent Harmon must've been thoroughly surprised to find me sitting on Brynn's desk and the two of us engaged in friendly conversation. He stopped dead in his tracks upon rounding the corner.

"Agent Harmon," I greeted with my most innocent smile. "Are you back already?

"Oh!" I exclaimed in perfect mimicry as if I'd just had a eureka moment. I flapped my arm between Brynn and Agent Harmon like I couldn't contain my excitement.

Finally pointing at Agent Harmon, I told him, "You should come too!"

Knowing what I referenced based upon the fact that it had provided our sole topic of conversation for the last ten minutes, Brynn nodded excitedly. I'm sure she would prove more than happy to have a familiar face at the party, obscured as it might be.

Fliting his eyes between my beaming smile and Brynn's vigorously bobbing head, Garth wondered, "Come to what?"

"My Halloween party tomorrow night," I answered chipperly.

Perhaps too chipperly.

Though he struggled admirably to contain himself before anyone could notice his expression and ask questions, I saw the fury flash across my husband's eyes. Hoping desperately to dig myself out of this hole, I fell back on my conflict avoidance knee-jerk reaction: I kept talking.

"I'm hosting a costume party tomorrow night and have just extended the invitation to Brynn and Thad." Pointing to Brynn, I added, "Apparently, she loves them and already knows what she's gonna wear. You should come too."

"I'll have to check with my wife." Garth's answer came curt and forced.

I recognized the deep breath that followed as Garth tried to calm himself.

He also realized that his voice had become sterner than he should have allowed. After removing his jacket and dropping the file on his desk, he said, still seething more than he wanted:

"Miss Bonnie, would you come with me? I need to speak with you. In private."

I quickly hopped off Brynn's desk and awaited Garth to show me where to go. Though unwise to appear eager, I knew coy aloofness would not go over well. He grabbed my arm as we began passing an isolated alcove and threw me inside.

Though Garth never had the slightest thought of hurting me, his frustration had got the best of him, and he'd gripped my arm harder than he'd realized. I ignored the dull throbbing in my arm. I resolved not to massage it, else Garth might ask questions.

Having had a final look to ensure no one stood nearby, Garth whirled on me, demanding, "What is wrong with you?"

"Concerning what? You'll have to be more specific." Though not the wisest choice in responses, I had to maintain my humor to keep from breaking.

"What could've possibly possessed you to invite Brynn and Thad to the party?"

"Don't forget Moller."

Garth stared at me with questioning disbelief, setting me off on another ramble.

"I intend to invite him too. It seems rude to invite everyone else and not him."

"We just talked about this not two hours ago." Garth had to pause, consciously lowering his volume back to a seething whisper for fear of alerting passersby. "How could you blatantly ignore my very legitimate concerns like that?"

I opened my mouth but discovered I'd temporarily lost my speaking ability. I cleared my throat and directed all my attention to my cuticles.

"Would you believe me if I said I had forgotten and didn't think about it?"

"Yes, Kati, I would believe you," Garth snapped back.

I dropped the shamefaced grimace I had tried to use against him after offering my excuse.

"I guess there's nothing to be done for it now?" he asked, more as a rhetorical accusation than searching for an answer.

"I can't very well revoke their invitations. That might cause even more questions," I pointed out.

With another exacerbated sigh—

Those seem to happen more frequently

—Garth closed his eyes and pinched the bridge of his nose. He pressed his fingers into the area around his eyebrows and tear ducts. Sighing again, this time in resignation more than anger, Garth informed me:

"Sometimes, it is far too much trouble to be in love with you."

"But you still are?" Though I had no doubts about the answer, I still needed to hear him say it.

"Most unfortunately, for my blood pressure," he assured with a subdued snort.

"We'll deal with the party—only because we don't have another option—" he made sure to inform me, "but, Kati, you cannot take unnecessary risks like this. Promise me, and do not forget again," he added with a stern finger in my face.

Fighting the urge to swat away that schoolmarmish finger, I promised him I would. "But you might have to continually remind me," I confessed with another attempt at a sheepish smile.

Having said his piece and knowing I meant no disrespect in my honest forgetfulness, my husband finally broke. He allowed a genuine smile to crack his face. Shaking his head with utter disbelief, I watched in real-time as he once more surrendered to those same quirks of mine with which he had fallen in love initially.

"What am I gonna do with you?" The rhetorical question lingered happily between us.

He asked the question I knew burned inside him, "Why'd you tell them about the party, to begin with?"

With a noncommittal shrug, I explained, "I thought it'd be fun."

"You have a strange sense of entertainment. You do realize that there will be people at this party who know that we're—" He stopped short, looked around once more to ensure nobody came nearby and whispered quietly: "That we're married, right?"

"I suppose it's a good thing we'll be wearing disguises, then," I whispered back.

Having pressed closer together to keep our voices as low as possible, I elucidated upon an observation.

"A quick word of advice, dear. You should probably wear tighter slacks if we work together like this."

"Garth?" Fortunately, Brynn's voice came from down the corridor, and she hadn't yet found us tucked away in the alcove.

Stepping in front of my husband, I poked my head around the corner and called to Brynn. "Did you need me?"

"Well, yes," she answered, surprised to see me. "You as well. Is Garth with you?"

"Right here," he affirmed, stepping out into the hallway. Apparently, my diversion had proved sufficient time to allow him to do whatever required to properly contain himself.

"We simply had some growing pains to address," he explained with an abrasive sneer at me. "What do you need?"

Brynn seemed blissfully unconcerned by why Agent Harmon had chosen such a secluded place in which to scold me. Whether from naivety or cognitive dissonance, I could not say.

With complete formality, she said, "A package arrived for Miss Clyde."

I looked at her with a scrunched face of confusion, believing she must be mistaken. "For me? From whom?"

"We don't know," she replied. "There's no label on the box."

"Who delivered it?" Garth inquired.

She shook her head. "We don't know that, either. It appeared while I had gone to the restroom and Thad to the vending machine."

The precise timing and secrecy of this delivery and limited awareness about my working on this case caused Garth and I to share an unabashedly concerned look. That no one should be able to connect my latest pseudonym to me did little to calm our nerves.

Using Garth's pocketknife to cut open the packaging tape, all three agents stood around my nearly empty desk. Only the mysterious box sat atop it. A slice of Styrofoam lay directly underneath the cardboard flaps.

Handing back Agent Harmon's knife, I slid my fingers into the nearly nonexistent gap between the Styrofoam and cardboard sides. I pushed the foam piece away, flipping it out of the box.

My entire body froze.

All oxygen left the room as time itself vanished.

Had the sight which greeted me not so absolutely terrified me, I would surely have forgotten all pretense and collapsed into Garth's arms. As it was, my mind and body had gone into such shock that I couldn't even faint.

Looking up from inside the box was C4's severed head.

He still wore his eye patch. Someone had cut out his tongue.

Chapter Eleven

In Which No Good Deed Goes Unpunished

I sat alone in the interrogation room, but my mood could not be further removed from the first trip. Before, I had played, flirted, and generally enjoyed myself. I commanded the room and provided the answers to questions only as they suited and amused me.

This time...

This time, I sat distant and broken.

I'd experienced far more debilitating blows in my life, but C4's fate had broken me in the way of dull, lingering pain. It's like watching a psychological thriller with a twist ending. Once you realize what's happened, you can't escape the sinking feeling crawling beneath your skin from its underlying terror.

The delivery of C4's head with his tongue cut out told me everything I needed to know about this case. I knew who stood behind it all, what they wanted, and why they wanted to scare me.

And he'd succeeded.

Garth entered the interrogation room. I didn't look up. C4's murder had rocked me, but not nearly so much as the knowledge of what would come next. I knew it was terrible to admit, but C4's life paled compared to what *el Barón* ultimately wanted from me.

"Miss Bonnie?"

Garth's gentle prompting pulled me from my introspection into the interrogation room. My breath shuddered as I inhaled, having forgotten to do so as I sat alone.

Meeting my husband's worried gaze took all my self-control to avoid rushing over to him and embracing him in a desperate hug. I needed his comfort and the assurance that he remained safe with me.

Both would have to wait.

"Miss Bonnie, are you ready to tell us what's happened?"

I took another tremulous breath and nodded slowly. Agent Harmon clicked open his pen, preparing to take notes on my story.

"Whenever you're ready," he gently prompted again.

I closed my eyes and took one more breath to steady myself. Once placated, I began my tale.

"The victim's professional moniker was C4, but his real name was Chi Fu. I'm one of only about half a dozen people who knew that. He used to work for the Chinese government doing something demolitions related. After years of service, something happened, and he became blacklisted. He made the wrong person mad, I think.

"They kicked him out of the country. Under fear of retaliation, the government took Chi Fu's family as hostages. They kept them in the complex of one of their officials. Chi Fu and I had worked together before, and he hired me to break them out and get them to safety."

"Why would he hire you to transport people?" Garth wondered as both probing investigator and curious husband. "I thought you worked in inanimate objects."

"I do, but I'd stolen something from that complex a year prior. Chi Fu wanted to capitalize on my preexisting knowledge of the layout and security. He wasn't willing to wait for someone else to prepare."

Desperate to add some levity, I attempted to smile. "I also have a good relationship with an excellent smuggler." I failed.

"So, I did the job. I got his family out of China and smuggled them to Budapest. We all laid low there for about a month while a third party obtained the paperwork in order so his family could safely flee to London. Everything came together, and Chi Fu said goodbye to his family, never to see them again."

"What's any of this to do with his murder?"

"I met him at Piedmont Park two days ago, and he told me about the 85 bombing. He said that he still owed me for Budapest."

Agent Harmon's ears perked at this potential break in the case. "What did he tell you?"

"That he was hired to carry out the bombing."

"Hired by Mancini?"

I did not listen closely enough to determine if he asked his question to confirm the FBI's initial assumption or mine. My mind still felt muddled by the impending fallout. It kept me from focusing and deciphering the tone and body language, something of which I would typically make sport.

I simply shook my head in reply.

"Hired by who, then?"

My breathing hitched and became labored again. I could feel the tears welling, and I struggled to fight them down. I saw Garth jerk towards me, wanting nothing more than to protect and comfort his wife, but he remembered our location and stopped himself. My body shook as I thought of the dangers to come.

I would tell Garth the truth, tell him everything, and hope that would allow us to keep each other safe, but I couldn't do it here. Not around all these cameras and people who couldn't know about us. I needed to tell, not Special Agent Harmon, but my husband. I needed his comfort and protection as much as he felt compelled to give them.

Brightside of my consuming terror meant Garth could end our meeting without anyone growing suspicious. They only had concerns over this phantom that could break my veneer and send me into a panic.

"Let me take you home, Miss Bonnie." Though he attempted to phrase the chivalry as an option for me to take for keeping up appearances, I knew he wouldn't allow me the choice. "You're in no state to drive. Let me take you wherever you need to go."

I lifted my eyes to meet Garth's with a terrible meekness that arose from the abject terror that the amends I had once tried to make for my sins had now found me, and my husband would pay the price. A single tear escaped as I weakly nodded.

Garth ran lights and sirens the entire drive to the manor. Weaving and bobbing in and out of traffic, running red lights, and speeding as much as possible, the whole trip likely fell under the category of 'abuse of power', but he no longer cared. He only possessed the concern of a husband protecting his wife.

The commute passed in silence. Garth needed to focus on the road, and I hadn't yet reached a place of safety in which I felt ready to elaborate and explain everything. Garth jumped out and ran around the car to help me after pulling into the garage.

I grabbed his hand, not for assistance, but for the assurance of my hand safely held in his. Half supporting, half carrying me into the house, Garth led me to the first couch in the sitting room off the side of the main entryway.

"Do you need anything to drink?" he offered once I had settled safely on the couch. I shook my head a few times before finding my voice to tell him no.

My husband sat beside me, our hands never breaking from each other's grasp. Before trying to ask any further questions or find out what he needed to do to protect me, Garth knew what he needed to do to comfort me.

He sat as close as possible and gingerly pulled my head to rest on his chest. Leaning back against the cushions, he held me and kissed my head as he bobbed in a gentle rocking motion. I don't know how long we remained like that, but it wasn't long enough. It's never long enough.

Finally, Garth continued questioning when he felt confident that he wouldn't indelicately press me by pursuing the issue.

"What's going on, Kati? How can I help you?"

"I know who's after me," I told him, my voice muffled by his chest.

"After you?" I felt his body tense as he said the words. "What do you mean 'after you'? Are... are you in danger?"

His body shook slightly as I nodded. My head rose and fell as he took a deep breath. He calmed his mind so that he might address the situation rationally: as an impartial FBI agent, not an emotionally invested husband.

"Who's after you? What do they want?"

"He wants what I stole from him two years ago."

"Who is 'he'?"

"*El Barón.*"

I heard Garth's breath hitch and felt his body tense once more. He knew the name but prayed that I meant someone else.

"The cartel kingpin?" he asked, hoping I'd correct him.

Again, I could only silently nod.

"What on earth could he so desperately want that causes him to track you down two years later? What did you steal from him?"

After a solemn pause, I answered, "His daughter."

A long moment of silence passed. Garth had to wrap his head around what I'd just said. Even then, he still couldn't understand.

"You," he paused, unsure of the words about to come from his own mouth.

He continued hesitantly, pausing after every word as he struggled with what I'd told him.

"You stole his daughter? What does that mean?"

"Do you remember how I postponed our wedding and disappeared for three months?"

"Of course. You had me terrified that something had happened to you, or I'd scared you off, or some other awful thing. You said there was something you had to do before you could marry me and asked me to trust you. I did. And I respected your decision and never asked questions once you returned."

I lifted my head to finally meet his eyes. "You were amazing for all of it. And it's not that I didn't want to tell you. It's that I thought you would be safer never knowing."

Dropping my head, I mumbled, "But that doesn't matter anymore. I fear we're both in danger now, and it's time I tell you the truth."

I pushed myself off Garth's chest to sit up and tell him the story. I never let go of his hand.

"After finishing in Paris, I returned to Budapest to steal a necklace from the Austro-Hungarian crown jewels as a present for *el Barón's* daughter. That man would never legally buy what he could pay to steal. Even if the thief's fee amounted to a higher price than the item itself.

"As part of my payment, *Barón* let me stay at his compound near the US-Mexico border. I left after a few days, lying about why I had to leave early. That's when I first encountered my convictions, but it wasn't until I spent more and more time with you that I paid them any mind.

"*El Barón's* compound stood on a bluff jutting out over the sea and was built like a medieval battle fortress. With his armed security crawling over every inch, I've never felt closer to being in prison.

"A narrow causeway was the one accessible route, but it also had secret boat access. Rumors circulated about tunnels and dungeons buried within the cliffs. Only *Barón*, his guards, and his victims knew the truth.

"At the time, *el Barón's* notoriety and how he conducted business meant little to me. He always upheld his end of the bargain and fairly paid for services rendered. As far as I cared, that's all that mattered.

"Going back to my room after dinner one night, I experienced what soon became a tipping point in my life. I was unexpectedly alone after passing the guarded door of the bedroom wing. Typically, I would revel in the moment of isolation—especially in a place such as *Barón's* compound—but I felt terribly ill at ease.

"So much so that I leapt out of my skin when I saw someone.

"Expecting to see a guard, my uneasiness grew when I realized it was a young girl. No older than eleven or twelve, her face looked ghost white, despite her clearly Hispanic heritage, and tear-stained. She looked terrified, as though I was the phantom stalking the halls. Then she turned and disappeared around the corner.

"Not doubting that that place housed ghosts, I chalked the experience up to that and called it a night. But I realized something about her as I was unable to sleep. She wore the necklace *el Barón* had hired me to steal for his daughter.

"My suspicions were confirmed at dinner the following night. *Barón* had her join us. My stomach lurched, and my skin crawled with how he displayed her like a show pony. I threw up everything I'd eaten when I made it back to my room. She looked so destroyed and didn't even try to hide it.

"I left in the morning. Returning to the villa, I asked Uncle César about *el Barón* and his daughter. He told me that he didn't know anything. Still, no small number of stories circulated about the way *Barón* loved his daughter and the affection he showed her.

"With the hesitation in his voice and the disgust in his eyes, I knew Uncle César referred to a vastly different love and affection than the kind he had shown me.

"However, those who knew fell into any combination of categories: they didn't care; didn't think it their business or problem to deal with; or didn't want to risk the ire of *el Barón*. It was into the final two that I fell.

"No matter how desperately I tried pushing the poor girl from my mind, I could never forget her. The image of her tear-streaked face and the inescapable terror consuming her beneath the lace and jewels haunted me every time I closed my eyes.

"Those images became more poignant and convicting the more time I spent with you." I raised my eyes to meet my husband's gaze for the first time since beginning my story.

"Your sense of duty and honor and commitment to doing the right thing and helping people tore away at me as I thought of what I did. And what I hadn't done. I knew the hell that girl lived in before I ever spoke with Uncle César; it was written all over her being. And I just walked away.

"I abandoned her, just like everyone that had ever come before me. When you proposed, I couldn't stand it any longer. I knew I couldn't marry you until I made this right. Until I did something to make me even remotely deserving of you."

"That's the three months of disappearance?" he confirmed.

"I needed the time to find how to successfully steal her away and figure out what to do with her afterward. I couldn't have any distractions or risk you finding out anything about what I was doing in case..."

"In case Baron came after you," he finished saying what I could not.

Again, I only nodded my head. "It seems, after four years of searching, he's finally found me, and he wants her back."

"Can he get her?" Garth wondered. "What did you do with the girl?"

"I gave her to a small church that found a perfect home for her and kept me entirely out of the process, so I wouldn't know anything."

"What was the name of the church?"

"Grace Gospel Church."

I felt his contented smile as he considered the coincidence of the name.

"That's the name of my church growing up."

I looked up at him again with a weak, bittersweet smile. "I know. They did such a good job with you. I hoped they'd do just as right by her."

He turned his content smile on me and gently stroked his fingers across my cheek. Several moments of silence hovered between melancholic happiness and abject horror.

Garth returned to his natural pragmatic tendencies and asked if we should cancel tomorrow night's party. I don't know what prompted it, but his question caused something to further strain within me, and I reached up to grab hold of his hand, still caressing my cheek.

"No," I answered. "We should keep up appearances and not react until we must. The girl's best chance of safety is anonymity. If we rally around her, it makes it significantly easier for *Barón* to find her."

I took a deep breath and squeezed Garth's hand. I've always found it easier to convince myself of things while clenching my fist. Once the decision had been made, the slow release of tension relaxed me and made my mind feel at ease.

"We continue life as usual," I reiterated.

Again, the heavy silence hung in the air. Garth's hand vacillated between squeezing mine, releasing the tension, and embracing again. He took several breaths, preparing to speak, as his mouth gaped and closed like a fish. Finally, he steadied his hand and found his voice.

"I don't want to push or sound callous," he hesitated again, "but why didn't you think of the Baron earlier?"

I couldn't fault him for asking when I'd spent every moment of lucidity over the last few hours berating myself for that very point. We could have set a plan if I had thought of *Barón* sooner. We could have begun moving into action and protecting everyone in danger. C4 might not have died.

"I think..." my voice trailed away as I considered a possible justification for my egregious, costly oversight.

"I think I never considered *el Barón* because I had purged all memory of him from my mind. After it was done, I made a conscious effort to forget. I couldn't think of him or the girl.

"I couldn't remember them because, if I did, the fear and paranoia would drive me mad. If I let myself realize that our safety hung by the thinnest of threads that could snap at any moment, none of us would ever know peace."

My body began to quiver as any final amounts of stoicism to which I had clung vanished. I couldn't hold out any longer. Reminded of everything I had purposefully forgotten, I began thinking of *Barón* and his daughter. How he treated her and the atrocities she had experienced. He stole her innocent childhood.

Everything inside of me broke. I felt distraught, enraged, terrified, and overwhelmed in a way that made me believe my body would tear itself to shreds from the inside out. I began shaking violently as my seldom-seen tears gushed forth.

"What?" Garth asked, desperately trying once more to calm me. "What is it? What's happened?"

"I— I— I just can't—" my words fell out in a stuttering, blubbering mess.

I couldn't find the air to fill my lungs to speak. I struggled even more with trying to explain, beginning to hyperventilate from the onslaught of overpowering emotion. The more frantic and hysterical I became, the more my husband's concern and terror built.

I mumbled through most of what I attempted to say to the point that I may have well skipped over it for all the good it did Garth in trying to figure out what was happening. Finally, I stumbled upon the deep-seated core of the breakdown with enough breath and control to form mostly coherent words.

"And when I think of that monster being allowed to have a child and we— I ca—"

"Shh." Garth immediately set upon me, wrapping his arms around every inch of my body and squeezing me tight.

He now realized the truth and remembered the heartache alongside me. Setting aside his own pain, he took up the mantle of husband with admirable vigor to comfort me in my time of desperation.

"Shh. It's okay, Kati. It's okay. You did a good thing. You rescued that girl. You gave her a good and true family. And I could never be prouder of you or happier about what you've done."

"You can still be saddened by what I can't do," I pointed out as my tears soaked through his shirt.

"But never at you," he promised me. "Never at you."

I cried myself to sleep in my husband's arms that night. Never once did he stir or release his hold of me.

Chapter Twelve

In Which Plans Began to Take Shape

I slept poorly that night and awoke early. I would have let Garth sleep, but we had an appointment to keep. Though my husband didn't detest mornings in the same way I did—he really had no preference one way or the other—he did hate anyone waking him.

Handily for him, Garth had developed a magical ability to wake up naturally when choosing a time to do so the night before. If he fell asleep without setting his mind, he'd just—as the saying I'd learned from my husband goes—'sleep until I wake up'. With the emotional turmoil of the following night, I doubted Garth had set his internal alarm clock.

No matter. Though I rarely awoke before my husband, I had learned how to wake him without incurring his ire. In fact, he'd never once so much as complained.

Tossing aside my mobile phone onto one of our over-plush armchairs, I sauntered my way over to the couch where Garth still snoozed. Even though he remained fast asleep and had no concern for how I walked, I couldn't help myself. Any seduction deserves proper completion to the full extent of one's ability, regardless of whether or not the mark has any idea of the temptress' efforts.

I smiled as I stood over him. My husband had stretched out on his back, leaving him in a position of easy access. My lips pursed as I considered my plan of attack and how much time we had before we needed to go.

With a sigh of only mild dejection, I decided we didn't have the time required to fulfill my desires. Not all of them, anyway.

Gracefully lowering myself to the carpet, I knelt beside my husband. His floppy hair was all a mess from a restless sleep. Not my fault, for once. Until I ran my fingers through it.

His hair wasn't long enough to fall into his face, so I had no need to move it out of my way. I merely wanted to feel the soft plushness of my husband's hair against my skin. It only served to muss his hair more and generate some static electricity.

His unconscious smile suggested he didn't mind. Leaning forward, I placed my lips on his Sleeping Beauty style. I knew Garth instantly awoke when I felt his lips responding to my own. Much unlike the fairy tale princes, I didn't pull away. And neither did he. Tangling my fingers deeper into that silky, milk chocolate hair, our lips squeezed tighter into each other.

He won't move his hands. The lazy bastard is more than content to lay there and let me do all the work.

Or so I thought. Suddenly, I heard myself squeal as I tumbled backward under the force of Garth's strength. Using his intentionally unoccupied hands, my husband caught himself so that he pinned me beneath him without crushing me into the carpet.

That crafty devil had planned to trap me as soon as my lips met his.

I smiled, despite my lips remaining otherwise engaged. As my husband steadily lowered himself to press more tightly against me, I had to comment on his change of location.

"While I realize I did a fantastic job choosing our flooring, the couch does not threaten carpet burns."

"And here I thought you always enjoyed that extra rush."

Having kindly moved his amorous attentions to my neck so I might speak, I felt the vibrations of Garth's reply against my skin more than I heard it. I only brought his lips back to mine as response. Any other reply would prove a lie.

Pressed firmly against me now that he had little need to continue supporting himself, I felt my husband's hand sliding underneath the waistband of my skirt. I pulled away with a bittersweet moan at the feeling of his deft fingers ready to explore that most sensitive skin.

"Unfortunately, we haven't time for that now, dear," I lamented. "We have an appointment to keep."

Garth's confusion made pushing him off and shimmying out from underneath him significantly easier.

"Appointment? What appointment?"

"Oh, good, you're already here," I greeted Darcy as I walked through the condo door.

She set aside her current edition of *The Economist* with a casualness that belied her arrival before us to our own home. She'd also let herself in, even though she didn't have a key.

Throwing aside my keys, I dove into why I'd summoned her at this unconscionably early hour for the likes of us.

"CliffsNotes: C4 was hired by *el Barón* to scare me because, two years ago, I stole his daughter and hid her away. Now he's somehow found out it was me and wants her back."

"It be making sense," Darcy agreed without the slightest hesitation. "Baron be having the money ta hire someone with C4's price tag, and he ain't exactly known for being forthcoming."

Taking her first moment to consider what I had said, Darcy remarked, "Didn't know the Baron actually be having a daughter."

"He doesn't anymore."

I looked at Garth, whose face suggested that he struggled mightily between trying to silently comfort me while also addressing his own utter confusion.

"It's a long, complicated story. I don't want to go into it again."

Darcy held up her hands. "No need. I heard the rumors, and if you went through the danger ta steal her away, I know the stories didn't suffice. What ya be thinking fer ya next move?"

"Hold on!" Garth's confused voice came out of my mouth. "What is going on?"

Turning to Darcy, he demanded, "Why are you not remotely confused or fazed or concerned about any of this? And why do you suddenly sound like Bob Marley?"

"Seriously? Bob Marley? He be the only islander ya can think ta name?"

Garth stumbled over his shock and attempted apology under Darcy's harsh stare. She rolled her eyes.

I responded with a head shake and the universally condescending, "Americans."

Reclaiming whatever authority we allowed him, my husband ignored our disapproval and demanded, "Who are you?"

"Darcy Rigby, at your service," she announced with a mock bow.

Garth dropped into his favorite recliner with an exasperated sigh, pinching the bridge of his nose. "Yeah, I got that much. How are you helpful to us in this situation? How has nothing Kati has said sounded like new or uncontextualized information to you? And how did you get in our house!"

"Darcy and I have a preexisting working relationship that allows us different insights the other might not consider," my voice echoed inside the refrigerator. I had stuck my head inside to grab my breakfast and reappeared with my yogurt cup. Shoveling in a spoonful, I continued, "We run in similar circles, with different perspectives."

Garth looked like a gasping fish as he pointed between us. Finally landing on Darcy, he found his voice to clarify, "You're a thief?"

"Strictly speaking, no. But I often be assisting many of them," Darcy answered.

He again scrunched his face and pinched the bridge of his nose.

"Okay. Let's try this one more time and see if we can't manage just a simple, straight answer: who are you!"

"I'm the head of Dawnwall Shipping."

This answer clearly did nothing to assuage my husband's concern.

"Excuse me?"

Darcy nodded.

"No." The force of his convictions prompted Garth to stand. He even pointed at Darcy like a parent scolding their teenager. "No, you are not allowed to be the head of Dawnwall Shipping."

"Why not?" I asked through another scoop of yogurt.

He marched over to me, thoroughly flustered by the nonchalance of the atmosphere.

"Because the Dawnwall Shipping Corporation is regularly under investigation by every stable government."

"Really?" I marveled. Looking past Garth, I said, "I'd think you'd be more careful about things like that."

"I run a shipping company," Darcy protested. "When be the last time ya cared if A.P. Moller–Maersk Group be involved in a scandal?"

"I don't even know who that is."

"I be resting my case."

I shrugged in agreement before continuing with my breakfast.

"Besides, no matter how many ongoing investigations plague Dawnwall, we never be worried about facing real danger."

"And why is that?" Garth snapped.

"Because the world economy be relying too heavily on my company," Darcy answered. Her voice held no hint of pride or boasting. What she said was a mere statement of fact. "My company, alone, be handling forty percent of the world's legal shipping and transportation of goods."

Garth had become a lovely shade of tickle-me-pink that steadily darkened towards beet red.

"And what percentage of its illegal shipping?"

"Ya know, I ain't really sure. It be estimated ta be about sixty-five to seventy percent, but that be a lot more difficult ta get a concrete number on."

I continued enjoying my breakfast while Darcy returned to her copy of *The Economist* without the slightest bit of concern. Garth, however, did not slide into such sanguinity towards our casual conversation concerning illicit activity.

"I quit. I'm done," he announced.

"Done with what?" I asked.

He threw his hands up in the air. "All of this!" Waving them wildly between Darcy and myself, he continued, "I can't know these things anymore. I'm done being your husband."

"You can't just be done being my husband," I remarked.

"Yes, I can. I quit the FBI. I'm done being your husband." The longer he complained, the closer he made it to the door. "I'm just gonna go be a hermit in the mountains. I quit. I'm done."

The door clicked closed behind him.

Darcy stared between the closed door and my apparent lack of concern over my husband's sudden departure.

"Do ya think ya oughta go after him?"

"Meh," I shrugged, scoping out my final spoonful of yogurt. "I give him ten minutes."

I threw away my depleted cup and let my spoon rattle around the empty sink. Using a washcloth to clean away any remnants from my mouth, I moved on to pressing matters.

"You've had more direct dealings with *Barón* than I have; what is his next play?"

"I smuggled his cocaine and opium. We ain't exactly be spending time discussing our plans of attack for enacting personal vendettas. I didn't even know he actually had a daughter."

Knowing her response had proved less than helpful, Darcy did try directing the brain trust to acquire beneficial knowledge. "What be your first instinct?"

I slumped onto the couch and confessed, "I have no first instincts. I've no idea what to do in this situation."

"This be precisely why we ain't ta be getting involved."

"I'm only back because an innocent young girl is in danger!" Garth announced as he flung open the door and marched back into the condo. "As soon as she's safe, I'm walkin' out and going full Thoreau on you people."

"Blame him for that," I told Darcy to explain my initial personal involvement.

We spent the next hour discussing possible options for what to do and how *Barón* would respond. Ultimately, we ended up with nothing. *El Barón* had always proved something of an elusive, loose cannon.

Not even the combined knowledge of a thief, a pirate smuggler, and a cop provided enough insight to build any sort of acceptable profile. Throw in the added challenge that no one had ever dared cross *el Barón* in such a direct, personal way, and we remained entirely in the dark.

After much deliberation and consideration, we finally decided the only feasible option was to continue with my plan of business as usual. *El Barón* meant the explosion to force me to scramble. He would then observe where I went to protect or ensure the girl's safety. If I didn't respond, *Barón* couldn't learn anything.

Though we had finally decided that it proved our best option, neither Garth nor I liked the decision. Garth feared that an ineffective first attack meant the Baron wouldn't wait long to make another and that the second would prove even worse than the first. And likely more direct. As for my part, I've never liked sitting still.

With nothing left to discuss, Darcy collected her magazine and prepared to leave. She promised she'd continue thinking of any possible options. She would gather whatever intel on the Baron she could from her lieutenants before tonight's party.

Before disappearing into the hallway, she reminded me that she'd always help any way she could. I thanked her but never stood from the couch to see her out.

Garth and I sat in a long, permeating silence in the minutes following Darcy's departure. My mind swam with everything we had discussed and how we all seemed so helpless to do anything. Even though we—I—solely possessed the knowledge *Barón* remained so desperate for, he still seemed to control the entire situation.

I couldn't do anything for fear of what that might reveal to whoever *Barón* had spying on me. After all, someone had to have watched when C4 met with me. There's no other way he would've been punished so quickly. That meant *Barón* knew I was in this city. He very well may have already discovered where I lived. Garth was right; it wouldn't be long before *el Barón* came after me, and he would come with a vengeance.

I won't sit idly by and do nothing. I have to take the fight directly to him.

And then my husband stood from his chair.

Though he went directly into the kitchen, his simple movements reminded me I was not the only person *Barón's* future attacks would destroy. Unless I went on a counterattack and overplayed my hand, *Barón* would never find the girl.

But if he'd found me, he'd also found my husband. If he didn't know yet, it wouldn't take *Barón's* spies long to learn the truth about my relationship with Garth and the ferocity with which I loved him. After that, nothing would hold *el Barón* back, and I could only allow this to end one way.

"Of every woman in all the world, why did I have to fall in love with you?" Garth wondered, hunched over the bar separating the main room from the kitchen.

He had his regular breakfast banana on the counter, but it remained unpeeled and abandoned. The horror of what *el Barón* might do to him paled compared to how Garth might respond to me after ensuring the girl remained safe.

Had introducing him to Darcy pushed his cognitive dissonance too far?

"Do you regret your decision?" I braved.

"Most unfortunately..."

He lifted his face out of his hands to rub his temples and massage away the growing headache. I couldn't tell if my heart pounded or quit beating as the pause prolonged.

Finally, raising his face to meet my gaze, I recognized the bittersweetness in his eyes. I had crossed a line by revealing the truth about Darcy, but he couldn't betray me because of it.

"No," he promised.

Rising from the seat I'd held for the past hour, I moved to join my husband in the kitchen. Standing behind him, I wrapped my arms around his chest and rested my cheek against his back. His warmth rippled through me as I inhaled every bit of scent from him.

With the combined smells of his shampoo and body wash—mine, actually, since he ran out the other day—and pheromones of his cologne and aftershave, he smelled something like a campfire burning after a summer thunderstorm on a relaxed Caribbean Island.

Holding him tight, I said, "You are an amazing man, you know that? And every day, you make me better for it."

"And every day, I question your influence on me," he replied.

Though his retort held some truth, I felt him chuckle, and his body relaxed as he said it. Resigning himself to our shared fate, he observed:

"Ah, who knows? Maybe having Darcy and Dawnwall as allies'll one day prove advantageous. Besides, with the level they operate at, it's more INTERPOL's concern than the FBI's. Just promise me something," he requested.

"Hmm?"

"Don't introduce me to any more of your friends."

Our bodies vibrated as my laughing shook us both. I squeezed him tighter into me with a smile I couldn't contain. I had my husband back.

"What about Uncle César?" Garth wondered.

"Hmm?" I hummed, not paying attention to anything that did not concern my body against my husband's.

"What about Uncle César?" he repeated. Spinning in my arms, Garth turned to face me and wrapped his own arms around me to return my embrace.

"What about him?" I wondered.

"How many of your, ilk, know about the relationship between the two of you?"

Thinking for a quick moment, I shrugged. "Basically, everybody."

Considering this information, he asked, "Is that somewhere the Baron would suspect you've hidden the girl? Think about it. Knowing that you took her, there's three criteria for where you'd leave her."

Though he never released his hold of me, I could feel his fingers ticking off the three options against my back. "One, it has to be somewhere safe; there's lots of options. Two, it has to be somewhere he couldn't get her; that narrows our possibilities quite a lot.

"And third, the most exclusive of the criteria, it has to be somewhere you would trust leaving her. There's an extraordinarily low number of people you trust, with Uncle César chief among them. I've heard that he's untouchable even by your own kind."

"You are actually chief among them," I corrected.

"I should hope so," he affirmed with that boyish grin. "But the Baron wouldn't know about me, thus, couldn't suspect me of hiding the girl."

My smile momentarily died as I prayed that remained the case.

Shifting back to the matter at hand, I informed Garth, "But *Barón* knows he can't get to Uncle César. So, even if he thinks that's where she is, he still can't get her back. But, of course!"

Garth jumped at my sudden outburst right in his face.

"That's how Mancini fits in! I think you're right, and he suspects I left his daughter with Uncle César."

I pulled my husband into me again—he'd moved slightly away when I excitedly yelled in his face—and commended him on his investigative logic.

"You're pretty good at this whole investigative, detective thing. It'd be a shame for you to give it all up."

His smile assured me he had no intention of releasing anything he currently held.

"Just one more question. Would you mind if I come and visit you in your shack on the pond?"

The kiss with which he responded suggested he would not mind the company.

Chapter Thirteen

In Which Costumes Removed Our Masks

Ding dong.

The doorbell altered me to the arrival of another party guest. All Fox Glen ladies and dates had arrived, as had Brynn. Much to my surprise, she actually showed up. Garth wouldn't ring the doorbell, even when trying to keep up appearances.

Mentally checking everyone else off my list as I skittered through the hodgepodge sea of costumes on my way to the door, I couldn't come up with who had arrived. A gasp of delight erupted from my soul as I opened the door to Special Agent Thad dressed up as Major Healey.

"Well," he whistled upon seeing me. "Isn't this a coincidence?"

"My dear sir, it is positively providential!" I agreed in my best Scarlett O'Hara impression.

The coinkydink to which we reacted arose from the extraordinary fact that both of our costumes came from the old TV show *I Dream of Jeannie*. I had donned the pink crop top and pantaloons of the titular character and dyed my hair blonde for the occasion. Of course, I also had to invest in a wig to achieve the proper look of the crazy top bun and ponytail.

Returning to my voice, I marveled, "Why, Major Healey, your costume looks remarkably realistic."

"That's because it is!" he explained, taking a step back and holding out his arms so I could adequately appreciate his effort. He even added a twirl for flourish.

"I was in the Army before joining the FBI. The uniform is all mine, and I spent years collecting the authentic paraphernalia to dress up as Major Healey. I use it as my go-to costume for finding the other cultured attendees of any party."

Holding out my hands to draw attention to my own costume—not that the eyes of men needed any help—I told him, "Clearly, I am the most cultured of them all."

"I wouldn't doubt it for a second," he affirmed with a kiss on my hand.

I began to make a snarky comment about how Garth would prove poor company for discussions of refined culture but caught myself before revealing my heart. As an acceptable recovery of my nearly stumbled words, I directed Thad inside.

We had a brief tour of important locations, i.e., the bar and the bathroom. Thad gave a quick salute and disappeared into the crowd. I topped off my cabernet before ascending to the landing that overlooked the condo's main room. I gazed down upon them all from my perch.

The bird's eye view allowed me the best vantage point for observing the costume parade. Jaylyn and Janko were still saddened that their youngest son's illness forced them to skip their annual trip to New Orleans. They came decked in their purple, gold, and green *Mardi Gras* attire.

Alexandria surprised us all by appearing in a costume the very definition of humble and modest: she wore a nun's habit. We all assumed she must have lost a bet with someone outside our Fox Glen circle to consign herself to wearing something so frumpy. As expected, we teased her viciously for it all night long.

In contrast to the unexpected prudishness of the typically suggestive Alexandria, Brynn had arrived in a witch's costume with cleavage to spare. Though I joked with Thad when he arrived, the surprise of Brynn's attire left me dumbfounded.

I unabashedly took my time in allowing my eyes to examine every part of Brynn as she stood awkwardly in my doorway. Though not as naturally curvy as myself, Miss Jolene knew how to flaunt what she had when presented the opportunity. She had even let down her hair from that constricting bun to let it flow in sleek waves over her shoulders.

I trapped her under such a stunned stare for so long that she asked if something was the matter. I assured her everything was fine and allowed her to enter.

Madeline and her husband, Alcide, attended as Bonnie and Clyde. Darcy and I had to summon every ounce of self-control—a task enormously difficult for the pair of us—to keep from doubling over in hysterics at the thought of these two clean-cut, law-abiding citizens playing as two of America's most notorious felons.

Still, we couldn't deny how perfectly they looked the part. Madeline, with her slim build and *ingénue* doe eyes. Alcide's chiseled jawline and sunken eyes made him appear far more threatening than imaginable. All told, no one could deny the historical resemblance. With no knowledge of my pseudonym, their choice in costume just tickled me all the more.

As for Darcy, she came decorated to the hilt as a pirate stepped right off *Queen Anne's Revenge*. Unlike the irony of Madeline and Alcide's costumes, Darcy's was a masterstroke of telling the truth to make everyone think you're bluffing. Her attire evoked nothing more than a sly smile and a silent nod of approval.

Her escort—a pirate, but obviously no captain like herself—never walked beside her but always remained a step behind. He never touched her, not even when whispering something in her ear. His hands stayed clasped behind him in a military stance.

He had the bronze skin, charcoal hair and eyes of someone who grew up in a Middle Eastern desert. His body and face shared similar features of an exposed rock carved by an unguarded wind and hardened in the relentless sun. His eyes continuously scanned the room with an even greater sternness.

I recalled spying his leather bracelet on one of my party sweeps and noting the symbol for *Krav Maga* pressed into it. Looking the man over in his sleeveless pirate attire, I wouldn't question if he'd found a way to elevate the brutal fighting style of his homeland to an art form.

Studying the man more closely, I realized I had met him before; he was one of Darcy's lieutenants. I couldn't, however, recall his name. It occurred to me that I was likely never told it.

Thad made quick friends with everyone in attendance as he fluttered about between each group with the effortless ease of a butterfly. Perhaps glibber than Major Healey, Thad proved no less quick-witted regarding snarky commentary.

At some point—if I ever manage to find him alone—I'll have to corner the man and ask him a few questions of my own.

Those inquires, however, fell promptly by the wayside as I caught sight of my final guest. As soon as I began inviting his coworkers, I told Garth that he'd have to take his costume to the manor and dress there. He'd then have to come to the condo as a typical guest and couldn't arrive early.

That proved the most challenging stipulation of all. That man always had a pathological aversion to arriving places late. I don't think he possessed the physical capacity to do so. I wonder how long he sat in his car in the parking garage. How many seconds did he count until I had deemed it an appropriate time for him to come in without stirring curiosities?

Garth quickly scanned the room and made his salutations to the people who caught his eye, but he couldn't be bothered to engage anyone in conversation. I'd kept my costume a secret from him, and he'd burst with desirous curiosity to know what I'd dress as.

More than that, whenever not entering a location together but knowing the other would be there, our eyes instinctively sought each other. Neither of us could rest without verifying the other had safely arrived. Even though I never left the condo and only Garth returned, old habits die hard.

My husband could not locate me engaged in conversation during his initial sweep of the room. He knew there was only one other place to look if I couldn't be found socializing. Bending his neck upward, he raised his eyes to see me standing above them all, surveying the kingdom of my own making.

But, at that moment, only one of my subjects interested me. Garth had the most advantageous physical asset of flashing a pair of dimples whenever he smiled. Coupled with his good-guy, genuinely-interested-in-what-you-have-to-say persona, no one questioned if he ever displayed a false smile for appearances.

That blind faith led to many a time where I required a delicate cough or glass of champagne to hide my own smile from the unsuspecting audience. But I possessed the intimate knowledge that allowed me to recognize his genuine smile and the tell-tale sign revealing it.

The way my husband's eyes crinkled whenever he donned that hidden smile reminded me of how I'd managed to fall in love with such a man.

He knew better than to wave or do anything to draw attention to us and contented to offer nothing but that knowing smile. I sighed, despite myself, as those gold-flaked, cinnamon irises found my inconsequential green ones once more.

Intentionally and extraordinarily begrudgingly, I set my mind to examine his costume instead of continuing along with the train of thought I had naturally pursued. He came dressed as a character from some fantasy realm. Probably *The Lord of the Rings*; Garth always loved those stories.

Who were those characters? Not Legolas.

I paid little attention when Garth forced me to sit down and watch the super-extended-endless-director's cut version of those movies. Still, I'll never forget a young Orlando Bloom.

What was Viggo Mortenson's character? Something connected to Spain?

But what truly caught my attention came from the sword hanging off his hip. Garth actually knew how to wield his, unlike most people who collect authentic replica swords or liked to wear them for costume parties, Renaissance Festivals, and Comic-Cons.

As a boy, Garth behaved as most boys, running around barefoot, picking up sticks, and flailing them like swords. Apparently, he never grew out of that fascination. He discovered a fencing class on campus at uni and picked up the sport with virtuoso speed.

He even managed to place in or win several inter-colligate competitions. As soon as he found himself stationed in Atlanta, Garth found a fencing club to join. He even proved instrumental in connecting that club and Fox Glen.

Thinking of my husband's prowess with one sword only drew my mind back to the other, which he also wielded with surpassing talent. Without thinking, I bit my lip as my imaginings and anticipations ran away with me.

So much for controlling my thoughts and keeping my distance.

After Darcy left us that morning, I implored my husband to stay with me a while longer and did my best to convince him why he ought to remain. I thought my lips and tongue—which I no longer used to form words—had perfectly formulated how I would make not yet disappearing into the woods worth his while.

Until Garth stepped away from the counter. Thanks to lifting, spinning, and finagling, I now sat atop the counter while my husband stood before me. I flexed my legs to trap Garth and keep him in my clutches, but he readily overpowered me and casually slipped beyond my reach.

"I have to go into the office," he'd said. "There'll be a bunch of questions about what happened yesterday."

My momentary amnestic reprieve shattered as reality smashed headlong back into our kitchen.

Darcy knew nothing of the full extent of my personal pain and torture concerning *Barón's* daughter, and I'd intentionally never revealed my own inadequacies and failures. I could never stand to see someone like her pity me.

Talking with Darcy about the girl was only a matter of business: how do we find out what *Barón* knows and, in light of that, how do I continue to keep the girl safe?

With Garth, the matter became much too personal for my comfort. I loved my husband and desired to never keep secrets from him. But, since marrying him, I'd discovered that particular pains sting more when someone else understands why you winced at a seemingly innocuous comment.

I've never determined if that sting lessens or becomes more acute when that person not only understands but shares your same pain. Garth must have known my thoughts when I could no longer look at him. He wrapped his arms around me in a comforting, revitalizing embrace.

I fiercely returned his grasp, burying my face in his collar to quash my brimming tears. I felt his hand smoothing my hair and his lips moving to kiss my cheek. I leaned into that kiss, desperate that it should never end. We spent either five minutes or an hour silently holding each other and Garth's delicate butterfly kisses.

"Are you sure you need to go into the office?" I asked.

"Did you have other plans for me?" he inquired, his lips drifting from my cheek down my neck.

I have always loved my husband's understanding that sexual healing is a very real, very potent tool in emotional recovery.

"I'm—"

My breath shuddered as Garth's fingers slid along my thigh and found the edge of my panties.

"I'm sure I can think of something."

"Unfortunately, as always, I do have to go."

"Then why bother teasing me like this?" I groaned.

"Because I was taught delayed gratification suggests that the longer we wait to satisfy our appetites, the more pronounced—"

He pushed my panties aside with practiced fingers and slid them in.

"—and hungrier they become."

And I certainly was that.

My husband returned his mouth to more important matters as his fingers and tongue worked in a delicious concert that sucked all the air from my lungs. But in that moment of glorious rapture building and building to nearly bursting, even death would have come as sweet release.

My back arched as I wrapped my legs around him, desperate to bring him deeper into me. I used the pressure of his own pelvis to pin his wrist and force his fingers in. My fingers, tangled in his milk chocolate hair, squeezed his lips against mine.

My body screamed with desire for his tongue and fingertips to meet. And amid that scream, I heard my husband chuckle. He slowly removed his fingers and tongue and stepped away with a lingering kiss.

When finally I could breathe again, I wondered, "Think you can keep hold of that appetite until after the party?"

"Who said anything about waiting until after?" he asked.

Reaching for him, I breathed out, "Oh, you delectable tease of a man."

"I learned from the best."

Much to my chagrin then, my husband proved an excellent student. He knew precisely how to force peak desire to linger. He departed, leaving me with a tantalizing wink and a smile. After remembering how to breathe and believing enough time had passed for my knees to have solidified from their gelatinous state, I hopped off the counter and set about freshening up.

Aragorn! That's the character's name!

I smiled, knowing my husband would be proud of me for remembering the character's name. He readily recognized the change in how my eyes and body surveyed him and me in his. I almost summoned him upstairs to make good on his promise that very moment.

In fact, I would've done had Thad not proved an exceptional special agent by looking up when most people never think to. He followed my determined, thirsty gaze to Garth with surprise in his eyes. I knew I needed to run quick interference and take his mind off whatever he thought he saw.

I scampered down the stairs with as much dignity and poise as one can conjure in such desperate circumstances. My arm slipped around his elbow before he could ask Garth any questions.

"So," I began as I guided Thad onto the balcony to enjoy the view of the city.

I desperately wanted to look back and assure Garth we hadn't already blown our secret wide open, and I would handle the flub to protect us both. But any backward glances would only cause problems.

Knowing the best way to make people forget about others is by having them talk about themselves, I began my inquiry.

"Thaddeus James Wilmington IV, what's your story?"

"I'll tell you mine if you tell me yours," he countered with a seductive wink.

"Okay," I agreed.

"What?" His seduction vanished.

"I was raised a simple Amish girl in Pennsylvania Quaker country. On my very first trip into the big city, I became separated from my kin and lost to them forever.

"I had to find some way to make money so I wouldn't freeze or starve, so I made friends with a peddler and started selling things I found on the street. I discovered that rich people buy sketchy things just as tourists on the corner do.

"Armed with such knowledge, I switched targets and brought in far more money with each fence. It was also exceedingly more entertaining."

We both took a drink of our libations in silence. Thad pondered my story while I waited to hear his response. Without too long a pause, Thad asked:

"Why don't I believe you?"

"Because you're a wise man," I replied with the same wink he'd given me. "Your turn."

"Do I get to make something up too?"

"But you're an honest man," I countered. "Dishonesty and making things up are how I make my living. Besides, I'm sure I could just find out on my own."

"Then why ask?"

With a dismissive flick of my fingers, I answered, "I like to give people the allusion of providing me new information. And I like hearing people tell their stories; it adds more flavor than a measly personnel report."

"Ahh," he replied with a nod of understanding. Catering to my whims, he reported, "Born and raised in Savannah. Skidaway Island."

"Ohhh," I approved. "I've visited that neighborhood."

"Business or pleasure?"

"One in the same," I reminded him.

He chuckled at me. "Grew up in the same house as the previous four generations."

"Is that where the 'fourth' comes from?"

"Convenient coincidence. Anyway, it happened that my dad inherited the house just about the same time my mom returned home to visit *abuela,* and the old woman got sick. My mom wasn't due to start her new job for a couple of weeks and decided she could help out.

"She cleaned houses for the week *abuela* was sick. It was while cleaning his house that my parents first met. Thinking her nothing other than a pretty new cleaning lady, my dad got quite the shock when he learned the truth."

"What'd your mom do?"

"Still does," he corrected. "She's a prosecuting attorney."

I exaggerated a recoil. "Do remind me to steer clear."

He only laughed cordially again. "They started dating that same week, and that was that."

"Well, aren't we modest?"

"What do you mean?"

"A name like Thaddeus James Wilmington does not go unnoticed by one such as me. You, my friend, failed to mention your family's historic wealth. The name of Thaddeus James Wilmington is one of old, deep south money."

"Yeah," he sighed, " 'old' and 'historic' referring to when my family had that money. If not for my *mi madre,* that ancestral home would've been sold years ago."

I briefly considered the information.

Such a shame.

Continuing, I inquire, "Why aren't you there?"

"One: my parents are still there and healthy. Two: FBI put me in Atlanta."

"Any plans to continue the tradition?"

"Nah, I don't wanna be tied down like that," he added with an adventurous smile. "Leave that to *mi hermanita.*"

My ears perked. I've always loved listening to people discuss their families.

"You've a younger sister?"

He nodded as his smile shifted from wanderlust to contentment. "And she'll put us all to shame. Famous, she is. Not actually, but, in her field, she's a rockstar."

Recalling my self-inflicted crusade to find Marína a romantic entanglement, I inquired:

"Do you have a girlfriend?"

Thad gave me a funny look, but Alexandria's interruption saved him from responding.

"There you are! Darcy's looking for you. Something about a delivery."

"Don't think yourself off the hook," I warned Thad. "I will find out."

I left Thad but noticed that I didn't leave him alone.

"Hey! That's my gelato!" I remarked upon sneaking into the second kitchen.

This room, the only one downstairs with walls and a door that separated it from the rest of the open floorplan, had acted as the catering kitchen earlier in the day. It now stood empty since I had promptly dismissed the catering crew after they finished. Jaylyn and Janko—who consider it a sin to waste time arriving late to any party—knocked on the door as catering walked out.

Anyone with good taste, fine-tuned manners, and no secrets to discuss would never leave the other guests to pass through the closed door. Alas, Darcy sat on my countertop, eating my authentic gelato with her lieutenant standing guard just inside.

"I procured you this gelato," Darcy countered through a spoonful.

I opened my mouth to complain further but could formulate no argument. After all, she was the only reason I had that gelato, and she had smuggled it for me herself instead of entrusting her underlings.

Seeing the great gelato matter settled, Darcy turned her attention to her stoically waiting lieutenant. She said nothing, only flicking her chin towards the door. The chiseled, sand-blasted man disappeared into the party with neither word nor nod of acknowledgment.

Once he departed, Darcy continued, "I've been thinking about your predicament, and I've an idea fer reconnaissance and establishing how ta proceed."

I felt myself losing balance and falling forward as Darcy took a dramatic pause to ingest another spoonful of gelato. I hadn't realized I'd shifted all my weight to my toes while Darcy spoke.

Finally discovering mercy and putting me out of my anxious anticipation, Darcy said only two simple words:

"The Gala."

"Of course!" I shouted as the lightbulb blasted on in the dark recesses of my mind.

I should have kicked myself for not even considering the obvious answer on my own. Uncle César would surely scold me soundly if he ever learned of my egregious oversight.

"*Barón* knows I'm guaranteed to attend this year. After you left, Garth suggested that *Barón* might suspect I left the girl under the protection of Uncle César. You two would make a good team," I observed.

Darcy simultaneously gagged and scoffed. I thought we might see her gelato return.

"Don't ever insult me like that again," she chastised.

Darcy's lieutenant returned with Garth directly behind him. The lieutenant did not linger but slipped through the door leading back into the party. I've no doubt that Darcy trusted that lieutenant beyond all others and would have allowed him to stay with a matter less delicate. This, however, was not her secret to tell, and this circle needed to remain as tight as possible.

Upon entering the second kitchen, Garth stopped short. He had, apparently, not yet seen Darcy's bold costume. He looked up and down—no lengthy task given her diminutive stature and position on the counter—with a pained grimace on his face. The shock and bruise of learning the truth about her clearly remained tender.

"You're mocking me, aren't you?" he asked.

She slipped into the Received Pronunciation accent she'd adopted while attending the London School of Economics.

"Oh, darling, you aren't high enough on anyone's payroll for me to concern myself with you." She flashed him a sardonic smile and enjoyed another helping of gelato.

Garth turned to me, biting his tongue on whatever else he might have said.

"I see why you two are friends."

"But enough pleasantries," Darcy slid in before I could respond. "Gyps and I have a plan."

She shifted her trenchant gaze to me, calmly waiting for me to do my job and explain said plan.

"Right," I verbally hiccupped. "The Thief's Gala."

I didn't think to say anything more, momentarily forgetting that my husband was the odd man out in this insider conversation.

"Yeah, you've mentioned that a few times," Garth recalled as he chewed at the inside of his cheek. "What is it? How does it help us?"

"It's an invitation-only event that occurs every few years for those of our ilk"

—Garth suppressed a titter at my intentional use of his word from that morning—

"To enjoy each other's company. Naturally, we don't tend to congregate out in the open. It's something of a family reunion, complete with all those cousins you long to see and those you long to punch in the teeth."

"And the Baron has an invitation?" Garth incorrectly surmised.

"Not really," I corrected.

"So, again, I ask, how does any of this help us?"

"We," I flapped my hand between Darcy and myself, "are confident that he will crash the upcoming Gala."

"Why? How is this one any different?"

"Well..."

"Oh, fer heaven's sake, woman!" Darcy erupted, finally annoyed with my uncharacteristic skirting of the issue. Wielding her spoon like a pointer—or a sword—Darcy exploded into an expositional tirade.

"César be hosting the Gala this go-round, meaning that Gyps, here, be guaranteed to attend. With the Baron knowing or suspecting or whatever the case may be that Gyps be the one who stole away his daughter, he be likely ta suspect the girl be hidden away under César's protection on his estate.

"Even if da girl ain't being there, Gyps will be, and the Baron will have his chance ta confront her."

"Then you can't go," Garth decreed without the slightest hesitation. "There's no way any reward of this plan outweighs the risk. The Baron is a man known for his sadism."

Though I understood my husband's fear—I shared it every time I considered the possibility of *Barón* coming after him—the situation required an uncomfortable level of risk.

"I can't just not attend."

"Why?" he demanded. "Is the girl there?"

My heart sank at his question. I'd lied to my husband about the gravest, most consequential secret I'd ever borne for two years. Even now, after finally unburdening myself to the one person I wanted to share my baggage with, I still couldn't allow him to fully help me bear that load.

He stood before me, his arm metaphorically extended to take that final piece of luggage, and I couldn't let him help. That he understood why and would never force me but forever stand with his arm patiently extended for whenever the weight broke me seemed the burden that would break me.

But that's the thing about secrets. Whether we keep ours for good or bad, someone eventually learns of them. Someone eventually looks at us with either pity or scorn, and everything we fought to hide comes to a head. Our demons care nothing of our intentions, only our actions.

"You know I can't tell you," I finally whispered.

Garth took a long, steadying breath. He sought to calm both the conversation and himself.

Darcy had remained silent and still ever since ending her monologue. Had she the ability to slip out of the kitchen unnoticed and leave my husband and me to our loving struggle, I believe she would have.

Garth nodded to the thoughts formulating in his head.

"Well, if she is with Uncle César, she's safe. Right? In fact, if the Baron dared to show his face at the Gala, then César would probably shoot him? Yeah?"

I nodded with a weak smile. "Javier definitely would."

"Then we don't have anything to worry about," Garth lied.

Despite his steady voice and confident eye contact with Darcy and me, we all knew it was a lie. Thanks to Garth's presence and influence on my life, I had everything to worry about.

Chapter Fourteen

In Which Devised Plans Became Complicated

The remainder of the party passed as a dull, gray-scale blur. Jaylyn popped her head into the second kitchen to jokingly scold me for abandoning my guests. I assumed a brave face and wore an eager smile for the rest of the evening, playing the perfect hostess flawlessly. I can't recall with whom I talked or any conversations.

Much to my allayed joy, the party wound to a natural conclusion around 2300. Couples had to relieve babysitters; ordinary people had to go back to work in the morning. Thad made his goodbyes—rather extensive for someone who met virtually every person he spoke with that same night—and departed near the middle of the pack.

Garth left with him. He saw going with Thad as an inconspicuous way to show off his departure by leaving to talk shop for those who would ask questions because he left. He returned at midnight after calling to ensure Brynn had left. Surprisingly enough, she had remained as my final guest.

All amorous ideas were dashed thanks to the exhaustive worry from the impending confrontation with *el Barón*. Garth merely slid into bed, held me tight, and we fell asleep with a goodnight kiss.

As Garth and I dressed for our mutual career/hobby, my thoughts remained consumed by how to proceed with the Gala. I'd rested poorly again, my sleep fitful and plagued by disturbing visions. I awoke exhausted and emotionally drained from nightmares I couldn't even remember.

While I've never leapt out of bed or acted remarkably spry in the mornings, that specific morning, I haunted the bathroom as a specter, trudging listlessly in and out of my closet.

My first attempt at dressing saw me don a green miniskirt and an orange gameday sweater. Upon recognizing my fashion monstrosity in the mirror, I disappeared for another try.

Next, I wore an adorable sundress. As I emerged from the closet, I heard the weather report ringing clear from the bedroom. A cold front had blown in overnight, and my sundress attire that suited me just a week ago became an ill-advised encore.

Giving up, I slid on a pair of jeans and a light sweater. I no longer cared if anyone found me sexy or glamorous.

"What?" I asked. I had heard Garth's voice say something for the first time that morning but hadn't understood what, so lost in my stupor.

"I said, I don't want you going to the Gala. Especially not without Darcy going."

Darcy had informed us that, though she typically attended the Gala, a prior engagement would keep her from the party this time. She offered no further details.

"It's too dangerous a gamble."

Before I could reply, Garth held up his hands in defense and shushed me.

"I understand why you think you need to go. I get it, and you're not wrong. But the Baron knows you. He'll go to the party looking for you, and heaven only knows what he'll do once he finally gets you.

"I don't care that César is the host," he cut off my beginning attempts at protest. "The Baron is ruthless and vile. If he's hunting you, going to him under any pretext is foolhardy and suicidal."

Knowing that my husband only spoke against me from a place of love and protection and that every word of his assessment was correct, I did not try to fight him.

"Then, what would you recommend?"

"I go in your stead. Undercover and alone."

Our atmosphere shattered, ripping away all the oxygen from my world. I felt myself gasping for air. Fish snatched out of the water had nothing on the face I made as I fought to breathe.

As a child, I often ran around the property with Uncle César's retired hunting dogs. He never let me touch those who still worked but allowed me to smother and spoil the retired ones.

One morning, two dogs fought over which one would return the ball I had thrown. The wrestling led to a toppling head over heels that knocked my feet out from under me and sent my chest flat against the gravel driveway.

The impact immediately knocked all the wind out of me. I lay on the ground, heaving, unable to fill my lungs. I couldn't feel the cuts on my knees or chin. My mind had no concern for the blood trickling down my legs. Pebbles lodged in my hands as I attempted to break my fall didn't register for what seemed hours.

My body convulsed from the terror that I would never find my breath and fall to suffocation as a young girl. But the inability to breathe becomes all the worse when it isn't your own life for which you fear.

"No."

My head shook of its own accord. My mind still focused all its power on having me breathe again.

"No, you can't go. And certainly not alone."

I crossed the bathroom in a single step to reach Garth. I needed to feel him in my arms. Needed to have the assurance of his touch that he remained safe and unharmed.

"If *Barón* ever found out about you, he wouldn't hesitate to use you to get to me. I can't let that happen. I—"

My husband pulled me tighter into him. The strength of his arms and the desperation with which he held me forced all the air I had managed to collect back out of my lungs. I didn't mind this inability to breathe.

"That's why I'll go undercover. We can even get César to help sell me as an invited thief. I'll be safe."

"You can't promise me that."

"But it is the only way I can protect you. That is my greatest concern."

I gripped him tighter still. Nothing would dissuade him from this course of keeping me safe, and I loved him all the more for it. But I loved him too much to let him go or risk himself without me.

I waited an hour after Garth left before joining him at the office. Not only did we need to arrive at different times, but I also needed the time alone to collect myself and prepare for the day's role. Our maintaining appearances carried real, devastating consequences beyond the intrinsic horror of allowing people to see us without face paint or costumes.

Thankfully, Gloria had front desk duty again. I engaged her in a lighthearted conversation to fully reset my playful mood before I joined Thad and Brynn upstairs. Gloria and her husband had attended a neighborhood party last night.

She told me of the excellent turnout of costumes ranging from ghosts and ghouls to superheroes and sports stars. Even an appearance by a Supreme Court Justice and a child claiming future presidency. The potluck food overflowed, and her descriptions were enough to set my mouth to water.

I would attempt to convey them, save that cooking never was a forte of mine, and my descriptions would only put hers to shame and retroactively impart a stain upon me.

When I expressed my surprise at her teenage son accompanying his parents to the party, she explained that he had quite the crush on a classmate that lived down the road. Someone had told him she would be there. Unfortunately, she stayed only a short while before her friends picked her up for another party elsewhere.

I told Gloria to tell her son he needed to set up an excuse to talk to his little friend. Have one of his friends bump into her and knock something out of her hands. Her son could then rush over to help pick up her things, complement her attire, and walk away. Gloria protested that it sounded complicated for a clumsy high schooler, but I assured her he could manage.

"People manage impressive feats of questionable sanity when they're in love," I reminded. "Just look at me."

Gloria graciously laughed without understanding, and I walked away before she could stop me to explain.

"Good morning, my honest companions!" I greeted with as much show and gusto as I could manage at such an hour.

Thad greeted me with a groan, and Garth with an apathetic, though cordial, "Miss Bonnie." Brynn, alone, seemed happy to see me.

"Thank you so much for inviting me to your party! I just had the best time!" she announced, dancing from behind her desk and throwing her arms around me.

Startled by this display of affection, I somewhat jumped at her enthusiasm and failed to return any form of embrace. Brynn became embarrassed by my lack of response and realized that emotion had overcome her. Seeking to rectify that momentary lapse in decorum, Brynn jumped away just as quickly as she had engulfed me.

Her cheeks glowed a fabulous shade of red that I wanted to capture for use as my next hair dye. She made some mumbling, sheepish apologies and excuses for her outburst as she disappeared behind her desk. Though I can't fathom how she did it, Brynn seemed to sit a little lower behind her desk than before.

"I am glad you enjoyed my party," I assured Brynn, hoping to calm her nerves. "Your costume was fantastic!"

The lady visibly brightened and sat straighter at my compliment.

"And what of you, Thaddeus? You certainly seemed to enjoy yourself. Make new friends, did we?"

He groaned again. "Your bartender and I got a little too close. Man! that girl, Alexandria, can drink!"

I couldn't contain my laughter at the trouble Thad had to endure for his efforts at courting my romantically elusive friend. The idea of any man thinking he could impress Alexandria by going toe-to-toe with her and her liver set me to full-on cackling in the middle of the office.

Thad winced. "If you're going to mock me, can you at least do it quietly?"

"A true Major Healey," I remarked. My laughing continued as I turned my attention toward the only quiet party.

"What about you, Agent Harmon? What did you think of my little *soirée*?"

"I found it tastefully amusing," he dryly responded. Without even looking away from his computer, he added, "Which, knowing you, came as something of a surprise."

Placing a hand on my chest, I properly feigned insult. "And what were you expecting, may I ask? Some wild *Eyes Wide Shut* kind of orgy?"

"Merely something that catered to a less savory clientele," he shot back.

I glared at him in response, hoping the snarling face wouldn't oversell our charade. Finally making my way to my desk, I plopped down in my chair with a decided *harrumph.*

The scowl I wore, however, quickly shifted into a bittersweet grin. Garth had just granted me the perfect segue to ensure he couldn't attend the Gala alone. I knew he would forgive me in time; perhaps he wouldn't even be mad at me, understanding why I did what I was about to do.

Fat chance.

A shudder ran across my skin as I considered how he may initially respond. Leaning casually back in my chair and making an effort not to look at Garth, I prepared for my next performance.

"Well, if that's the sort of party you like to attend, there is always the Thief's Gala."

Out of the corner of my eye, I could see the enraged shock on his face that my husband struggled mightily to contain. It didn't matter. I had already dropped the bomb, and nothing could be done to return it or prevent the impact.

"The what?" Thad wondered, suddenly forgetting the scathing headache from his hangover.

"The Thief's Gala," I repeated with all casualness.

My eyes must have looked like I had recently snorted a kilo of cocaine with the way my pupils kept bouncing between Garth and anything but Garth.

"What's that?" Brynn asked next.

"Am I stuttering? What do you think it is? It's exactly what it sounds like. It's a gala for thieves. Honestly! and they call you people detectives," I added with a disparaging headshake. "It's the most impressive gathering of crooks and criminals outside of Congress."

"Why bring this up?" Agent Harmon demanded.

A valid question, even with the others having no inkling that the question carried extra weight or that it came from both the FBI detective and my husband. Without acting questionably, I allowed my excessively diverted attention to land wholly on Garth, no longer able to ignore him.

He had achieved the herculean feat of returning his facial expression to one of apathetic curiosity. However, his eyes still burned with an unquenchable frustration. I also noticed how white his knuckles had become as they gripped a stress ball he kept in his desk.

So much for my hopes that his understanding would immediately supersede his annoyed anger.

"Not only did you bring it up by discussing the moral vagueness of my friends, but funnily enough, it pertains to our case."

More blood vessels than I knew existed in the human arm cropped up on Garth's hand and wrist as he moved as if to pop his stress ball. Blissfully granted the opportunity to redirect my attention, I spun around in my chair to look at Thad and Brynn.

"I assume Agent Harmon has briefed you on what occurred concerning our curious package the other day?"

They nodded. I didn't know what Garth had told them. I did know it was sufficient that I could discuss *el Barón* and the Thief's Gala without discussing his daughter or my specific involvement in the matter. I suspected they would believe any story I told them about someone upset at me for something I did.

I knew Garth certainly would.

They learned all about the vagaries of how I expected *el Barón* would attend the upcoming Gala and how I was all but required to do so.

"Why would you be required to attend when *Barón* is only expected to?" Thad inquired.

"The individual hosting this year's Gala and I have a particular relationship. They would feel thoroughly insulted if I did not attend," I somewhat explained.

"So, are you proposing we go undercover to set up a sting to arrest the Baron?" Brynn wondered.

"No," I admitted. "Such is my understanding that you have no jurisdiction outside of the US and, most certainly, none in Argentina."

"Then why bother bringing any of this up?" Agent Harmon questioned.

His voice seethed with frustration. Now able to display his complete annoyance without fear of raising suspicions, he made no attempt to contain himself. The intensity with which he stared me down—far different than how he usually looked at me with such intense emotion—sent a shiver down my spine.

Also, a long league's distance from how he typically made me squirm.

I cleared my throat and struggled to wet it again, so I might speak. An unnatural pause accompanied every word as my mind raced to formulate what my mouth would say.

"As we have established, I am attending the Gala. And I thought it prudent to inform all of you of this in case you might try to get me in trouble for leaving the country unannounced."

"Moller wouldn't take kindly to it," Thad agreed. He looked at Garth as he spoke.

Garth's phone rang, saving us all from how he might have responded. The conversation ended quickly. Ignoring Thad and myself, Agent Harmon looked to Brynn.

"Moller wants to see us."

He lifted his suit jacket from the back of his chair to put on but stopped mid-motion. Turning directly to face me, he used his body to block out everything else and force me to pay attention only to him. Under different circumstances, I would have found the domineering seductive.

"Do not leave this desk," he commanded.

I nodded sheepishly. Jokes and contradictions would have shattered an already tense situation.

"What do you think that's about?" I asked Thad.

"Could be anything," he unhelpfully answered. "We're always juggling multiple cases."

"Why weren't you invited?"

"Someone has to stay here and look after you."

For the first time since I dropped the bomb about the Gala, I smiled and felt like I could breathe again. I relaxed, leaning back in my chair, relishing the simple joys of deep breaths and unforced smiles.

Thad's banter and innocent flirting had helped remove a boulder from my heart. I now only needed to once again have Garth engage me without a scowl to wholly lift my spirits.

"There's one case the two of them have been particularly involved in for years now, but I don't know any details," Thad continued. "Might be that."

"Why would they handle a case without you?" Seeking to continue the banter, I jested, "Thought you guys were an unbreakable team."

"Somethin' like that," he chuckled, "but they were already involved in that case before I joined their team."

Recognizing the severity of this mysterious case, I transitioned to earnestness to ask, "Why not bring you in? If it's years in the making, I would think they could use the help."

"Maybe," he shrugged, "but, from what I've gathered, seems like the case is pretty intense. I think they want to keep the circle as tight as possible."

I wondered what would constitute an intense case that required remaining a secret even amongst team members. And if they had been working on this case for years, how had I never heard anything about it? Had Garth been keeping his own secret mission for as long as I had kept mine?

The thought of dealing with two draining cases simultaneously—perhaps even more—gave me a newfound respect for my husband.

Now, he has to actively worry about me on top of all of it.

Needing to steer my thoughts back to lighthearted matters, I re-engaged Thad in our interrupted conversation from the proceeding evening as though no time had passed.

"So, back to my girlfriend question."

"When did we discuss your girlfriend?" Thad shot back. "I know your friend gave me a hangover, but I'm confident I would've remembered *that* conversation."

I wadded up a blank sheet of printer paper and threw it at him. The shot bounced off his shoulder, but that didn't stop Thad from clutching his chest like he'd taken a bullet in the trenches. Laughing it off, he returned to typing up a report.

"Why does my love life interest you so much? Are you trying to ask me out, Miss Bonnie?"

Pausing from his work, Thad stared over the top of his monitor at me, trying his best to make his eyebrows dance in an alluring sort of way. Far from seducing me, his limber facial hair only sent me into a much-needed laughing fit.

As I watched him behaving with such unabashed goofiness, I wondered if he could tell I needed the release. I had seen him interacting with people at the party and knew he possessed a debonair suaveness that could easily beguile any fair maiden.

"Heavens, no," I squeaked out through fits of laughter. "Nothing against you, of course, but I have found that I am, perhaps surprisingly, a one-man kind of woman."

His silly flirtation ceased, but he did not appear upset. Instead, curiosity piqued his voice. "Oh?"

Consciously—even more deliberately than when Garth sat there mere minutes ago—I forced my eyes to avoid looking in any direction close to Agent Harmon's desk.

"Unfortunately, he and I move in substantially different circles. I fear an ultimately healthy romance between us nigh on impossible."

Thad slid out from behind his monitor to look directly at me. He had to move a stack of folders to achieve unhindered eye contact. Leaning forward, he rested his crossed arms on his desk and stared intently at me. He seemed to study me as though he could determine my mystery man's identity by peering into my soul's depths.

I let him observe without any attempt to help or hinder. After a long moment, a smile crept along his face until it covered the entire bottom half.

Expecting him to begin making blind guesses as to my beau, I couldn't contain my own smile at what he eventually said.

"But isn't that how all the best stories start?"

Any further discussion halted as Agent Harmon and Brynn returned from their meeting. Garth still wore a scowl, but my conversation with Thad had rejuvenated me enough that I no longer minded. He had every right to remain angry at me for how I blindsided him. He would forgive me eventually.

Taking no time for pleasantries, Agent Harmon walked to my desk and announced:

"Despite my protests and his annoyance, Moller acknowledges that we have no authority to keep you from leaving. However, I am going with you to ensure you don't violate our agreement while on your little vacation."

I nodded contentedly along with this final decision. I still didn't like the idea of Garth attending the Gala and running the risk of placing himself on *Barón's* radar, but it was far better than him going alone.

Realizing that Moller may now have information he shouldn't, I hurriedly clarified, "You didn't tell him what it is, did you?"

"We only said you wished to take an international trip to visit family," Brynn answered.

"I'm going to lunch," Agent Harmon announced. "Miss Bonnie, would you care to join me?" Despite the clock not yet reaching 1000, his tone brokered no argument.

"Do I have a choice?"

The glare with which he responded also left no room for suggesting otherwise. I grabbed my purse and silently followed him to the garage.

We drove in silence to Piedmont Park. Garth kicked the door open after throwing the car into park. He paced around the parking lot, waiting for me to crawl out of the vehicle. The moment I opened the door and began to exit, he rounded on me, yelling at the top of his lungs without caring who might hear him.

"I feel like I've asked this question a lot recently, but it just bears constant repeating: what is wrong with you! We had a plan!"

"No! You had a plan!" I reprimanded, slamming my own door closed. Marching over to him with an accusatory finger, I reminded him:

"You had a plan with a possible price that I was unwilling to pay! But, the more I thought about it, aside from my own terror of what could happen if we went with your plan, it wouldn't work anyway!

"The only thing Uncle César told me on the phone was that he did not believe Mancini was behind this, but I always felt he knew something more! The only way he will reveal whatever else he knows is an in-person conversation with me. He won't trust even you to relay those details!"

All our energy spent, Garth and I stood nearly touching noses, panting as our adrenaline faded. Everything that had brewed since yesterday morning and had come to a boiling point this morning was released. We could finally air everything we hadn't been able to or were scared to formulate and give voice to.

Once my breathing returned to normal and I could talk again without yelling, I admitted, "We have to do this together. There is no other way."

I took his hand in both of mine and pulled his wedding band to my lips. "Fortunately for us, we already promised 'til death do us part'."

He drew his finger along the chain around my neck. "For better or worse."

"For now and forever," I promised.

We embraced in a reconciliatory hug.

With a kiss on my head, Garth reminded me, "I'm terrified to lose you, too, you know?"

"I do," I assured, squeezing him tighter. "Which is why, if neither of us is willing to let the other go alone, we must protect each other."

"This could all end very badly."

"It will if we don't seize the opportunity to catch *Barón.*"

"It's not about catching the Baron," he lovingly corrected. "Not in Argentina. As you said, I have no jurisdiction there. We don't even have an extradition treaty."

"I know. Why do you think Uncle César is so proud of his home country?"

My heart lightened as I felt him smiling against me.

"It's about getting information from him, right? Finding out what he knows before we proceed with anything."

"Yeah," Garth breathed unconvincingly, "if we can."

"What do you mean 'if we can'? What's the other alternative? We just discussed how you can't arrest him. If you aren't going to arrest or interrogate him, your only other option is to..."

I pulled away as I realized the only other option. The prospect didn't scare me, but the determined callousness with which my husband had set his mind did. I had never known him, never imagined to know him, so resolute in a matter so grave.

"Garth, were you going to kill him?"

"Only if I had to. We have no extradition treaty, and César will do anything to keep you safe. I fall under that protection by proxy. I wasn't gonna let the Baron come close to hurting his daughter again, and you can be damn sure I was never going to let him hurt you."

He pulled me tightly against him again. I believe he needed to feel my body, whole and unharmed, against him more than any need to comfort me.

"No matter what it took."

Chapter Fifteen

In Which I Took a Boy Home for the First Time

The minutes of the hours of the days of the fortnight leading up to the Thief's Gala crawled by with the agonizingly grueling pace of a herd of turtles stampeding through peanut butter.

Garth set me to devising all foreseeable options for how *Barón* might attempt to confront me or ascertain if Uncle César had the girl. It helped to pass some of the time. Mostly, however, it set me to philosophical ponderings and melancholic musings.

For the foreseeable future. What an odd concept.

As though anyone can know, or even accurately guess, what will happen to us in the impending seconds. Had someone told me less than a month ago that I would not only spend my days inside an FBI office building but do so voluntarily as an approved guest, I would have mocked the fool to their face.

Then again, had anyone predicted I'd fall in love with an honest man who arrested people like me for a living... Well, I honestly don't know how I would have responded. Dumbfounded shock at the ludicrous stupidity of the very idea, most likely.

Yet, there I sat in an appropriately drab suit as two FBI agents worked with blissful unconcern across from my desk. And my secret FBI husband, who now feared any unprompted sidelong glances from his friends, sat beside me.

By the week prior, I had given up on my attempts to convince Garth to stay home and let me handle the gala situation alone. I repeatedly attempted to inform him that his presence would only serve to put him in danger, but my pleas fell on deaf ears.

My tactic of using sex to persuade him seemed to backfire. Apparently, the fact that he enjoyed and wanted to continue having sex with me significantly fueled his desire to protect me.

"You alright, Bonnie?" Thad probed.

I think he had passed the last several minutes dividing his attention between watching me and attempting to continue his work. As I had spent that time paying attention to absolutely nothing within my visible vicinity, I couldn't say for sure.

"I'm fine," I lied. "Just lost in my own excitement imagining the glories of the Thief's Gala," I continued bending the truth. "Why do you ask?"

"You were biting your nails."

So he did observe me.

"I'm no body language expert, but I'm pretty sure that's something people only really do when they're anxious."

"Anxious with excitement," I told him.

I rested my chin on my hands in a conscious effort to keep them near my mouth and avoid the additional body language suggesting guilt or self-conscious behavior.

"After all, Agent Harmon and I fly out tonight."

"Speaking of," the man himself popped in, "you still need to check-in."

Leaning back in my chair with a casual yet confident regality I learned from Darcy, I scoffed at his middling travel plans.

"Maybe you do. Charter flights don't have "check-ins"." I added air quotes for optimum annoying pompousness.

Garth played his role with aplomb, rolling his eyes, and returning to work.

"Wait," Brynn chimed in, "Didn't you have to submit proof of your purchased plane tickets to Moller?"

Unable to contain my giddy joy, I snorted as I said, "Yeah! And you should have seen his face when he saw we were going to Argentina. Oh! It was art! Gave Michelangelo's *David* a run for his money."

"Miss Bonnie," Agent Harmon gently scolded.

"What? Does it make you jealous to hear me call another man pretty?" I teased.

"But how are you flying charter if Garth is flying commercial?" Brynn questioned. "I thought the entire purpose of him accompanying you was to ensure you didn't violate the terms of the agreement."

"What am I supposed to steal on a plane?" I mocked.

Considering the option, I mused, "Although, that would make for a fun challenge. Nevertheless, not biting the hand that feeds you also applies to not robbing your friends who own jets.

"But not your friends who own *the Jets*; it's perfectly fine to rob them. However, with the butt fumble in their repertoire, it's not like their playbook would go for anything on the open market."

Thad out-and-out cackled at my joke. Brynn gave him a sideways look, the entire reference sailing over her head. Though he fought valiantly to hide it, I saw the slightest proud smile crack across Agent Harmon's face as he tried to ignore us.

Shaking her head as though she could erase the joke she didn't understand and bring everyone back on track with such a simple action, Brynn moved on to what she meant to ask.

"But how are you allowed to take separate planes?"

"Because the FBI isn't willing to foot my bill for a private charter, and we don't actually have the authority to make her do what we want unless she violates the terms of the agreement," Agent Harmon explained.

I merely pointed at him as my answer.

He began saving documents and closing windows on his computer as he continued, "And, on that note, I have to go home and pack."

Clapping my hands together, I exclaimed, "Oh, good! That means I don't have to be here anymore, either."

Agent Harmon shrugged on his jacket and collected his briefcase. Stepping out from behind his desk, he told Brynn and Thad, "See you in three days."

Performing my best chameleon impression by copying Garth's movements, I, too, addressed my new co-workers.

"I might see either of you again. Hold the elevator, Agent Harmon!"

I slipped through the closing doors at the last possible moment, rather proud of myself for reaching the elevator before it closed in heels. As the lift descended towards the lobby, I leaned over to Garth and whispered:

"Just so we are clear on one thing, you do have all authority to make me do whatever you want."

He turned his head slowly. His eyes examined my attire and what it concealed before resting on mine. The smirk he previously attempted to hide surveyed me with unhindered desire.

"I'm gonna like Argentina, aren't I?"

"They don't call their airport EZE for nothing."

The elevator *dinged* as I met his gaze and slipped through the doors into the lobby. I winked over my shoulder at him as the lift doors closed to carry him to the parking garage.

At 0800 the following morning, I stood at the arrivals gate of *Ministro Pistarini* International Airport in Buenos Aires, waiting for Garth's plane to land. I feared Gustave might rescind his never-ending offer to help when I asked him for a ride to Argentina that I needed to arrive early in the morning. It seems that even I underestimated his desire for those celebrated dancers.

I tried convincing Garth to ditch his commercial flight and join me on Gustave's private plane, complete with its own bedroom. He wanted to join me; I saw the desire in his eyes and tightening slacks. Alas, he would never break the rules and risk falling into trouble should something unexpected occur.

I suppose I should have felt flattered by the display of chivalry since my husband utilized such caution to protect me, above everything. But accepting the flattery of chivalry remains exceedingly onerous when one has a craving for the knight sans his armor.

Having finally wandered his way from the terminal to where I eagerly awaited him, Garth sauntered up to me and wondered, "Did you miss me?"

"Eh," I shrugged.

I couldn't tell him I had imagined nothing else since we went our separate ways at Hartsfield-Jackson. Or that I tossed and turned all night for dreaming of him once more disrupting my sleep.

"We go this way," I informed him, pointing away from the exit doors.

I brushed past him to guide us to our next leg of the journey but didn't make it far. Garth's strong hand gently grabbed my arm and yanked my body into his. He cradled the back of my neck in his elbow and dipped me as he buried his lips against mine a la the famous V-J Day kiss photo.

I knew people gawked and commented at us, but I didn't care. The pleasures of my husband's satin lips pressed into mine consumed my concerns. Quickly as he had dipped me, he pulled his lips away and set me back on my feet.

After finally opening my eyes from savoring his long-awaited kiss, I saw him smiling at me like a little boy who'd just gotten away with something. His kiss killed all nonchalant pretense. I couldn't help myself.

"Now, *that*, I did miss."

Leaning in close, my husband teased, "You have no idea what all you've missed."

That bastard will force me to freshen up before we leave the airport.

Standing erect—

As I'm positive he was.

—he took my hand and asked:

"Now, where to?"

Knowing of my arrival, Uncle César had sent his helicopter to fetch Garth and me from the airport and transport us to his villa. Sadly, we shared a comms channel with our pilot. That meant the tantalizing appeal of verbal foreplay plummeted with an audience.

Though I typically relish the sultriness of engaging in foreplay in public, half that fun comes from trying not to get caught. To see who busts first and gives away the game. When that subtlety and innuendo are destroyed from the outset of the circumstance, it kills more than half the fun.

My husband, however, would not be deterred from his suit.

Those inconveniences proved nothing more than mild speedbumps along the highway to what he ultimately desired. Unable to speak, he resorted to using another language to state his case. A language which, if I am to tell honestly, screamed volumes that the spoken word could never achieve.

He would move me to make great strides towards those volumes later that night, though.

Enclosing my hand within his, Garth began by intertwining our fingers. Remaining like that for several moments, we sat in perfect contentedness, enjoying the innocent eroticism of holding hands. Desiring something more, my husband loosed our shared grip and led his fingertips to trace invisible designs across the surprisingly sensitive skin of my palm.

Each kiss of his skin against mine sent a shiver of anticipation shooting up my arm and electrifying my heart. I believe I passed out from an inability to breathe, for the next thing I knew, our pilot informed us to brace for landing.

We landed approximately half a mile from the house. The ornate, wrought iron gate up the hill opened just as we touched down, and a baby blue 1938 Alfa Romeo came roaring down the gravel drive to meet us. A black, armor-plated Land Rover accompanied it with far less enthusiasm.

Our pilot couldn't finish saying it was safe to disembark before I had thrown off my headset and seatbelt and jumped out. The Alfa Romeo's elongated nose drifted to a stop only a few feet away. Its back wheels locked, digging two divots out of the pebbles and sending up a mist of dirt.

Uncle César threw open his door and bounded out of the low-ridding car with impressive nimbleness for a man plagued by arthritis.

"¡Mi pequeña ladróna!" he yelled with arms outstretched.

We launched ourselves at each other, embracing to make up for the time since our last encounter. I couldn't respond. Both from the overwhelming emotion and the inability to breathe as he mostly lifted my feet off the ground. My toes still touched, unlike when we were both younger and smaller, and Uncle César would heave my feet up above his knees as he spun me around in the South American sun.

"I have missed you, *mi hija.*"

"*Yo tambien,*" I agreed.

We squeezed each other tighter.

As the Land Rover came to a gentler stop behind Uncle César, I pulled away to check on my own entourage. Garth stood beside the helicopter with our overnight bags on either side; he hadn't taken a single step but to move beyond the door's swing.

My husband smiled at me with perfect happiness. All burning, amorous desires had passed to the back of his mind. The smile that lighted his face and shone through his eyes looked like nothing I had ever seen.

Sanskrit has a word with no direct, proper translation into English or Spanish: *muditā.* 'Vicarious joy' would prove the most accurate translation. Still, I have always felt that connotation loses some of the intensity of the emotion behind *muditā.*

It is, in essence, the pleasure that comes from delighting in another person's well-being. Personal pride is nonexistent in *muditā;* the person experiencing the feeling remains entirely outside the situation, gaining nothing from the occurrence. Quite simply, *muditā* is a pure joy unadulterated by self-interest.

I had never understood what all that meant—most certainly had no idea what it looked like—until I saw how my husband watched Uncle César and me in that moment. Garth left our bags and took my outstretched hand. Our fingers fell into place, intertwining in each other's grasp.

"Uncle César," I began as I pulled Garth tight and wrapped my arm around his. "I'd like you to meet Special Agent Garth Harmon, my husband."

"It's an honor to finally meet you." Garth extended his hand.

"A pleasure," Uncle César reciprocated.

Releasing his grip, Uncle César let his eyes evaluate Garth before saying, "So, you are the honest thief?"

"Sorry?"

"The honest man who managed to steal *mi pequeña ladróna's* heart."

My husband only smiled at me.

"Very first time she told me of you, I knew she was in love," Uncle César continued.

I returned Garth's smile. The moment held us captive in overflowing appreciative love. The kind of love where you feel no need to talk, no need to make love, no need at all save allow yourself to fall deeper in love.

"You could have, at least, told me when you were getting married," Uncle César lightheartedly complained.

Garth and I laughed, knowing the moment shattered but in no way diminished.

"In all fairness," Garth explained, "*I* didn't know when we were getting married, either."

Uncle César cocked his eyebrow and looked to me for an explanation. My husband provided it.

"Kati had some...personal debts she wanted to settle before we wed. She showed up at my apartment one night, said she was ready, and we were married less that same night."

"Your parents did not mind?"

Garth allowed his head to sag for just a moment. "Both my parents died several years ago."

Uncle César sympathized as he crossed himself.

"Gracias."

Though he incorrectly stressed the 'c' and made the word three distinct syllables instead of a fluid sound sliding off his tongue, I smiled at my husband's attempt to meet Uncle César.

"Come! Lunch will be ready soon. Leave your bags," he said as Garth turned to retrieve them. "That's why we have staff. *¡Vayan!"* he called out with a snap of his fingers.

Instantly, one of the men from the Land Rover trotted past us to collect our suitcases. Uncle César, Garth, and I—me sitting on Garth's lap—piled into the Alpha Romeo and puttered up to the villa as the Land Rover steadily climbed the hill behind us.

My husband froze as he stepped out of the car and saw the full glory of Uncle César's villa for the first time. As the only home I had ever known before building one with Garth, I found the opulent splendor comforting in a way few have throughout history.

The awestruck dilation of his pupils and absentminded drooping of his mouth told me Garth felt taken aback and unsure how to respond to his new surroundings. He let out a long, low whistle as he concluded his surveying of the villa.

"This makes the manor seem modest," he commented.

"And you've not even stepped inside," I replied.

I reached down and gave his gorgeous butt a quick squeeze to get him moving. Fortunately, everyone had already entered ahead of us, and no one saw how we looked at each other as my hand slid into the pocket of his jeans.

Uncle César called to us, waving emphatically from the front door. He insisted on giving his guest a full tour of the villa before allowing us lunch. Knowing he would hold food hostage from me, I removed my hand from Garth's back pocket. I contented myself to lace my arm through his as we made our way to the double, opaque glass doors waiting open for us.

Stepping across the threshold of my "childhood" home with my husband, memories flooded my soul in a way I hadn't anticipated or ever experienced when returning alone.

When Garth saw the polished, mosaic floor of the foyer, I remembered a gangly 13-year-old girl scurrying down the grand staircase in bare feet and ignorance of a freshly waxed floor. The instant my feet touched that ground, I shot across the entryway, flailing like a baby giraffe on ice skates. I smacked into the far wall and sent myself tumbling down.

My scream of surprise and resounding impact with the wall drew a crowd of bodyguards—some with guns already drawn—rushing to my rescue. Amazingly, I didn't injure myself. We all went about our day with only mild embarrassment as I had to explain what happened.

Uncle César explained the history of the fountain he had relocated from some Ottoman palace into the sunken courtyard that consumed most of the main floor. I watched as my younger self tackled one of his guards into the fountain basin.

I had recently devised a new training exercise for them by introducing Nerf guns into the house. Uncle César then turned my idea into a multipronged attack where I could train in my future profession. It became my task to sneak into the villa and steal anything of my choosing; it became security's task to catch me. If I won, I got to keep whatever I took. If I lost, the guards got to keep their jobs and heads.

That was how I came to own my first car at only age 14. I stole the keys to Uncle César's 1963 Corvette Stingray and drove it down a service road into the heart of the ranch where no gates could stop me.

He claimed to curse the day he taught me to drive a manual transmission as he watched me speed away. Yet, I distinctly remember seeing him smiling and laughing from the balcony through the cloud of dirt I left in my wake.

During one of our exercises, I made a mistake and got caught. In overwhelming frustration for having acted so carelessly and exacerbated annoyance at the barrage of Nerf darts pelting me, I snapped and bull-rushed the nearest guard. Unfortunately for us, he stood in front of the fountain, and our impact ended in a splash.

For such a big, open house, I've run into a lot of things in it.

We turned upstairs to the semi-private second floor where the kitchen resided. Uncle César set my mouth to watering with descriptions of the food that awaited us: *asado* of the beef, pork, and lamb varieties, *chimichurri* for topping, and *alfajores* for munching.

I licked my lips as I thought of the roasting meat marinated with the tangy, garlicky green salsa that country put on everything. We would have *helado con dulce de leche* to shovel in by the spoonful for dessert.

"As I recall," Uncle César inserted into his own monologue, "you spent a fair amount of time in the kitchen as a teenager."

"You don't cook," Garth said, protesting any suggestion that I would occupy my time near a stove or oven.

"Oh, no, it was not the food that interested her," Uncle César corrected. "It was the young, dark, and handsome Rolando."

"Really?" my husband attempted to tease.

In truth, he was far too interested in learning all the quirky, intimate details about my adolescence that I never shared. I believe he enjoyed discovering all details that proved I behaved like any child my age all the world over. How I grew up may have been odd and exceedingly unique, but I was still a typical girl.

"In love with the kitchen boy, were you?"

"Apprentice chef, thank you very much," I sassed. "And a fine better cook than you could ever hope to be."

"Hey! I make a mean bowl of cereal."

"Except when you use buttermilk."

"That was one time!"

Refusing to dignify my culinarily decrepit husband, I asked Uncle César, "How is Rolando? Do you keep in touch?"

"I just sent a christening gift for his newest daughter. *Donde comen dos, comen tres ¿no?"*

"Esos son los católicos para ti."

Uncle César howled with laughter as he unlocked the door to the wine cellar.

Does it still qualify as a cellar if it isn't underground?

Garth stared blankly, waiting for a translation.

"No birth control for Catholics," I offered.

He got the gist without understanding the whole joke.

Emerging from the sealed room with a precisely chosen bottle in hand, Uncle César announced, "For the wine..."

He twisted the bottle for us to see the label. I gasped in delight at what I saw.

"Our Malbec?" I tenderly placed my fingertips on the sketch of the villa's silhouette, afraid that any excess pressure may shatter the glass. "I thought we had long ago finished all these."

"Five years ago, I set aside this last bottle and promised myself we would not drink it until you brought home the man who made you smile." His eyes flicked to Garth, but mine remained glued to the wine bottle.

"And here we are! Now, it is time for lunch." Uncle César collected a firm grip on the bottle and led us to the balcony to dine.

Wrapping his arm around my waist, Garth pulled me close and whispered, "What's with the wine?"

"Uncle César owns a small vineyard and sells a select number of world-class malbecs each year. But that year, he refused to sell a single bottle. He forewent several thousand dollars of revenue to keep every last bottle for his own cellar."

"Why? What was so special about that year?"

"That was the year Uncle César and I met. The year we became a family."

"Ahora," Uncle César said, clapping his hands together after we finished our lunch. "What has brought you to my humble home?"

"The Thief's Gala, of course," I responded without a thought.

"That, I think, is not the only reason."

"Why would you say that? I always attend the Gala," I protested.

He pointed at Garth. "But he does not. Why bring him now?"

"You've always said he's a thief," I offered.

"But an honest one," Uncle César clarified. "Honest, to quote you, 'as they come'."

He said nothing more. Instead, Uncle César looked at me with his stare to compel anyone into bending to his will. I squirmed in my seat, trying to avoid his gaze, but it did me no good; it never did.

Unable to withstand the pressure, I blurted out, "We've come to catch *el Barón*!"

This news took Uncle César aback. "*El Barón*? He never attends the Gala. Why should he come this year?"

My eyelids felt heavy as I looked at Garth. For the first time since I was a 12-year-old intruding stranger in this house, I was scared to tell Uncle César something. Garth silently nodded his encouragement. Recognizing I needed more, he reached out to envelop my hand in his.

The sun beat down on us. There wasn't a cloud in the sky to block the burning heat. Though the weather had been delightful when we arrived and as we ate our food, I suddenly found myself concerned for my husband's fair skin.

Uncle César and I had nothing with which to concern ourselves. Our skin tones were designed for the sun of the Argentinian grasslands. Garth, however, tended not to fare so well without the diligent help of high SPF sunscreen.

Intellectually, I knew Garth had nothing to worry about. The day was not so hot, the sun not so bright, and the time spent on the balcony not so long that his skin would appear the slightest bit different from our foray on the porch. All the same, I desperately sought something to distract me and an excuse to manipulate.

The pressure of Garth's hand gently squeezing mine brought me back into the present moment. Both the men in my life watched me with vested concern: my husband because he knew and understood; my father figure because he did not.

Returning Garth's flexed grip, I took a deep breath, squared my body against Uncle César, and began my tale.

Chapter Sixteen

In Which We Explored the Various Incarnations of Chess

Our conversation with Uncle César lasted for the next few hours. I gave him more detail than I had told Darcy, but even he did not learn the whole story I had relayed to Garth. No one else would ever know that tale. I related to Uncle César only how I had learned of the girl and my decision to free her, leaving my motivations to discern for himself.

He guessed that *Barón's* daughter was the 'personal debt' I wanted to settle before marrying Garth. He pressed no further in questioning details I did not provide. When I finished explaining what C4 told me about Mancini as the fall guy, Uncle César finally jumped in with commentary and corrections.

"I know why Mancini was framed," he announced. He paused, taking a long sip of his wine as Garth and I leaned forward, waiting for his eruditeness. "*El Barón* framed Mancini because he knew he could without any repercussions. Mancini died nearly a year ago."

I collapsed into my chair. My eyes closed. The lids suddenly became too heavy for me to continue holding open. Much like a child who misunderstands the hide-and-seek concept, I hoped that my inability to see my problems meant they couldn't see or find me either.

Garth sighed beside me but ignored his own disappointment to place a hand on my shoulder and prompt me back into action. I ignored his nudge. Knowing we couldn't do anything to solve our critical situation by sitting on a porch beneath the Argentinian sunshine, Garth asked:

"How did he die?"

"Heart attack," Uncle César told us.

That, at least, relieved our fears of how widespread *Barón*'s conniving might have run.

I opened my eyes but remained slumped in my seat for several more moments of silence. Finally leaning forward, I held my head up by resting my elbows on the table and pressing my fingertips into each temple. The weight of it all still proved too much to support without aid. Taking a deep breath, I rejoined the world.

"Obviously, *Barón* did not actually want Mancini to take the fall for the bomb. So why would *Barón* frame him? What is the purpose?"

When Uncle César provided no thoughts, Garth spoke up. "I have a theory. Learning more about your relationship, specifics about the Baron, and the situation, at large, this is what I've determined:

"The Baron has likely assumed that Kati gave his daughter to César to protect her. The Baron went after Kati for two reasons: to cause her to react; and because César is untouchable. The only way to get at you," he again pointed at Uncle César, "is to have you come to rescue her."

Instead of merely pointing at me, Garth laid his hand on my arm. He lightly gripped it, silently reminding me that Uncle César was not the only man who would come to my rescue. I'm not sure he realized he did it. He continued.

"From what I have gathered, Kati and Mancini had some dramatic falling out, which means there is personal contention. If the goal was for César to become involved, is there anyone besides Mancini who would cause that response?"

Uncle César and I looked at each other for any ideas. Though Mancini proved the most obvious, we couldn't afford to jump to conclusions and ignore other possible options. Unable to think of anyone else, we shook our heads and told Garth he had no other choices.

Nodding along to his own logic train, Garth deduced, "Because you didn't call for help, the Baron has to go to plan B, which is the Thief's Gala."

I stared at my husband in disbelief. He couldn't possibly be implying what I reasoned. "You think *el Barón* would have raided the villa for his daughter when Uncle César came to my rescue?"

"I do."

"How?" Uncle César asked. "How would he know I had left? And, if he is so willing to storm the castle, why wait until I am not home? *Barón* is not a man bothered by torture."

"He probably planned on you going full protective mode and taking your small army of security with you to protect Kati. The tunnel vision would make you ignore the common sense to leave plenty of men here to guard the house. He reasoned it would be his best chance of making it out alive, with the girl unharmed."

Uncle César threw his napkin on his empty plate as the chair screamed across the stone. "*El Barón* was right about one thing; I will kill him, myself!"

I stood from my seat to catch Uncle César and calm him. "No. No, Uncle César, we don't want to kill him. We want to arrest him. Justice—"

"This would be justice!"

"Justice done properly," I clarified. "Garth's justice." Shaking my head, I added, "Not ours."

I led Uncle César in a breathing exercise he taught me many years ago to calm myself when emotions and nerves ran high on a job. Three seconds of deep inhale, three seconds of controlled exhaled, and two seconds before beginning again.

Our racing hearts calmed, and the blood in our veins returned to a gentle simmer—the blood of Hispanics never cools beneath a simmer. We finally took our seats again.

Returning his napkin to his lap, Uncle César grabbed an *alfajor* from the depleted platter with the grace of an unperturbed debutant. After taking a bite, he used his small wafer sandwich to point at Garth.

"He has made you better."

I wanted to say something, agree with what he had said, and commend Garth for the incredible man he was, but I could not. My mouth had gone dry, my throat clogged with emotion, and my mind overwhelmed by this highest of praise from Uncle César. I could only smile at my husband and intertwine our fingers beneath the table.

Uncle César finished his snack, wiped his lips with the napkin, and restarted the conversation. "Since you seem the professional best suited to our situation, what now? How do we proceed?"

Garth squeezed my hand as he began. "You and Kati play the same part you always would. The Baron knows both of you, or enough about you, that neither of you could get away with any act."

"And you?" I asked.

I hadn't realized how terrifying the possible answer was until I heard the quiver in my own voice. Both Uncle César and Garth looked at me, having recognized the shakiness. I only watched my husband.

Beneath the table, he parted our hands just enough to stroke his thumb across the inside of my palm. Unlike during the helicopter ride, when he meant the motion to arouse and tease me, he only sought to comfort me. His eyes never left mine as he spoke.

"I'm going to ingratiate myself to the Baron. Appeal to his darker, less guarded nature, and find out what he knows and plans next."

I tried to object, but Garth continued speaking to cut me off.

"For this to work, neither of you can know me for the duration of the gala. César can approach me only as a gracious host." He paused to take a breath, then hesitated.

The words could not be forced out of his mouth. He struggled to swallow, clear his throat, and make his mouth form the words. His eyes dropped to watch our fingers, still intertwined. Only then could he say it.

"Kati cannot approach me at all. We must be and remain complete strangers throughout the gala. No matter what happens."

"What do you expect to happen?" I demanded.

Prying his eyes from our hands, Garth struggled to raise them to meet mine. I had never seen such concern in them before.

"No matter what happens," he repeated.

Next thing I knew, the sun had sunk to rest upon the horizon. Garth and I sat alone on the balcony. I do not know when Uncle César left us.

When Garth and I finally came to our senses and realized that the world still spun, the fatigue of travel crashed into us, and we recognized how tired we had become. Rising from our chairs, I showed Garth to our room—the same one I had occupied growing up and during every subsequent visit.

We never relinquished each other's hand.

I requested Uncle César's chess set delivered to my room. I knew our overwhelming emotions would mockingly keep us from desperately desired sleep.

Feeling Garth's eyes on me, I told him, "I thought a casual match might relax us before bed. Help to clear our minds, anyway."

He raised our interlocked hands to his lips.

The chess set arrived after I changed into my pajamas, but Garth remained in the bathroom, preparing for bed.

"Wow," my husband remarked as he emerged from the bathroom.

I knew he paid me no mind in my flannel sleep shirt and floor-length silk robe. His eyes filled with the light reflecting and refracting off the fully displayed chess set. Garth took slow, careful steps forward as though the pieces might enliven and flee at the approach of a stranger.

"This is gorgeous. How did César find such a magnificent set?"

"How do you think?" I remarked. "He custom ordered the whole thing. Well, I guess, technically, the board itself isn't a custom order, just from a limited line."

"Very limited," Garth breathed, still awing over the sight before him.

Once again, the richness and beauty of the set seemed commonplace to me. I had learned to play chess on this board. My husband, however, saw something immaculate and perhaps ostentatious.

The board and each piece had been handcrafted from flawless specimens of ebony and ivory Waterford crystal. The Irish masters of crystal craft created an impressive set. Still, Uncle César had to include his mark on the set to create something entirely unique in the world.

And Garth wonders where I get my ostentatiousness.

"Do the stones mean something?" Garth asked.

"Of course," I replied. "Have a seat. I'll explain as we play."

We took our regular seats: Garth, the white knight; me, the black queen.

The invaluable inclusion that Garth had noticed in the set was the gemstone embedded within each piece. Chosen for their historical symbolism in myth and art, Uncle César selected the stones himself from across the world to create this masterpiece. I have always believed the chess set his most prized possession.

Though white historically goes first, my husband's chivalry of 'ladies first' dictated that, whenever we play, I always begin the game. Moving my first pawn forward, I explained:

"The pawns have no stone because they aren't valuable enough for such extravagances."

With a half-hearted frown, Garth mirrored my move. "Seems a bit rude."

I shrugged. "Such is life." Lifting my knight into the fray, I said, "The knights bear a ruby for its Latin association with the planet Mars and, thus, war."

"What of the rook?" he questioned. "They also have red stones."

"Ah! very good," I exclaimed, clapping my hands together. "You're as uneducated as the rest of them!"

Garth cocked his head at me but did not interrupt.

"The rooks have a red garnet with less brilliance than the rubies because Uncle César is a jerk."

Doubly insulting both the men in my life in a single breath caused Garth to look even further sideways at me.

I elucidated, "When learning to play chess, I always confused the knight and rook. Even now, I sometimes have to stop and think about it before I speak. In his great and endless sympathies, Uncle César saw fit to choose two stones easily confused by the untrained eye to represent my two problem pieces."

In defense of my husband, he did cover his mouth and kept it closed in his attempt to not openly laugh in my face. Even still, his eyes shone, and his body shook as the halting grunts of a suppressed chortle escaped him.

"Other than a personal slight against you, does the garnet have significance?" he wondered.

"Yes," I replied through a stuck-out tongue. "The varying colors of the garnet mean varying significance, but the red, again, connects it with Mars and war."

"So, César just really wanted to screw with you?" Garth confirmed with a beaming smile. I nodded my head, and he burst into laughter. "At least now I know where you get it. What about the bishop?" he asked, flawlessly moving along the conversation and the match. I moved my knight to take a pawn.

"Bishops have a sapphire because the clear blue stone has often related to the heavens and the Throne of God. More specifically, Catholic cardinals wear a sapphire in their ring of office."

"Why not use the stone worn by bishops?" Garth wondered as he capitalized on my mistake and used his rook to take my knight.

Taking more time to read the board before my next move, I spoke slowly, my mouth often interrupted by my brain evaluating. "Because they wear amethyst. Amethyst is a quartz, which is crystal, which is what the main components of this set are made of. Uncle César wanted something unique and precious."

Seeing my opening, I slid my bishop halfway across the board, putting Garth's queen in danger. Readily seeing the danger, Garth effortlessly slid his lady from harm's way.

"And the queen?" he asked, mocking me with his smile and question.

"She wears a diamond; because what else would a queen have?"

He only smiled.

Though neither had moved, only one piece remained for an explanation.

"Why are the kings different? Each other piece has the same regardless of black or white. Why make the kings singular in their decoration?"

I lifted my own king to examine him and the stone within. Despite the darkness of the crystal used to craft the piece, the perfectly white circle buried deep within him shone through without the slightest resistance.

"The others were chosen for color and symbolism; the kings' stones were chosen only for the meaning of the color. The black king has a milky white moonstone; the white king has the darkness of pure jet. These represent dualistic nature. The idea of yin-yang battling against itself.

"Uncle César always taught me that chess is more of a battle against your own mind than your opponent's." I returned my king to his square and studied the board once more.

As I studied, Garth asked a question that I know must have bothered him since he learned to ask it. "Now that I know the truth of Darcy's occupation, I wondered, is Darcy Rigby her real name?"

"Beats me," I incuriously replied with a shrug. My rook took one of his pawns.

"Why's she call you Gyps?"

"It's short for Gypsy."

"That did nothing to answer my question."

"Green eyes and my skin tone aren't super common, but they were historically associated with the Romani people. I guess Darcy thought it an appropriate comparison."

"And Darcy just happened to know that historical association?"

"Darcy just happens to know a lot of things. Some of which are really unsettling."

"Isn't Gypsy supposed to be considered derogatory?"

"Something Darcy has never concerned herself with. Something tells me that when you run an international smuggling enterprise, political correctness is not high amongst your concerns."

"Thanks. Just rub that in." He paused, needing the shift in tone to permeate the room before proceeding. "What happened between you and Mancini?"

Despite the seriousness of the question, the circumstances surrounding it, and the truth of the story, I couldn't help myself. Out of equal parts conscious flirtation and instinct, I responded with sarcasm.

"Well—promise you won't get upset—but you must remember that I was an impressionable young woman who wanted to make my mark in our world. Mancini, despite the age gap, was..."

The look of dumbfounded horror on Garth's face broke me and sent me into a laughing fit.

"I'm sorry. I can't. I tried, but, oh, your face!" Collapsing back into my chair in my hilarity, I assured him, "No. No, it was nothing like that." I laughed for a few more moments and had to repeatedly clear my throat so I might bring myself back on track for discussing a serious issue.

I moved a pawn forward, hoping to trap Garth in an easy capture. The added moment allowed me to calm down and silence to settle across the room so I might tell the real story.

"What actually happened was a difference in ideology. More accurately, a change in *my* ideology."

That piqued his interest. "What do you mean? Was this because of me?"

I nodded. "The last job Mancini and I did together was at the Louvre. We meant to recover a painting and provide it to a particular auction. As I began scouting the museum, this old woman sat on a bench staring at another painting for what must have been hours on end. One day, I noticed her crying.

"She cried with a very calm, controlled, single tear; the kind of way you cry when emotion so overcomes you that your body doesn't know what to do. You have moved past the point of hysteria and reside in some sort of numb, persisting shock.

"I thought the painting merely moved her on a profound level. It's not an uncommon sight to see in museums. But I examined the piece and realized it was a stylized family portrait. I thought it strange that a family portrait of six random people could so touch this woman.

"I left but couldn't stop thinking about that woman. I couldn't sleep for my confusion. I returned to the Louvre the next day. I wasn't supposed to go that day, but I just had to talk to that woman and somehow knew she would be there. I sat down beside her, and we started talking.

"Though she continued to cry the entire time, she was gracious and glad to talk. I learned that she had moved from a small town in Poland to Paris just for this painting. When I asked why the image meant so much to her, she told me it was a family portrait: her family portrait, painted by her late father.

"I asked why she would donate this piece, beautiful as it was, to the museum when it obviously held such importance to her. The tears staining her face hardened into something like diamonds as she lifted her frail body and said, with a defiance forged in the hottest of fires, that she had done no such thing.

"This painting had been stolen from her home when she and all her family were rounded up, thrown into cargo containers, and she was forced off at Ravensbruck Concentration Camp.

"At this point, I could no longer speak. What do you say to something like that?

"She didn't mind, though. I had got her on a roll, and off she went. Her finding of the painting happened merely by accident. She had come to Paris on holiday, and a friend brought her to the museum. She had thought the picture forever lost and broke down in the middle of the gallery when she saw it.

"The museum curators spoke with her about the painting, but she didn't have any paperwork to prove ownership. Her father had painted it because he wanted to. He never meant it to leave their family.

"When she exhausted all resources, even hiring a private investigator, she moved to Paris to be near them. No one else in that painting had survived the Holocaust. That portrait was the last thing that remained of her family outside her memories.

"We stayed on that bench until the museum closed as she told me countless stories about each person in the painting. Before we parted that evening, I had her give me her address. I promised her that within the month, that painting would hang in her living room, and she would have the paperwork to ensure no one could ever take it from her again. And I did."

"But what does any of this have to do with Mancini?" Garth inquired.

"We only planned to steal one painting," I explained. "All the research we had done on security, our movements, escape, timing, and everything else allowed us the perfect window we needed for one painting. I had no idea how to acquire that woman's portrait, but I knew I had to.

"My opportunity came when Mancini broke his foot two days before the heist. We had planned to go in together, but he obviously couldn't now.

We didn't have time to bring in anyone else before the auction, so I went alone.

"I had already set about putting a rush order on the paperwork needed for my side project. My forger got the files to me just two hours before the heist. So, I stole one painting.

"But it never arrived at auction, and Mancini never saw it. Apparently, he intended that painting to erase a debt he owed, which explained his fury when it never arrived. Our falling out was rather public, especially for our world, with countless death threats made. Mancini and I never saw each other again."

Garth's face blanched as a horrible thought invaded his mind. "Mancini wasn't indebted to the Baron, was he?"

"No," I assured. "If you miss your deadline for paying *Barón*, you get no second try."

"Not much of a bookie, is he?" The slightest whisper of a bittersweet smile flitted across my face.

"Money is no object to *Barón*." I moved my queen into position. If Garth made his next move as I anticipated, he would put himself in check. "He values power and control over anything else."

Readily reading my plan, my husband, instead, moved a pawn to block my queen. He would lose the little guy, but it kept his king safe.

"When did all this happen?"

My hand hovered over the board as I tried to determine what to do next. Taking his pawn seemed too easy a move. He had to have preordained a trap for me.

"Before I began my first day scouting the Louvre, I wanted breakfast from a little café I knew in *Jardín des Tuileries*." Seeing my move, I sent my remaining knight into position. I jumped when my husband yelled:

"Hold up!"

"What?" I yelled back. Pointing at my knight, I defended myself. "That's a legal move!"

"No, I don't care about that." He insisted with a dismissive wave of his hand. "I'm about to win, anyway."

"What?"

He paid no mind to my confused interjection. "When we met, you said I'd never find Mancini in Paris."

I sighed in realization at his protestations. Though his certainty at having essentially already won kept my attention glued on studying the board. "Technically, he wasn't there yet," I offered. "And I wasn't lying when I said he's a Francophobe."

"But you did lie that he'd be in the city."

"Yeah," I breathed defiantly as I moved my queen again to take his pesky pawn. Whatever trap he had laid, I could not find it. Thinking myself clever and within reach of actually beating my husband at chess, I asked, "You gonna do something about that?"

He only smiled, not hesitating for a moment to reevaluate as he slid his queen the length of the board and trapped my king between her and a knight.

"Checkmate."

I opened my mouth to protest but could only make irritated noises as my lips flapped about in a most undignified manner. I finally huffed, conceding to yet another one of his chess victories. My king fell with a vengeance that knocked aside Garth's queen as I flicked the useless man to lay face-first on the board.

Slumping back in my chair, I asked, "Now what?"

Despite the long day, the chess match and conversation had done more to wake me than lull me into desiring sleep. My husband continued smiling at me in an 'all-hail-the-victors' way. He wore a mischievous glint in his eye that told me faster than could any words what he intended to do next.

"The laws of battle dictate that a conquering king may take the conquered queen for his own."

"Is that so?"

He made no reply. The way his eyes looked through my silk robe and flannel nightshirt to what waited beneath proved answer enough.

"Well, then, your majesty," I let the words linger and drip from my lips in equal parts tantalization and mockery. "Claim your spoils. Do with me what you will."

And did he ever!

Chapter Seventeen

In Which Trees Revealed Their Magic

"*¡Buenos días!*" Uncle César greeted us with the abominable perkiness of someone who enjoys mornings. He held up a mug of black coffee to welcome Garth and me as we slogged to the veranda table.

Though I dragged my feet and longed to return to bed, I did not arrive at breakfast as sleepy-eyed as usual. I had already been awake and active for some time, you see.

Garth plopped down across from Uncle César and grabbed the coffee carafe. He poured a mouthful into the cup and downed it like a shot. I watched with eager anticipation for how his body would respond.

Unaccustomed to the strength of Argentinian coffee and having no reason to expect Uncle César preferred *café doble*—

Because who needs sleep?

—my husband's reaction proved just as entertaining as expected.

His eyes shot open with more expression than I knew possible for anyone who wasn't an anime character. He grabbed the side of the table, bracing himself for a gasp of air, desperate to quell the burning sensation consuming his mouth and throat.

The full-mouthed force he exhaled reminded me of a dragon spewing fire on an unsuspecting castle. A hacking fit followed. Deciding that he had not put himself in imminent danger by killing my husband, Uncle César teased:

"Awake now?" He had watched the ingestion with equal curiosity to my own.

"Good lord," Garth heaved once he could finally speak. Looking at me, he wondered, "Is this why you don't drink coffee?"

I shrugged unhelpfully as I plucked a grape from a nearby bowl and popped it in my mouth. Not entirely unsympathetic to my husband's plight, I did pour him a glass of orange juice and passed it over before helping myself.

Trying to be helpful, Uncle César welcomed us to sit and enjoy the morning.

"You know I prefer night to mornings," I reminded him.

Recovering from the shock to his system, Garth began selecting foods with which to pile his plate.

Motioning to my husband, Uncle César insisted, "But mornings have breakfast!"

"So do twenty-four-hour diners," I countered.

"Yes, I remember." Turning to Garth, he explained, "She always liked going to a diner after a big score. Strange girl. I remember when we were in New York once, and we had just stolen one-hundred million dollars' worth of jewels—on a job she designed, mind you—and all she could talk about was going to some diner down the street so she could eat pancakes."

My father and husband laughed at the story as I privately mused, "Those were some delicious pancakes."

Never one to sit down when I can wander, I selected a deliciously golden *medialuna* from a serving platter and took the rum-and-sugar glazed croissant in one hand. With my orange juice in the other, I leaned against the railing and looked out across the *pampas* glowing golden in the rising sun's light.

Continuing with his commentary of my perpetual disrespect to mornings, Uncle César informed us, "I thought to come and wake you, as we still have much to do before this evening, but I was concerned about what view I would see upon entering your newly shared bedroom."

Fortunately, I faced away from the men and had my glass of orange juice to hide my smile. No clerical hermit, and a widower, to boot, Uncle César knew all about the ways of the world. He made no attempts to avoid the knowledge of what likely happened on Garth's first night visiting.

Even still, a certain cognitive dissonance exists between knowing something likely occurred and accruing unequivocal confirmation by the cheeky smile of a canary-stuffed cat.

Given the paternal love towards his *pequeña ladróna*, I don't think Uncle César would have fared so well should he have seen my face as I thought back to what he would have observed not a full hour ago.

45 Minutes Earlier...

I stirred as I began to wake. Trying to roll from my side to a supine position, I found a solid pound of flesh plastered against me that kept me from doing so. I had fallen into blissfully exhausted slumber as we engaged in our post-coital cuddle following the chess match, and so had my husband.

His hand cupped my exposed breast with one arm draped across my side. His knees followed the bend in my legs, and our feet intertwined in a resting game of footsies.

I wondered how we could have found this position comfortable for sleeping before recalling our preceding lengthy and exuberant exertions. My husband slept like the dead afterward.

Men tire easily like that.

I didn't have the strength to move against him when tangled in his embrace. Not that I typically wanted to. My stirring evidently woke him, for I felt his fingers flexing as they checked for blood flow.

With his hand holding my breast, flexing his fingers meant he switched from a passive resting to an active squeezing. Responding to my accelerating heart rate beneath his hand, he squeezed more and began kissing my back and neck.

This reprise proved lackluster and echoed the sentiments of this lazy morning but in no way lacked the passion of last night's main event.

I frowned as he drew his hand away from my breast but soon had another reaction.

He entered me slowly and gently. The tempo of his sliding remained calm, relaxing, and slumberous. I wondered if he had awoken or if this was merely his natural reaction to stirring naked in bed with me.

Returning his hand to my breast, we continued in this entrancement until we inadvertently rocked ourselves back to sleep.

As I said, the night's expenditure warranted prolonged recovery.

Reawakening only ten minutes later, with Garth still inside me, we set out with a vigor to complete the task we had lackadaisically begun.

Who needs an alarm clock when they have an amorous lark of a husband?

With an efficient façade that arose from exponential instances of practice, I stifled my smile. I turned back to the men at the breakfast table. But, before I could manage to open my mouth, Garth spoke.

"When will the guests begin arriving?"

"Sundown," Uncle César answered.

I elaborated, "We have plenty of time; whenever on a social call, thieves always arrive fashionably late."

"Will you need anything?" Uncle César inquired.

Garth assured him he had everything. When Uncle César reminded him that the Thief's Gala is a black-tie event, my husband promised that he had an acceptable tuxedo to wear. I had forced him to buy one for our proverbial nights-out-on-the-town.

I frowned, realizing that this night might end with Garth still wearing his tuxedo. A terrified shudder ran down my spine as I forced my mind blank. I couldn't allow myself to consider whatever he had planned.

Uncle César observed me with crinkled eyes. The morning air hung much too warm for me to shiver. *"¿Estás bien?"*

"Por supuesto," I lied.

The lack of an easing expression on Uncle César's face suggested he didn't believe me. Still, he didn't press his concern. Likely knowing what sent me into a momentary fit, my gallant husband deftly shifted Uncle César's attention back to him.

"Actually, there is one thing I'll need to borrow."

Uncle César's garage lights aroused with a *kathunk* sound before settling into a steady buzz of industrial illumination. They sounded nothing near as loud as those that lit the hangar, but the noise still drove me mad after only a few minutes.

My husband had the enviable quality of selective deafness and could deliberately ignore sounds he had no desire to hear. He often swore that he never used this skill against me. My narrowed eyes and pursed lips revealed that I never believed his protestations.

His attempts at innocence only made him smile sheepishly at me through his enviably lush eyelashes—

Honestly! why did God see fit to grant men the most naturally beautiful eyelashes? I shall never forgive Him.

—which tempted my lips to purse for a different reason. Our debates over Garth's talent never lasted particularly long.

I, on the other hand, always found that sounds became malignantly sentient when I sought to ignore them. Much like a spoiled toddler, the more I struggled to ignore the noises distracting me, the louder they became, and the harder they fought to subdue me to their will.

On this day, however, it mattered not how long I had to remain under the incessant buzzing of the fluorescent light fixtures. I needed to stay with Garth while he chose the car for his grand entrance. The vehicle itself made no difference to me. Only spending every possible second with my husband did.

With each minute ticking by on that fateful day, I felt a looming portend creeping closer. Like a venomous spider crawling along my skin, it pulled us closer to a terrible end. But, for now, we needed to choose a vehicle in which Garth could arrive at the Gala alone.

"As you can see," Uncle César began with a sweeping hand and a beaming smile, "I have accrued quite the collection. What sort of vehicle did you have in mind?"

In addition to the Alfa Romeo, Corvette—

The very same I won by successfully stealing but never removed from Uncle César's herd.

—and a small fleet of Land Rovers, Uncle César also owned an authentic Mini Cooper that had raced in the famous 1964 Monte Carlo Rally. Upon seeing Garth examining the car, Uncle César hurriedly informed him that the Mini was a display vehicle only.

Referencing the beating any rally or endurance car suffers during a race, Garth insisted that he would never think of driving such a legend. Moving onto cars he might actually utilize, Garth surveyed an utterly inconsequential silver '98 BMW coupé and a 1957 plum Mercedes-Benz convertible.

Deeming the Mercedes as too ostentatious for the aesthetic he wanted, Garth opted in favor of the Beemer. Drawing a key from his pocket, Uncle César attended to a lockbox near the door between the interior and the garage to fetch the key for Garth's chosen vehicle.

"What aesthetic do you want?" I asked while we waited.

"Someone who wants to look like they have more money than they do but isn't foolish enough to draw extra attention to themselves," he explained.

He provided more information than I had expected. Doubling down to push my luck, I inquired, "How did you come by your money?"

He then looked at me the way I had expected initially. Garth's face drooped dolefully. His eyes sagged with a rueful heaviness that made me more greatly afeared for whatever he had planned.

"Surely, you can tell me something," I begged. My words caught in my throat, choking me as they falteringly tumbled out of my mouth. "*El Barón* doesn't know about us. I can help sell your cover."

I held my breath to keep from weeping. My husband's refusal to answer the question panged him just as much as it did me. He held his fingers to my face, lifting the tear that had escaped from my cheek. Those fingers uncurled across my cheek, caressing my face in his hand.

I collapsed into that embrace, latching onto his hand and pressing my lips into his palm. My eyes clenched shut as I fought to hide from the impending unknown.

"I want to do something before I go." Garth whispered, "Take me to your favorite spot on the estate."

I nodded violently, shaking his entire arm as I kept my hold. He held up the keys for the BMW; I never noticed Uncle César's giving them to him. The garage door opened as we stepped into the car. In the rearview mirror, it looked almost like Uncle César wiped away a tear as he watched us pull out into the sunlight.

Ten minutes later, I pulled the car off the dirt road that led away from the house out into the expanse of the cattle's grazing area. A lone tree stood on the top of a small, singular mound that overlooked this far-flung part of the ranch. The villa had disappeared about a mile ago, and rotational grazing meant that this paddock had neither cows nor *gauchos.*

Garth and I had the surrounding acreage to ourselves.

Parking just off the road, I shut off the engine and waited for Garth to come around and open my door. I kept my hand grasping his as I led him up that small hill and what waited for us atop it.

A *palo borracho* tree towered above us as a beautiful, steadfast sentinel watching over the land from its elevated post. Since we sat firmly in mid-spring here in the southern hemisphere, the gorgeous white and pink flowers had not yet begun to bloom.

The first traces of sparring buds struggled to emerge from the thorny branches, but the beauty had not yet broken through. It would take several more months for that to occur.

Legend states that the *paol borracho* tree was once a woman. After devoting her love to a soldier who died in battle, her grief forced her to flee into the woods, and she became a tree. They say that the blood of her deceased lover spread through the flowers that were once her fingers. The red of the blood faded with time to become the brilliant pink color for which they were now known.

As a lovelorn teenager, I spent many hours sitting under that tree, imaging the strength of love it must have taken for the nameless woman to suffer such a fate. Standing under it with my husband's hand clasped firmly in mine, I finally developed that understanding.

Hanging from one of the tree's sturdy, outstretched branches, a porch swing swayed in the midday breeze. It was to that swing I took Garth. He sat first, using his weight to stabilize the swing while I crawled up beside him.

With my head resting on his chest and my legs tucked up underneath me, he controlled the gentle rocking motion that lulled us into a momentary sense of comfort and security.

Alas, a moment was all I could withstand.

"Garth, please," I pleaded once more. Prying my head away from where it rested over his heart, I begged, "You have to tell me something!"

"Wifey." He whispered that name.

"No!" I would not be deterred by his soothing sentimentality. "You cannot leave me entirely in the dark! I will go mad with worry over what should be happening and what is happening and what you want to happen, and I—"

My husband's lips forcefully stilled mine.

Relenting his embrace and iron will, he agreed to a partial acquiescence.

"I will tell you what to watch for, but, no matter what, you are not to intervene. Promise me, Kati, or I'll not tell you anything."

I nodded. He tucked a stray strand of hair behind my ear, letting his thumb linger on my cheek.

"My plan is to befriend the Baron and have him extend me an invitation to his complex. Better still, if I can trick him into stepping on US soil."

"How will you do it?" I pressed.

He remained steadfast. "That, I won't tell you." Pausing to concentrate on his caress of my face, he added, "We can't know anything about each other."

With the twitch of a bittersweet smile, I reminded him, "It's far too late for that, my love."

Garth mirrored the smile we couldn't bring ourselves to share. Still stroking my hair, my husband calmly forced my head back to rest over his heart. I did not fight him.

"There's nothing for you to worry over," he tried to assure me. "I will only make contact and make a brief connection before going about my own way. The morning will see us in each other's arms once more."

"What would you have me do?"

Though we had discussed this already—repeatedly—I hoped against reason that constant asking might eventually cause a different response. It did not.

"I told you: act normally. But don't approach the Baron. We need to remove as many variables as we can."

Considering an option we hadn't discussed, I sought his advice on a new choice. "What should I do if he seeks me out?"

My whole body rose with his chest as he took a deep breath.

"Behave like you normally would," he decided. "Don't admit to anything. Don't react to anything. Play the dimwit."

"You think I'm normally a dimwit?"

Again, my whole body responded, shaking to the rumbling of my husband's laughter.

"The furthest from it. You only play the fool when it suits your purposes." He kissed the top of my head. "Let it suit you tonight."

I snuggled tighter into him and his kiss. "Only you can do that."

He took another deep breath, releasing the tension coiling within him in a long, slow sigh. A shifting of the gears in his mind occurred during that sigh, as though he needed to take a moment to reset himself on a new track before safely proceeding. Once correctly positioned, he directed us down our new path.

"Since I can't allow myself to respond, tell me what dress you're wearing tonight." His kisses flitted across my hair. "I need to prepare myself."

"Oh, so, what?" I shoved myself off him, needing to challenge him face-to-face. "You get forewarning, but I can't have any?"

"Your surprised reactions aren't as visible or distracting as mine."

He made a valid point, but I wouldn't let him win. "Then wear a jockstrap."

Garth chuckled again at my recommendation.

Still indignant on my high horse, I explained, "I'll sometimes wear a corset; it's basically the same thing."

"Except that you in your corset causes even stronger reactions from me."

The arm that had remained wrapped around my waist drew designs traveling along my back and hips.

"You've still not told me what you're wearing, wifey" he coaxed. Thinking my comment may have provided a clue, I heard the excitement in his voice as he wondered, "Will you wear your corset?"

Giving up and sinking back onto his chest, I huffed, "I'm tempted to come in my pajamas."

He found this option amusing and not unappealing. However, he did remind me that Uncle César would not likely approve.

"True, but it is such terrible work to properly dress oneself to the nines. I'm often tempted to never wear fancy clothes again."

"I'd prefer you never wear any clothes again," my husband offered as the hand tracing designs slipped underneath my shirt.

I craned my neck to look at him but did not remove it from his chest.

"But I thought you always had such fun with unwrapping your present."

"Oh, I do." His smile assured me of the truth of his claim. "And, as you've taught me, delayed gratification is something wonderful to savor."

His fingertips tickled the bare skin of the small of my back. "However, it's not the dress that excites me, but the woman beneath it and how you smile in those dresses."

"Does my smile change with my wardrobe?" Though I modulated my tone to continue the flirtation, I did pose the question in earnest.

"It can. Mostly, though, you just have the smile of a seductress."

Cocking my eyebrows at that description, I told him, "Please do elaborate."

His explanations came in few-word spurts as his lips became periodically unavailable. Some kisses found my lips; others missed their mark, landing on my neck or cheeks. I couldn't complain about his poor aim.

"I used to think" *pause* "that you smiled" *pause* "like a cat" *pause* "playing with its food," *pause* "but I realized" *pause* "that's not it." *pause* "You smile" *pause* "like a woman" *pause* "who is toying" *pause* "with a man."

I hesitated in my response as my lips had become otherwise engaged.

"Is there a difference?"

"Depends on the woman." *pause* "Depends on the man." *pause* "You" *pause* "have the smile" *pause* "of a good time tease," *long pause* "the difference being" *pause* "that it's not a tease." *long pause.*

He pulled back just enough for our twinkling eyes to meet. "You fully intend to make *very good* on exactly what you smile about."

"And have I teased you recently?" I found the irony delicious that he spoke of me tempting him as his lips met mine again.

"Only every moment you're breathing."

The hand that had crept under my shirt found its way to the clasp of my bra. His hands slid down my back, resting with a gentle squeeze on my hips. I knew my husband was directing me to sit on his lap with that slightest prompting.

As I pushed off the swing to settle happily in my husband's lap, Garth lifted the hem of my lacy white dress away from where I would sit on it. He released the fabric to pool above his knees and my thighs.

We stayed for a moment in the sensual stillness. I did not rock my hips against his; he did not move his hands to grope either breast or butt. We neither kissed nor spoke. We only looked upon each other, falling profoundly and adoringly into the gaze of our only beloved.

A silent tear of joy welled on my eyelid as I thought about the beauty and strength of my husband, falling every day, every moment, deeper in love with him. He kept one arm pressed protectively against my back as he raised the other to lift away my tear.

I caught his hand before his finger reached my tear and brought it to my lips. I would not let him remove this trophy of the wonderful man he was. Continuing to hold his hand against my lips, I quoted:

" 'You run the risk of weeping a little if you let yourself get tamed.' "

Garth melted wholly into me as I recited from the transcendental children's story he had adored so much growing up. He clasped our entwined hands and pulled me close.

Our hearts pressed together galloped apace as our lips found each other with a tenderness that excited my senses beyond any seduction.

My body, my mind, my very soul burned for my husband. I was reminded again that no matter how effective the fountain of youth, I could never, for all eternity, have enough of this man.

The late spring breeze blew calm and cool against my back as Garth unzipped my dress. He lifted it over my head, wrapped it into a contained bundle, and set it across the swing from us. My bra I let slide from my shoulders and tossed into the grass behind me.

Having less care for his clothing, I dropped Garth's t-shirt on the ground with my bra. Garth paused in our swinging, and we added his jeans and our underthings to the growing pile.

Garth resumed our swinging. The rhythm of his flexing and relaxing legs slid me into place as we settled into a glorious cadence. The sky began erupting in a kaleidoscope of color as our kisses stopped, and we descended together from those heavens.

I would have remained forever with my husband in the moment if only God had given me the chance.

As it was, reality screamed in the distance, and we had a gala to prepare for. Not until later recollections of our time at the swing, did I realize what my husband had done. He did not specifically desire sex.

Not that he passed on the opportunity once offered.

Instead, he knew he needed to steer my mind towards lighter flirtations. He recognized, in a way not even I did, that my mind needed to be directed away from the Gala and required the assurance that he was still with me at that moment and safe. I would have enough to worry about during the event; it would do no good to work myself into an endless tizzy hours before it even began.

As I reflected on this and the incredible intuitiveness of my husband, I could not help but fall in love with him all the more.

Chapter Eighteen

In Which Set Plans Utterly Imploded

I spent thirty minutes pacing around the immediate vicinity of the front doors. The evening began with me 'helping' Uncle César greet his guests. After I ignored five consecutive arrivals, however, he sent me inside. My attempt to protest that it would be bad form fell short.

With the bittersweetness of tough love, he reminded me that the villa was no longer my home and, thus, no longer my duty to play hostess. Even with those I managed to adequately greet, my attention remained diverted as I desperately sought the arrival of Uncle César's borrowed BMW.

"Go inside," he gently commanded. "Get a drink to calm your nerves and socialize. You can see him safely arrive, but neither of you will be tempted with the forced proximity."

I opened my mouth to protest again, but his raised hand silenced me.

"Besides, you are not supposed to make contact with *Barón*. Go inside."

He reached his hand forward to stroke my curled, sandy-brown hair like he had while I was a child. The most minute twinge of comfort briefly invaded my tumult of terrified apprehension threatening to drown me.

"Your husband is a smart, strong man who loves you desperately. He will protect you and come back home to you at all costs. Go inside and await your white knight."

Uncle César wiped away the single tear that threatened to ruin my makeup. Stepping aside, he held open his hand to direct me inwards. I smiled at him, broken yet grateful, before leaving him alone on the terrace.

The first hour of the Gala passed as a blur. I spoke to various people, former associates, and even a few cohorts I considered friends but remember nothing of it. The brave face I displayed seemed convincing enough, for no one asked if I felt unwell or had some worry plaguing my mind.

To be sure, I behaved as far less the flitty social butterfly than I typically would at these spectacular events. Nor did I network or seek potential exploits. Even still, the difference seemed minor or nonexistent to the guests.

I suppose a society of unintentional narcissists with no social decorum can prove occasionally beneficial.

Exhausted from putting on my smiling, cheerful demeanor, I collected another glass of wine and made my way onto the balcony. I would have preferred something more potent on a night like that, but the inevitably numerous drinks would make for an unfortunate morning. I needed to remain vigilant for the arrival of both Garth and *el Barón*. As yet, neither had made an appearance.

The night bore down on me, hot, stuffy, and oppressive. The weather felt better suited to a swamp at summer's height after a storm. Argentina—my home—should not feel like this. Even the hot humidity of the summers never caused the discomfort of standing on the porch that night.

That evening, firmly nestled within the heart of spring, should have maintained the *status quo* by reminding me of the climate one would find in a fairy story.

A perfect, residual heat to comfort us in our wanderings accompanied by a slight breeze that joined the adventure as far more travel companion than a meteorological occurrence. I used to spend hours on this overlook, entranced and enamored of the endless grasslands during the day and countless stars at night.

I could not stand staying outdoors longer than a few moments that night.

I took a long draught of my wine and shuffled back inside for another pour. I never made it to the bar. As I crossed through the sunken courtyard and weaved between conversations and the fountain, Garth finally made his appearance.

My heart leapt into my throat upon seeing him. I grasped the wall beside me and steadied myself. Not until pulling away a wet hand did I realize that the wall was actually one of the fountain tiers.

Air couldn't suck through my windpipe fast enough to force my heart back into my chest. My head swam as my stomach churned into knots. It wasn't until that moment I realized I had secretly hoped that Garth would not arrive at the Gala.

I prayed he would fall into car trouble, or become lost, or experience an overwhelming conviction that he ought not attend. I had unconsciously pleaded that he would miss the event, only to crawl into bed with me several hours later.

Alas, life would not prove so kind.

Our eyes locked for the briefest of instances as he instinctively surveyed the room. Even across the entryway, I saw his pupils dilate when his eyes caught me. Garth pried his gaze away without allowing him time for further reactions to continue his sweep.

As he crossed to the bar, I finally found my breath. My hand went to the silver chain hanging around my neck and the two rings that hung safely tucked beneath my dress.

Unable to command my feet to stop, I continued my shuffle towards the bar with another empty glass to use as an excuse. Once again, I was not yet to return.

While my heart had sputtered and constricted when I saw Garth, the specter now darkening the doorstep stopped its beating altogether. Abject terror gripped my throat with icy fingers that stabbed and burned as it kept me trapped within its grasp.

Much as I secretly hoped Garth never arrived at the Gala, I had openly begged that our second guest of consequence miss the event. That cognitive dissonance between intellectually knowing a truth but not being forced to confront it head-on had implanted itself firmly within my mind.

I knew everything that had happened came as his handiwork and that this night could not possibly pass without a confrontation. Delusional, desperate hope had still allowed me to convince myself that safety could still exist.

The imposing silhouette of *el Barón* standing in Uncle César's foyer brought that hope crashing down around my ears.

My heart sank to my feet and leaked out of my open-toe heels, meddling with the soiled spillage of the terminally bleeding hope that someone had blundered, and none of this was really ever about me. If I were not the target, Garth would not face the danger of collateral.

A momentary silence fell over the party as *el Barón,* and his two accompanying bodyguards, entered. No one else brought their own security. The unspoken laws concerning the Thief's Gala marked the time and location of the gathering as a zone of safety. Only words and clothing could commit crimes within the confines of this time and space.

Caring nothing for the anxiety he caused amongst those gathered, *el Barón's* hard, determined eyes inspected the faces of every person who uncomfortably watched him. Some, I am sure, watched with curiosity, amazed that he should attend this event for the first time since its inception.

Others, undoubtedly, gulped down their liquid courage for the sight of him. Those who thought themselves in no danger here questioned the choices which led them to this night.

I chief among them.

Quickly as they ceased, though not nearly as organically, the smattering of diverse conversations overlapped and returned to filling the house with chatter. Those who thought it best not to incur the ire—or further disappointment—of *el Barón* formed a line to pay him their respects and kiss the ring.

Knowing he searched for me, I waited until these thralls obstructed *Barón's* attention. Bounding up the stairs three at a time, I placed myself at a safe distance for observing. Even I had underestimated *el Barón's* intimidation and self-established domineering within our world.

In retrospect, had I understood the total weight of what could come down upon me when I stole away with his daughter, I may not have possessed the strength to do what was required of me. I nearly spilled the wine left in my glass with the shudder that convulsed my entire being.

The steady stream of peons abandoning their conversations to pay homage to their warlord continued for half an hour. Some joined *Barón* for the extended, amiable discussions of old business partners discussing the volatile trends of stocks or struggles of demands and distribution. Others spent less than a minute in the presence of *el Barón* and never dared to look him in the eye.

The whole time, Garth remained at the bar, watching every interaction in which *el Barón* engaged with a scrutinizing eye. I had never seen the blank determination that consumed his face. His eyes never remained still, constantly shifting to take in every minute detail of every interaction.

I could see the list he compiled in his mind of every gesture, every movement, every word, and inflection that *Barón* made as he spoke with his varying audiences. With each new piece of information he collected, Garth fashioned, in real-time, his approach and angle for finally making his own introduction.

Garth made himself an unknown with no attempts to appear approachable or interested in conversation. His guise allowed him to pass the entire time of observation undisturbed by all except the bartender inquiring if he wanted another pour.

When the revolving door stilled, and it seemed everyone who cared to engage with the man had, *Barón* again set his sights to examining the room. He sought something and would not be deterred in his search.

He sought some*one*.

He sought me.

When he could find me nowhere on the ground floor, those cold, lifeless eyes rose to examine the interior balcony.

My heart stopped again. My whole body tensed as I recoiled from the banister. With that look of murder in his eyes, I knew, beyond all hope or doubt, that he knew what I had done and sought my head as payment.

As he took a step forward and I took another step back. Garth sprang into action. He all but leapt in front of *Barón*, cutting him off and loudly announcing himself in a drunk, hick voice.

"I been watchin' you, friend, an', after seein' the deference that e'r'body been payin' ya, I had ta come over an' introduce myself!" Sticking out his whisky-free hand, Garth announced himself with the name, "Wolf Campbell. But you can just call me Wolf."

Capitalizing on *Barón's* complete distraction, I slipped down a back staircase. Stationed at the far side of the bar, I listened to their conversation while remaining out of *Barón's* line of view.

I would do just as Garth had asked and maintain my distance. But that didn't mean I wouldn't continue watching him and keep an eye on everything he did that evening. I promised I wouldn't interfere, no matter what, but I'd be damned if I wasn't going to be prepared for the instant he allowed the façade to break.

When I took up my new position, *Barón's* gaze still rested on Garth's face and outstretched hand. He examined my husband like a real wolf might a yapping Pomeranian. Garth's adopted attitude and accent did little to impress *Barón,* as I'm sure was the point.

Without accepting Garth's waiting hand, *el Barón* wondered at his name. "Wolf?"

"Yes, sir!" Garth proudly owned his pseudonym, intentionally misinterpreting *Barón's* condescension. "An' with a given name like that, how could I do anythin', but what I do now?"

"What do you do?" *Barón* questioned. He cared nothing for what Garth—Wolf—actually did, only how he had managed to secure an invitation to this most exclusive of parties.

"You might call me a distributer."

"Of?"

"The finest crystal comestibles you ever have encountered."

"You're a meth dealer?" *El Barón* suddenly found Garth tolerably more interesting.

"Well, that's a bit crude sort o' way of puttin' it, but when you get to the root of it all..." Garth toasted his scotch and took a drink.

El Barón raised his own glass, one that a peon had provided to him as a peace sacrifice, almost imperceptibly, but did not join his new friend in a drink.

Encouragingly intrigued by Garth's cover, *Barón* asked, "Where have you based your operation?"

"Ah, well, if you're cookin' up the quality of crystals that we do, only one place ta do it."

El Barón waited for his answer. He wouldn't bite for any bait.

As though the answer was obvious, Garth told him, "Out in the boonies."

El Barón appeared unamused. "Yes, but which boonies?"

"I've found the best is Alabama."

At that, *Barón* became increasingly interested in his new friend.

Encouraged by this newfound interest, Garth proceeded proudly. "Yes, sir! Those boys couldn't pass no 5th-grade science—shoot! I don't think most of 'em even made it that far—but, I tell you what, they sure do know their chemicals."

El Barón snorted as Garth backhanded him on the chest before taking another swig of his whisky. Garth had found the first nibbles of *Barón's* interest. *Barón* set out to determine Garth's worth.

"You find the meth trade profitable, do you?"

"Well, I do think this a rather nice tux," Garth replied, examining his own suit. "But, tell you truth, I've grown tired of those stupid crystals."

"You could have fooled me," *Barón* replied with an eye roll. "You seemed rather proud of yourself."

"And that I am!" Garth defended boisterously.

Fortunately, this drunken outburst drew the curious gazes of most people in the foyer, and my covert examination of the situation became nothing of note.

"Don't let no man think I ain't proud of where I come from or the work I done to pull myself up by my own bootstraps!"

Undesiring of any audience, *Barón* turned his back to the room and replied with intentional quietness, "Then why admit you're tired of that work?"

I inched forward along the bar to better continue spying on the conversation.

Leaning in, Garth said, "Call it bein' more environmentally conscious."

Instead of not biting from stubbornness, *Barón* did not bite from confusion.

"The thing that always done bothered me so much 'bout them drugs is they are one-time use. Can't get nothin' else out of 'em."

"So you're interested in finding a reusable commodity to sell?" *el Barón* attempted to clarify. A horrible glint flashed in his eyes as he thought ahead to what Garth implied.

"Oh, no, sir," Garth corrected. "I already done got my reusable commodity. Funny enough, I's actually goin' back to my roots. Ya see, it's how I done found them boys, an' their crystal comestibles, in the first place."

"What exactly do you mean?" *El Barón* would take no chances of making assumptions and missing his mark.

Garth leaned in closer still. He had *Barón* on the hook and wouldn't dare lose the opportunity to sink said hook deeper. He glanced about them for show and whispered:

"I got a particular talent in findin' folk an' connectin' 'em with interested parties. An' what I've discovered is there ain't nothin' in the world more reusable than a human bein'. 'Specially them young ones."

I shuddered and nearly vomited into my glass at the precision with which Garth played his role. Had I known ahead of time what he planned, the impact wouldn't have caused such a visceral gut punch, but I now understood why Garth knew he had to keep me in the dark.

Delighted by what he heard, *el Barón* invited Garth onto the patio for cigars and a more private conversation. Knowing the terrace provided no hidden places for sneaking and eavesdropping, I had to let my husband continue alone.

Had I not already been immediately concerned with acquiring a Sprite from the bartender to calm my churning stomach, that one thought would have made me sick.

As I gulped down half the can in a single swallow, a thought of abject horror overcame me as I considered that *Barón* may have come for my head but would leave with my heart.

The Gala ended some hours later. I passed the last of it in the same way I had the time before Garth or *el Barón* arrived. I desired little more than to go to my room, curl up into bed, and sleep away the night waiting until my husband returned to me.

But I couldn't stand the thought of removing myself from the main room and remaining indefinitely ignorant of what Garth and *Barón* did. As it turned out, my perpetual hovering made no matter in me knowing what happened.

The final guests departed in the wee small hours of the morning as the first thoughts of light began to slowly banish the shadows from the world. I bid them good morning and watched the elderly couple—long since retired but still highly respected and sought as mentors within our profession—slip into their rented Aston Martin with surprising calm.

I knew that Garth would have left quietly after completing his task of "befriending" *Barón* and would purposely wait several hours before returning.

An unforced smile of content expectancy stretched gently across my face as I stood with Uncle César, watching our final guests depart. It would not be long now until that old Beemer came trundling up the driveway, bringing my beloved back home to me.

That calm contentment did not last.

"Uncle César?"

"Hmm?" His voice sounded drowsy. He had had a long, exciting night of socializing and reconnecting with old friends and rivals. His tired, arthritic joints longed for the comfort of a goose-down duvet.

"Why is your BMW still here?"

His sleepy eyes followed my pointed finger to where Garth had parked to the side for an easy, early exit. To calm me and allow himself the fastest route to bed, Uncle César offered:

"You are certain he left? He does not wait for you?"

I nearly shoved Uncle César aside as I raced up to the bedroom. The desperation that I might see Garth sitting leisurely at the chessboard, studying it like a book not yet written, spurned me.

He would look up at me panting and my heart pounding furiously within my chest, and flash that innocent, dimpled smile asking what took me so long. He wouldn't have time to stand as I launched myself into his lap, squeezing him against me desperately and covering his face in lipstick stains.

But the lights remained off, and the room was empty when I flung the door open. I slumped against the frame. My legs not even able to support that, they buckled, and I sank to sit on the floor.

"Something happened." I didn't have the strength to lift my head as I spoke to the approaching Uncle César. "He only intended to make contact. What if something happened? What if *Barón* made him?"

My voice remained surprisingly steady and monotone as I spoke. The exhaustion of shock kept me from crumpling into hysteria.

Uncle César's knees popped, and his whole body groaned as he struggled to kneel beside me. "Maybe Garth changed his plan for a more effective strategy."

"No," I countered. "He wouldn't have changed anything without telling me." No longer able to speak in even the shocked monotone that had plagued my vocal cords upon finding the dark, empty room, I could only whisper. "He knew I would worry otherwise."

Uncle César understood the exponential joy and suffering that came part and parcel of marriage. Still, his wife had died peacefully of natural causes. He knew nothing of the horror that your own actions may have condemned the life of your beloved.

Worse still, when those deeds had been committed from a place of goodness and honor.

Though we knew nothing definitively, we both understood the character—or lack thereof—of *el Barón* to recognize the hazy, poorly spelled writing on the wall. Neither of us would speak the likely reality, but neither would we dismiss it. Uncle César offered the only advice he could think to give.

"Lay down and try to rest. I am sure he will return soon."

"I can't." My whispered voice slipped into further croakiness. The words tore at the inside of my throat. "For over two years, I've not had a single good night's sleep without feeling him beside me."

Tightening the arms he had wrapped around my shoulders, Uncle César summoned what strength remained in him to gently lift me from the floor.

"Come, then. Let us have some *chocolate caliente* to calm you down. It always worked when you were a girl." He smiled, trying desperately to force happier times into my mind.

His efforts failed.

"Where is he?"

"Protecting you. Come." He half-steered, half-dragged me to the kitchen.

The hot chocolate turned cold in my hands.

I sent Uncle César to bed around 5 o'clock that morning. He protested chivalrously, claiming he could never sleep while I wallowed in such distress. Though I did not doubt the sincerity of the sentiment in his claim, Uncle César no longer was as young as he used to be.

He had repeatedly dozed off a few seconds at a time while my hot chocolate cooled. He waved off these *siestas* with the insistence that he simply rested his eyes. He claimed his mind remained sharp as ever and would remain with me until my husband returned.

After much coercion concerning his health, promises that I would be fine while he rested for a few hours, and him nearly landing face-first in my congealed hot chocolate mug, Uncle César finally acquiesced going to bed.

Unable to withstand the solitude of a sleeping house, I made my way to my favorite spot in—or on—the villa. I had not lied when I took Garth to the tree and claimed it as my favorite place on the entire estate.

Still, there existed one spot that I loved even beyond the isolated tree within the bounds of the house itself. However, this new location would never be shared with anyone save those who sought to fetch me from it.

As a petulant, emotional, broody teenager incessantly accosted by hormones and a most unconventional upbringing, I had learned how to climb from the balcony up the exterior cobbled walls. I climbed onto the flat, red-tile roof for a view of the estate that not even Uncle César had ever seen.

My discovery that I could climb the wall and the subsequent initial trip were spurred by mere curiosity and a lack of proper climbing trees nearer the house. We quickly realized that Uncle César's muscled security could not ascend behind me without damaging the stones of the wall or their bodies without fetching a ladder.

I then began utilizing the roof as a place to escape where no one could touch or interrupt me. It also proved useful in spying. More accurately, it used to prove useful.

I pulled my legs in tight, wrapped my arms around the jeans I had changed into, and cradled my body against itself. Garth's t-shirt draped across my shoulders fluttered in the morning breeze. If only I had planned ahead, I could have used the roof for eavesdropping on anything happening within the annoyingly spy-proof balcony.

Why hadn't I thought through this better and prepared for all possible needs? You're better than this, Kati. This is the kind of work you literally get paid to do.

The clattering of a ladder attempting to balance along the uneven cobblestones interrupted my self-reprimanding. It didn't matter; I had the rest of my life to hate myself for whatever was happening to my husband.

"I thought I told you to go to bed?"

My words stabbed at Uncle César infinitely more sharply than the pangs in his chest as he huffed and puffed up the ladder. I refused to look at him or offer a steadying hand as he balanced himself on the top rungs.

He had never been adventurous or foolhardy enough to attempt to join me on the roof. Clinging to the ladder and mumbling Hail Mary's were sufficient exhilaration for him.

"You did."

His voice remained calm and gentle. I was no longer a moody teenager to be reprimanded, and he would gladly accept all the slings and arrows I shot at him in place of a proper target.

"Do you not see the sunrise? I slept for a full hour."

He was right. The sun had fully risen over the horizon, and day had dawned upon the world anew. Though I faced due east, I noticed none of it until Uncle César forced me to look. A ponderous silence hung in the air of that crisp, unobstructed morning.

Not knowing what to say but desperate for some sort of conversation, Uncle César commented how much time had passed since he last ascended the heights to fetch me. I made no response.

Then, just as I felt myself slipping into an inescapable depression at the assumed, but not yet accepted, loss of my husband, my phone rang. Miracle of miracles, the number displayed—

I made a habit early in my life of memorizing every number I needed to know and never saving any contacts in my phone.

—was that of Garth's cell phone.

"Garth!" I screamed his name into the receiver. "What happened? Are you alright? Are you safe? Why did you leave me? Where are you? Do I need to come get you?"

Silence met my breathless pleas.

"Garth?"

The silence stretched unbearably, further marring what should have been a pleasant morning with frozen tendrils of terror.

"Baby?"

"Special Agent Garth Harmon cannot come to the phone right now. Terribly sorry to offer you any sense of false hope."

El Barón's voice graveled across invisible wires connecting the satellites that my and Garth's specialized phones wielded for communication. He spoke calmly with no detectible emotion. An audible sneer would have made me feel better instead of that cold calculation.

"What have you done to him?" Though I tried to sound equally collected and menacing, my voice shook with every syllable.

"Nothing," he insisted. "As of yet."

"What do you want?"

"I should think it obvious; you stole something that I love, and I have now stolen something that you love. As a businessman, I am more than happy to make an equivalent exchange of goods."

"These are human beings you're talking about! People of flesh and blood, not goods or commodities to be traded!"

"And if you want your beloved husband to retain his flesh and blood, I suggest you return my daughter to me."

"I can't. I don't know where she is. I have no way of contacting her." I only partially lied.

"Then I suggest you tap into your husband's 'particular talent in findin' folk'." He mimicked Garth's exaggerated accent. "And I suggest you do it quickly. I make no promises on how long your darling will survive for a trade."

Deafening silence signaled *Barón* had terminated the phone call. I nearly dropped my phone off the roof in the residing shock.

"¿Hija?"

Uncle César's voice sounded muffled and distant. Blood swirled in my ears. It pounded around my brain as the world around me slipped into shades of bleeding crimson.

Long, barely controlled clouds of steam poured from my nostrils as the pressure boiled inside me. I stared beyond the sunrise to the unseen lair where *el Barón* kept captive my husband.

A red flag waved by *el Barón* taunted me. I mentally stomped my foot into the dirt, churning up dust and mud as I prepared to charge towards my inevitable doom.

Chapter Nineteen

In Which New Plans Began to Take Shape

The front door of the federal building slammed into the far edge of what its hinges could bear. The *crack* resounded through the high-ceilinged, tile atrium. Everyone halted midbreath to observe with the morbid fascination of watching a car accident. Three AR-15 barrels rose against me as four 9mm Glocks hesitated in various stages of drawn and aimed.

I paid them no mind, storming through the lobby with no regard for anyone who dared stand in my way.

Fortunately, my new friend, Gloria, manned the front security desk on that fateful morning. Nothing good would have happened had an unknown guard sat in her place. Someone who would have delayed me in my pursuit of recovering my husband.

What could have ensued would only have made matters worse and easily pinned me into a dangerous position of getting myself and Garth into trouble after his rescue. As Gloria pressed the button to unlock the gate and let me pass, the guns returned to their resting positions. The world steadily recovered to normalcy after the tornado that was me finished passing through.

I did not bother waiting for the elevator but sprinted up the stairs three at a time until I broke through the door of the fifth floor. Wearing tennis shoes and completing regular cardio training made the ascent easy enough. The rage-fueled adrenaline burning through my veins made up for any lack of stamina needed for the climb.

Continuing my invigorated march, I made a brief stop by the desk space. In no uncertain terms, I commanded the surprised Thad and Brynn to follow me. I did not hesitate or look back to ensure they did. Without pausing, knocking, or in any other way showing respect or seeking permission, I barreled directly into Moller's office.

"What the—!"

Moller, who already had someone in his office for a private meeting, did not take kindly to my interruption. Not that he ever appreciated my presence, as a general rule.

Thad and Brynn hovered beyond the door, unwilling to show the same brashness as me. Their heads poked around the frame. They reminded me of two schoolchildren hoping to watch someone receive their comeuppance but needing to retain a quick way of escape should the ire turn on them.

"*El Barón* has taken Agent Harmon hostage," I announced without hesitation or, surprisingly, emotion. In retrospect, I believe my adrenaline had hopped me up and drugged me so that my brain had no processing power left for any other emotion.

The room fell silent. The air swelled with a heaviness that constricted everyone's ability to breathe. Moller, Thad, and Brynn stared at me in shock. The unknown woman's—a lovely lady with the delicate features of an immediate Korean heritage—face ticked in a nervous fashion that pulled at the corner of her mouth to look almost like a smirk.

The brevity and avoidance that marked our first meeting meant I did not initially recognize her. Still, my skin prickled as the back of my mind recalled her countenance.

Moller recovered himself and turned to the woman sitting across from his desk. "Agent Hayes, if you would excuse us?"

"Of course." Her voice betrayed her as the one agent who ignored me when all others came to investigate the first rumors of my arrival.

She stood before Moller had finished. I felt her eyes linger on me as she passed closer than required to exit the room, but I paid her no mind. My focus remained locked on Moller.

"You two might as well come in," Moller told Thad and Brynn. "Close the door. What happened?"

I relayed in excruciating detail everything that occurred the day of the Gala—beginning with Garth's departure after he and I visited the tree. They learned everything about his conversation with *el Barón*, the cover he had used, and what I suspected he had in mind for how to manipulate and capture *el Barón*.

I told them of Garth's unplanned departure, how the borrowed car—I purposefully never described—remained at the villa, and the subsequent call from *Barón*. Not until recounting the phone call did I realize that *Barón* had referred to Garth as both a federal agent *and* my husband.

I left out the part about him being my husband to the team. Though I kept half my mind focused on the conversations, theories, and plans that Moller, Thad, and Brynn concocted, my mind whirled with the information I didn't reveal.

How does Barón *know so much about Garth? Hardly anyone knows both men that Garth is. Only Darcy and Uncle César, to be exact. Everyone else knows him as either my husband, who does general, nondescript work for the government, or FBI Agent Harmon. We've spent the last three years meticulously cultivating the world's perception of us. How does* Barón *know information not even our closest acquaintances do?*

Tabling my private thoughts for later and forcing myself back into the public discourse, I noticed that Thad looked at me like a dog listening to a high-pitched noise. Though he contributed to the dialogue, he spent most of the time staring at me, only occasionally glancing at the people he spoke with.

"Why do you look so confused?" I asked. "What are you staring at?"

"You!" he exclaimed as though bursting. "You look like a bum!" He gestured to all of me.

I still wore the oversized Braves t-shirt Garth had won at trivia night. It hung on me like a sack. Not even tattered enough to look sexily disheveled but just frumpy and like a potato. My jeans, also, were the same threadbare, faded things that had become more of lounge pants than anything appropriate to wear in public.

"I've never seen you dressed to anything less than aloof, curated perfection," Thad continued. "You look almost like a concerned human being."

"Oh," was all I could come up with to say.

I hadn't considered that my attire would raise questions about my motivations. I hadn't considered anything, really. Frankly, I'm proud of myself for wearing any clothes. The single track which consumed my mind blocked out all other thoughts, and I honestly would not have realized I wore no clothing until someone pointed it out.

Moller and Brynn now stared at me, as well. With the drastic change revealed for all to notice, they wanted an explanation. Struggling to buy myself time, I thanked Thad for his compliment on my typical state of dress. Unable to conjure any believable story that would not cause them to ask even further questions, I went with as much honesty as I could spare.

"Truthfully, I haven't gone home yet. I thought it pertinent to come straight here after landing."

The three quizzical faces that greeted my explanation caused me to question if I had chosen the wrong option. Needing to distance myself from the notion that I might *care* about Garth, I hurriedly continued.

"It seemed only fair play, after all. Seeing as how it's rather my fault that Garth—Agent Harmon, rather—was taken for ransom."

"Good!" Moller boomed. "I'm glad you seem to understand the gravity of your life choices. Maybe now you won't fight when I eventually get to arrest you."

I grimaced at Moller's logic. "I wouldn't go *that* far."

He only glared at me. Once the focus left me, I released a silent sigh.

That could've ended very *badly.*

"Our biggest obstacle is getting the Baron on US soil," Moller announced. "Until we do that, we have no jurisdiction to arrest him."

"You prepare the case to arrest and convict him. I'll get him on US soil," I promised.

"How?" Thad asked.

"*El Barón* wants his daughter..."

The words caught in my chest. They carried a terrible heaviness that made it difficult to force them upwards through my throat and out my mouth. I took a deep breath to steel myself and summon the strength to raise them.

"She has to be our bait."

"We can't do that!" Brynn protested. "If half of what Garth told us about her life before you was true, we cannot inflict that kind of trauma back on this poor girl."

She spoke with an unwavering authority that surprised me. Even Thad seemed mildly impressed. Moller seemed unfazed. I wondered if he was just that impassive or if he had seen this side of her before. My mind drifted back to Thad's comments nearly a month ago about the intense, secretive case that Garth and Brynn worked without him.

"She won't ever be in danger," I assured Brynn, bringing my mind back to the present puzzle. "I won't allow her to be. Neither would Garth. He would never allow himself to be traded for an innocent person."

Themselves so consumed by the task at hand, none of the agents reacted to the wistfulness I spoke of Garth with, nor the intimacy of his character I described.

Before they could reflect on my observations, Brynn demanded to know what I planned and how I could ensure the girl's safety.

"It's probably best that none of you know," I replied. "Legality and plausible deniability and all that."

After I set up everything with *Barón*, I'd call one of them with the details and their roles. Moller then dismissed Thad and Brynn to prepare all the paperwork and whatnot—my word, not his—for convicting the Baron and sending him to prison for a long time.

Moller caught me before I followed the others out. "Miss Bonnie. Whatever you're planning, if it goes wrong and you get caught, I can't offer you immunity for it."

His voice's sincerity and distinct lack of ire gave me pause. He wanted me to do whatever was necessary to rescue Garth, and he wished he had the authority to grant me the ability to do so.

"It doesn't matter," I assured him. "I'll do whatever it takes to save Agent Harmon."

I hovered in the doorway as his voice stopped me again.

"Why risk your freedom to save an FBI agent? Your profile suggests you value freedom and the unhindered ability to do whatever you want above everything else. Why take that risk?"

"I've grown surprisingly fond of the man, despite myself, and would hate to have his blood on my hands. As I'm sure you recall, I'm right proud of my spotless reputation."

I turned to make another attempt at leaving but halted mid-step. Twisting back to face Moller, I said, "I thought I didn't have a file?"

"If you thought I hadn't started building one the second you stepped into my office, you deserve to get caught."

Though he did his best to hide it, that was one of the few times I saw Moller smile. I proudly returned his concealed grin and tipped my head forward in a respect-of-rivals manner before finally making my way entirely out the door.

Standing in front of the doors waiting for my elevator, I yawned. The involuntary action surprised me as I considered everything that had befallen me in the past 48 hours.

Had it really been so long and *so short?*

My body no longer possessed any intuitive sense of time. My circadian clock had become lost somewhere in the Twilight Zone. Someone could have told me the Gala had happened 20 minutes or 20 months ago, and I would have readily believed either.

As the elevator *dinged* and I stepped on, another yawn made me realize that all my terror- and rage-fueled adrenaline had burned up. Garth remained in imminent danger, and I knew *el Barón* did not threaten people without the plans and desire to make good on those threats. My heart still palpitated from the worry of what sort of state I would find my husband returned to me.

That said, progress had been made, and I did have a plan of attack. Perhaps even more significant, I had an army to march with me into battle. Albeit a small army. But what had G.K. Chesterton once written? 'It is the fact that the only kind of hope that is of any use in a battle is a hope that denies arithmetic.'

Garth's team loved him and would do everything to rescue him and stop *Barón.* Couple that with my lovelorn reckless abandon, and I'd either get my husband back or die in the attempt.

As I descended alone in the elevator, my thoughts drifted to Moller's evaluation of me. Credit where credit is due, Moller's assessment of who I used to be and the persona I still displayed in most public appearances was spot on. Sporadic, spontaneous, solo trips without a note or word of my plans marked my relationship with Uncle César like a pox.

He once scolded me for it, saying I was never to travel to another country without telling him where I was going or when I might return. Those promptly fizzled out when it became clear I did not possess the biological component required to remember such instructions, and he ultimately conceded defeat.

Even Garth knows not to call and ask where I am unless 24 hours have passed without him having seen me or possessing prior knowledge of my plans. I always informed Garth of my timeline for work trips, and, as it turned out, I much preferred taking non-work trips with my husband.

By and large, I began to take my brief solo trips to force my husband and me to spend a night or two apart. I can confirm with the utmost confidence that absence makes the heart—and loins—grow fonder.

Much like Uncle César, Garth once protested these departures. Garth also came to abandon his quest, but for reasons far removed from Uncle César's. More than once, he even turned my own tactics against me. I initially thought it very rude for him to force me to swallow a taste of my own medicine.

It didn't take long to discover how bitters can delightfully enhance a drink.

Chapter Twenty

In Which Remembering was the Final Stage of the Pleasure

Two Years Earlier...

A few months after we had married, Garth sent me a text message that his day at work was blisteringly hot and stale, and he would require a great deal to drink upon his arrival at the condo. We had recently acquired it to make his commute easier and for hosting socials, so he wanted to ensure that I would be there. He had no interest in wasting valuable time on excess commuting.

Because I am a terrible human being who gets my jollies from watching others suffer, I blatantly ignored my husband's instructions. I decided to take an overnight trip to my favorite mountain spa. Well, my favored one in Georgia, anyway. Switzerland would have taken much too long for the joke to work. I left him a note on the bar:

'*Your talk of grueling work made me feel rather desperate for some proper pampering. I shall return tomorrow after I have been satisfied. Until we meet again.*'

My only sadness came in my inability to see my new husband's face when he read my note. My husband had paid enough attention to my moods to safely assume that I would return from my relaxing spa trip just as thirsty as he had been. Armed with this knowledge, he decided, for the first time, to give me a taste of my own medicine.

Upon arriving home the following evening feeling pampered and ready to engage in marital bliss, I discovered one missing component required for my desires. My husband was not present. Thinking he might still be at work or had gone to the manor, I called his good phone to inquire of his whereabouts.

The granite countertop in our kitchen echoed the mocking lyrics informing me that I couldn't always get what I wanted. I narrowed my eyes at the inanimate object, staring beyond it to the boy it represented with appropriate levels of disdain.

'As I'm sure you've noticed, I am intentionally unavailable when you most desire me. I'm confident you recognize and appreciate the irony of my actions and accompanying ringtone.'

The phone shrieked with that most annoyingly shrill beep signifying the end of his voicemail greeting.

"You bastard," was all I could manage to say. Despite my furiousness with my husband, I smiled as I cursed him.

He knew that only I had the number to call the satellite phone I had provided him shortly after becoming engaged. As such, he could record the tease-specific voicemail message without alarming anyone else into raising questions.

The brazenness of his table-turning and inherent consummate skill with which he played the game only heightened my desire.

Delayed gratification, indeed.

When Garth finally returned home the following day, I sat at the far end of the main room in my most prudish, schoolmarmish attire reading *The Merry Wives of Windsor.* Rather, my clothing would have appeared stuffy and strict had I worn a longer skirt, pantyhose, and properly buttoned my shirt.

The black mini skirt, bare legs, and red lingerie peeking out beneath my white blouse added sexiness to the prudish outfit. My glasses and hair pinned into a bun properly fit the role, at least.

"You certainly did spend a significant amount of time at the office over the past two days," I scolded without looking up from my book as my erring husband entered the room.

"Did you even leave the building last night," I lifted my eyes from the page to glare at him over the rim of my superficial reading glasses, "or did you just sleep at your desk?"

"I'd never dream of sleeping at my desk," he corrected as he dropped his briefcase onto the counter with more force than strictly required. "We do have cots available for those agents who require them."

Unaware of this fact, the reveal took me by surprise. "Really?" I asked, entirely breaking character.

He only nodded the confirmation.

"Huh." Needing to reengage my enemy so as not to lose this battle of wits, I cleared my throat, returned to my not-actually-reading, and accused, "And is that where you passed the night?"

"Heaven's no." Having shed his jacket, Garth collapsed onto the couch beside my chair and began loosening his tie. "I went for a night on the town with one of my bachelor coworkers. It was quite an entertaining excursion."

"I suppose you ended up somewhere one could safely consider the utmost of class? The Claremont Lounge, perhaps?" I hissed the name with a truly appropriate level of disdain.

As anyone from Atlanta knows, the concept of 'class' and the 'Clermont Lounge' ought never be uttered in the same sentence. My response caused an honest chortle from my husband, which, in turn, elicited a smile from me. Both of our façades broken, we quickly buried our mutual smiles to properly continue the game.

"And what of you?" Garth accused. "What happened to you that first night, which set all this in motion?"

"You dare try to blame this on me!" I snapped. "I had an appointment to maintain. The likes of you"—I gave him a once-over seething with manufactured disdain—"was certainly not enough to keep me from my massage."

"Is that so? Well, I will let you know that while my coworker and I may not have ended up at the Claremont, we did have dinner at Twin Peaks."

For those in the class unaware, Twin Peaks is a restaurant that follows much the same business model as Hooters, only impressively leaving even less to the imagination. The food, however, is actually quite delicious.

I exaggerated my scoff at this revelation of dinner locales.

"And!" Garth interjected into my scoff. He sat up straight, scooting himself to the edge of the couch with an air of puffing out his chest and sticking out his chin.

"Both our waitress *and* the bartender were extremely interested in me and spent the whole evening flirting. They even offered me one of their calendars at a discounted rate. I actually considered taking off my wedding band for the meal."

That proved the final straw. With such a perfect opening, I could no longer withstand the playing of the game. It had come time for me to win.

Closing my book, I set it on the coffee table with the controlled grace of one too elegant to let their temper get the better of them and stood from my chair. Finally able to see me in the full glory of my sexy teacher costume, I heard Garth's breath hitch as I took a deep breath and pushed my cleavage forward.

"Tell me, dear, faithful husband, did those other women and their calendar really entice you?"

I shoved his back against the couch, opening his lap to sit on. Lowering myself to comfortably straddle his legs, I instantly noted that his hindered breath had not been his only reaction to my attire.

"Only in a general, conceptual sense," he teased back, pulling my hips firmly into his.

One of my heels clattered to the floor.

"Oh?"

I withdrew the pins from my bun, allowing my currently chestnut-colored hair to cascade down my back. Garth tangled his fingers in the soft lushness as he ran his fingertips up and down my spine.

"Only when I imagine you wearing those uniforms and posing in their positions. Then I start to think about all the marvelous things I would do to you."

"What sorts of things might those be?"

He removed his hands from my back to further unbutton my shirt and kissed my décolletage. My second heel bounced noisily along the floor as my toes curled. Unsatisfied with what I had pre-exposed, my husband set his fingers to wholly unbuttoning and discarding my blouse.

My head lolled backward as my husband buried his face in the abundance of my chest. He split his lips with his tongue, expertly utilizing every aspect of his mouth in his kisses. Delectable friction built between us as my hips rocked in response.

The final button undone, Garth pushed away the fabric, letting it slide down my arms and crumble on the floor around my discarded shoes. My husband was no longer willing to deny himself the tantalizing pleasures of partially-clothed foreplay.

He made short work of that mutually beloved, front-clasped, red bra. No sooner had it joined my other clothing on the floor than I snapped my fingers interlaced behind his head and held on for dear life. With no hindrances, Garth had moved to take all of me that could fit between his lips.

His diligent and expert use of flicking the tip of his tongue made me limp. My back arched as my head lolled further. I pressed my breasts upward so we might both enjoy Garth having his fill of me. Returning a hand to my back, Garth pulled me towards him, my chest pressed firmly against him.

His lips, unable to reach my breasts, accommodated his desires by leaving a line of nibbles along my neck. Letting his fingertips tickle the exposed skin of the small of my back, he drew designs leading to the hem of my black mini skirt.

Cupping a firm hold of my posterior, my husband lifted me from his lap to dump me on my back between him and the couch. Without those pesky heels in the way, Garth slid off my skirt with the slightest ease.

"I know you've just returned from the spa," his voice vibrated against my throat, "but how about I give you a *full* body massage?"

Before I could respond, Garth scooped me in his arms and carried me upstairs. He rejected my kisses as he climbed the stairs, opting to look to avoid dumping us across the faux-marble flooring. Once again on level ground, we passed a long moment without forward progress as our lips needed to make up for lost time.

"You haven't got any massage oils, have you?" he asked, returning me to my feet upon reaching the bedroom.

"You were serious about that massage?"

He nodded. "What did you think I meant?"

I stared at him precisely as I should for such an idiotic question. "Sex?"

He paused from his diligent work of folding down the bedcovers and gave a slight hum as though considering the option for the first time. Garth continued with his work.

"All in good time. First, you must remind me why I didn't flirt with those waitresses."

My head tilted further in confusion. "Isn't that more reason for sex? Or why I should massage you?"

The smile my husband flashed over his shoulder almost made me orgasm.

"What am I going to do with you?" I sighed.

Stepping away from the turned-down bed, he pressed his lips against mine. "A great many wonderful things." With one hand cupping a boob and the other squeezing my butt, it was neither a suggestion nor a request.

He let go and patted the bed. "Lay down. I'm gonna change."

I did as instructed but not as intended. My husband froze as he emerged from the bathroom in pajama pants and no shirt to see me lying on my back with my legs positioned invitingly.

"On your stomach. I can't massage your back while you're laying on it."

"But there are other things you can massage."

I resigned as he looked at me with loving exasperation.

"While I'm not complaining, I am terribly confused," I told my husband as he rubbed my shoulders. "Why, when you insist that I am the one who needs to atone, are you the one doing all the work?"

His hands moved down my back as Garth took a moment to respond. Once he did, he spoke with the tone and tenor as one giving an objective, scientific TED talk.

"Sex is like most things in life: preplanning and preparation are key to an optimal experience. Every wise man understands he must properly romance a woman to achieve the most sublime sex. And the man who refuses to be lazy will never regret it."

"And you know this from all your vast experience with women?"

"I am a very quick study." His hands glided across my exposed backside but did not grasp or linger on his way to my legs. "Don't worry your gorgeous self; you will atone."

His firm, capable hands lured me into an extraordinary level of relaxation and comfort that muddled my brain and kept me from responding for several minutes. Though I'm sure the trained masseuse did a markedly better job working out the knots and improving my circulation and flexibility, I had no doubts I would feel immensely more relaxed by the time my husband finished his work with me.

Finally remembering myself and continuing with Garth's stern teacher voice, I asked, "Are you my tutor, then? Schooling me so I might excel when the exam arrives?"

"I guess you can think of it like that."

"And, of course, the better the student performs, the more it pleases the teacher."

"I hadn't even thought of that."

"I'm sure."

His massaging of my feet lulled me into another silent appreciation. Though still desiring the initially expected sex, I couldn't complain about my second massage.

"When is this all-important exam to occur?" My words tumbled out with drowsy relaxation that belied my desire.

If Garth isn't careful, he might relax me out of my thirstiness...

"I'm afraid you still don't understand."

With the way his hands caressed my hips, I was quickly losing all sense of understanding.

"This exam is not a one-and-done situation." Garth instructed me to finally lay on my back with a gentle squeeze and slight twisting. His hands gladly supported my posterior with not strictly required aid as I flopped over.

I don't care how hard one tries; some movements simply cannot be made sexy. But he didn't seem to mind.

Standing at the foot of the bed, Garth returned to massaging my feet. "This exam takes a very long time and requires multiple sits to complete."

Using that massage as pretense, my husband yanked me towards him. My naked body slid across the sheet with the greatest of ease.

...Or not.

"And as all good teachers know," I said, "the best preparation comes from doing. If it pleases the professor, I believe I'm ready to take my first mock exam."

He clicked his tongue at me. "Patience, wifey." He left my feet, walked to the head of the bed, and crawled up. "I'll let you know when you're ready."

My husband spread his legs and gently pulled my head into his lap. There was quite a lump in my pillow, but his massaging of my temples felt divine.

"Can't have you getting in over your head before you're ready to swim. I'm going to make sure you're so overly prepared for your exam that you won't be able to stand your eagerness to take it."

"Heightening the delayed gratification?" I muttered in more relaxed drowsiness.

His hands traveled down my neck and across the top of my chest. He stopped short of my breasts.

"Now you've got it."

"You are too quick of a study, indeed. But don't think I'm confusing all these good things with altruism; I know you're doing this out of self-interest."

"Whatever makes you say that?"

My breath caught as he finally let his hands massage my breasts.

"The firmness of my pillow," I sighed.

My whole body shook with his chuckle, and I have never felt a sensation more wonderful. But enough was enough. I knew my husband and I had each other good and primed. I rolled over, carefully avoiding any parts I would soon need.

Garth smiled at me, equal parts joyous and ravenous. I smiled back in kind. One elbow balanced me while the other hand worked to slide down my husband's pajama pants. His excitement no longer contained, I lowered myself back to the bed and set about with my first test of atonement.

Up and down, my head bobbed like those Chinese birds drinking water. But, unlike those mechanical birds, my well did not run empty. My husband moaned with delight, listing my articles of penance.

Satisfied with the results of my first subject, it came time for me to take a break and for Garth to sit his first exam. We shimmied his pajama pants off. His lips and tongue began at my neck and worked their way down to the junction of my legs, taking no short time to linger at my breasts.

Each flick of his tongue and pucker of his lips brought a new article of penance from my own mouth. He quickly began work fulfilling those desires as his mouth reached that junction. I felt him smile with each greater arching of my back.

His goodly work complete, we longed for nothing more than the mutual giving of ourselves to each other. With no time to lose, his mouth leapt the length of my body to join with mine. He filled the space left by his lips as our tongues filled each other's mouths.

Gasping for air, yanking our lips together, grinding our hips, we eliminated all space between us. Our bodies and souls melted and reformed into one. Prayers of thanksgiving poured forth from every pore as every aspect delighted in each other.

When the pleasure became too rapturously sweet, we cried each other's name in one voice, together proclaiming all our indiscretions forgiven.

Garth and I awoke together from our post-coital slumber. Nuzzled against him and using his chest for my pillow, I felt his stirring.

"Good morning," he whispered.

Wisps of my hair trembled under his breath. Garth brushed them aside as I looked up at him.

"Good morning," I whispered back.

Letting my head rest again on his chest, my husband took to kissing my hair while his fingertips slid all over my naked shoulder, side, and hip. That lightest touch excited and delighted me perhaps more than last night's entire erotic massage.

I pressed my body into his and sighed at the pleasure of his touch. We remained in this lackadaisical pleasure, watching the sun rise with half-open eyes.

"Do you really want me to pose like those women?" I wondered as sunlight began lightening the room.

"What women?"

I smiled at his honest reply. I never worried that Garth had looked at their provocative calendar or considered removing his wedding ring like he'd teased me. I knew no woman could ever compete with me, not out of my own arrogance but because my husband had repeatedly assured me. Still, hearing him respond with complete forgetfulness about any other woman made me smile.

"Your waitresses from the other night. You really want me to pose like they do in their calendar?"

He hugged me tightly and kissed my head.

"You know I never saw those poses." His tone was neither defensive nor derogatory. It even lilted with an unrealized laugh.

"I do," I assured him, snuggling in tighter. "But that doesn't mean we can't design our own."

Pushing off his chest, I rose to meet my husband's lips. He wrapped his caressing arm around me, drawing our lips closer. Loathe to part our lips and tongues, I had to for a more extraordinary pleasure than kissing.

My husband did not look at me with sadness when I gently pulled away. He had learned I could only deny him to give him something better. I brushed my fingers through his hair.

"Shall we?"

Garth nodded almost imperceptibly. Flashes of anticipation once again danced across his mind. I smiled at the calm look of deep passion swirling in those cinnamon eyes. Like watching from shore as a storm brewed on the horizon.

You couldn't see the intensity swirling and building, but you could feel it deep in your blood. And when that storm finally made landfall, you knew it would consume you with its beautiful power, leaving you breathless in its wake. But unlike the ravaging, merciless storm, this consuming culmination was mutual and life-giving.

Just because we still played our game of atonement didn't mean both of us wouldn't also wholly give ourselves time after time after time.

"Go get your camera," I whispered.

He smiled again, then slid out of bed to fetch his equipment from downstairs. I lay on the bed for a moment considering my outfit choices. The photo shoot would, of course, end without clothing, but we couldn't start with nothing to build something.

We must begin with clothes—perhaps only lingerie—then work to less clothing. Next, utilizing bedsheets in place of clothing until we finally returned to nothing, where the only thing that covered me would be Garth's own naked muscles.

When my husband returned, I lounged on the bed wearing matching black lace bra, panties, and a black silk nightgown. A pair of heels sat on the floor beside the bed. I hadn't decided if I wanted to go through the effort of those. He stopped in the doorway to admire the view.

"I must say how appreciative I am of your recent fashion sense."

"What? This old thing?" I waved away the compliment with a nondescript aristocratic accent.

"That is no old thing," my husband corrected. He fiddled with his camera and took a few test shots for lighting and focus. "That is the set you bought for me for our one-month anniversary."

He set the camera down, freeing both hands for more important matters.

"No," I mock protested as Garth crawled onto the bed atop me. "I've washed this outfit far too many times to have only had it for a few months."

"We've made good use of it during those few months."

Our intertwined tongues kept me from any reply. Capitalizing on his lips moving to my neck, I asked:

"Aren't you going to take your pictures?"

Garth's kisses didn't pause as he wondered, "Why bother when I have the real thing right here?"

"What is it they say? 'Take a picture; it'll last longer'?"

Not that length or duration have ever been an issue.

"Maybe, but I prefer the fleetingness of the interactive experience."

He paused long enough to move his lips back to mine and enjoy a handful of boob. As he moved his attentions back to my neck, my head lulled to the side. The sun streamed through the floor-to-ceiling windows in a wonderful way that made one glad to be in the world. My naked husband helped with that sentiment. But the sunlight was genuinely beautiful.

"Darling, if we don't start now, we'll lose our lighting. You don't want to waste the golden hour, do you?"

He lifted his head to meet my gaze. The golden flakes in his eyes showed intense anticipation, reminding me why I'd had to wash these clothes so often.

"I have another idea for spending our golden hour, and, I promise you, it will not be wasted."

My back arched as the hand fondling my breast moved to explore the other piece of this lingerie set.

"But if you have your heart set on a calendar shoot..."

If all my mental acuity hadn't been turned to mush, I would've caught Garth's hand as it slipped away from my panties and not let him leave that bed. But by the time I recovered the slightest hint of consciousness, my husband had moved beyond my reach and taken his camera in hand to set up our first shot.

I started innocently enough with poses sitting on various areas of the bed. Leaning against the backboard, I opted for the innocently erotic with joyous smiles and my lingerie fully covered. I channeled the advertising campaign of a department store that wanted to look 'family-friendly sexy' as they displayed their new loungewear and the joys of a lazy morning in bed.

Moving to the edge of the bed, my cleavage made less of an implied appearance as I let the negligee part where it would. A series of poses leaning forward and resting my chin on my hand shifted the sexiness from homely to classy.

Next came poses lying on my side with my arm draped seductively over my waist. Then on my back, with my hands over my head and my hair sprawling in sexy dishevelment. A combination of legs straight or knees bent kept us in those poses longer.

I think Garth enjoyed the negligee falling out of my control in such poses. My cleavage becoming less and less concealed didn't dampen his spirits. Tired of fighting with the negligee, I discarded it altogether.

Slowly.

The shutter clicked at a frantic pace. My husband tried capturing every sensual moment of the silk draping off my shoulders, sliding down my arms, and pooling discarded around my hips as an invitation. My lip bite shifted to a smile as I collected the negligee and threw it at the camera.

With better skill than I could've asked for, the silk caught perfectly on the camera body to drape entirely over the lens and block further photos.

"Very cute," he smirked.

"Aren't I, though?"

Using the negligee as a silk covering, Garth wrapped it around the camera and set them aside.

"You can't be done yet," I teased. "You can usually go for so much longer."

"We aren't done. Not with photos or anything else."

He crawled onto the bed, but I refused to lay back and slide under him as before.

"How many more photos did you have in mind?"

Since I wouldn't lean back, he pressed his body against mine, forcing me to submit. I clenched my abs and fought back, thinking how excellent a core exercise this would make.

"You have at least three more outfits."

Garth's chest muscles tightened against my breasts, and I desperately wanted to fall back in total surrender. But like waiting for water to boil before adding the tea bag, we needed to let this pot simmer a little longer. And the game was just too darn fun.

"Those being?"

"What you're wearing now. Then less."

He lifted his pressure to place one slow kiss on each breast. My relaxed core gave way, so I sank to my elbows, whether I willed it or not.

Garth smiled. I knew I was done.

"And less."

His lips pressed against my hip bone above the edge of my lace panties. My sigh was not intended. Nor was my sinking further onto the bed. Nor the arching of my back as he left a trail of kisses up my stomach, between my breasts, and back to my lips.

"And maybe use the sheet for good measure."

My eyelids fluttered with his whispered breath.

"We have to remake the bed, anyway."

He wasn't wrong; the sheet we had tangled up and cast aside last night would make for an easy cover. I found my wits and words with no insignificant amount of effort.

"Why'd you stop if there's so many more pictures to take?"

Garth lifted his lips from where they caressed the nape of my neck. "You're the one who hindered my equipment."

I raised myself again to my elbows. My husband graciously moved with me.

"Something else I'll have to atone for?"

He nodded.

This time, Garth did not control himself but used the muscular superiority of his chest to press my back flat on the bed. But muscular superiority didn't mean absolute superiority, and I used my chest to remind him of that.

Not unlike the rat in that Disney movie, I discovered the surprising ease of controlling someone significantly stronger than yourself when you've got your fingers intertwined in their hair. Using that delicious leverage, I directed my husband to roll over, switching our positions.

Even contained—mostly—in a bra, Garth appreciated the reversal of my chest pressing into his. He did not, however, appreciate my pulling away and sitting up.

"Come on, then," I said. "I won't dress up for you again if you undress me now." My smile told my husband I clearly lied, but he accepted the ruse.

I repeated many of my poses from before: sitting on the edge of the bed, chin resting on my hand; laying across the bed on my side, my arm cocooned in the curve of my waist; and so forth.

Most of these poses returned for a braless third appearance. Perhaps a boring model for any proper photographer or photo shoot, my husband made neither protest nor complaint about my limited modeling range.

Utilizing Garth's bathroom break, I shimmied off my panties, grabbed the bedsheet from the floor, and wrapped myself up. I had only just finished my burrito-ing when he emerged.

Garth looked from me to my discarded unmentionables, back to me, gave the sheet a once over, and looked as though the school bully had just told him Santa isn't real.

My darling husband has always found such joy in unwrapping his presents. Not only as a prelude to sex. I think he genuinely enjoys taking my clothes off. Which is precisely why I had instructed him to remove my bra for me.

He wasted no time in gently unfastening the front clasp. Altruistic as ever, my husband felt it only right to use his hands to replace my bra's support. I unintentionally leaned backward as his thumbs and fingertips explored that tender tissue again.

No matter the countless times he had and would caress my breasts, my body's delightfully sensitive response to my husband's touch never ceased nor faded. So, when he found me fully shucked and wrapped in a sheet, Garth did feel I had cheated him of a bit of his fun.

Raising puppy dog eyes to mine, he said, "You skipped an outfit." His voice had the tone and tenor of that same Santa-less boy finding no presents under his Christmas tree.

With an exaggerated sigh, I confessed, "It seems I have many faults I need to apologize for."

The disappointed dejection in his eyes faded rapidly.

"Can't imagine why you'd ever marry such a problematic woman."

Garth's face lit up anew with Christmas come early. He leapt the few feet from the bathroom to the bed, tackling me down with him. My teasing smile turned to unadulterated joy and giggling. Brushing my disheveled hair from my face, my husband educated me.

"She must've had some impressive positives for me to overlook all those problems. But I'm not sure I didn't underestimate those problems and overestimate those positives."

"Pretty sure that's a double negative."

Undeterred by the thin sheet, Garth returned his hands to the enjoyment of boob. "Pretty sure that's a double positive."

I scoffed and squirmed at his ridiculous pun and terrible pillow talk.

"Aren't you going to take the rest of your pictures?" I asked when he showed no signs of stopping his enjoyment a second time.

Garth's eyes shone as he shook his head. "And I won't be robbed again."

His fingers moved from my breasts to where I'd tucked the bedsheet into itself like a towel. They found the edge of the sheet and slowly followed it down, pushing the fabric aside.

Putting on my most ignorant, innocent voice, I asked, "Robbed of what?"

With the sheet pushed fully aside, my husband proceeded most unexpectedly. Instead of using his fingers or tongue to get his due, he rolled us around until the open sheet wrapped around him. He had successfully burrito-ed us together in a bedsheet cocoon.

"I must confess, this is not where I expected that to go," I told my husband. But laying against his body with his arms wrapped around me was not an unpleasant alternative.

Our entire cocoon shrugged with him. "I know."

I sighed in utter contentment. This man kept me on my toes in the most delightful of ways, and I couldn't help but love him for it.

"Whatever am I to do with you?"

Garth cocked his head. "Thought we already discussed that last night."

Lowering my lips to his, I whispered, "Remind me what we said."

For untold moments in which could have passed hours, days, or years we stayed wrapped securely around each other with our bodies pressed tight and cozy and kisses abounding. I could have spent my whole life in that moment and never grown tired of it or had enough of my amazing husband.

The morning ended the same way as it began: a quiet, comfortable intimacy that flowed with natural gentility into lovemaking like a river into the sea. The mountain stream it began as took its time babbling over rocks and traipsing through the meadows, sometimes winding far beyond a straight path to explore somewhere new.

The stream had no worry about reaching the sea, for it knew there was nowhere else it could possibly end. It would achieve this most natural of conclusions in good time and delight just as fully in enjoying the journey to its climax.

The sheet gradually fell away as our bodies rocked and settled against each other. His hands slid down my back to caress my curves. My hands gripped the muscles of his arms as his fingertips traced the outline of my hips. I ran my fingers through his hair.

He wrapped his leg around mine, and I delighted in the entanglement. As our positions switched, we left the sheet behind; the fire rushing through our veins and our hearts beating in time kept us plenty warm.

"I love you, my husband."

"I love you, my wife."

Garth's back flexed under my fingers; mine arched at his entrance. Our sighs and moans filled the morning like sunlight streaming through the windows: warm, renewing, and glorious. Our delight in each other became palpable as our pleasure built and built.

Holy incense flooded the air, the bed, our very bodies and souls as they mingled, intertwined, and became one. Bodies and hearts pulsed in time as the mountain stream surged into a mighty river, finally making its long-desired arrival in the sea. The storm and stream met with such fearsome beauty that no force could contain it.

I lay beside my husband, our bodies still tucked tightly together. Our chests heaved, and the sunlight showed a glean of sweat across our bodies. It didn't matter, though. No imperfection could spoil the ecstasy of this moment.

My racing heart had barely begun to calm when I lifted my body onto his and pressed myself closer. I kissed his face, his neck, his chest, his lips. I kissed every inch of his body my lips could reach. Garth's eyes watched me with amazement, but over my stamina or his luck... who's to say?

An amazing thing about the sea: no matter how many times a river flows into it, it never becomes full.

Chapter Twenty-One

In Which I Implored for a Terrible Sacrifice

The tires of my Porsche Cayenne crunched over the gravel that demarcated the parking lot of Grace Gospel Church from the dirt road wandering beside it. The charcoal paint job of my car had become spackled with brown dust, covering the vehicle from bow to stern. After retrieving my husband, I'd have to find a car wash somewhere in this Podunk town so I might restore my Porsche to its proper glory.

For now, though, a bit of dirt seemed more than a fair price to pay for having my husband returned to me. After all, I never expected to make it out of this predicament without getting my hands dirty.

Grace Gospel Church looked precisely as I recalled from my only visit two years ago. The white paint remained cracked and chipped in the same places, while the clock beneath the belfry still sat stalwartly at 0940. The atomic clock in my car read 1125.

The church consisted of the chapel and a single back hallway leading to three classrooms, one serving as the nursery, and a fellowship hall the size of my condo's kitchen. They had converted a broom closet at the front of the chapel into a reception area, but it sat empty.

As though time had not progressed in this sleepy hamlet, the frail, white-haired pastor still stood at his pulpit, enraptured in his notes and scripture as he prepared for next week's sermon. I can't recall on which passage his monologue centered during either trip. I feel like I ought to know.

Though he expected only one other person on the property at that time—a doddering blue hair who acted as church secretary—the pastor still wore a coat and tie. A product of generations who took to heart John Wesley's infamous proclamation that cleanliness is next to godliness, this gentleman had probably never stepped foot inside a church without wearing a suit in half a century.

Because I don't know how to enter a building—especially one in which I am unexpected—in anything but absolute silence, the pastor had no knowledge of his audience. As I moved closer to the pulpit, my Converse-clad feet fell silently along the single red strip of faded, worn down carpet that bisected the two columns of pews.

Still unnoticed when I crossed the halfway point, I made my presence known. "Pastor?"

He looked up but did not act startled. I wondered how frequently his parishioners sought personal guidance beyond Sunday mornings.

"Hi, sorry to interrupt, I'm not sure if you'll remember me—"

"How could I forget?" he asked, removing his reading glasses from the edge of his nose. He laid them atop his open Bible before twisting closed the cap of his fountain pen and placing it on the outcropping holding his legal pad in place.

"A little country church like this don't get too many people droppin' off terrified twelve-year-old girls lookin' for safety and a good home." Even without projecting, the singsong tenor of an accent also frozen in time rang crisply through the wooden rafters.

With a reassuring smile containing no flash, only genuine interest, he said, "Though I would like to actually learn your name at some point."

When I did not respond, he continued, "What brings ya here, now? I would ask if you've come to hear one of my convictin' sermons, but you're a few days early."

I paused a moment longer. Not out of desire but necessity. I struggled to speak more during that autumn than in any one season for the rest of my life.

Finally, I muttered, "I've come for the girl." Trusting the pastor wouldn't cave at that simple request, I told him, "I need to speak to her."

The elderly man straightened his decaying spine. He peered at me with stolid eyes over the impermeable, mahogany podium.

"As I recall, you were very adamant that we never see each other 'gain, an' you know nothin' 'bout the child's whereabouts."

I could not lift my head to meet his stare.

"Yes, I was."

"What's changed?"

"I need her help."

"Ain't nobody else can help?" The pastor had lost the singsong cadence of his voice. Each word came as a sharp, detached sting.

Eviscerated by his condemnation, I whispered, "Unfortunately, no."

I heard him exhale slowly. My eyes lifted just enough to see the reprimand burning through his gaze. Instead, he had shrunk back down to his usual frail form and observed me with tempered sympathy. He motioned with his hand, inviting me to sit in the nearest pew. As I did so, he carefully began descending the few stairs of the altar.

"Ya know, in the time she been here, she still ain't told me nothin' 'bout her life 'fore you brought her here. I don't know what you took her from, how it happened, how on earth you ended up here," he opened up his arms, gesturing at the overall isolation of his parish, "or anythin' of the sort.

"But I do know that she regards you, whoever you may be, as her personal hero. She's asked numerous times to try gettin' in contact with you. But each time I told her that, for her own safety, you two couldn't never see nor talk to each other ever 'gain."

"And I know that," I announced, standing from my seat. "There is nothing I value more than her continued safety and peace of mind—"

"Well, there must be somethin' you value more if you've come here willin' to risk that continued safety."

I sank back into my pew.

Steadily closing the distance between us, the pastor wondered, "What do you need her for? What do you want?"

I forced my head to rise and meet his wrinkled eyes.

"I want my husband back."

The old man sank into the pew beside me. I couldn't tell if his reaction came in response to the effort required for him to sit without collapsing or from my answer.

"Of everythin' you could say, it had to be that."

I received my answer, though I didn't understand it. My head cocked, and my eyes crinkled on their own accord as I stared at the side of the pastor's face. For once, he did not look at me. No doubt, years of counseling granted him the third eye to recognize my confusion.

He explained, "She's often talked 'bout marriage an' her desire to find a husband who will care for her, protect her, an' make her a better woman than before she found him." He lifted a finger with joints gnarled from a lifetime of hard work, belying the idea that he only ever offered a metaphorical hand.

"Now, the 'mazin' thing is that she started talkin' 'bout those sorts of things shortly after she got here. Ain't many pastors I know who've had twelve-year-old girls talk to them 'bout marriage with such reverence and respect. Most of 'em wanna find a prince or a popstar and still view love and marriage as a fairytale."

"Her ability to see life as a fairytale was stolen from her," I informed him. "She does not have the luxury of innocence."

He nodded sagely. I could see him wandering through his memory palace. He'd recorded and cataloged every scrap of information granted him as he patiently worked to unpuzzle his flock.

"All the more surprisin' that she should speak with such maturity and admiration. Most children of comp'rable circumstances have a painfully skewed view of life an' cannot understand what it ought be with such clarity."

I wanted to ask him more questions about how he knew these things and how a man of seemingly surprising education ended up way out here in the sticks. Time, however, was of the essence, so I made the painful concession of forcing myself to remain on topic.

"Why are you telling me this?"

He turned to meet my gaze, and I didn't pull mine away. "I am explainin' to you why I'm ignorin' your first orders in favor of this new request, which goes directly against what you initially asked of me."

My eyes crinkled at him again. "Your explanation did very little to explain."

He smiled at me. "You ain't the first person to accuse me of bein' longwinded. Just ask any of my parishioners on a pretty Sunday."

I couldn't keep myself from chuckling at his goodhearted humor. I then understood how he could correct and protect someone in a single conversation. He returned to the serious matter at hand.

"She said neither of you talked much during the relocation ordeal. Even if you did, she don't remember. She says she don't remember nothin' 'bout that time. Only bein' where she started then wakin' up here and findin' a new family. But what she remembers, with the utmost clarity, is your answer when she asked why you were helpin' her. You said—"

" 'The inherent goodness of the man I love has convicted me to no longer turn a blind eye.' "

"An' that's what she wants. She wants a man to love and to love her, where the two of them will be iron sharpenin' iron. If she ever learned that your husband was in danger, she had the ability save him, an' we didn't let her try," he shook his head, "ain't none of us would ever hear from that girl 'gain.

"Now!" he clapped his hands on his knees before grasping the pew in front of us to help him stand. "You wait right here, an' I go give 'em a call. Make sure they home an' all."

"Thank you," I breathed. My hushed tone no longer arose from shame but an overwhelming sense of relief. I had moved one step closer to retrieving my husband.

Which reminds me.

"How long have you been the pastor here?"

Having shuffled his way back to the altar steps, he proudly announced, "Thirty years, next week."

"Then you'll understand why I chose your church."

He took half a step towards me. His tired eyes sparkled at a question he had held onto for over three years.

"My name is Mrs. Garth Harmon."

Just as I had hoped, that name meant a great deal to the old man. His body straightened with a sharp intake of breath. He held that breath for several moments as his mind raced to process this new information. Finally, bringing his eyes back into focus, he steadied himself.

"Anythin' any of us can do to help you save Garth, you just say the word. Everyone here loved him dearly."

I nodded a sad smile. I had condemned this remarkable man to the weight of my terrible choice. Suddenly, he no longer solicited advice about a hypothetical situation.

Without understanding anything about the particulars, I knew the pastor recognized that I played chicken with two people's lives. If I found myself inexplicably lucky, both of those lives—and my heart—would make it out safely.

Evening approached. The sinking sun bathed the rolling hills of central Alabama in a honey glow as the sky exploded in a kaleidoscope of color. Billowing clouds heavy with collecting rain towered from beneath the horizon to beyond the scope of my windshield.

Following the dips and bends of the old, gray blacktop, I briefly wished I had driven Hermie to Alabama instead. Nothing simultaneously relaxes and excites in quite the same way as a delightful drive through the country on a beautiful day despite anything else occurring in the world.

The wind swirling through a topless convertible blows away all troubles and woes. Your only concerns become nothing of greater consequence than the radio's next song or where to stop and eat.

Without considering my solitude, I reached my hand across the center console, expecting Garth's hand to readily accept my invitation. He did not, and I found my exposed hand lying in an empty seat. My eyes drifted from the road to consider the void left by my forcibly absent navigator.

The treated leather felt foreign and coarse beneath my touch. The color appeared dull and faded from wear. A small slit had torn where the edges of his pocketknife had steadily carved into the material. I made no mental notes to have the stitching repaired.

I did resolve that, as soon as I had reclaimed my husband into my arms, we would take a long weekend to travel out into the country, wandering wherever the road took us and leaving our mobile phones at home.

A pothole jolted me back into minding the road and reminded me why I decided to leave the Cobra in Atlanta. I had remained at the church for several unplanned hours, even enjoying a delicious homecooked meal of down-home soul food provided by the pastor's wife.

Over fried chicken, mashed potatoes, collard greens, and cornbread, the pastor explained he had called their house phone. I nearly choked on my sweet tea at the revelation that people still had house phones. But the pastor received no answer. He left a voicemail asking them to call him back soon as they could and invited me to stay at the church for as long as I liked.

Lunch brought with it a myriad of conversation topics. I learned about the upcoming Iron Bowl—the members of this church had a robust and good-hearted rivalry between Auburn and Bama that made the event quite the church social; even the pastor and his wife found themselves on opposite sides of the fray.

They wanted to know what I did for work to how Garth and I met. I told the honest folk my usual employment answer and said only that Garth and I met while on a work trip. To the gentleman's credit, he never once asked about the girl or attempted to wile any details from me.

After lunch, and with still no return call, I passed the next two hours by exploring the pastor's surprising library. He had the expected books of various Bible translations—including tomes in Hebrew, Greek, and Aramaic—various commentaries and explorations into apologetics and assorted theological topics.

I was impressed with the range of psychological texts—including the most recent edition of the DSM—and treatises on morality and ethics from the unexpected likes of Voltaire stretching through David Hume. I desired to inquire how such a seemingly learned man had found himself in the backwoods of Alabama for so long, but he came to me first with far more pressing concerns.

"They've got home, and she'd love to see you," he informed me with a smile. He handed me a page torn from his legal pad. "This is their address. Just down the road, make your first right, and it's at the end of the street. Can't miss it."

I thanked him with all heartfelt sincerity, but my mind had already sprinted out the door and cranked the engine. The house at the end of the lane looked like the perfect picture of an idyllic country home. A traditional white picket fence separated the front yard from the rest of the world.

Nestled inside was a modest single-story ranch house with blue shutters and a front door with only the slightest red frame surrounding the glass body. Two horses neighed in a call-and-response in a pasture somewhere behind the cozy abode.

The light illuminated the entryway—hardly large enough to be called a foyer—so I might see the main family room before ever stepping inside. A pallet of sky blue, muted yellow, and cream created the cheerful and inviting kind of home in which a child ought to grow up.

I had not even reached my hand out to ring the bell when the front door flung open with a *whoosh* of air. A beautiful, thriving young woman of 15 stood before me with tears of joy sparkling in her vibrant brown eyes.

Not having the slightest idea of what one ought to say in the circumstances of such a curious reunion, I opted for the universally simple:

"Hey."

She only stared at me, too overcome to respond. Uncomfortable in this most awkward of silences, I began to ramble.

"I wasn't sure if you'd want to see me or even remember me. I thought maybe you would have blocked all these memories from your mind—"

I coughed out the final consonant as she barreled into my chest and smothered me in a hug she'd held onto for two years.

With her voice muffled against me, she wondered, "How could I not want to see you? How do I forget the woman who saved my life?"

Exhaling as best I could within her grasp, I relaxed into the child's embrace and returned her hold.

"Don't just stand there an' squash the poor lady!" I heard a man's voice call out.

"Y'all come on inside an' I'll get dinner started," a woman announced. Though the couple stood just in the doorway, their voices came to me as though miles away.

I discovered something in that grateful embrace of a girl I barely knew yet managed to impact her life forever: all terrible beginnings need not have terrible ends.

Due to our blatant ignoring of them, the girl's new father called again to her in a voice stern but by no means cruel. "Anastasia! Bring her inside. Don't want y'all gettin' caught in the rain."

I gently forced us apart, not feeling the girl relinquishing her hold over me by the slightest measure. "Anastasia?"

She—Anastasia—nodded. "After I started feeling comfortable here, when I felt safe and at home, I wanted to change my name," she explained, whipping away the tears that hadn't absorbed in my shirt.

"Did you choose it, or did your new parents?"

"We chose it together. They suggested it for what it means, and I made the final decision."

With one hand to keep us connected remaining on her back, I inquired, "What does it mean?"

" 'She will rise again'. And the shortening of it to Anna means 'a woman graced with God's favor'. We thought they'd be comforting and encouraging for me."

"It seems you've found good people," I told her to encourage both of us.

Anastasia nodded with unbridled enthusiasm.

"Y'all comin' in, or what?" Anna's dad asked, reappearing in the doorway. He smiled as he questioned us.

I wrapped my arm around Anna's shoulders and let her guide me inside.

Anna gave me a tour of the house with all the pride and joy one would expect if discovering a sprawling mansion rather than a 1,500-square-foot abode. *Barón's* compound had more than one room in which Anna's entire new home could fit with space still to spare, yet her smile and the stories she told proved she thought this modest building the pinnacle of high living.

The smells and crackle of frying chicken wafted down the home's single hallway as Anastasia showed me her room. I didn't have the heart to comment about having already eaten the same for lunch.

As she showed me her growing display of blue ribbons for various equestrian events, I inquired, "You don't mind living out here in Podunk, Alabama?"

Anna's smile faded as she diligently examined the ribbon she held. "I've come to know more people in two years here than twelve years living in *méxico*."

Her accent only appeared when saying a word in her native language. I wondered if she had fought to suppress it. She glided her thumb across the gold lettering, declaring her and her horse the winners of some unnamed contest.

"This is the only thing I kept from my old life."

She spoke so softly. I wasn't sure Anna meant for me to hear. But I believe she needed to unburden herself to someone. Someone who knew something about her life without her having to explain.

"I loved ridin' horses. It was my only freedom. The only thing he let me do on my own. I wanted to take my horse and ride away every day, but I was twelve and had nowhere to go. I didn't even know where I was."

Tears had begun forming in her eyes anew. A pang of guilt stabbed me through the heart. Though I had saved Anastasia from a life of continued horror, I abandoned a terrified twelve-year-old to figure out her new world entirely on her own.

Holding her with that desperate grip she had greeted me, I embraced Anna. I hugged her tight, hoping she would not see my tears and think me too weak to help her. In truth, I was too weak. I had abandoned her, claiming I did so for her protection but truthfully for my own convenience.

I didn't know how to take care of her, or anyone else, for that matter. This wonderful couple could still have cared for her. I needed only to remain nearby as someone with whom she could talk. Perhaps that was all I could ever be: always a removed companion, never an immediate nurturer.

"So," Anna began, pulling away from my embrace. I hurriedly dried my eyes as she turned away to place the ribbon she still held back on its display. "You haven't said what made you finally come see me."

"Nothing," I lied.

Perhaps I couldn't return to when she needed me most those years ago, but I'd be damned if I willingly endangered her now. Come hell or high water, I would find another way to save Garth.

"Nothing, in particular, anyway. I just wanted to see how you were doing and thought maybe enough time had passed for my appearance to not open old wounds."

She nodded once in apparent acceptance of my answer, but something about the heaviness in her eyes and the way she wouldn't return my gaze made me question that acceptance.

Having spent a lifetime practicing lying to people's faces with a smile, it lightened my heart to see her inability to do so. That same heart cracked and fissured with terror for my husband.

I sat on the edge of the guest bed, shaking as I silently bawled into a washcloth, trying desperately not to drown the sheets or borrowed pajamas. Though my decision to lie protected Anastasia, I couldn't help feeling terrified that I had destroyed my only chance at saving my husband.

Ever the perfect embodiment of the white knight, Garth would never allow any innocent person's life traded for his. He would even call me brave and say how proud my sacrifice made him. Still, nothing could stop me from believing I betrayed and abandoned him if I couldn't rescue him.

Perhaps I could call *Barón* and lie. I could tell him I found the girl, meet him alone, and pray that, in his rage, he would shoot us both and allow Garth and I to die together. I knew the plan was folly, but I reached for my phone, all the same.

A timid tapping on my door stayed my hand. Without waiting for an invitation—no doubt she heard my tears through the closed door—Anna pushed it open and slipped inside.

"What are you still doing up?" I asked, using the washcloth to wipe away my tears with all the forced casualness as though I had just washed my face and needed to pat dry the excess water. "I thought everyone else had gone to bed."

"I couldn't sleep," she answered, sitting on the ottoman of the oversized chair in the corner.

"No?" I asked, sniffling back the flow of snot that accompanies a good cry. Ignoring my woes and feigning as though she had not just walked in on me in a puddle of my own tears, I wondered, "What's the matter?"

Raising her eyes to meet my blotched face, she casually told me, "You lied to me."

Of all the things I thought she might say, that had not made the list. My sniffles hiccupped at my confusion. "What?"

"You lied to me," she repeated.

Without allowing me time to preemptively defend myself, Anna explained how she knew before asking why I had come. "Pastor told me. He wanted me to know that you wanted something from me before I agreed to see you. He didn't know the details, only that it involved your husband.

"As I thought about it, I figured you could only need my help if your husband was in trouble with *Barón*."

"And you agreed to see me anyway?"

She nodded, and my mind went blank. What could I say? This girl knew I came to her intending to ask her for a terrible favor, and, still, she not only let me come but greeted me with an unguarded hug. Fortunately, she spoke again.

"This husband, he's the one who made you decide to save me?"

More tears began to well as I gave her a broken smile and nodded.

"What's marriage really like? Is it really wanting to be better for someone else's sake?"

With a smile struggling mightily to heal, I told her, "The best marriages are. In truth, marriage is imperfect, and it is infuriating," I paused, watching her flinch at each negative word. She wanted me to tell her how wonderful it was, and I would not lie to her.

My smile fully healed with a contented joy I could not contain as I said, "And it is the magic of this world. It is sexy and beautiful and inconvenient, and you will drive each other mad in every conceivable way. All the while, even as you temporarily hate them, you'll do anything for each other.

"It is lunacy in its wisest form and selfishness in its noblest incarnation. It is simultaneously both noun and verb and a conscious decision, daily made, and every moment adhered to. Above all things, marriage is finding simultaneous strength and weakness in someone else's arms."

"And you know all that from one man?"

I shrugged while still smiling. "One is all you need."

"I want to help you. I really, *really* want to help you," she dropped her head, unable to look at me, "but I can't face him."

I rose from the bed to sit beside her, leaping to her aide. "I know. It was wrong of me to ever come here and think to ask it of you.

"The instant I saw you," I brushed a stray strand of her curly hair behind her ear, "saw the beautiful young woman you had become and the height you've flourished to in this new world." I sighed. "I knew I could never ask such a terrible request of you. Can you ever forgive me for even considering it?"

She threw her arms around my shoulders and buried her face in my chest again. My phone ringing cut my return embrace short. Returning to the bedside table, the number appearing on my screen belonged to Garth's satellite phone.

My heart somersaulted until my brain knocked it down, mid-flip, realizing that the call came from *el Barón*. My gaze returned to Anastasia as the phone continued to ring. I had no time to send her away. Based on her face's worry, I realized she wouldn't leave. I answered the phone.

"*Barón.*"

Anna sucked in her breath as her face lost some of its natural tan.

"Have you found my daughter?" his gravelly voice crunched through the receiver.

"No," I lied. "I've not been able to find her."

Anastasia's eyes focused again on mine. She looked as though about to cry.

"That is a shame." *Barón* spoke with all the emotion of reading a list of ingredients. "I grow tired of waiting and do not have confidence that your husband can withstand much more of my hospitality."

My hand shot to cover my mouth and stifle the cry threatening to erupt. All notions of maintaining a brave face for Anna's sake shattered with

Barón's threat. I could barely manage to keep *Barón* from hearing my fear; hiding it from Anastasia became impossible.

Watching my heart crack in real-time, Anna madly waved both hands.

"What?" I mouthed to her. She eyed my phone leerily as she whispered,

"Tell him you have a lead. That you're confident you can find me in a day or two."

"No!" I shook my head and opened my mouth wide to enunciate the silent word.

"I trust you," Anastasia told me. "You protected me once; I know you'll do it again."

I felt terrible as no small part of me breathed a sigh of relief.

Knowing I couldn't dissuade her and selfishly not wanting to try, I told *Barón*, "If you can wait a few more days, I've found a lead that I'm confident will guide me to her."

"Well, why not start with that?" he inquired. "In the spirit of fair trade, you have bought your husband 48 hours of respite. After that, you will have found the end of my patience. Talk soon."

"Wait!" I yelled into the phone to keep him from hanging up on me. "*Barón*! I just have one question for you: how did you know? How did you know about him? About us?"

"Oh, I don't think that information is pertinent at this point," he taunted. "Tick-tock, Kati. You're 48 hours have begun."

The phone went silent.

"What did he say?" Anna questioned as I lowered the phone from my ear. "What's gonna happen?"

"We have two days to make our plan," I told her, staring at my phone's black screen. My mind raced with all I must do and how to do it. First things first, I needed to be alone.

Meeting her scared eyes with steeled determination, I told her, "You should try to rest. I have much to do."

CHAPTER TWENTY-TWO

In Which an Ending Loomed Heavily

I stood alone in the steeple's early morning shadow, waiting for *el Barón*. I returned his call 24 hours after his ultimatum with the instructions for him to meet me at the church, and we would conduct our hostage exchange.

When he protested about making the journey, I explained that I couldn't convince his daughter to go very far with me. It ran the risk of *Barón* discovering his daughter's location on his own and the entire plan dissolving into ash. I gambled that he had grown so desperate to recover her that he would take the bait.

Turns out, I gambled correctly.

In an abundance of caution, Darcy stood by at the crop-dusting airstrip to smuggle Anna and her family out of the country and set them up with a new life elsewhere.

Brynn crouched, hidden in the belfry with the crosshairs of a modified AR-15 and a sniper scope trained on me. She wore a headset that transmitted the feed of the wire taped beneath my dress, giving her the power to make the fatal decision once *Barón* arrived.

I insisted that she not do anything rash until I had Garth safely returned to me. Judging by her reaction when I informed them of the situation, I had little confidence she would do as told. A radio in the sanctuary allowed Thad and Anastasia to listen to all that happened outside.

I had protested having Thad as Anna's keeper, afraid that his most basic resemblance to *el Barón* might set her on edge and keep her from trusting him. My concerns proved accurate, but everyone insisted on Brynn's superior marksmanship. I would never allow someone I didn't know to stay with Anna, so Thad it was.

When Thad, Brynn, and a dozen unknown agents arrived at the house the night before, Anastasia retreated to her room. After living with *el Barón*, she still did not take well to strangers in her home. She need not know anyone else, but if Thad had the task of directly watching over her, Anna did need to know him before we found ourselves in the midst of it.

"Anastasia?" her mom gently knocked on the closed bedroom door. "Anna, there's someone Mrs. Kati wants you to meet."

Anna never invited us into her room, but the lack of denial seemed enough acceptance for the three of us to enter. Mrs. Charlotte went directly to the bed, allowing Anna to latch onto her instead of the body pillow she used to hide. I entered second and followed her mother to the bedside but did not sit.

Thad remained by the door, waiting for acceptance.

I squatted beside the bed and explained, "This is Special Agent Thaddeus James Wilmington IV of the FBI. He's going to be the one directly protecting you tomorrow."

"Hi, Anastasia," he greeted with a wide, warm smile. "You can call me Thad."

Anna curled tighter into her mother. The coffee-colored skin, glossy black hair, and brown eyes reminded her too much of *Barón*.

Watching Anastasia, she reminded me far too much of the little girl I had stolen and not the young woman I had met the other day. I placed my hand on her leg, giving her a comforting squeeze.

Undeterred by Anna's reaction, Thad calmly grabbed the purple office chair tucked under her desk and casually rolled it out to have a seat. He remained on the far side of the room, never moving closer to Anna than necessary to fetch the chair.

"Before anything else," Thad began as he took up a reclined posture in the chair. He spoke in a mellow voice as though recalling some inconsequential afterthought. "I just have to tell you how courageous you are."

"Really?" Anna wondered.

Thad nodded. "You're quite possibly the bravest girl I've ever met. And I was in the army, so I've met a lot of brave women. But I don't know that one of them would do what you've agreed to do tomorrow.

"In fact, from what Miss Bonnie has told me, you decided to face *el Barón* on your own. Is that right? Did you tell Miss Bonnie that you wanted to do this?"

Anastasia's death grip on her mother began relaxing. She made a feeble nod before looking at me as though seeking either permission or affirmation.

Smiling at her, I told Thad, "She sure did."

He whistled slowly. "That's just about the most courageous thing I've ever heard. It takes a certain bravery to stand down an unknown threat. But to volunteer to face a personal enemy eye-to-eye," Thad exhaled in awe, "that's a kind of bravery I don't even have."

Taking a chance, Thad rolled forward the length his outstretched leg could pull him. Anastasia did not relax further, but she also did not retreat. He leaned forward, resting his forearms on his knees.

"You know, this man that we're going to rescue tomorrow, Garth, he's a friend of Miss Bonnie's, and he's a real good friend of mine, and I will do just about anything to get him back.

"But, no matter what, even if it means losing my dear friend, I will never let *el Barón* to touch you again. I don't care what the cost; that monster will never put you in danger again."

He paused for a moment, letting the promise sink in. "Do you believe me?"

Taking a long moment to consider his words, Anna nodded slowly.

"Good." Thad smiled and sat back to his relaxed posture.

Gesturing his thumb at me, he added, "And if I break that promise, Bonnie here'll shoot me where I stand."

"You bet I will," I assured with a smile.

My body tensed, pulling me from my reverie, as an unseen car kicked up a cloud of dust along the road. Despite four cars having already driven harmlessly down the dirt road beside the church—

So much for an unpopulated, sleepy hamlet.

—my body coiled, my heart pounded, and my fists clenched with each one. The horrible anticipation had only worsened with every passing vehicle. Like waiting for an exam you knew you'd fail, the prospect of waiting haunted far worse than the outcome of the event itself.

"False alarm," I spoke into the wire taped between my cleavage as the dust cloud faded and the car disappeared down the road. I had no earpiece with which the others could speak to me, so I imagined they had probably grown tired of my unhelpful commentary.

Thad and Anastasia could see nothing within the church. Its stain-glass windows were too opaque for anything other than sunlight, and Brynn could see everything happening with her eagle-eye scope.

It didn't matter; I always talked aloud whenever bored or nervous. These comments would still occur, wire or no.

Finally, a dust cloud larger than any that morning billowed and grew on the horizon. Either a semi had lost its way and came barreling down our dirt road, or a small caravan of SUVs approached.

In that morning's dense, expectant silence, I heard the clicking sound of Brynn chambering a round in her rifle. She must have studied the arriving dust storm and made her evaluation.

When I told the team I wanted a sniper posted in the belfry, the immediacy with which both Moller and Thad said Brynn's name made me jump. I pulled the phone away from my face and stared at it as though the device had become possessed and had begun spouting idiocies.

Carefully returning the phone to my ear—worried that a demon might crawl out and try to eat me—I acted as if I hadn't heard what the men said and asked them to repeat it. Hearing Brynn's name again with unmistakable clarity, I could not stop myself.

"Really?"

"Oh yeah!" Thad insisted. "She's incredible with a rifle! How many times have you won the office shooting competitions?"

Brynn said nothing, even as Thad spent the next few minutes trying to coax an exact number out of her. Tiring of this unhelpfulness, Moller's booming voice cut in to assure that this task was best suited to Agent Jolene and inquired what else I would need.

The herd made its way over to Alabama, and I explained what I intended to happen the following morning. I tried finding the time to pull Brynn aside and have some girl talk, inquiring about this apparent sharpshooter skill. Alas, we all remained rather busy and had no opportunity for such frivolities.

Another time, then.

The cloud approached. Within the swirl of dust, I could now distinguish three black Escalades. If this somehow proved anyone other than *Barón*, we would undoubtedly find ourselves in for a curious day. The three SUVs turning onto the church's side road confirmed this caravan as the rest of our party.

"Look alive, everyone. It's showtime."

The vehicles skidded to a stop in sparks of gravel and another cloud of dust. I kept my eyes locked on the second car, ignoring the dust biting my eyes. Eight men with semi-automatic rifles barreled out of the lead and follow SUVs.

Two kept their guns locked on me while the other six scanned the surrounding area for any threats. None of them moved more than three feet from any one vehicle.

El Barón, alone, stepped out of the second car, from the driver's seat, no less. Apparently, he had not left anything involving the transport to chance. He stared into the sky, observing the cross standing stalwart atop the steeple.

"Curious place to meet," he commented, still looking upward. "Do you suspect I'll behave here out of a fear of God?"

"I suspect you don't fear anything," I remarked. Needing a quip to knock him off balance, I added, "Expect what I can do to your daughter."

Barón finally brought his gaze to meet mine. The corners of his mouth twitched upward in the slightest shadow of a bemused smile. His sunglasses kept me from seeing his eyes. I chose to believe that an intentional choice so they might not betray any emotion.

He studied me for a long moment before remarking, "You have had two years to do with her what you will." His smile grew. "If you've done nothing yet, you won't ever do anything."

"Oh, I don't know," I mused. "Leverage only works so long as you apply pressure."

Barón's smile faltered. Instantly recovering, he said, "Speaking of, I notice a distinct lack of what I came for."

"I'll show you mine if you show me yours."

"You're not my type," he retorted with a nasty scowl.

"I'm about twenty years older than your type," I shot back.

In truth, the assertion that I was approximately 30 years of age came as a complete guess, based upon an evaluation by Uncle César's doctor shortly after we met.

El Barón's gravelly voice became a growl with my accusation. Encouraged by his unraveling, I pressed forward.

"I have a gun trained on your daughter. Show me Agent Harmon, or I'll have a bullet put in her skull."

"That would destroy all hope of him returning to you."

"I'd rather lose them both than allow that girl back in your clutches."

When *Barón* hesitated in an attempt to call my bluff, I raised my hand in the air. Only Brynn could see me, and we had not predetermined that as any signal, but *Barón* didn't know any of this.

"I close my fist, and you'll hear a girl's scream followed by the discharge of a 9mm."

"You'd never dare." *Barón's* response came as more of a plea than a command.

"Are you sure? You've never been much of a gambling man. Are you willing to bet now?"

My fingers flicked in anticipation of movement.

"Bring him!" *Barón* barked over his shoulder.

The backdoor of the middle Escalade opened, and out stepped another gunman. Yanking on something still hidden inside, Garth came tumbling out, crashing into a pile in the gravel. The guard gripped Garth by the neck and wrenched him to his feet. Maintaining the vise grip around my husband's neck, the guard shoved him to stumble forward.

I clenched my entire body. My tightened diaphragm kept me from breathing. Even my blood seemed to stop as my veins contracted. I had to stifle any reaction and quash the overwhelming desire to rush to my husband and take his battered and bruised body into my arms. I had chosen my dark sunglasses for the reason I suspected of *Barón's.*

Garth's hair looked knotted and oily and had lost its natural sheen. His left eye remained swollen with the sickly yellow color of an old, deep bruise. He could only open his eye about halfway; I knew it was previously swollen shut.

The nauseating discoloration around his eye highlighted the golden flakes of his irises in the same way jaundice highlights golden-blonde hair. The thought of the bruise marring the beautiful eyes of my husband angered me more than the violence against him.

However, the aspect of his appearance that nearly caused me to become sick came from his right eye. Seemingly untouched by hand or fist, dried blood caked a wound from his hairline to where it dripped off his chin. A precise, deep gash that had not begun healing created the blood flow.

The red stripe passed no more than a finger's width from the outside corner of my husband's eye.

"You're lucky you called when you did," *el Barón* said. The pallor of my face had revived some of his confidence. "Had you delayed any longer, the next cut would have seen him lose an eye. I've had enough games now. Bring me my daughter."

Ignoring *Barón's* threats, I asked Garth, "You feel any better than you look?"

The attempted nonchalance of his shrug shattered with the wince that accompanied the movement.

"Not to worry," I said before Garth could steady himself to make a response. "You were never all that pretty, anyway."

He winced again. The laughter intensified the pain of his bruised ribs.

"Enough!" *Barón* mercifully cut me off before I could say anything inappropriate in the mixed company. "Bring me my daughter!"

I did not pull my eyes from Garth. "She can't come to you. She's not here," I lied. "I've already had her smuggled away somewhere new."

I forced my gaze from my husband to meet *Barón's* concealed eyes. "You have no hope of ever finding her."

"Now, I know you're bluffing."

Without hesitation, *Barón* drew a pistol from the shoulder holster under his suit jacket, turned, and shot Garth in the leg. We both screamed as Garth's guard released his hold and let my husband collapse again into the dust.

Barón tangled his fingers in Garth's hair and ripped him off the ground. Holding his gun to my husband's head, *el Barón* manically shouted:

"Give her to me!"

Before I could respond, the figure of Anastasia came sprinting out of the church.

"No!" I protested after my brain processed what my eyes saw, but it was too late. She already stood, with arms raised, between *Barón* and me. Thad chased after her with his own handgun drawn.

"Please don't hurt him!" rang out Anna's shrill, terrified voice.

"Hija," Barón whispered from shock.

"You don't get to call me that!" she told him.

Tears streamed down her face as she stood face-to-face against him.

"Are you alright?" he insisted.

Had I not known the truth, I would have thought *Barón* a sincere father.

"You don't get to ask me that! You don't get to ask me anything!"

In a move that surprised everybody gathered, Anastasia drew her own pistol from where she had it tucked in the waistband of her jeans. Eyes wide, I stared at Thad, wondering if he had given her something to protect herself in hopes of endearing himself to and calming her. The shock he looked back with suggested he had done no such thing.

I recalled how Anna had insisted on wearing her jacket, which I thought odd considering the unseasonal warmness of the day. Now I understood why.

"You don't get to say anything to me! You don't get to speak to me or look at me, and you never get to touch me again!"

She held the gun with both hands, struggling to keep it from shaking. She failed.

"Brynn," I whispered into my wire. With everyone's attention locked on Anna, no one worried about me muttering to myself. "Brynn, we can't let Anna live the rest of her life with the weight of killing her own father, regardless of circumstances."

I knew Garth remained in danger as *Barón* still held him as a human shield.

Maybe she has an angle around him.

I swallowed where my heart stuck in my throat. I couldn't allow tears to form as I watched my husband sway on the edges of consciousness from blood loss.

"Take the shot."

I sighed with relief when no response came. No attempt on *Barón* meant no risk to my husband. That relief came short-lived when Anastasia began yelling again.

"You'll never get to hurt anyone again!"

Anna locked her elbows to steady her trembling arms and pulled the trigger.

Her gun clicked harmlessly. No bullet fired. No pop signaled the internal explosion of gunpowder.

She was stunned by her own tenacity—failed though it had. Anastasia stared at the defective gun in her outstretched arms. No one had taught her about the machine's safety mechanism.

Several things then happened all at once.

During the pause of confusion, Thad snatched the opportunity to rush Anna and bring her back under his protection. Doing as he should to protect his employer, one of *el Barón's* men raised his rifle to shoot at the girl who just tried to kill his boss. This man did know about safeties.

Recognizing the impending attack, Thad's feet left the ground as he tackled Anna to the gravel in a diving leap. She screamed in surprise, and Thad yelled in pain. Blood oozing from his shoulder wetted the rocks beneath them.

Upon realizing someone had just tried taking a shot at his daughter, *el Barón* released his hold on Garth. My husband promptly collapsed into the dirt in a state of semi-lucidity.

El Barón turned to face his men. Focusing on the one holding the literal smoking gun, *Barón* did not hesitate to fire three bullets into the man that dared threaten his daughter.

Again, had I not known the truth, *Barón's* apparent sincerity as a father may have moved me.

The instant Garth fell out of harm's way, I screamed loud enough that I did not need a wire for Brynn to hear me.

"Take the shot!"

Two short *cracks* followed by a compounded, resounding *boom* echoed off the surrounding hills as two bullets fired from the steeple.

Pandemonium broke out.

I dropped to the ground as more shots rang out from the steeple, accompanied by gunfire from all sides. The agents-in-waiting with Brynn and Thad joined the fray, helping Brynn pick off *el Barón's* men while providing cover for the four of us caught in the middle.

I army crawled my way over to *Barón's* crumpled form. Giving a quick inspection of Garth as I passed, I knew I couldn't let *Barón* die without getting an answer from him.

Pushing myself to my knees, I grabbed *Barón* by the lapels of his tailored suit and demanded, "How did you know? How did you learn the truth!"

"I didn't," he admitted through gurgles of blood. "Someone told me."

That answer proved worse than any reasoning I had imagined.

"Who!" I yelled.

If *Barón* did not learn but was told, Garth and I remained in a patient, impending danger.

"Who told you!"

El Barón only smiled before coughing up another mouthful of blood. His head snapped back into the dirt.

I wanted to make some 80's action hero quip about *el Barón* now having a fear of God and steeples. My own fear over how he learned about us fogged the quippy, sarcasm centers of my brain.

My job at the crime scene ended with *Barón* dead and all his men in body bags or handcuffs. A terrible prickly feeling crawled across my entire body as a stream of FBI agents incessantly asked after me and wanted me to give my statement for the records.

I always purposefully avoided such places after they leapt from innocuous to consequential.

Worst of all, I could only watch from afar and with a decidedly passing interest in the medical field examination conducted on Garth. Fortunately, Thad's injury and concurrent evaluation allowed me to spend some time around them without drawing suspicion.

Better still, Anna had not left Thad's side since they helped each other off the ground. Apparently, him literally taking a bullet for her proved how unlike *el Barón* Thad was.

Thad's bullet had not passed clean through but lodged close enough to his collarbone that the paramedics could easily retrieve it in the back of their ambulance. I offered to acquire the boys a fresh bottle of moonshine to cleanse their wounds and for some liquid strength.

We are in Alabama, after all. It may not be Tennessee, but it seems only logical we could find an honest still tucked somewhere in these hills.

While Thad appreciated my humor, Garth had fallen so far out of it that he didn't even know who I was. That probably proved the best option for not blowing our cover after all the effort to make my actions seem honest and not personally motivated.

The paramedics loaded up their patients after completing the furthest extent of medical care they could in an ambulance in a church parking lot. They drove them back to Atlanta for further treatment.

Anastasia asked the paramedics and accompanying agents four times to go with Thad. When they refused, she pleaded to let her know which hospital they headed for and when she could come visit him. FBI protocol did not allow anyone to tell Anna the answers she desired.

But, just before they closed the doors on him, Thad promised her that he would let me send all the information needed for her to send him a 'Get Well Soon' card.

As the crowd began to disperse, I escorted Anna home to her parents. They greeted each other with hugs, kisses, and joyous tears of relief. I felt my body pulled into the group hug as Anastasia clasped a free hand around my wrist.

My offer to have Darcy move them out of the country still stood, but with *Barón* on his way to the morgue, Anastasia no longer feared him finding her. She had finally found a safe, loving home, and she swore she would never give it up for anything.

With the day rapidly ending, Charlotte and Neil offered me my room again. The prospect piqued my interest as all the adrenaline fading from my system lured me into slumbering comfort, but I declined. I craved my own home and desperately desired to make covert inquiries into my husband's status.

Though only forcibly separated for some 72 hours, it had seemed a lifetime since I last held my husband in my arms. I knew my heart would not take kindly to prolonging that separation.

Chapter Twenty-Three

In Which My Heart Learned to Beat Again

Evening approached. The sinking sun bathed the rolling hills of central Alabama in a fiery glow as the sky exploded in a kaleidoscope of color. Lifting my eyes upward through the open convertible top, the sky seamlessly faded into ever-darkening shades of blue.

Early, eager stars danced high above my head in the cloudless sky. Hermie followed the dips and bends of the old, gray blacktop perfectly as a song about only wanting you for Christmas rang through the speakers. Without considering my actions, I reached my hand across the center console, expecting Garth's hand to readily accept my invitation.

My heart fluttered as I felt his hand enclosing mine. Letting my eyes drift from the road, I considered the man sitting beside me and the haunting depression which would have consumed my life had I lost him.

He slid his fingers between mine before giving my hand another squeeze. He reminded me that he had not died and it was no ghost occupying my passenger seat.

"You really don't mind the scar?" He asked his daily question since his discharge from the hospital.

The doctor had kept Garth two days for observation after sewing up his face and leg to ensure no dormant injuries sprang up. The bullet missed Garth's knee and lodged in his thigh muscle, miraculously doing as minimal damage as possible. But he needed to hobble around on crutches for the next few weeks.

Still, the doctor insisted that the injury should cause no significant long-term effects. Less than a week stuck at home after his discharge, Garth started developing cabin fever. With Christmas approaching, Moller insisted Garth take the next month off to recover.

He threatened to arrest him for insubordination if he set foot in the office before the new year. I mentally questioned whether he had the authority to do that outside the military. Although, I wasn't about to protest having my husband all to myself for an entire month.

"I have already told you that scars are incredibly sexy," I assured. "And if you had lost your eye and required an eyepatch," I shrugged, "that would've been pretty great, too. You know I like pirates."

Garth lifted my hand to his lips. He held it against his kiss for a long moment, his eyes closed as he savored the feeling, taste, and smell of me back in his grasp. Satisfied for the moment, my husband let our hands drop to rest again on the center console.

I released a long, slow sigh of perfect contentment as we shared a smile. Forcing our fingers straightened but never apart, I downshifted as we came out of a dipping curve in the road and took us gleefully speeding into the setting sun.

"You still haven't told me where we're headed," he said.

"That's why I called it a surprise," I teased. "Consider it an early Christmas present."

I turned off the road onto a dirt driveway with a familiar idyllic farmhouse resting at the end of the lane. All their Christmas decorations on display, the farm looked as much the picture of holiday perfection as any location without a powdering of fresh snow could achieve.

"Where are we?" my husband asked as I shut off Hermie's engine.

I bit my lower lip in a futile attempt to contain my smile. "There's someone who wants to meet you. Someone I want you to meet."

Hurrying out of the car, I fetched Garth's crutches from the trunk and met him as he pushed open his door. My husband leaned on me as he righted himself and settled into his crutches.

I did not notice the front door opening or the glowing young woman who stood under the icicle lights. Only my husband's nod shifted my focus away from him. Leaving him by the car, I met Anna with a joyous embrace halfway to the door.

But I was not the person Anna most desired to see.

Promptly breaking our hug, Anastasia craned around me to look at the man hobbling towards her. Garth smiled warmly despite the discomfort of crutches and his fading painkillers; the magic of Percocet held no comparison to the euphoria of this moment.

Glancing between us as though requiring confirmation, I nodded my permission, and Anna left me to greet my husband.

"Anastasia, I want you to meet my husband, Garth Harmon. Garth, this is Anna."

Garth lifted a steady hand to shake Anna's trembling one.

"It is a pleasure to meet you, Anna."

Anna tried returning the greeting but couldn't find words. Instead, she continued smiling at him with that insatiable, beaming grin.

How marvelously resilient the human spirit is.

Watching my husband finally meet the little girl he had unknowingly moved me to save, I experienced my own sensation of *muditā.* No Christmas ever held more magic.

"Mama and Daddy have dinner ready." Anna dropped Garth's hand, only seemingly now realizing she still held it. "Come on."

She had bounced halfway across the yard before she remembered Garth could only move so quickly. I called for her to go on ahead and assured I'd help Garth. She didn't wait for a second prompting before disappearing inside.

"I think you've made the poor girl nervous," I remarked.

"She's just excited, is all. Can't blame her."

"Neither can I," I said, wrapping my arm around him and pressing my body against his.

Luckily, my husband had already steadied himself on his crutches, and I did not send us toppling. Again.

"Meeting you did get me all sorts of excited."

"That's not exactly what I meant," he corrected through a matching smile. He paused, allowing me a moment to still my roving hands. "I know why you never could before, but it means the world that you're letting me meet Anna now."

Cocking my head, I wondered, "Did I have a choice? After this whole scenario blew out her anonymity, would you ever have let it rest?"

His smile shifted. "Of course not. 'But love given unsought is better'."

My eyes shone with equal parts desire and pride. "You just had to go and quote Shakespeare, didn't you?"

His kiss provided answer enough.

Taking a few taunting steps ahead of him, I observed, "It's poor form to keep our hosts waiting. Hobble along, Tiny Tim."

"Who you callin' tiny?"

My raised eyebrow and half-smile dissuaded any self-consciousness.

The delicious turkey dinner passed with cheerful conversation and countless stories between tellers. No one uttered a word about *el Barón*, Garth's injuries, or the preceding weeks' events. I believe that, if only for those few hours, not a single person gathered at that table even remembered how we found ourselves there.

Anastasia's smile beamed without the faintest hint of shadow. Garth relaxed at the table as would any able-bodied guest. Anna's parents told stories of their daughter as though no time existed when they were not together.

Garth and I recounted tales of our various escapades, from international travels to quiet evenings at home, all sprinkled with euphemisms to spare. Details or questions of illegality never arose, nor did the topic of my employment or that every FBI Agent had referred to me as Bonnie.

I have always thought that Anna's parents must have possessed some idea that I worked in a career field they did not desire for their daughter but would never dare ask. We had performed a miraculous service for each other, and that was all we ever need know.

As the other adults sipped their post-dinner coffee, Anna and I enjoyed our own cups of peppermint tea. Before our leaves had even completed their steeping, a whinnying from the paddock reminded Anastasia of someone whose dinner she had neglected in the excitement of the evening.

Asking Garth and me if we would like to meet her treasured horses, our entire party ventured into the world of stars and Christmas lights beyond the back porch.

An impatient Appaloosa gelding snorted and stamped a hoof into the ground as Anastasia and I approached the fence. The animal calmed instantly under the girl's touch. Garth hobbled behind us in timing with the chestnut mare trotting lazily to investigate the party at the fence.

My husband and I remained at the fence with the mare happy to keep us company as we stroked her nose. The Appaloosa dutifully followed Anna in the direction of the feeding trough. Anna began her dossier on each animal, returning with a bucket of oats and the Appaloosa still trotting behind.

She didn't miss a step or falter when Curtis nudged her for taking too long in her feeding. Lucille still had no care for food when she had new friends to pet her. Anna made the shy, calculated remark that Garth would probably have to come back if he wanted to go riding.

Her smile returned when I agreed we would do just that. Anna told us she loved riding Curtis for freedom, speed, and jumping. Lucille's gentler nature made for more relaxing days of exploration and thinking.

They didn't pause when I left Garth and Anna under the pretense of needing more hot water for my tea. In truth, I had the strongest urging to stand away and watch from afar as they got to know each other. I couldn't ignore a prompting inside me whispering towards the loveliness of such a sight.

I never made it inside for my hot water when I joined Charlotte and Neil in a rocking chair on the deck. Several minutes of contented silence passed between the three of us. Anna's parents heard that same whisper that guided me to the porch.

Eventually, Charlotte's matronly voice gently slipped its way through the quiet. "Thank you."

Though no longer a hesitation than necessary for processing brainwaves, I seemed to hear the words lingering before recognizing them. They settled which such ease into the sentiment of the moment that I did not realize anyone had broken that sweet silence. As the words awakened my mind from its reverie, I turned to their speaker.

"For everything that you did," Charlotte continued.

Though only she spoke, the incalculable gratitude of Neil's eyes as he held his wife's hand echoed every word.

"We never did have the chance to say it before. Thank you."

Smiling back at them, I could only bring myself to say, "Likewise."

"Whenever it happens for you, you'll be amazing." Charlotte's smile twitched as she spoke the delicate encouragement.

Consumed in the moment, I could not follow the tiptoe in her eyes.

"When what happens?"

"Your own child. When you become a mother."

My breath caught. I made no attempts to conceal it.

"After our Issac died... we already had such trouble conceiving him, and we didn't think we had any more hope. Above it all, I didn't think my heart could take the risk of losing another."

Her shattered smile slowly returned as Neil grasped her hand tighter.

"Then, years later, Pastor calls with the strangest request and an even stranger explanation. We couldn't say no."

Forgetting me entirely, Anna's parents looked to the paddock's edge. "The moment I set eyes on her, my heart burst with a joy I thought impossible to feel again. What you were willing to do, to risk, for her..." Charlotte's voice trailed away.

Returning her gaze to my glistening eyes, she told me, "You will be wonderful."

My body and breath shuddered as a tear escaped. I couldn't ever allow myself to believe or accept it, but I felt that this woman had spoken the truth of a promise over me.

Alone in the bathroom, I stared at my reflection as I brushed my teeth. Charlotte's words haunted and encouraged me in equal measure. The longer I stared into the reflection of my own eyes, the closer I brewed to critical mass.

"I think it's time for a change," I announced.

"Of?" The word came as a wince as Garth studiously positioned himself on the bed.

I took a breath and dove in.

"We have no real Christmas traditions. There are things we usually happen to do each year, but nothing we make a deliberate point towards."

"I beg to differ. There is one activity we make a regular point towards, particularly at Christmas."

I poked my head out of the bathroom. My husband had delivered his remark with admirable deadpan in his voice, but his eyes never had quite mastered hiding emotions.

"That is not what I meant. And, besides, we don't make a point for that; it just happens." I shrugged. "Christmastime does things to me."

"I know. Why do you think it's my favorite holiday?"

I made a smirk but dare not lie to call him mistaken.

After disappearing into the bathroom, I heard him ask, "What new tradition did you want?"

Without the second-guessing I anticipated, my reflection smiled back at me. "This one. A family one." I switched off the bathroom light but stopped before reaching the bed.

"I want to visit Anna and Charlotte and Neil every year. Maybe even invite them to the manor."

The love of my husband's gaze shifted to shock. "You'd tell them about the manor?"

I nodded; Garth smiled with a silent 'wow'.

"I think it'll be good for both of you," I defended, knowing he required none. "You each need someone to talk to about me."

"I think it'll be good for you, too." His smile widened, knowing I never would have admitted it, even to myself.

Finally making my way to the bed, I crawled in beside him, careful not to disturb the painless positioning he had settled upon. Sidling to rest against my husband, I forced myself to leave as much space between us as I could stand so as not to risk accidental aggravation to his injuries.

My body sprawled across the bed, and my head rested on Garth's chest. We laid in that comfortable, innocently erotic silence with only the sounds of crickets and our tender taken breaths.

"They told me, when you were still saying hi to Anna's horses, Charlotte and Neil told me how good of a mother I'll be someday."

"They aren't wrong."

"We've tried," I reminded, pushing myself off his chest to look at Garth's face. "Twice, we've tried."

Brushing a stray hair from my face, he corrected, "Oh, we've tried far more than that."

I smiled at his attempt in lightheartedness but could not hold it.

"What if Anna is the closest I ever get?"

With no hairs left in the way, he moved to stroke my face without pretense, his fingertips flowing across my skin in a sweet glissando, despite the callouses and bitten nails.

I leaned into that touch, desperate for whatever embrace my husband could presently provide. I needed to feel him for the sake of himself as much as for any comforting on my part.

He paused and lifted my chin, forcing me to meet his determined but not harsh gaze.

"Then you did a damn good job with what you got. And I could never be prouder to call you my wife."

I leaned further into him and settled my lips against his for a deep, healing kiss. Snuggling again with his chest for my pillow, I drew my fingers in lazy outlines of his subtle torso muscles.

"You know, they say that being in a positive space and being around good energy can help with the conception."

"Do they?"

"And I'm hard pressed to think of a place more positive and filled with good energy than this."

"So early in my recovery? It could cause negative consequences," Garth teased, running his fingers through my hair.

"Actually, your doctor did say that regular activity and keeping your blood flowing would decrease your recovery time. Even assist in making your recovery more complete."

"Well, it is foolish to ignore a doctor's direct orders."

"Isn't it just?"

"And it is Christmastime."

"And we have discussed what that does to me."

We met each other's smiles, instantly sharing the same conclusion. Delightful as it is to banter and more delightful, still, to follow through on that banter, Garth's body had not yet recovered enough for that. He knew he had to deny both of us our desire. That wounded him more than both the bullet and knife.

Leaning across his chest, I kissed my husband's face, my lips gently caressing the healing stitches.

"Then again, it does seem rude to soil someone else's home," I decided so he wouldn't have to give it voice. "After all, we don't know them *that* well."

His dimpled smile shone in full force. "That's why we have next Christmas."

"That's why we have now and forever."

I lay on his chest, listening to my husband's heart beating its steady cadence. My eyes grew heavy with contentment as the purse of his lips repeatedly pressed against my head.

I had my husband beside me and the surrogate child he had given me the strength to rescue dreaming of her own man just like him down the hall. A final sigh whisked me away into the bliss of perfect sleep, which comes from knowing that never in all the world could the hope of a dream compare to my present reality.

"I realized something in my codeine-induced dreams," he said. "You can't get immunity from former crimes if no one knows you did them.

So, either you didn't think through your demand, or you never expected a reward."

"You asked for my help. What else was I gonna do?" I told him with another gentle kiss. "Speaking of," I announced, momentarily rousing both of us, "I got a message the other day. It seems somebody desires my services."

After making him jump and groan, Garth kissed my head and made a final request, settling back into his preferred position. "Do me a favor? Wait until the drugs kick in before saying anything else."

My husband's gentle snoring confirmed the drugs' quick work before my lips left his cheek.

And so ends our first adventure, sweet reader.
Until we meet again.

Acknowledgments

Thank ya kindly to all my friends and family for your encouragments and critiques. To my parents for teaching me that marriage is worth celebrating. Constable, for all the things. Rachel, for your editing prowess. Joyce, for all your guidance through the publishing weeds.

All glory be to Christ, for He is our Guide, even unto the end.

About the Author

Though fantastic at basically everything else, Kati failed spectacularly writing her own story. So, she hired a ghostwriter from the FBI records named Emily Copeland. Love & Theft is Emily's first novel, but Kati liked her spunk at nearly getting arrested for trespassing to play on a swing set. Emily sleeps in a different city most nights with an ever-changing entourage of men—as a flight attendant, you delightfully gutter-minded reader—but she collects her mail in Atlanta. You can follow her on Facebook and Instagram and keep up with all things to come at 718stories.com. Until we meet again!

www.ingramcontent.com/pod-product-compliance
Lightning Source LLC
LaVergne TN
LVHW090555110826
845146LV00001B/141

* 9 7 9 8 9 8 8 4 6 2 7 0 5 *